PACKART'S ORCHARD

A David Allen Murder Mystery

WENDY SCOTT-ETTINGER

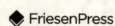

One Printers Way
Altona, MB R0G 0B0
Canada

www.friesenpress.com

Copyright © 2024 by Wendy Scott-Ettinger
First Edition — 2024

All rights reserved.

No part of this publication may be reproduced in any form, or by any means, electronic or mechanical, including photocopying, recording, or any information browsing, storage, or retrieval system, without permission in writing from FriesenPress.

ISBN
978-1-03-919638-4 (Hardcover)
978-1-03-919637-7 (Paperback)
978-1-03-919639-1 (eBook)

1. FICTION, MYSTERY & DETECTIVE

Distributed to the trade by The Ingram Book Company

PACKART'S ORCHARD

CHAPTER 1

ANNA LISTER'S FATHER, PAUL JACKSON, DIED IN the orchard twenty years ago, and although she was only four and a half, Anna would never forget the day her daddy stopped coming home for dinner. There were others that died in and around the orchard back then too. Anna had heard her mother talk about them over the years. There was never any definitive answer to what had happened to them. Her mother had never forgiven the police for not looking into any of it. They'd chalked the deaths up to natural causes or accidents and left it at that.

Mr. and Mrs. Packart had closed the business and left town for over two years after five men died in similar ways around the orchard. Even after they returned and tried to reopen the orchard, The Packart's business never thrived the way it had back then. The deaths did stop though, and the townspeople began to forget about what had happened. Life in the small town of Windsmill went back to normal.

Now, twenty years later, Mr. Packart hired Jack Lister to try to bring the orchard back to life again. Jack and Anna had fallen in love in college, married and lived on the coast with their five-year-old son. She was thrilled when she'd heard they would be moving to her hometown of Windsmill. Everything was going so well for them. Johnny loved kindergarten and was looking forward to being with the big kids in grade one in the fall. Everything seemed perfect until another victim was found on the outskirts of town. Hector Lightfeather lived and worked in the Orchard. Everyone called him Red because of his flaming red hair that never seemed to get longer but never looked like it had been cut either. Red maybe drank too much on occasion, but he was a hard worker, doing chores for Jack, and Mrs. Packart, and small jobs for the town council. The coroner's office could not find a definitive cause of death so blamed the mishap on his heavy drinking the night before, possibly causing a fall. At least that's what the local grapevine was saying.

Jack was worried that he had stirred something up in the orchard with some of the changes he and Mr. Packart had started to make, but Anna assured him that whatever had happened to Red wasn't his doing. She prayed she was right, and that the same thing that had happened to her father was not starting up again.

But a month later, as the blossoms on the trees started to show, her husband Jack was number seven in the horrible string of deaths. She was the only one to hear her husband's last words. He had told her about monster bugs three times the size of any he'd seen before. "It came from the apple trees," he said. "Came down when I was eating lunch. Thought it wanted my sandwich at first but came straight for my head." He rubbed the large welt on the side of his jaw and shivered. That's all he would say about it, no matter how much Anna pushed. The only thing he said for two days after was, "Anna, if this thing kills me, don't ever let Johnny go into that orchard. Please promise me you'll leave town with the boy and never look back".

Anna believed she knew what had caused them all. It was the same bugs her dad had told her mother about. And they needed to find them before anyone else died.

A few days after she buried her husband and got her son settled back into school, Anna went to the police with her husband's story, but Sheriff Harper told her that it was nonsense. "He was likely delirious, Anna. You told me yourself he was shivering, and all broke out in a sweat when he was telling you these stories. I'm sorry for your loss; I really liked Jack. Maybe you should listen to your husband and get out of town for a while. Go visit your relatives in Allensville or take a long vacation. Someplace warm, maybe." Harpy knew this story from over twenty years ago. Mary, Anna's mother, had come in with the same story after Paul had died. Whatever these men were seeing out in the orchard, it hadn't changed in twenty years.

"Thanks for nothing," Anna had murmured under her breath as she turned to leave. She was afraid to go any further with the sheriff, knowing they thought she was just a grieving woman making up stories. She left the sheriff's office not knowing what her next step would be, but she wasn't prepared to let it go. She decided to go to Dr. Redding's office down the street to make sure he had done an autopsy on her husband like she'd requested. He said he was waiting on the toxicology results before he could finish up his finding. Anna hoped it would give her some information on what really happened to Jack. Her mother had never requested one in 1990, and because Anna's father had died in a hospital they weren't done automatically. As a result, the family had never had any answers or closure.

Later that week Anna decided to go to Bellcom City, where she hoped to find someone that would help her. Bellcom was only about an hour's drive, but it was the biggest city in the area and had more resources. She'd try the police station first in hopes of a more professional response than what Windsmill police had provided.

"I'm sorry, Mrs. Lister, but we can't help you," the sergeant said. "First, because Windsmill is out of our jurisdiction. Secondly, because ... well ..."

"Because you don't believe me. Isn't that what you're trying to say?" Anna exclaimed in frustration.

"Yes," he said. "It's not that I don't want to help find the reason for your husband's death, ma'am. Someone will have to come up with a better answer than monster bugs before city council will let anyone touch the case. Believe me, Mrs. Lister, I know they won't waste any resources on this case."

"You knew about this story before I told you?" Anna questioned.

"Mr. Packart came in with it over twenty years ago, after his son died. His explanation was basically the same as yours. I don't know why you've waited this long to come to us, though, Mrs. Lister. Hasn't it been a month since your husband died."

"First of all, it takes time to get an autopsy completed and burial arrangements made and a son to calm down and get back into a routine and an inept police officer in Windsmill to tell me to take a holiday to feel better. That's 3 weeks sir! And excuse my bluntness, Sergeant, but you don't look old enough to have heard Mr. Packart's explanation twenty years ago." Anna glared at the police officer.

"No." The sergeant looked at her pointedly. "My father was a sergeant here back in those days. He used to tell me about that one case; you know, the one that never gets solved but sticks with you. It always bothered him that the investigation went nowhere. There just wasn't any proof of a crime."

"I didn't believe it at first either, Sergeant. But the more I think about it, the more it makes sense. All the people who have died from this horrible thing either worked in Packart's Orchard or were found close to the orchard boundaries. I remember when my father died. Mother was very upset about it and sent my brother away. He was never allowed to come home or even visit. She never said why, but I think my dad must have said something to her about getting him out of town, just like Jack begged me to do with Johnny."

"But Mrs. Lister, don't you think that there would be an unusual bite mark on the body or some type of venom in the bloodstream? Something?"

"I thought about that too. My husband did have a bite on his jaw, but working in the orchard there are a lot of different insects. The coroner thought nothing of the bites on his body. And as for venom, every insect leaves a deposit of some type in the bloodstream when it bites. I would think that these monsters would leave similar venom to what we're all familiar with. We'll see what my husband's autopsy says."

"It sounds plausible, but I still can't do anything to help you. Perhaps you should go to a private investigator or something. Someone who's not afraid to tackle these types of cases and isn't restricted by law and politics."

"You mean someone who needs the money more than they care about being embarrassed to ask around? Thanks for nothing!" Anna stormed out of the police station.

The sergeant shook his head, thinking, *Sometimes I wish there was something I could do for these people. But the coroner's office hasn't ruled these deaths suspicious, so there's nothing we can do.*

ANNA SAT AT THE COFFEE SHOP SCROLLING through her phone for information on investigators in the Bellcom area. She was surprised to find so many listings. Some only specialized in areas like divorce and cheating, finding parents or children from adoption situations, and lost or missing children or pets. Some looked promising, though, and after finding a half dozen that looked good, she started making calls. She was ready to give up after the fifth one gave her the same response that the two police stations had. Some didn't even hold back their laughter as they told her she needed a different kind of help than what they offered.

One more and then I have to get back to Windsmill to pick Johnny up from school, Anna thought as she dialed the last number on her list.

"Allen and Associates Investigations. David Allen at your service. How may I help you?" The man on the other end of the line sounded young and eager. *Maybe too eager*, Anna thought.

She explained her situation and what she was looking for. With or without this investigator, she was going to look into all of this, but she didn't tell Mr. Allen that.

David indicated his interest in helping her with her dilemma and asked when and where they could meet to discuss the case in more detail.

Finally, she thought. *I have someone on my side.* She looked at her watch and realized she didn't have time to meet Mr. Allen today. "I have to be back to Windsmill to pick up my son from school. Could we meet sometime tomorrow instead?" Anna asked hopefully.

David agreed to call her in the morning to make arrangements to meet, and Anna thanked him again. She raced to her car and headed home, a little lighter in her step and a little more hopeful that she could finally solve this mystery. She had found someone that was at least willing to listen to her.

CHAPTER 2

DAVID PHONED ANNA AS SHE WAS GETTING into the car to drop Johnny off at school the next morning. They agreed to meet at his office in Bellcom and he gave her the address and directions on how to get there. The building she arrived at about an hour and a half later was an old, two-storey brick building with a Vietnamese Pho Restaurant on one side and a fast-food sandwich joint on the other. Not the best area of town, but not the worst either. There was a bright-blue door just as David had described which she walked through and up the staircase to get to a glass and wood door with *Allen and Associates Investigations* etched in gold on the frosted glass.

"Come in, the door's unlocked," came a voice when she knocked. Anna turned the doorknob and entered. The man sitting behind the large oak desk was slender and looked to be in his late twenties. His dark curly hair and striking crystal blue eyes were just like Anna's. His face seemed familiar, though she couldn't place it. She didn't think she'd met him before.

"David Allen at your service, ma'am." His voice was very pleasant. "You must be Mrs. Lister." He stood up and stuck out his hand to shake hers. *He's very tall*, she thought. She had to look up to see his face.

"Yes, that's right." She smiled and shook his hand. "You're willing to help me?" Anna asked hopefully.

"Frankly, Mrs. Lister, I'm not sure. I'd like to know more about it before I commit. But I'm sure there is something I can do for you, ma'am. Coffee?" he asked and pointed to the small coffee counter to his right.

"No, thank you. And please, Mr. Allen, call me Anna. We look to be about the same age, and "ma'am" makes me feel so old." Anna chuckled.

"Okay, Anna. I'm David – Mr. Allen is my dad." He smiled sheepishly. "Now let's sit down and discuss this a bit further, shall we?"

They sat down, and Anna started to explain her story while David listened and jotted down notes as she spoke. She told him about the five men that had died more than twenty years ago, including Mr. Packart's son and her own father, and how they all worked in or around the Packart Orchard, except for the last one in 1990. She told him how after the stranger died it all just stopped.

"No one died the same way again and everyone in town forgot about it. That is until about three months ago, when Harry, that's the school bus driver, he found Red – sorry, his real name was Hector Lightfeather. He was found dead just outside Windsmill about a mile from his cabin in the orchard."

"And what about your husband? What happened to him?"

"He died just three weeks ago. High fever, shivers, convulsions. Some say he was delusional at the end, but I don't believe it. He had a small lump on his jaw just below his ear that he kept rubbing. Not like it hurt or itched or anything, just like he was thinking about how it happened. That's when he told me the stories about the bugs."

"And you told the police about all of this, right?" David stated.

"Yes, I told the police in Windsmill and when they wouldn't help me, I went to Bellcom City Police. It was the sergeant in Bellcom that told me that Mr. Packart had gone to them just after his son died in 1990. Sounds like they started to look into it, but nothing came of it. At least the sergeant wouldn't, or couldn't, tell me anything more. They all worked at or around the orchard; they were all young men between the ages of twenty and thirty years old; they were all in good health until just before they died; and they all died suddenly – within a couple of days or less of falling ill," Anna stated emphatically.

"Sounds interesting. What about the other workers in the orchard or young men in Windsmill? Have any of them mentioned seeing these monster bugs or whatever they are? Have any had illnesses even remotely resembling the symptoms that the others died from?"

"Not that I know of." Anna began to feel disappointed again. The questions were good ones, but there just weren't any answers. "No one has talked about all of this for years now, and if there was an investigation when Mr. Packart came forward, no one ever told me about it. Mind you, I wasn't even five yet when my dad died, so I likely wouldn't have heard about it anyway.

"There are so many loose ends, and if the police already looked into this years ago ..." Anna hesitated. "Maybe I should just drop it like they told me to." She hung her head to hide the tears welling up in her eyes.

PACKART'S ORCHARD   7

"Don't be so quick to give up on this!" David exclaimed. "This is just the beginning. I think we should start at the Packart residence; see if Mr. or Mrs. Packart can shed any light on any of this. That is, if you still want my help."

"Yes. Yes, of course I want your help." Anna jumped up from her chair. "I want to know what it is that killed these men. They were all so young and healthy. I want to make sure that others, including my son, are safe in Windsmill." Anna grabbed her purse and headed for the door.

David grabbed his jacket and car keys and ran to catch up. "How about I meet you back in Windsmill at about noon? We can have lunch and figure out our game plan."

Anna shook her head. "No. We have a game plan, so let's just do it!" She had already waited too long to get this started.

"Fine, then we can take my car. We can come back later and get yours if that's okay," he said as they left the office building and headed for the parking lot. "We can go over our plan and make sure I have all the details before we get to the Packart's place." David approached a beautiful sky-blue Mustang convertible with black racing stripes and a navy leather interior.

"This is your car?" Anna asked. "Business must be good." She chuckled.

"Graduation present from my folks." David shrugged as he opened the passenger door for her.

THE DRIVE BACK TO WINDSMILL SEEMED LONG, though it was less than fifty miles. Even though David said he wanted to continue to go over details, he seemed deep in his own thoughts and so there wasn't any more talk about the situation they were about to dive into. Anna had pushed hard on everyone she'd talked to about her husband's death, but now she was having second thoughts. Maybe she was making more out of this than there really was. Maybe the police were right, and she should take a holiday. Pack up and move her and Johnny somewhere else. But how could she leave her mother and all her lifelong friends? She'd never lived anywhere else, except when she went to college on the coast, and her and Jack first got married. She wouldn't know how to start over again.

"Do you have any family in Windsmill?" David asked conversationally.

Anna jumped with a start. "Sorry, what?" She looked at David, dazed.

"Sorry, didn't mean to startle you. I was just asking about your family. Do they live in Windsmill?"

"My mother does. And my son, of course. He'll be six next month."

"Do you have any siblings? Brothers or sisters that might remember anything?" David asked.

"What does my family have to do with any of this?" Anna snapped. "No, I don't have any brothers or sisters," she responded absently.

"Well, the first one to die was your father, and now twenty years later your husband. I think your family is well involved, Anna. Don't you?"

"Yes, I guess you're right." Anna stared out the window as the trees and brush passed by the car. Should she tell the man any more about her family? She barely knew him, but there was something so familiar about him. She sighed deeply. "I had a brother, although I don't remember much about him. Mother sent him away and I believe he was adopted by someone else. Mother goes to Allensville to see her sister all the time. I suppose that David is still in that area somewhere." Anna stopped her rambling and suddenly directed all of her attention to David. It dawned on her why the man driving the car looked so familiar to her.

"Stop the Car! NOW!" she screamed at him. "You can't go to Windsmill!"

"Anna, what's wrong?" He pulled the car off to the side of the road. "Why are you stopping me? Why can't I go to Windsmill?" He was confused and didn't know quite what to do next.

"Where are you from?" The question was sudden but demanding, and it startled David.

"You stopped the car to ask me that?!" he said indignantly. He was angry with the sudden change in attitude.

"Just answer me!" Her voice began to quiver. "I have to know. Please," she pleaded.

"Okay, if it's that important to you. I was born in Windsmill but don't know who my biological parents were or what happened to them. I was adopted by Mr. and Mrs. Allen in Allensville and yes, before you ask, the town was named after my dad's great-grandfather. I was seven years old when they adopted me, although I'd lived with them for a couple of years or more before that. I don't remember much before I lived in Allensville, and no one ever talked about it.

"Anyway, I was sent to Hedley College in Bellcom where I studied criminology and paranormal psychology. I now live in Bellcom City and own and operate my own investigation company." He looked straight into Anna's face. "There. Now you know. Can we go now"? he asked sarcastically.

"NO!" Anna screamed at him. "You CANNOT GO TO WINDSMILL! Mother promised Dad that she would never let you into the orchards, and if we pursue this investigation any further, it will lead you straight into the middle of them!"

"Anna, you aren't making any sense! I don't even know who your mother is, so how could she promise anyone where she would or would not let me go?"

"David, don't you understand?! Mr. and Mrs. A. J. Allen are my aunt and uncle. Aunt Jennie is my mother's sister; you may know her as Aunt Mary. You are my brother – my twin. Mother sent you away from Windsmill because of the promise she made to our father on his death bed. She didn't want you to look for us or come back to Windsmill. Ever. So, she took you to Aunt Jennie's and they must have agreed that they would adopt you as their own." Anna was getting excited but scared too. She had finally found her brother after all these years, and now she had gotten him into something that neither of them understood. Something that could kill him!

"Wow!" David leaned back on the driver's seat and rubbed his face. "That's a heavy statement, Anna, especially when it's all assumption." He knew the statements she made, the names she knew, the facts she told him, were much more, but this was too much for him to take in all at once.

"It is not all assumption! When I first saw you, you looked so familiar, but I couldn't place where or how I would know you. I couldn't place the resemblance, but now I do. You are the exact double of the picture of my dad that Mom keeps on her nightstand. David, you are my brother!"

"Okay, okay. I'm still going to find out what is killing all these men in Windsmill! I need to know more now than ever what's going on, and I don't intend to let it kill me either! Now let's go, okay?!"

Anna hesitated. She didn't want to lose her brother like she did the other men in her life. Especially since she just found him again. But looking at the determination on David's face, she knew he was going to investigate this with or without her. "Oh, alright! But David, please promise me that you'll be careful and stay away from the orchard. Please!?"

David shook his head. "I think your family makes too damned many promises!"

CHAPTER 3

ANNA ASKED DAVID TO STOP AT HER mother's place before they went anywhere else. She wanted to ask her mom to pick up Johnny from school while they carried on to the Packart's place. David told her to call instead. He didn't think it was a good idea to just pop in on Anna's mother after what he'd just found out.

"What's she going to say when she sees me in Windsmill"? David asked Anna pointedly. "Does she even know that you're looking into all of this? Isn't this whole thing going to open up a whole lot of scars and sadness from her past?"

"Yes, I suppose so. But I think we need to talk to her about this at some point. Find out what she knows and what Dad actually told her about what was going on." Anna looked down at her phone. She knew David was procrastinating about meeting mother even though he already knew her as Aunt Mary. She was having a hard time processing all that had just happened, even though she had known about him. She couldn't fathom what David was thinking. He hadn't even known she existed.

"We'll stop by after we talk to the Packarts. We'll have more time to sit down and let her know what you and I are up to. I think it will be a long and emotional discussion, so we need to make time for it."

"Okay, let me call Mom about Johnny. Then I'll give you the directions for the Packarts' place. Hopefully they're home. I haven't seen either of them around much for the past few months except just after Jack died, of course, at the funeral and all. Maybe they've gone away for a while or something. I don't know. Maybe we should call first and make sure. I could look up their phone number, and we can go from there. I'm just not sure if we should just pop in on them …"

11

"Anna!" David stopped her rambling. "We'll stop by and if they aren't there, we'll talk about plan B. How about you call your mother, then we'll stop someplace and grab a bite to eat, then I head out to the orchards? Now, the address please."

Anna pointed out a drive-thru eatery and, while David ordered two burger combos, Anna called her mother. It was a short conversation and she knew, when she got back home, she'd have to explain everything. She'd cross that bridge later.

After eating like she had never seen food before, Anna dictated the directions to the Packarts' house from memory. David drove until they got to a metal security gate in front of a large southern plantation style house on the edge of a beautifully landscaped and well-maintained acreage. David looked around for a buzzer or security system that would allow them access through the gate. Anna jumped out of the passenger seat, punched in the key code on a post by the gate, and it swung open effortlessly. David looked at her, mystified.

"My husband was the orchard manager and horticulturalist. I often came to meet him for lunch, or to bring him tools or information when he needed something. I guess I forgot to mention that."

David gave her a sideways glance. There were so many questions he needed answers to. Everything about this situation seemed to be so intertwined, it was going to take a lot of time and talking to get it all untangled.

They drove up the winding driveway until they came to a wide parking area by a grand-looking entrance. The whole house reminded David of pictures of plantation houses down south he'd seen in books. They were always so magnificent. Something about them looked so familiar to him, though he'd never seen one in person until now. At least, not that he remembered.

Anna ran up the steps and used the big knocker to rap on the door. When there was no response, she pressed the doorbell to the side of the big double doors. She could hear faint footsteps coming from behind the door and a voice saying, "I'm coming, I'm coming, hold your horses!" Anna smiled. The voice was so familiar to her. She reached over and turned the door handle and swung open the massive wooden door.

"Mrs. Packart, its Anna!" she said as she stepped into the foyer of the big house.

"Well, come in, dear, come in. How are you feeling these days? I'm so sorry about Jack." Mrs. Packart looked behind Anna as David walked in behind her. Her face went completely white, and her knees began to buckle. Anna rushed over and caught the woman in her arms. After sitting her on a small velvet chaise beside the door, Anna ran to the kitchen to get a glass of water for her.

When Anna returned, she noticed Mrs. Packart hadn't moved; she sat on the chaise staring at the door as if she'd seen a ghost. Then Anna realized what she was staring at. David had remained in the doorway, not leaving but not fully entering either. His silhouette with the sun behind him gave him a surreal, almost apparition-like appearance. He wore dress pants and a light pullover sweater, pushing the sleeves up to the elbow to stave off the heat of the afternoon sun. He looked just like Anna's father.

"Mrs. Packart, this is David Allen," Anna said quickly, gesturing toward David and waving him into the house. "He's helping me look into the strange deaths in the area."

"Nice to meet you, ma'am," David said as sweetly as he could muster. He stuck his hand out to shake the woman's hand, but she didn't move. He walked closer to where she was sitting. "Anna and I have some questions about the orchard. We thought you or your husband might be able to help us out."

Mrs. Packart began to shake her head slowly. "No, no, no!" she exclaimed, "you can't be here! You can't be in the orchard! Go away!" She stood up and walked quickly toward the back of the house.

David and Anna raced after her, afraid she was going to fall and hurt herself. They caught up to her in the kitchen. It was brightly lit and open, with a huge island. A double-door fridge stood majestically beside the ovens, and a stove top with ten burners graced the counter. Sitting at a table in a nook by a bay window was Mrs. Packart, tears running down her face as she stared at the landline telephone on the wall next to her.

"If you don't leave immediately, I will call the police," she said, staring pointedly at David. "You can't be here. How could you bring him here to the orchard, Anna? After everything you've been through, I would have thought you of all people would be smarter than that!"

Anna took a step back, not knowing what to say or do. David realized that he would need to calm the woman down and keep Anna from running, or they'd never get to the bottom of all this.

"Mrs. Packart, please." David placed his hand on her shoulder. "We just want to figure out what's going on so that we can stop whatever it is. Please,

PACKART'S ORCHARD   13

Mrs. Packart, can we just sit and talk about what's going on; ask a few questions? We won't stay long." David guided Anna toward the chair beside Mrs. Packart and then sat across from the two women.

Mrs. Packart nodded, tears streaming down her face. "Fine. You can stay a bit, but you need to be out of here before the sun starts to set. You need to get as far away as you can before dark." She pointed at David. "You look just like him, you know. Just like your father," she said, wiping away the tear streaks from her cheeks.

"So Anna has said. He was the first to die in the orchard?" David asked quietly.

"Yes, him, and then the Faulkon twins, then Darren after that."

"Darren?" asked David.

"My son. We thought at first it was something the two of them got into. They were always getting into trouble, those two boys, since they were in elementary school. But after the medical report for Darren came back undetermined, we figured something more was happening. That's when Albert – that's my husband," she directed to David. "When he went to the police, they just sent him home and told him to come back if he had anything concrete for them to look at." Mrs. Packart sighed and pushed herself up from the table. "I'll get some iced tea," she said, but Anna gently pushed her back down.

"I'll get it." Anna walked over to a cupboard and found glasses then pulled the pitcher of iced tea out of the refrigerator. She filled three glasses with ice then poured in tea. She set the glasses in front of them, leaving the pitcher in the middle of the table.

"What did he suspect was happening that the police could help with? Have you seen anything in the orchard that might be responsible?" David took a big gulp out of the cold glass.

"Yes." She began to shiver. "I have seen things. No monster-sized bugs or anything like that, if that's what you mean, but there have been things happening around here for years."

"Ma'am, if you don't mind, can you describe what you've seen?" David asked as he jotted notes in his notebook. He was recording the conversation on his phone but liked the old school way to help keep his thoughts on track of what to ask about next.

"I do mind!" Mrs. Packart said. "I want you gone. So, if you don't mind, you can just go away! And don't come back!" She pushed past Anna and started to walk toward the staircase at the end of the kitchen.

"NO! I do mind too, Mrs. Packart!" Anna screamed. "Listen, you have known me and my family for years now. All my life, as a matter of fact, and most of my father's life as well! He died because of this orchard, and so did your son. Now my husband is gone too! Mrs. Packart, you can help us find out why!"

"Fine." Mrs. Packart sat back down across from David and glared at him. "You two aren't going to stop, are you?" She watched as Anna sat down beside her. "Fine. I will tell you what little I know, but then you have to leave." When they both nodded in agreement, she continued. "It started about a year before your father died. It was very strange, and it still frightens me at times, especially now that I'm here alone and all."

"Alone?" Anna questioned. "Has Mr. Packart gone away?"

Mrs. Packart waved her question away. "Well, anyway, Albert said he knew what it was but that it wouldn't hurt anyone and would likely go away on its own. After Paul died …" Mrs. Packart hesitated. "After your father died, I told Albert to get rid of whatever it was. He told me to not be silly, that it wasn't the orchard that killed Paul, it was likely a flu-bug or his heart, like the doctors told us happened. The orchard wouldn't hurt anyone, especially a family friend like young Paul, Albert said."

"What was in the orchard that you wanted him to get rid of, Mrs. Packart?" David looked at her suspiciously. She knew more than she was willing to tell.

"I don't know. He never said." She turned to look at Anna. "After those two brothers died and then Darren, well, Albert began to believe that the thing was out to kill everyone in the family. And then the investigator at the hotel downtown that Albert had been talking to, well, that's when he went to the police in Bellcom City. The police told him he was crazy, that there was nothing in the orchard that was killing those men. But all the medical reports were inconclusive. No one knows what was killing them. After the investigator died, it just stopped. No more deaths, no more sightings, nothing! But Albert wouldn't let it go. He said we had to be diligent and make sure there was no one else that would get hurt."

She looked at David with sadness in her eyes. "That's when the families got together and decided to send the young male family members away from Windsmill and Packart's Orchard. To try to stop the deaths!" She closed her eyes to stay the tears. "My daughter-in-law took my son's boys up north where her family was from. I get to talk to them on Facetime but haven't seen them in person in years." Tears flowed freely now. "Your mom sent David away too, but not as far. She didn't want to leave Windsmill at the time because her dad had just died a couple years earlier, and her mother was still here in town on her own. After David was gone for a couple of years, Mary and Jennie decided that Jennie and AJ would adopt him as their own. It was to try to keep you away," she said to David. "To keep you safe.

"When Red was found a couple months ago, and then Jack died this month, it was too much for Albert. His heart gave out, and I called an ambulance. He's in hospital in Bellcom, but it's the mental issues that are keeping him there. He keeps telling everyone that the monster needs to be stopped. Everyone thinks he's crazy."

"He's never told you what it was that he is so afraid of?" David asked.

"I already told you that he never said what it was! Don't you listen?"

"Yes, of course I've been listening. I just thought maybe after your husband broke down, he …"

"He never said anything!" Mrs. Packart stood and started to walk back toward the front door. Anna and David followed her. "Now go away! Please, leave me alone." She flung the big wooden door open dramatically and pointed outside. "Leave, and if you were smart, young man, you'd leave Windsmill and never come back! Before you end up like the rest of them, dead or too scared to come to work!"

As they walked toward the car, they heard the door slam shut. That was all they were going to get out of Mrs. Packart today, David thought.

"I'll take you to your mother's, then I'll come back and look around the orchard, see what I can come up with out here." David gestured toward the acres of long rows of fruit trees and outbuildings visible from the parking lot. The shadows that were cast on the pathway by the afternoon sun made it somehow seem more ominous. He knew that cabins where Anna told him Hector Lightfeather had lived, were at the end of orchard, and there was likely more to see at that end of the property as well. He might have to drive around the back acre to see what was out there too.

"You can't go out there now! Not after what Mrs. Packart just said about getting out of here before dark!" Anna said incredulously. "David, come on, we'll come back another time."

16   WENDY SCOTT-ETTINGER

"Oh, Anna, stop it! When people say those things, they're just trying to frighten everyone away. There is usually a very reasonable explanation for things that go bump in the night. People see monsters where there aren't any. Dust bunnies and light reflecting off the bed legs makes people believe in monsters under the bed. A wind rustling the tree leaves or the irrigation pipes banging before they start or stop. There's likely a very logical explanation." David opened the car door to let Anna in.

"Dust bunnies under the bed, rustling wind, and rattling pipes don't kill people, David!" Anna grabbed the car door and slammed it shut again. "And if you think I'm going home like a good little girl while you wander around aimlessly in this orchard getting yourself killed, you have another thing coming!" She walked toward the apple trees then stopped and turned back to David. "Well, are you coming?" she asked sarcastically, before turning back to the shadows.

"Damn it, woman!" The words stormed out of his mouth before he realized what he was saying. "You think that I'm going to let you go into this mess too? One of us has to stay behind in case something does happen to the other ..." He stopped himself. "Look, Anna. I don't mean to sound chauvinistic or anything, and I'm trying not to frighten you, but if something does happen to me, you'll need to take the recording I made of our conversation with Mrs. Packart to the authorities. I'll send it to your phone, and I'll be making a video of my trip through the orchard as well. The conversation recording will give the police something to start with, at least, and will give me something to review once I get back to the office, if I make it that far. Now please, Anna, please! Just at least stay here in the car and wait for me. I won't be long." He opened the car door again and she walked back toward him.

"Fine. But you better not be long. Leave me the car keys." He handed her his keys and walked in the same direction she had started to go. "I'll be back in an hour; hour and a half, tops," he said over his shoulder. *Or at least I hope so,* he thought as he walked into the shadows.

She didn't like the idea of staying behind and letting him go into the orchard by himself. *What if something does happen to him? I would never forgive myself for getting him into this,* Anna thought as she scrolled through her phone for something to occupy her mind. She sat in the car for what seemed forever, but according to her phone he'd only been gone thirty minutes or so. She looked up at the mansion and noticed the front room curtains moving. *Just the wind, like David implied about all strange things,* she thought. *The window must be open.*

PACKART'S ORCHARD 17

AMELIA PACKART LOOKED OUT THE FRONT WINDOW and watched as David and Anna argued about something. *Why did all of this have to start up again? Why now?* she thought as she watched the twins pace back and forth. Then Anna got into the car and David headed out toward the outbuildings. Another death was coming soon, she thought as she turned from the window. She could feel it. She walked down the staircase, through the kitchen, and out the back door. She'd follow the cedar trees up to the highway and back. They should be gone by the time she finished her walk.

ANNA LISTENED TO THE CAR RADIO AND must have changed the station a hundred times. She remembered the recording David had sent her of their conversation with Mrs. Packart and began to listen to that. She had never seen Mrs. Packart as on edge as she was that afternoon. Anna searched the car for a pen and paper so she could make some notes and jot down further questions but couldn't find any. *Of course not*, she thought, *his note pad is likely in his pocket*. She turned on the Notes app on her phone and jotted down some questions as she listened to the recording. This sitting doing nothing wasn't in her nature and would drive her crazy if he didn't return soon.

Anna sat there for what seemed like another forever, then finally got out of the car and headed in the direction David had gone. The curtains in the front window waved again, but she dismissed it. She walked through the trees cautiously, watching every little movement around her.

The sun was dipping in the sky by the time Anna found David. It was going to get dark soon. He was hunched down in a small bush, peering out of the leaves at her. "Anna"! His voice boomed out over the silence. "What in god's name do you think you're doing"?

"David! You scared the crap out of me!" Anna jumped in the opposite direction. "I was bored stiff sitting in the car, and I was worried ..." she trailed off. She could tell by the look on his face that he was angry. "Please, just let me help. You've been out here forever," she pleaded.

"I scared you?! You were worried?! If you can't sit in a car for an hour without getting into trouble you should have let me take you home. Damn it, Anna, I've only been out here about fifty to fifty-five minutes tops!" David was so angry he could barely put a sentence together. He was stammering and muttering under his breath as he grabbed her arm to drag her back to the car. "If you had waited a few more minutes, I would have been back at the car. Now, let's get out of here. It's getting too dark in the trees to see anything more today!"

"So what were you doing in that bush, anyway?" Anna asked curiously. "You looked foolish jumping out of there." She chuckled.

"I thought I heard something, so I was trying to hide but still get a good look at what was making the noise. Turns out it was my long-lost sister coming to save me." David's voice dripped with sarcasm.

"You can let go of my arm now, David." Anna looked down at his hand on her elbow. "I'm not going to run back into the trees."

"Fine." He dropped his hand and quickened his pace. The sooner they got out of here, and he could get her home and himself back to Bellcom City, the better. Maybe it wasn't such a good idea taking this case after all.

AMELIA CLEANED UP THE KITCHEN AFTER SHE returned from her walk. The fresh air always made her feel better, and the exercise was good for her. She turned off the lights on the main floor and went back up the back stairs to her sitting room. She spent a lot of time up here watching. She looked out the window and realized David's car was still there. Anna was no longer sitting in the passenger seat staring at her phone, as all young people seemed to do these days. Amelia scanned the garden area and then looked toward the orchard. All was quiet; at least for now. But this wasn't over yet. Someone could die tonight, but it wouldn't be David. She looked down at the needlepoint in her hand and began to sew.

Amelia glanced from her sewing to the trees and back again as she continued surveillance, and a few minutes later David and Anna reappeared. "Anna may have saved a life tonight," Amelia said as she walked back down the stairs and pushed the button that would open the gate for them. *No use taking any chances*, she thought as she went back to her room.

THEY GOT INTO THE CAR WITHOUT SAYING another word to each other, both lost in their own thoughts. David drove down the long driveway and realized the gate was still open. Did they leave it open when they came in earlier? Maybe Mrs. Packart had opened it when they left the house but wouldn't it have timed-out and closed again. *Strange* he thought, as he pulled up to the highway and watched the gate auto-close behind him. He shook his head as he turned toward Windsmill one more time.

PACKART'S ORCHARD 19

CHAPTER 4

IT WAS DUSK AND GETTING HARDER TO see, so David flipped on his headlights and turned west toward town. He was about to ask Anna for directions to her mother's home when he noticed something off the side of the road just after a rest stop. *What was that?* he thought. Something was lying in the long grass, not quite in the ditch. It looked like someone threw a laundry basket full of clothes out of a car window. David stopped the car and walked up to what he was looking at.

"Where are you going?" Anna asked as she climbed out of the car.

"Get back in the car!" David said as he looked down at what he'd thought was a bundle of clothes "And call 911."

"What is it?" Anna asked as she leaned over his shoulder to see what he'd found. She scurried back more quickly than she thought she could ever move. "Oh my god! It's Marty Faulkon, Marvin and Becky's son." She covered her mouth to try to keep from screaming. "Is he … is he dead?" she stammered.

"Can't find a pulse, so yes, I think so. But he's still warm. Now call the police, Anna. Now!" he yelled when she didn't move. She ran back to the car and found her phone sitting on the seat where she'd left it. She dialed 911 and within seconds the operator answered. Anna explained what they'd found and where they were, and the operator asked her not to hang up until emergency services had arrived. She was sitting frozen to the car seat with the phone still to her ear when David got back into the driver's seat.

"Did you get through?" he asked as he turned the car back on and turned up the heater. He knew it was the shock of what he'd just discovered, but he was shivering like a baby right out of the bath water. He looked over at Anna and realized she was looking like a deer in the headlights too.

Two police cars, an ambulance, and a firetruck came roaring around the corner, lights flashing and sirens blaring.

"They're here," Anna said flatly into the phone.

"I heard the sirens," the operator said, "if you no longer need my services, I'll disconnect now," and before Anna could say anything, the line went dead.

As David reached for his door handle, Anna grabbed his arm. "Please stay in the car! Whatever killed Marty could kill you too." Fear covered her face and tears welled up in her clear blue eyes. "Please," she pleaded.

"I have to talk to the police, Anna, and let them know what's going on." He peeled her fingers from his shirt sleeve and was about to open the car door when a flashlight shone through the side window into his face. He blocked the light with his arm and rolled down the window.

"You call emergency?" the police officer asked.

"Yes, we found a body over there in the grass. Thought it was just someone's laundry or something but when I got over there, I realized it was a body." David gestured toward the ditch.

"It's Marty. Marty Faulkon," Anna said. "He's dead, Officer, just like Red. Just like Jack." She put her face in her hands and began to sob.

"Did either of you touch anything?" asked the officer matter-of-factly.

"Just touched his wrist and then under his chin looking for a pulse. Didn't touch anything else, sir," David explained.

"What are you two doing out here this time of day, anyway? You look familiar," the officer pointed at David, "but I don't think we've met."

"I'm David Allen. I run a private investigation business out of Bellcom City." David reached out the window to shake the officer's hand, but they backed away from the window and reached for the gun hanging in a holster under their jacket. "Sorry. Sorry. I wasn't thinking. Just trying to be friendly. Break the tension and all."

The officer relaxed their hand. "Okay, just stay in the car and don't leave until I've told you it's okay to do so. Understand?"

David nodded. "Can I get some jackets and water out of the trunk please, sir?" he asked as politely as he could. This officer was jumpy.

"Pop the trunk. I'll get whatever you need out," the officer responded. David didn't like the idea of the police searching the trunk and his belongings. They'd find his gun and his investigative equipment, and they might think he had something to do with the dead guy.

PACKART'S ORCHARD 21

"I'd rather do it myself if you don't mind. It's pretty messy back there and you'd need a map to find anything." David chuckled nervously.

"Got something to hide, sir?" The officer looked at David with suspicion and started to reach for the gun again.

"No, sir, just trying to not hold you up too much from your duties." David nodded toward the body and the emergency team scurrying around it.

"Fine, but don't do anything stupid or you could end up beside Marty in the morgue." The officer walked away before David could say anything else. He was beginning to hate Windsmill more and more as the day went on. The sooner he could get out of here and regroup, the better he'd feel. He jumped out of the car and headed for the trunk. He rummaged around and found a jacket for himself and one that wasn't too dirty to give to Anna. He opened the cooler and found water, juice, and some snacks, because he thought they could be here awhile and he was already getting hungry again.

As David was putting his stash between the front seats of his car, something caught his eye. The flashing lights of the emergency vehicles were illuminating the trees around the rest area, but they were so intermittent that it made it hard to see anything but shadows. There was definitely something there, though. David tried to look closer, but he couldn't see anything. He pulled his phone out of his pocket and turned on the flashlight feature. Not the strongest light in the world, but better than nothing, he thought as he stood up again and aimed it at the trees over the roof of his car.

The police officer walked over and stood beside him. "Something wrong, Mr. Allen?" the officer asked as they stared over the car's roof in the direction of the light.

"Thought I saw something in the trees. Probably my imagination," David said as he stuffed his phone back in his pocket. "This light isn't helping at all, and the flashing lights make it hard to see much of anything."

The officer nodded. "We'll be searching the area in the morning. If there is anything out there, we'll find it. Now get back into your car so we don't have to be out here all night." The officer walked back over to greet yet another police vehicle pulling into the rest area.

An older, grey-haired man, likely in his late fifties or early sixties, stepped out of the squad car. He was stout and about 5' 8" tall with his thumbs in his belt loops and an easy smile on his face. "Looks like one of those sheriffs out of the old movies," David said to Anna as they watched the scene unfold.

Anna chuckled for the first time in a while. "That's Sheriff Harper," she said, "and he's friendly. Doesn't get out of the police station much anymore, I don't think." She smiled at her old family friend.

THE SHERIFF WALKED TOWARD THE OFFICER. "WHAT we got, Charlie?" he asked as he looked down at the body.

"We believe it's Marty Faulkon, sir" the officer answered. "Anna, er, Mrs. Lister, identified him when her and her private eye friend found him."

"What in the world is she up to now?" The sheriff asked no one in particular. "Who's the dick with her?" he asked curiously. His counterpart in Bellcom City had told him that Anna had been into their office yesterday, and that his sergeant told her to hire an investigator, but Harpy didn't think she'd actually find someone. He shook his head.

"He's David Allen. Has a PI outfit in Bellcom City. Had one of the MT's run him while we were waiting for the go to load. Coroner's not coming out this way tonight. Said he'd meet the ambulance at the morgue when we're ready."

"Okay. You can tell the MT's to load up whenever they're ready to do so. Tell them to get hold of Mason on their way into town and let him know I want a report on my desk in the morning."

His voice became less formal as he questioned with a smile, "So what did you find out about Mr. Allen and his investigation services?"

Charlie turned her back to Harpy as she responded, "I'll just let everyone know they're cleared to clean up the scene and go. I'll give Jeff the keys to the cruiser, and I'll head back into town with you, if that's okay? I'll let you know everything we've found out here, and about the guy in that car, when we get going." Charlie walked with purpose back to the waiting team.

The sheriff sauntered over to the shiny blue sports car, scanning the ditch and tree line as he walked. He rapped on the driver's window with the end of his flashlight, still looking over the car's roof into the trees, where he'd seen Charlie and the civilian staring. When he heard the whirring of the window descending, he glanced down toward the face of the man sitting in the car and almost passed out. He stepped back from the car and reached for his gun. He felt dizzy and confused. He pulled his gun and ordered, "Get out of the car – NOW!"

David looked at the strange man and saw the fear in his eyes. "Is there a problem, Sheriff?" he asked slowly. "What's happened?" He reached for the door handle and pushed the door open. He moved with purpose, never breaking eye contact with the sheriff as he exited the car. "Sir, are you alright? You look like you've seen a ghost." David heard the passenger door open and shut quickly. *She's going to get me killed sooner rather than later, isn't she?* he thought, hanging his head and shaking it vigorously.

"Not now, Anna, get back into the car, please," he said, returning his gaze back to the sheriff's face.

"Harpy, are you okay?" Anna asked gently as she rounded the front of the car, ignoring David's demands. "You're very pale and shaking like a leaf. You should really put your gun away before you shoot someone by accident." Anna said soothingly. The sheriff broke eye contact with David for the first time, and he smiled at Anna. She reached over and pushed his arm down so the gun was pointed toward the ground. "Sheriff, is everything okay?"

The sheriff shook his head and tried to compose himself. "I'm fine, Anna. Are you okay?" He put his arm around her shoulders and pulled her close. "It's been a hell of a few weeks, hasn't it?" he said to her. Then he glanced back at David.

"You can't be who I just saw in that car," he said to David. "So, who are you and what are you doing out here in the middle of nowhere with Anna in tow?" His authoritative stance and voice were back.

"I'm David Allen of Allen and Associates Investigations sir." David reached out to shake the sheriff's hand. "Pleased to meet you, sir." The sheriff waved it off just like his deputy had. "Mrs. Lister hired me to look into her husband's death. She and I spent a good portion of the afternoon with Mrs. Packart talking to her about what's been going on around the orchard." David didn't know what, if anything, he wanted to tell the sheriff just yet. Then he heard rustling in the trees behind him and he shivered. "Perhaps we could go somewhere a little warmer, and not so dark, to finish this conversation?" he asked.

The sheriff was still suspicious, but he nodded in agreement. "Are you okay to continue your journey home with this man?" he asked Anna as he pushed her to arm's length without letting her go. He was staring into her face to make sure he didn't see anything he didn't like. It made Anna feel like she was a kid again.

"I'm fine, Harpy. David would never hurt me. I trust him completely. But I agree with him that we shouldn't be out here in the dark like this. Can we come into your office in the morning to finish this conversation?" she looked up at him hopefully. She needed time to think and to talk to David about what he'd seen in the shadows of the trees, without the prying eyes and ears of the law.

The sheriff agreed to let them go, with the strict understanding that they were to be in his office at nine o'clock sharp. If either of them didn't show, he'd put out a warrant for their arrest. They nodded in agreement and quickly got back into the car. David didn't want to give the sheriff time to change his mind. He just wanted to head back to his office and review everything that had happened that day.

After getting directions to Anna's mother's place, he carefully pulled his car out onto the highway and headed towards Windsmill. Neither of them said anything until they pulled up in front of a very small but well-cared-for two-storey home. It tweaked a faraway memory in David's subconscious of a tire swing hanging from a big old willow tree. Those flashes of memory were happening a lot today. He turned toward Anna, waiting for her to exit the car.

"Aren't you coming in with me?" Anna asked. She tilted her head slightly and looked at him in the same expectant way he was looking at her.

"No, not now," he said. "I'm tired and my head is spinning from everything that has happened since you and I met at my office today. I just need some time to go over my notes," he added non-committedly. He wanted to listen to their conversation with Mrs. Packart and view the video he'd taken in the orchard and the one he'd started when they'd found the body and didn't end until the sheriff had gotten back into his squad car. He needed time to sort out who he was and whether it was a good idea to continue this investigation with Anna, or to even see Aunt Mary or be in Windsmill at all. "I'll meet you tomorrow at the sheriff's office," he said as he looked away and waited for her to get out. "Unless you need me to pick you up. We can go together," he added, remembering her car was still in the parking lot by his office.

Anna knew he wasn't going to budge, so she didn't push him. She confirmed she'd be at the sheriff's office at 9:00 a.m. sharp and got out of the car. Being away from David would give her time to go over everything that had happened and try to figure out what, if anything, she was going to tell her mother. She'd have to ask her mom if she could borrow her car tomorrow. That was going to cause a barrage of questions as to why her car was still in Bellcom City.

She stood on the big porch steps and watched as David's car lights disappeared around the corner toward the highway. She prayed he'd make it home safe, then entered her mother's front door and hugged the little boy rushing toward her from the kitchen.

CHAPTER 5

WITH ABOUT FIVE MINUTES TO SPARE, DAVID pulled into the parking lot of the Windsmill Sheriff's Department and jumped out of his car. He'd fallen asleep at his desk rereading the notes he'd taken from all that had happened the day before. He woke with a start with just enough time to wash his face, change his clothes, and head out of town again. He was really hoping the police coffee was not as horrible as all the stories he'd heard, because he could really use one about now. He was about to open the door to the station when a familiar voice called from behind. He turned around in time to see Anna skipping up the steps, a cup of coffee in each hand.

"Looks like you need this a lot more than I do this morning," she said as she held out the cup in front of her. "You look like hell." She giggled.

"Thanks!" he said as he grabbed the cup from her hand and took a big swallow, immediately regretting it, as it burned his tongue and throat. "Ouch! Did you ask them to boil it again before putting it in the cup?" He held his mouth open, hoping the cool morning air would help.

"Maxine always makes the best coffee, but you do need to wait a bit before drinking it. I should have warned you. I keep forgetting you're really not from around here." She reached around him and pulled open the door. "We should get in there before Harpy sends out the cavalry." She smiled over her shoulder at him.

As they walked toward the reception area to announce their arrival, a very pleasant-looking woman in uniform stopped in front of them. "About time you two showed up," she said with a tight smile. She was a tall, slender woman with straw-colored hair and the greenest eyes David had ever seen. He glanced down at the name on her chest and then immediately looked

26

back up at her. *It couldn't be!* he thought as he looked at the name and the face again.

"I'm Deputy Sheriff Charlene Carter, but most people around here call me Charlie." She smiled again, amused at the confused look on David's face. "And yes, I'm the officer in charge at last night's little party. You know, the one where I really wanted any excuse to shoot you," she added as she turned and started to walk down the hallway. "Follow me. Sheriff Harper is expecting you."

They followed Charlie down a long corridor and into a small conference room across the hall from a large office with "SHERRIF'S OFFICE" embossed on it in gold.

"Are we being interrogated?" David questioned formally. "Should we be requesting legal counsel?"

"Not unless you've done something wrong." Charlie sneered back at him. "Harpy thought this would be more comfortable since he's asked me and the medical examiner to join you for this little chat." Charlie rapped lightly on the door and then opened it without waiting for a response. The sheriff was sitting at the head of a long conference table, chatting quietly with a man of about forty in a black suit and white dress shirt. He looked more like the undertaker than a doctor, but being in a small town, he could be both, David supposed.

"Aah, you finally made it." Sheriff Harper stood up and stuck out his hand to shake David's. "It's nice of you to come in this morning," he added.

David shook the sheriff's hand and nodded at the man now standing beside him. "And you are?" David asked as he held out his hand to the other man.

"Good to meet you, David." The man took his hand with a firm grasp. "I'm Dr. Mason Redding. I'm the town's family doctor, coroner, medical examiner, and occasionally the mortician." Mason smiled up at him, then looked over at Anna and added, "Good morning, Anna. How's that son of yours? I bet he's growing like a weed."

"Good morning, Dr. Redding. Johnny is doing fine, all things considered," Anna responded.

"Please have a seat and we'll get this party started, shall we," Harpy interrupted. "Charlie, close that door please and have a seat, everyone."

Harper asked David and Anna to explain what they were doing out by Packarts and what made them stop at the rest stop. David reiterated what he'd told them the night before about Anna hiring him to help her investigate her husband's death, and that they had decided to start by talking to the Packarts. David said he wasn't going very fast because it was dusk, and the trees tended to block out most of the sunlight at that time of day. He said he was about to pull over to punch Anna's mother's address into his GPS when he spotted what looked like a large pile of clothing. He decided to investigate, and that's when he asked Anna to call 911.

Anna confirmed what David had just said and added that she hadn't known why David had pulled over but got out of the car to see what he was looking at. That's when she realized it was Marty Faulkon's body. There wasn't much more she could add to David's explanation.

After a few more basic questions about how they had come to meet up and what Anna was thinking bringing David to Windsmill, let alone to Packart's Orchard, Charlie finally spoke up for the first time. "What exactly where you looking at over the car roof last night?" she questioned David.

"I honestly don't know. I thought I'd seen something move just inside the tree line. But like I said last night, with the flashing lights from the emergency vehicles, it was hard to see anything out there. I decided it wouldn't be a good move to get out of the car and move closer to the trees, lest I get shot" he smiled sheepishly at Charlie, "so I just stood there staring for a while. Could have been the wind moving the trees. Could have been a deer or another animal of some sort. Could have been my imagination." David shrugged as if to say that was all he was saying on the subject.

"Have you been out there since you were told to leave last night?" Charlie questioned David with a cold stare.

"No. I dropped Anna off at her mother's place immediately after leaving the scene, and then headed directly to Bellcom City. I stopped in at the restaurant in the same building as my office, and then reviewed my notes before making a few phone calls. I came directly from my office in Bellcom City this morning to this office, as directed." David was becoming defensive and wasn't sure where the officer was going with her questions.

"What calls did you make? Who did you speak to?" Charlie questioned authoritatively.

"The hospital where Mr. Packart is currently staying, to inquire about visiting hours and any visitor restrictions. My father, Mr. AJ Allen, to discuss a few more personal issues." David glanced over at Anna as he said this. "I then called a couple of other clients to reschedule their appointments for later in the week."

"Did you mention the body you found or the name of that person to anyone?" Charlie continued.

"No. What exactly are you digging for, Deputy?" David gave her the same tone she had been taking with him. "Do I need to call my lawyer?"

Charlie ignored David's question and turned to Anna. "And how about you, Mrs. Lister? Did you go back out to the rest area after Mr. Allen dropped you off?"

"No, of course not!" Anna said, surprised at the line of questioning. "And before you ask, I didn't leave my mother's house after David dropped me off. Johnny and I stayed the night at Mother's place. We, my mother, my son and I, had dinner and then I read a story to Johnny, bathed him, and put him to bed. I talked to my mother about everything that had happened yesterday, including about finding David." She glanced at him as she continued. "My mother tried calling her sister shortly after that, but the line was busy, so she said she'd try again this morning, after Johnny and I left the house." She glanced at David again and he nodded to acknowledge what she was saying mostly for his benefit. "Neither she nor I spoke to anyone else the rest of the evening. And just for the purposes of full disclosure," Anna glared at Charlie, "I went to bed early, about nine-thirty p.m. The day's events took a big toll on me emotionally, and I was quite exhausted. Now, if that's all," Anna stood up, gathering her empty coffee cup and a note pad she'd brought with her, "I have other more pressing things to think about besides being accused of unknown offenses."

"Mrs. Lister," Mason spoke up. "I have the reports from your husband's autopsy as well as a Permission to Release form, so I can release same to Mr. Allen if you'd just sign the paperwork before you leave. I assume you'll be looking for information regarding the deaths of Mr. Lightfeather and Mr. Faulkon as well?" he questioned, looking at David. After receiving nods from both, and Anna's signature on the release form, Mr. Redding continued. "I'll need to get formal permission from the families before I'm able to release any of those reports. If and when I receive those permissions, I'll let you know."

"Thank you, Dr. Redding. I appreciate your assistance." Anna picked up the envelope he had set on the table in front of her and walked toward the door, brushing past Charlie and ignoring Harpy's outstretched hand. The niceties were over.

David stood up as well and thanked Dr. Redding, who handed him an envelope with the report in it. "If I have further inquiries, may I call you directly, or are there other protocols in place for that?" David asked the doctor in the most professional voice he could muster.

"Yes, of course, just give me a call. If it's a more detailed discussion you're after, we can make an appointment. My card is attached to the report. It has my direct line on it." Dr. Mason smiled knowingly at David. He stuck out his hand and David shook it with a strong grip.

"I'm sure we'll be speaking again soon," David responded. Without another glance at either of the police officers, David grabbed his jacket from the back of his chair, gathered up the cup and papers he'd brought, and quickly left the conference room.

When he descended the steps of the police station building, he spotted Anna pacing beside his car.

"I walked here from Mother's this morning," she said as he approached. "Can you give me a ride home, please?"

This is going to be an interesting ride to Mother's house, he thought.

SHERIFF HARPER THANKED DR. REDDING FOR JOINING them and taking the time to get the report ready for Mrs. Lister. They chatted a bit about when Harpy might expect the autopsy results for Marty Faulkon, and then the doctor left for his own office. Before Charlie could leave with the doctor, Harpy called her back into the conference room.

"Charlie, if you have another minute?" he asked politely. "Please come on in and close the door."

Charlie was red-faced and pacing as she looked over at Sheriff Harper. "So?" she said like a bad-tempered teenager.

"Deputy Carter, please have a seat" Harpy pointed at a chair. "Now. Please," he said in a more commanding voice when Charlie didn't move.

As she sat heavily in the chair, he asked, "Want to tell me what the hell that was all about?" He waited.

Charlie looked at him obstinately and after a few seconds finally broke the silence. "I was back out to the scene earlier this morning. There were vehicle tracks over those that had been there last night when we left the scene. It was obvious to me that someone had beat us out there. There was boot prints in the ditch and up the side of the hill toward where Mr. Allen had been staring the night before. Both myself and Officer Parent, who accompanied me this morning, took pictures of these disturbances and made a formal report of same. They should be on your desk now, sir."

Harpy stared at Charlie for a long time without speaking. He breathed deeply and then said quietly, "What time did you head out to the scene this morning?"

"Seven-thirty a.m., sir."

"And did anyone else in the precinct know you had gone out there?"

"No, sir, Parent and I were the first ones here as far as I know, sir."

"Did you pass any vehicles going out or coming back into town?"

"No, sir. We saw no traffic."

"What time did you get back to the precinct this morning, Deputy?"

"Approximately eight-thirty a.m., sir."

"So, you must have typed up your report with posthaste in order to be waiting for Mrs. Lister and Mr. Allen at the door at eight fifty-five a.m., Deputy Carter." Harper's tone was becoming more formal and authoritative with every statement. "Or did you happen to have it dictated to my secretary while you were in the cruiser on your way back?"

"I, we, I ..." Charlie hesitated. She'd forgotten how early the Sheriff and his secretary got into the office every morning. She assumed, wrongly, she realized now, that he would be late getting in today because they were so late getting out of the precinct the night before. "I dictated my report to Sarah's voicemail and requested she get a hard copy of the report to you as early as was possible, sir."

"I'm aware of your voicemail to my assistant this morning, Deputy Carter," the sheriff said. "As a matter of fact, she and I listened to it together." He watched his deputy's face fall and her 'I'm-smarter-than-you-are' attitude drop away. "Since you were so busy waiting to try to intimidate our only two potential witnesses to a possible homicide this morning, rather than coming to talk to me about the meeting ahead of their arrival, you wouldn't know that I also had additional information regarding those tire and boot prints that you and Officer Parent found on your unauthorized jaunt to the scene of a potential crime." Sheriff Harper flipped his boots up on the table and leaned back in his chair.

He stared at Charlie, waiting for her response to his statement. When she simply sat in the chair with her hands folded on the table in front of her, and her head hanging to her chest, he continued. "As a matter of fact, the extra boot prints are most likely from my feet, and the car tires are from Sarah's car. She picked me up on her way to the office this morning, as I'd caught a ride with a fellow officer who was leaving shift this morning. I had him drop me at the scene and since Sarah lives up a ways from the orchard, I asked if she could pick me up. We stopped at the café for coffee, so we must have just missed you as you went on your little jaunt before our meeting." Charlie didn't flinch or move from her position, so Harper simply asked, "any comments so far, Deputy Carter?"

She shook her head and quietly muttered, "I screwed up."

"What was that?" Harpy prodded.

"I screwed up, sir." Charlie lifted her head and stoically stood up. "Am I suspended, sir?" she asked quietly.

"What? No, of course not." Harpy looked at her with pity and quickly added, "But if you ever treat potential witnesses like criminals again, you'll be more than suspended. You'll be emptying out your desk. Do I make myself clear?" Harper stood up and started to move toward the door. "Now go get yourself in a better frame of mind and then go apologize to Officer Parent for putting him in this position along with you. I'll expect you back in my office before lunch to decide the best course of action with this case going forward. Understand?"

"Yes, sir." Charlie turned toward the sheriff. "And thank you, sir, for your consideration. I appreciate it."

"Don't take it lightly, Deputy. I won't be this lenient again." He hesitated, then added, "You're a good policeman, Charlie. Damn good. You wouldn't be in the position you are at such a young age if you weren't. I don't know what possessed you to do what you did today, but I expect you will let me know when you're ready to tell me."

They left the room together and went their separate ways. Harper watched her walk confidently down the hallway and heard her holler at Officer Parent to come with her as she headed for the door. He assumed, and hoped, she was taking the officer for breakfast and a quick apology. At least, that's what she'd better be doing. He'd wait to see what she had to say later that day.

Harper decided to make a few phone calls. He hated having to let the families know about the death of a loved one. It was especially difficult when it was a child that had died, and even worse when the child's parents were kids he'd grown up with. "Damn it," he muttered, then asked Sarah for the Faulkons' phone number, and a strong cup of coffee to go with it.

Sarah brought the phone numbers for home and both businesses, as well as a cup of coffee, into Harpy's office. She asked quietly if there was anything else she could do for him. He shook his head. "Not at the moment, Sarah. Thank you." She left Harpy's office and quietly closed the door behind her.

She'd worked with him long enough to know that this was going to be a nasty day all around. Sarah thought he should have made the deputy make these calls after the fiasco she'd made of the meeting today, but she understood why Harpy had to do it himself. By the time he'd got out of the coroner's office last night he felt it was too late to call Marvin and Becky. Then, with the stupidity he had to deal with this morning before and after the meeting, he hadn't had the chance to catch them.

Harpy picked up the phone and decided to call Marvin first to see if he was in the vicinity of City Hall. If he was, they could both meet Becky there and he'd break the news in person. It was always better to do it face to face, and Becky would need the support.

CHAPTER 6

ANNA AND DAVID DECIDED TO STOP FOR coffee and maybe a bite to eat before heading over to her mother's place. Anna knew it was a stall tactic on David's part, but she gave him the directions to Maxine's Coffee Shop on Main Street, and they parked down the street so that they could walk a bit in the fresh morning air and clear the anger that both felt from the attitude they'd gotten from Deputy Carter.

"What a battle axe that one is!" David said. "What the hell is her problem, anyway?"

"I've never seen her treat anyone like that before. It was like we were the ones that killed Marty or something. I'd hate to see how she treats the real criminals." Anna's anger was not settling, and the more they talked about it the angrier she became. "I have a mind to file a formal complaint against her and ask for her head on a platter," she exclaimed.

David realized that feeding the anger wasn't going to get either of them anywhere. They might need to get some cooperation from the police in town before all of this was over. "Let's just get something to eat and another one of those delicious coffees. Then you can show me around town a bit before we go back to your mother's place."

"Fine." Anna stormed up the street toward the café. "But I'm not kidding about that complaint," she added.

"I get that. But just consider that we don't know all the facts yet, and we may need police cooperation to help us get them. Filing a complaint is only going to stir the hornet's nest a little more."

At the café, David reached over and swung the door open and motioned for Anna to enter ahead of him. "Ladies first," he said, smiling.

Anna walked in and looked around. It was pretty much dead downtown during the week, and today was no exception. "Hi, Max!" She waved at the pretty blonde behind the counter.

"Back already?" Maxine smiled at Anna. "And bringing handsome strangers with you." She smiled at David as well.

"This is the man I told you I was meeting earlier. He liked your coffee so much he asked to take me for another." Anna winked at her friend. "I'll have the usual with a cinnamon bun please, and…?" She looked over her shoulder at David.

"I'll take a coffee, black with a half teaspoon of sugar, and do you have any breakfast sandwiches or something?" he asked as he scanned the chalkboards above the counter.

"Special orders are always welcome this time of day," Maxine responded. "What would you like, and I'll let you know if I have the ingredients to make it."

"Wow! Now that's service!" David exclaimed happily. He gave her his order and then looked around for Anna. She was sitting at a table by the big front window, absently staring out. David sat down across from her and did the same.

Maxine brought two coffees and Anna's cinnamon bun to the table. "Penny for your thoughts, you two," she said cheerfully. "Hey, did anyone ever tell you that you two look alike? You could be twins." Maxine looked from one to the other and waited for a reaction.

"Well," they both started together, and then laughed. "We kind of are," Anna finished, looking at David to see what, if anything, he wanted her to divulge.

"What?" Maxine looked at her, then started to laugh. "Funny Anna. I assume you're related, but I know I've never seen him before."

"True. We are definitely related, but we haven't seen each other in years. We share a birthday, so we think of each other as twins," Anna explained.

"Okay, now it makes sense. I'll be right back with your sandwich, sir. Is there anything else I can get for you two 'twins'?" Max chuckled.

"Not at the moment," David responded as Maxine walked into the back room of the café. "She's very nice." He turned to Anna.

"Yes, she is. Max and I were in school together from about grade five on. She was my best friend from the first day we met. She worked at the café from the time she was about sixteen. When the owners decided to retire and move to Florida, they asked Max if she wanted to buy it. Long story short, she changed the name, and it's been booming for about five or six years now."

"Wow. She's got a great place here," David said as he looked around. "Hope she has lots of traffic at other times of the day," he added, realizing they were the only ones in the shop.

As he said that, the door opened and in walked Charlie and another officer. Charlie stopped short when she spotted Anna and David, wishing she had seen them before they opened the door. She quietly turned to Officer Parent to see if he wanted to go down the street to the 7-Eleven for their coffee, but it was too late. Officer Parent waved at Maxine as she entered the room from the back.

"Hi Max," he said. "How's the coffee this time of day?"

"My coffee is always good and always fresh; you know that, Marc." Max smiled back at him. "You want anything with that coffee?" she inquired.

Charlie walked up to the counter "Make that two coffees, please, Max, and two cinnamon buns." She looked over her shoulder at her junior officer. "Good enough?"

"Yep. Nothing better than Maxine's cinnamon buns!" Marc replied with a big smile on his face. "And even better, the Dep is paying today." He chuckled and walked toward the back-wall table, a habit most police officers had was to keep their back to the wall so they could see the entrance and the other patrons. Not that they needed to worry so much in Windsmill, but the training was ingrained. Charlie joined him but put her back to the room, which was unusual. Marc scowled. "You sure you don't want to sit over on the other side, Dep?" he asked her.

"No, I'm fine here. You got my back, right?" She shrugged.

He looked over her shoulder and spotted Anna and David at the table by the window. They didn't look very happy about the new patrons, but too bad, Marc thought as he gave a small wave to Anna.

"Max, can you make David's sandwich to go, and can I get two to-go cups for our coffees as well, please," Anna called out to Maxine, who emerged from the back room with a cinnamon bun in each hand.

"Sure, no problem. Would you like your coffees topped up before you go?" she asked over her shoulder.

"Sure, that would be great," Anna said as she picked up her sweater from her lap and walked hurriedly over to the counter to gather up their order.

"What's up?" Maxine asked as she looked at the anger building up in Anna's face.

"Nothing," Anna responded curtly and glared at the back of the senior officer. "We'll talk soon," she said to Maxine as she turned to see if David was ready to go. She was surprised to see him walking toward the officers rather than away from them.

"Don't burn your mouth on that coffee, Deputy," he drawled into Charlie's ear. "We wouldn't want that big mouth of yours to get too sore." David smiled at the other officer, then turned and walked away.

Officer Parent looked over at his partner with questioning eyes. He noticed Charlie's face turning red, and the anger in her eyes was enough that he didn't question the exchange.

Anna could hardly hold her laughter back as they exited the café. She rounded the corner toward the big city park, hoping they'd find a table to sit and finish their breakfast. Once she was out of earshot from the café, she burst into fits of laughter. She laughed so hard she had tears running down her face and was holding her sides. She plopped herself down on a bench and continued to laugh.

David just stood there smiling at Anna like a Chessy Cat. It felt good to get rid of the anger and the solemn mood that had taken over since they'd met the day before. It was so easy to be with Anna, like she finished him somehow. He'd never felt like this before, but it was kind of nice.

They finished their breakfast in the warm spring weather. The sky was so blue it almost didn't look real. There wasn't a cloud anywhere, and the slight breeze felt good. David closed his eyes and just listened to the quiet noises of a sleepy town in the middle of a spring day. There was laughter coming from somewhere in the park; there was a vehicle driving slowly behind them on one of the few town roads; and there was footsteps of someone walking on a sidewalk close by. He loved trying to figure out who was around him and what they might be doing. The lack of movement here made it that much easier, he thought.

Suddenly, he was pulled from his quiet with the wails of a woman and the call of a frustrated yet sad-sounding man. "What is that?" he said, opening his eyes and standing up. As he turned toward the noises, he saw a slender, well-dressed woman in business dress carrying a pair of heels as she ran toward the park in her bare feet. Her curly salt-and-pepper black hair was pulled off her face and her chocolate-brown eyes, filled with grief, poured tears down her cheeks. Close behind her was a very tall dark man calling after her. Tears tore down both his cheeks as he determinedly tried to catch up to his wife.

"Becky!" the man hollered, "Becky, please slow down. Please stop." The man's breathing was laboured, but he didn't slow down. "Beck, please!"

The woman slowed to a stop then fell to her knees. She put her face in her hands and sobbed uncontrollably. The large man sat down behind her, wrapping his arms around her as they sobbed together.

David looked over at Anna. She started to walk toward the couple when David put his arm on her shoulder to stop her. "No, Anna, leave them," David said to her. "They need this time to grieve alone."

Anna looked up at David with her eyes full of tears. "It's the Faulkons," she said. "Harpy must have told them about Marty."

As she spoke, Marvin looked toward the voice and froze. His face went pale, and he blinked rapidly.

"Anna," he called, "is that you?" he asked, trying to ignore the man standing beside her.

"Yes Marvin, it's me." She stepped closer to the couple. "Are you and Becky okay? Can I get you anything? Here, come sit on the bench and I'll go get you a coffee or water or whatever you want. I don't know what to say. I can't imagine what you're going through. I'm so sorry," Anna rambled. David reached over and touched her arm. She took a deep breath and stopped talking.

"Anna?" Marvin questioned again. "Who's with you?" he asked, looking pointedly at David. It couldn't be who Marvin was seeing, could it? Was he seeing ghosts now too?

"Oh, I'm sorry, Marvin," Anna spoke softly as she continued to step closer to them. "This is David," she said, pointing to her brother. "You remember David?"

Marvin stared at David for a long time and Becky finally looked up to see what was going on. She knew that David was no longer in Windsmill. No one had said anything about him being back. She looked up at him and then fainted straightaway.

Marvin grabbed his wife up from the grass and started to walk back the way they had come. "I need to get her home now, Anna. We'll talk soon." Marvin walked away, then turned back and looked directly at David again. "You look just like him. You look just like Paul," he said.

David nodded in agreement and watched as Marvin carried his wife away.

"Am I going to get that kind of reaction from everyone I meet in this town?" he asked Anna.

38   WENDY SCOTT-ETTINGER

"I'm afraid you will, from anyone that knew our dad," Anna replied.

"Your dad," David corrected. "My dad and mom are planning on coming into town later today. Said they'd meet us at Aunt Mary's place. I'm going to walk back to the car. I need to get away for a while and think. Can I drop you anywhere?"

"No. Mom's place is just the other side of the park. I'll walk over there. You can come by whenever you're ready." Anna turned away from David and headed through the park toward a row of houses in the distance.

David watched her walk and then glanced at the trees lining the fences at the back of the park. There was a small gap where a gate was added into the fence. A sudden fear struck David. The one he used to get as a kid when he had those horrible nightmares. Mom would wake him up and tell him that he was safe. That the monsters in the trees couldn't ever get him. Were these the trees in his dreams?

"Anna," he called out to her, but she was moving too fast to hear his calls. "Anna," he hollered more loudly. She turned to look at him and put her hands up in a shrug as if to ask "what?" He waved at her as if to say "see you later" and walked back toward Main Street where he'd parked his car. *Don't be silly, David,* he told himself. *It's just the wind, or birds, or ….*

When he rounded the corner and started to walk toward his car, he spotted a police officer leaning on it and looking around. He quickened his step and hollered, "Is there a problem with my vehicle, Officer?" When Charlie turned to look at him, he added, "Or are you making up some more trumped-up lies to ticket me now?" He scowled at her.

Charlie put her hands up in a surrender motion. "I come in peace," she said when he'd gotten close enough to hear her. "I thought I'd wait and apologize for this morning's meeting. I was out of line."

David stopped short and stared at her. He wasn't sure what her game was, but he wasn't buying it. "Can you get off my car, please, you'll scratch the paint with all that crap hanging off of you." He walked to the driver's side of the vehicle. Charlie straightened up and stood on the sidewalk.

"Anyway, that's all I had to say." She turned to walk back toward the precinct, then stopped and looked back at David. "Someone was out at the scene sometime between when Harpy and I left and when I got out there at approximately seven-thirty a.m." She sounded like she was giving a report to a fellow officer. "Whoever it was, was looking through the ditch and up toward the tree line where you had been looking last night," she continued.

PACKART'S ORCHARD   39

"And you assumed that it was me?" David raised his eyebrows at her.

"Yes," she stated flatly. "Harpy, you and I, and possibly Anna, were the only ones that could have known your interest in that particular spot."

"Or the killer was still there and was looking around to make sure they hadn't left anything incriminating. Or there could have been someone else watching what was going on," David pointed out to her.

"Yes. Or that," Charlie admitted. She wasn't going to tell him that it was Harpy that had been up there this morning, or he'd really think the Windsmill Sheriff's Department was incompetent. "Anyway, I'm sorry I jumped to conclusions. It was unprofessional of me to treat you that way."

"Why the about face, Deputy? You didn't look very happy to see us in the café earlier, and believe me, if Anna has her way, you'll be looking for a new profession." David emphasized the last part of his statement.

Charlie looked down at her boots and scuffed a piece of broken cement from the sidewalk onto the road. "I'll talk to her too. Where is she?" Charlie looked around to see if she could spot Anna.

"Heading to her mother's place. She was still upset, and seeing the Faulkons didn't help the situation."

"Right, well …" Charlie hesitated. She looked up at David and tried to smile. "I'll head back to the precinct now and get some work done while I still have a job."

David smiled at her uneasiness. "And Officer," he said with a smirk as he hit the remote start button for his car. "You might want to remember if you 'assume,' you make an ASS of U and ME." David laughed at the confused look on her face. "Write it down," he said before closing his car door and driving away.

Charlie watched the little blue sports car drive down Main Street and turn toward the highway. He'd better not go out there now or she'd kick his ass, she thought. She listened to see if she could tell which way he'd turned and smiled as she could hear him head out of town toward Bellcom City.

Yep, better get back to the office, Charlie. You have some work to do, she told herself as she walked back toward City Hall and the precinct.

CHAPTER 7

DAVID CALLED HIS DAD'S CELL PHONE FROM the car on his way back into Bellcom City. "Hi Dad," he said when his dad's voicemail answered. "It's about noon. I'm heading back into Bellcom and to my office for a bit. Give me a call when you and Mom are heading into Windsmill, and I'll meet you someplace. I'd like to talk to you about this morning's meeting with the lovely Windsmill Police before we go talk to Aunt Mary. Anyway, talk soon." He ended the call and turned onto 2nd Street to head to the office. As he parked his car, he noticed a piece of paper stuck under Anna's car wipers.

"Shit." David got out of his car, locking it with his remote as he walked over to Anna's car. He looked down at the piece of paper. "Not a ticket. Good," he said out loud, "and not a flyer either." He pulled the paper off the windshield. It was a plain white sheet of paper, the kind you'd find in any printer in town. It was folded like someone was going to put it in an envelope but changed their mind. David unfolded it. It was a type-written note that said "STOP LOOKING. YOU'LL BE SORRY."

"What the hell?" David read the note again, then pulled his phone out of his jacket pocket and dialed the Bellcom City police station. "Hi, this is David Allen. Is Sergeant McCall in today?"

"One moment, Mr. Allen, I'll see if he's available."

A few seconds later a deep male voice answered. "Hi, mate. You looking for a drinking buddy tonight? Haven't heard from you in what? A week or more?"

"Hi Mike, I'd like nothing better, pal, but this is an official call. Can you or one of your work friends come down to my office parking lot? I've found something and I'd like another opinion."

41

"You trying on girls clothes again?" The sergeant laughed. "I'm sure we can find someone to help you out."

"Funny lad, aren't you? I'm serious. I'm working this case for this lady who turns out to be my twin sister. Anyway, she left her car here the last couple of nights and I just found a note on her car windshield. I'd like to have you guys look into it for me."

"Your sister, hey?" David could hear the smirk through the phone. "That's what you're calling them now, are you?"

"Okay. Fine, I'll call a real cop," David said indignantly. Before he could hang up, Mike told him he'd be there in ten- or fifteen-minutes tops and they both disconnected.

David looked around the parking lot for any security cameras. Then he looked back at his office building to check if the businesses would have had any. He should have had that security system put in when he took over the management of the building like his realtor suggested. He'd figured he'd get to it when he had the time and money to spend on it. "Damn," he said under his breath. *I really need to spend some quality time on this place.*

He leaned on Anna's car and waited for his friend to show up. He closed his eyes and rubbed his face with his hands. *This doesn't make sense,* he thought. *We haven't even talked to anyone yet. Other than the police and Mrs. Packart, no one even knows.* David looked up as a police cruiser entered the parking lot. Hopefully it was Mike, and he didn't send one of the rookies. He really needed someone to talk to besides Anna.

A tall, redheaded police officer folded himself out of the cruiser, then turned and smiled at David. "You're looking tired," he said to his friend. "Hopefully it's fun that's keeping you out of bed."

"I wish!" He smiled back at Mike. "Thanks for coming out here so quickly. This is kind of a weird situation and I'm not sure what, if anything, can be done to track the person responsible. I'll leave that to you and yours for now." David handed him the piece of paper he found on Anna's car.

Mike unfolded the paper and read it, frowning. "STOP LOOKING. YOU'LL BE SORRY," he read out loud. "This mean anything to you? Since you don't have a sister, who is the owner of this car really? How do you know them?"

"The car belongs to Anna Lister of Windsmill. She came in a couple of days ago to ask me to investigate her husband's death."

Mike raised his eyebrows at the last part of David's statement. "Wait, you mean she actually took my advice and hired a private eye? And that PI is you!" Mike started to laugh. "Could this get any crazier?"

"Oh, believe me, it can and has," David said somberly. "Turns out that Anna is my biological twin sister. Her mother apparently sent me to live with Mom and Dad after my biological father died the same way Anna's husband has – mysteriously in Packart's Orchard. Anyway, her and I ended up talking to Mrs. Packart yesterday afternoon. Not a happy lady by any stretch. Her husband is currently in Bellcom General Hospital after a heart attack believed to be caused by Jack Lister's death. He's in psych right now under observation."

Mike tried to interrupt to ask questions, but David held up his hand. "Just wait until I get this all out," David said, then continued. "On our way back into Windsmill from the Packart place, I spotted what I thought at first was a pile of clothes on the side of a rest area pull out. I stopped to take a look and discovered a twenty-ish- year-old man. He was dead but his body was still warm, so he hadn't been out there that long. Anyway, we called 911 and the emergency response team, including a Deputy Sheriff Charlie Carter, and later the sheriff himself. They questioned us briefly at the scene. While I was waiting for the word to leave, I spotted something in the bushes on the other side of the ditch by the tree line. I couldn't tell what it was, and I wasn't about to go looking as both the deputy and the sheriff were pretty jumpy. Anyway, after dropping Anna off at her mother's, I came back here, made some phone calls, and then did some digging on my computer. I woke up with my head on my desk at about eight a.m. I had to be at the Windsmill Sheriff's Department at nine a.m. sharp or risk the sheriff's threat of having me arrested."

"Was the note on this car when you left?" Mike asked. He was feverishly writing in his notebook.

"Not that I recall seeing, but I was in a real hurry and hadn't been awake for long, so I really didn't notice."

"So, this note could have been here anytime from sometime mid-morning yesterday until now?"

"Sure, I guess so. The thing is, other than a small group of police officers, old Mrs. Packart, Anna, and her mother, no one else knows about us looking into anything. Anyone that may have seen us at Packarts would just think we were visiting. Mrs. Packart has known Anna since she was born. Who would leave this kind of note on Anna's car? Unless this has nothing to do with this case." David shrugged and wiped his face with his hands again.

"Do you have the keys for this vehicle?" Mike asked.

"No, Anna was going to come back and get it yesterday afternoon. Obviously, she was not in any condition to drive last night after everything that had happened, so I was planning on driving her back here after the meeting with the police. That didn't go well either."

Mike raised his fire-red-coloured eyebrows again. "Care to explain?"

"The deputy went back out to the scene before our meeting. Apparently, she found evidence that someone had been out there between the time they cleared out last night and they got back out there this morning. She came on way too strong, accusing Anna and I of tampering with a crime scene. All but accused us of killing the kid."

"Sounds like something Charlie would do. She can be pretty hot-headed when she gets a bee in her bonnet. Sounds like you and her didn't get off to a good start." Mike smiled at his friend. "What? You hit on her or something?" Mike laughed.

"No! Didn't even realize she wasn't a man until this morning. It was dark and I wasn't paying much attention to her face. She was jumpy as hell and kept putting her hand on her gun like she was going to shoot me at the slightest provocation, so I was more interested in her gun hand than anything else. Anyway, she's definitely a hot-head!"

"Okay, I'm going to take this back to the precinct and see what I can find. Other than your fingerprints, since I assume you hadn't gloved up to remove it?" Mike questioned.

"No. Wasn't thinking straight. Actually, haven't thought straight in this whole situation so far. I have to get a handle on my emotions and start acting like a professional."

"You want to take a photo of this for your records before I head out of here?" Mike held the paper open and turned it toward David. David pulled out his phone and snapped a shot. He thanked Mike again for all his help and told him he'd call him later that night. Mike folded back into his cruiser and headed back out of the parking lot.

David looked at the two restaurants on the main floor of his building. As usual, they were both hammered with the lunchtime rush that seemed to start at about 10:30 every morning and not end until 2:00 p.m. He wanted to talk to them about what they may have seen in the last twenty-four or so hours and find out if they had security systems or cameras that might cover the parking lot. He didn't want to interrupt them while the crowds were still lined up. He looked at his watch; it was almost 1:30, so he could wait a half hour before talking to them. He thought of going up to his office but just didn't have the energy, so he climbed back into his car, turned the radio on, and promptly fell asleep.

"Sir? Sir, are you okay?" A rap on his car window woke him with a start. An older man of maybe sixty-five or older stood by his car. He had a sandwich shop bag in one hand and a set of keys in the other.

David rolled down his window slightly and smiled at the man. "Yes, I'm fine, thanks. A couple of sleepless nights, is all." He reached over and turned off his car and climbed out. "Sorry if I gave you a start," he said to the man.

"No problem. As long as you're okay," the man replied as he walked toward an old, rusty brown, or maybe it used to be red, truck and climbed into the driver's seat. David watched as the man drove away. There were a lot of strangers around this area, he thought as he locked the car and started walking toward the building. He'd start with the guy that ran the pho place, he thought. He was a young guy, about David's age. More likely to have a good modern system installed.

He talked to both tenants and found that while both had alarm systems installed, neither had any outside cameras. He promised that he'd look into a better overall security system for the building. He started heading toward his office door when his stomach reminded him that he hadn't really eaten anything in the last few days, except the small pho soup last night and the breakfast sandwich he'd only eaten half of that morning.

David needed another coffee too, so he decided he'd head to the local Starbucks. He dialed his dad's phone again to let him know where he was headed and find out where they were. Still no answer. He left a message: "Hi Dad, it's David again. I'm just heading to the Starbucks down the street from my office. How about you and Mom meet me there and I'll buy you a coffee before we head into Windsmill? It's been a crazy couple of days."

Hopefully he'd have a chance to review the recordings and videos he'd taken over the last couple of days before the folks showed up. He ordered a strong grandé regular coffee black with sugar and a croissant with ham and cheese, then sat in a corner of the café with his back to the wall. The last thing he needed right now was for someone to sneak up on him while he was reviewing his recordings. He plugged his earphones into the phone and started the recording of their conversation with Mrs. Packart. He pulled his notebook out of his pocket and got lost in his review. He jumped and pulled out his earbuds as someone sat down in front of him and then realized it was his mother.

"Mom, when did you get here?" he asked, bewildered. "I just sat down."

"We've been here a few minutes. You phoned Dad about an hour ago and told us to meet you here. Are you okay, David, you don't look good?" His mother reached over the table and grabbed his hand. "You look very tired. Are you sure we should be going to Mary's place today? We can go another time, you know."

"No. No. I'm okay," David stammered. The sooner they got this whole thing over with the better off they'd all be. "I need to talk to her about her husband's death and what exactly happened leading up to it. Anything she can remember may help Anna and I out with this case."

"I know you're anxious to get this done, but David …" His mother stopped and looked over her shoulder to see if AJ was bringing the coffees and pastries yet. "David, this isn't just a normal case, and you and I both know it. This is you meeting your biological mother for the first time since you were four years old. This is you going back to your family home and getting to know your twin again. This is going to be a very emotional meeting for everyone, especially you." She squeezed his hand and then reached for the coffee that her husband set down in front of her.

"Everything okay?" AJ asked as he sat down beside his wife. "Jenny, what's going on?" He looked concerned at the emotions in his wife's eyes.

"I was just talking to David about how tired he looks and about the meeting with Mary," she said.

"David, you said in your voicemails that things are getting a little crazy. Want to tell me what's happening?" AJ took a bite from his pastry and looked concerned for his son. This was going to be a hard situation for everyone today. "We can postpone if you want to. We don't have to go back into Windsmill."

"Okay, look. I need to go. I need to find out what the hell is going on, or nobody is really going to be safe. So, can we just drink our coffee and get the hell out of here?" He gathered up his notebook and phone and stuffed them back into his pocket as he stood up from the table. "Sorry," he said and sat back down. "I'm a little on edge."

He began to tell his parents about everything that had happened over the last two days. When he got to the part about the Faulkon boy, his mother gasped.

"Oh no!" she exclaimed with tears in her eyes. "Poor Becky. I hope Marv was with her when she found out. I can't imagine losing a child like that."

David stopped his story and looked up at his parents for the first time. "You know the Faulkons?" he asked.

AJ put his arm around Jenny and squeezed. "Yes. Knew them is more like it. Before Paul died, we'd go out to their place a lot. Jenny and I were still hoping to have kids of our own back then and loved coming out to Windsmill for visits. They usually had a house full of people and lots of kids around. Becky and Marvin were pregnant for their first when Paul died. Then Darren died not long after that, and of course Marvin's brothers, or was it his cousins? They died before Darren did, I think. It was a bad time for everyone back then. Darren's wife took her boys and went back up north to live. Marvin took Becky up north to help with all the arrangements for the boys, and well, everything just kind of fell apart after that. When you came to live with us, we believed it was best for everyone that we not go out there anymore." AJ hung his head and pushed his pastry plate away.

"I think we should get going," AJ said finally. "You driving with us, or taking yourself out there?" he asked David as they all gathered their cups and plates and headed toward the clearing station by the door.

"I'll drive myself." He hugged his mother and looked up at his dad. "You two okay to drive or do you want to come with me?"

"No, I'm good. The drive out there will help settle my nerves. We'll meet you at Mary's, if that's okay."

David nodded. "I'm just going to get another coffee to go. I'll see you there."

Man, this is a tangled web, he thought as he watched his parents get into their car and drive east toward Windsmill. *How did I get myself in the middle of this?* He grabbed his coffee off the counter and headed for the door, realizing he had been in the middle of this since before he could remember.

PACKART'S ORCHARD 47

CHAPTER 8

MARY PACED BACK AND FORTH FROM THE kitchen table to the front door and back again. It was past four o'clock and they still weren't there. "Maybe they changed their mind?" she said out loud.

"They could have, but wouldn't they let you know if they did?" Anna replied from the kitchen table. She sat with Grade 1 homework in front of her. Johnny had a pencil up to his lips, thinking about the question his mother had just asked him. He was so much like his father, Anna thought as she ruffled his hair.

"Only three more questions and you can go out back and play on the swing for a bit before supper," she said absently. Johnny smiled up at her and started hurriedly writing down numbers on his worksheet.

"There, done," he said as he headed for the door. Anna looked over at the worksheet and smiled. He'd done that so quickly he obviously knew the answers before she'd sat down to help.

"Why didn't you do that a half hour ago?" she asked Johnny as he pulled his sneakers on.

"You looked like you needed to help," he said, and then ran out the door.

Anna picked up her phone. "Do you want me to call David and see what's holding them up?" she asked her mother.

"No. I think I see their car coming down the street now." Mary swung open the door and stood on the porch, waiting for her sister to get out of the car. She waved at them, then frowned as she saw the emotion on their faces. She held the door open and hugged them both as they entered the porch door. "Is everything okay?" Mary asked.

"Yes, we're fine," Jenny responded. "David just told us about Becky and Marvin's son before we left the city. It was a shock, is all."

48

Mary hugged her sister tightly. "I know it is. I was going to tell you yesterday when I was talking to you but didn't know whether the police had told Becky and Marv yet. I'm sorry I didn't mention it." Mary walked her sister into the kitchen with her arm around her shoulder. "Sit, I'll make some coffee."

"No thanks, not for me, anyway. We stopped at Starbucks with David before we left the city. I'm all coffee'd out." Jenny smiled at Mary. "AJ, you want coffee?" she called after her husband.

"No, thanks. Not right now," AJ responded as he sat on the loveseat in front of the TV. "I haven't seen this old place in forever," he said quietly as he looked around the living room. "Lots of great memories in this place." He chuckled to himself. Just then he heard another car pull up in front of the house. "Must be David," he said and stood to look out the window.

Anna stood at the front door, half listening to Mr. Allen talk to himself and half watching for David's sky-blue car.

"There he is, finally," she exclaimed as she flung open the door to let him in. "It's about time you showed up," she yelled out at him. "What took you so long?" She smiled.

"It's not that late, it's only," David glanced at his phone, "okay, so it's later than expected. Sorry," he said as he walked up the sidewalk. He looked at the front of the house. Plants were starting to come to life again in the front gardens. He got a flash of a garter snake and chasing a little girl, both of them giggling. "Was there a snake?" David asked Anna as he started up the stairs.

Anna gasped. "You remember that?" she asked, with her hand over her mouth.

"Not really," David responded quietly. "Just a flash, maybe?"

"We'll talk about it later." Anna held the door open. "Come on in. Welcome to our childhood home." She gestured for him to enter.

David walked up the steps and into the screened-in porch at the front of the house. Another half memory flashed in front of him. *This was going to be a very hard evening*, he thought as he entered the front foyer. "At least they're happy memories so far," he said to Anna as they walked into the living room together.

Mary glanced over her shoulder as Anna and David entered the kitchen, and gasped. Her face went completely white, and she put her head on the table to keep from passing out.

PACKART'S ORCHARD   49

"Are you okay, Mom?" Anna rushed over and put her hand on her mother's back.

"Yes. Yes, of course. I'm fine. It's just …" Mary trailed off and lifted her head slowly off the table. "I'm sorry," she said as she turned to look at David. "You looked so much like your father standing there. It's a bit of a shock." She stood up and smiled. "How are you these days? I haven't seen you since your graduation from Hedley. That was such a proud day."

"Yes, Hedley. I remember. That was a few years ago." David looked at the woman in front of him. So tiny, just like his mom. They looked so much alike. He glanced out the big window behind the kitchen table. It looked out onto a large back yard, which appeared to back onto the park. A little boy was playing on a big tire swing. There were more flashes of memory, and then something hit him. He sat down on the chair that Mary had just vacated.

"David, what is it?" Anna questioned; her face furled in concern.

"Is that the park we were in this morning?" he asked.

"Yes, why?"

"Has that gate always been there?" he questioned.

"Yes. I think Dad put it in so Mom could walk to the town square and not have to drive over all the time. Why?"

"There used to be a grove of trees lining the fence. On the other side." David pointed over the fence. "There," he said.

"Yes," Mary responded. "I had the city take most of them down after." She stopped and looked over at her sister for support. Jenny nodded and AJ wrapped his arm around Mary's shoulder. "After your father, Paul. After he died," she finished.

"Why? What was in the trees?" David asked her flatly.

"Nothing that anyone ever found," Mary answered. "Paul insisted that someone or something was watching the house back then. Neither Anna nor I ever saw anything. Not that we knew what we were supposed to be seeing. But he and Darren both saw something out there. They saw it in the orchard too."

"I saw it too, didn't I?" David asked as he turned to look at Mary. His mother, he thought as he stared at her waiting for an answer. She really was his mother, wasn't she?

"Yes," Mary said slowly. "You used to look out the window of your bedroom upstairs and cry. You were so scared of whatever it was." She looked at his face. *So much like Paul,* she thought as she stared back at him. "So analytical and straightforward. But loving and caring too," she said.

David gave her a questioning look. "What was that?" he asked.

"Oh, I'm sorry. I was just thinking out loud. You are very much like your father was. Even now when you've been away for so long. You are very much like him," Mary answered.

She might be tiny, David thought, *but there's strength and determination there too.* "Will you tell me about him? About what happened those many years ago? What happened to him, and Darren and the Faulkon boys and all the rest?" David raised his eyebrows at her, waiting for her to turn him down, but she didn't.

"Yes, I'll tell you and Anna everything I know about what happened. I'll tell you all of it," Mary responded. "Anna, do you want to bring Johnny in now and have some supper before we start this journey? It's a long story, so perhaps we should wait for him to be put to bed before we start?" She looked at David, rather than Anna, for a response. He needed to hear all of it, but Johnny didn't. Not yet anyway.

"Sure, that would be okay, I guess." David nodded. "Do you need help with him, or with supper or anything?" he asked Anna. "I need to keep busy," he added before she could say anything.

David walked around the backyard and looked at all the gardens. He remembered seeing a woman, his mother, he guessed, down on her knees weeding all these gardens and watching he and Anna playing. She'd tell them to take turns on the swing and to not get too dirty. He remembered running out to the front of the house before supper, watching for a blue truck to appear. It usually came just before supper, but sometimes it didn't, he recalled. He loved seeing that truck turn onto their street. He couldn't wait to see his dad and tell him all the stories about their day. He loved sitting on his dad's knee and listening to him tell them about the work he was doing in the orchard. All the plans he had to upgrade the place. Wow! It was all flooding back. How could he remember so much from such a long time ago and not have remembered before today?

David pushed Johnny on the swing and asked him about his day. He didn't have a father or a grandfather to tell him stories anymore. AJ had always been a good dad to David. Took him to work with him when he could. Always told him about his day and asked David about his. He wondered what life would have been like if he'd stayed here in Windsmill with Mary and Anna.

PACKART'S ORCHARD   51

Would AJ still have played the father figure for him, or would it have been someone else that took on that role?

Anna called them for supper, and David and Johnny hurried up onto the back deck. David felt a strange but somehow familiar shiver up his back. Like someone, or something, was watching him. He turned around to look over the fence, but only saw what looked like teenagers walking up a pathway in the park. David shook his head and turned back toward the house. *It's just been a long and strange couple of days*, he thought as he looked at his sister. She had an inquisitive look on her face as she watched him from the doorway.

"You see something out there?" Anna questioned quietly as he passed her.

"Later," he said as he walked into the kitchen, smiling at the adults around the table. "It smells delicious in here." He sat down beside Johnny. "What are we eating tonight, Johnny?" he asked the little boy.

"Was 'posed to be burgers and fries tonight," Johnny glared at his mother, "but someone changed it."

"We will have hamburgers tomorrow night. And the word is supposed to, not 'posed to," Anna corrected her son. "We're having meatloaf, salad and what's left of last year's potatoes," she answered David. "Mom has a big garden every year, and we keep all the root vegetables in the cellar under the shed. They keep all winter out there without any problems." She said as her mother put all the food on the table. "This is much tastier than burgers and fries, anyway." She looked at Johnny.

The evening meal was a wonderful, boisterous family discussion, with everyone talking about various different aspects of their lives and laughing at each other's foibles. It was as if they'd all known each other their entire lives. David stopped for a minute and watched his parents and Mary as they reminisced about their college days and how they had met. How dad and his father had met the Strickland sisters and fallen in love immediately. The men spent many summers working together at the orchards or at the cannery, while the ladies worked at restaurants or shops in Bellcom City or around Hedley campus. They talked about the weddings, the families they'd met and had become. David realized they had known each other for all their adult lives and had watched Anna and David grow up and become the people they were now too. This really was his family. His world.

Before Anna put Johnny to bed, she showed David the upstairs bedrooms and told him that the room that Johnny was now staying in used to be David's. He walked over and looked out the bedroom window Mary had told him he'd looked out with fear as a small boy. It was dark, and the park appeared to be quiet this time of night. He supposed it was always quiet here at night, being such a small town. There didn't appear to be anything to fear as he let the curtains close and turned back to Anna. She was standing at the bedroom door.

"Anything?" she asked.

"No." David shook his head. "Hi Johnny, is it time for bed now?"

Johnny bounded into the room and bounced on the bed. "Book, please, Mom," he begged as his uncle left the room.

Anna read him a book and tucked him in. Then she headed downstairs to hear a story from her own mother. Mary sat at the end of the couch, where she did every night. She had her legs pulled up underneath her and a cup of tea on the table beside her. Instead of a book in her hand, she had an old journal and a picture album on her lap. Jenny, AJ, and David sat around the living room with drinks in their hands.

"May I record this?" David asked Mary, as Anna sat beside him in an easy chair.

"I suppose so." Mary looked at him and then smiled. "I suppose you'll want to take some notes and ask questions as we go."

"I'll try not to interrupt unless it's important," he responded professionally.

"Okay, well, we might as well get started then." Mary turned to the papers and albums on her lap. "This journal is Paul's. He always kept it with him and jotted down whatever was happening or things he thought about over time. I'll leave it with you when we're finished here today," she said directly to David.

"Paul loved the orchards," she began ...

CHAPTER 9

PAUL'S STORY — 1990

THE TALL, SLENDER MAN STANDING IN A grove of trees just south of the main Packart house was Paul Jackson. He was a young family man, twenty-eight years old, with dark curly hair that was just long enough to always look windblown, and striking crystal-blue eyes that contrasted with his leathery suntanned skin. He was currently the foreman for the orchard staff and had been in and around the Packart Orchards for most of his life.

He stood staring out at the orchard stretching out in front of him, lost in thought. He loved this place as if it were his own and was glad that Mr. Packart had hired him after he came back from Hedley College in Bellcom City. He had taken horticultural technology there and learned a lot about orchard growth, propagation, and GMOs, as well as chemical and natural pest control methods. Some of the old methods still being used at the orchard really needed to be upgraded. The Packarts had a hundred acres of trees, mostly apples, but some cherries and apricots as well. They'd been growing and harvesting fruit for two generations now. It would soon be handed over to Paul's best friend Darren when he got back from university. That would make the third generation of Packarts one of the larger employers in this part of the valley.

The orchard's irrigation system was in bad need of replacing. He'd talked to Mr. Packart about it a few times, but Mr. P. said it was just fine and not to worry about it. Some of the trees weren't producing as well as they used to, and with acreage yields dwindling, they'd have to come up with some solutions if they wanted to continue to feed three families full-time off of it.

He and Darren would figure it out together when he got back, Paul thought. They always did.

Darren was coming back from Northern University after finishing his B.Sc. in earth sciences and entomology. Paul had wanted to go with him, but life and lack of funds got in his way. Paul worked his way through college, working in the orchard in the summer months and in the cannery in Allensville when he could get the hours the rest of the year. The Allen family were good people and had been good to Paul. Paul had become friends with AJ, Mr. Allen's only son. They were the same age and ended up at most of the same college parties. Paul didn't know which one of them fell in love with a Strickland sister first, but they both ended up marrying one.

Paul saw stars the first time he met Mary, and that was it. They were married the following spring after he finished his studies and graduated with honours. Within the year, they had twins on the way. Paul had bought a small, two-storey house on Meadow Creek Way. It needed lots of work, but Paul figured they would get it fixed up eventually. An old willow tree had been planted in the middle of the backyard. Maybe a tire swing for the kids eventually, Paul thought when he'd seen it. For now, a good coat of paint inside and out, and new screens around the front porch, and it would be good to live in.

And it had been. Mary and the twins loved being in the backyard. The twins would be five soon, he thought absent-mindedly, and spent more summer days playing on the tire swing Paul had strung up in that old tree than they did on the fancy new playset their grandparents had bought them. School started in the fall and before he knew it, they'd be off to college or university and whatever else life held for them.

He turned to walk back up toward the mansion and almost mowed Mr. Packart down.

"Oof, I'm so sorry sir," Paul muttered as he caught Mr. Packart from falling. "Are you alright? What are you doing out here this time of day?" he asked.

"I was coming to ask you the same question Paul." Mr. Packart pointed at the sky. "It's getting dark. Shouldn't you be heading home to that cute little family of yours."

Yes, I guess I'll be late for dinner again tonight," Paul smiled. He thought about how angry Mary would be if he messed with the family routine.

Mr. Packart turned back toward the mansion, and Paul followed him as far as the parking lot. Mr. Packart had to be fifty or more. His salt and pepper black hair and the wrinkles around his deep black eyes showed signs of age and worry, but other than that he was as young as the rest of them. Paul had to walk a little more quickly than he usually did to keep pace with Mr. Packart.

"Then off you go," Mr. Packart said as he walked. "I suppose whatever you're thinking about will wait another day or two. When Darren get's home you two can hatch up all the crazy changes you think this place needs."

"Will you miss being involved in the orchard on a daily basis once Darren gets his head into it?" Paul asked him conversationally.

"Don't count me out just yet Paul. Darren and his new wife haven't even decided whether they'll stay permanently in Windsmill or not."

Albert hadn't told anyone else about Darren's indecision about the family business, not even his wife. Amelia would be terribly upset if she found out that the new Mrs. Packart was more city and less country than Amelia would have liked.

Paul started to ask why Darren wouldn't want to stay but didn't think Mr. Packart was ready to talk about it, and it was too late in the day to start something Paul wasn't prepared to think about himself yet either. As they got to the edge of the parking lot, Mr. Packart waved to Paul and headed up the walk to the wide stairs that led to the front of their wonderful mansion. "See you tomorrow, Paul. Give Mary and those adorable kids of yours a hug for me."

Paul waved goodbye to him and watched as he entered the house and closed the door. As Paul turned toward his work truck, he thought he saw something or someone standing in the shadows just inside the grove of trees he and Mr. Packart had just exited. Paul stopped and leaned slightly toward the shadows, hoping to get a better look at what it might be. But there was nothing. He stood stock-still, hoping to spot anything. But whatever it might have been, was gone. Paul shook his head and mentally berated himself for being so silly. Some days he just fell into that rabbit hole filled with the town's superstitions and started seeing monsters in the trees where none existed. He climbed into his bright-blue pickup.

Paul drove down the winding drive and jumped out of the truck to open the big gate that blocked the entrance. It was a form of security that Mr. Packart had installed a few years ago, mostly to keep wayward travelers from coming up to the house thinking it was a motel or one of those new bed and breakfast places that had started popping up all over the place. He pulled out of the gate and jumped back out to close it again when he saw the same shadows moving in the hedges to the left of the gate.

Paul shook his head again and jumped back into his truck. He must be tired or something. He was jumping at shadows.

Darren showed up the next day and Albert brought him to the treehouse office out back by the old cabins. He hadn't been home since Paul and Albert had had a contractor come out and build a real house in a tree, out of the old treehouse. He walked up the stairs, and when Paul opened the door, he flung his arms around him and hugged him tightly.

Darren walked into what could very well be the coolest office he'd ever seen. There was a large oak desk in the middle of the floor. Paul had pictures of the orchard all over the walls. Old ones; new ones; pictures of trees; pictures of all the buildings; architectural drawings for some of them; blueprints of the old irrigation system and the watermill. He had more blueprints spread over the top of the desk. A black leather office chair sat behind the desk and another not-so-comfortable-looking one sat in front. There was a small table with a coffee pot, mugs, sugar, and creamer on a shelf above it, and a small tea pot and a box of mint tea beside the mugs. A mini bar fridge sat in the opposite corner, with a houseplant of some sort sitting on top of it. A picture of a beautiful blonde with curly hair sat beside the plant, and there was another photo of the same blonde with a boy and a girl on each side of her. Their crystal-blue eyes gave them away instantly. They must be Paul's kids.

Darren smiled and pointed to the fridge behind Paul. He asked if there was any beer tucked away in there. Paul chuckled and asked if Darren was having fun with his walk down memory lane. He then checked his watch to see what time it was, and with a grin pulled the fridge door open and removed two bottles of Lucky beer, the same kind they had stolen from Mr. Packart all those years ago. Paul informed Darren it was a little early in the day to be drinking, but he knew they weren't likely to get any real work done that day anyway.

He handed one of the bottles to Darren, who laughed at his choice of beer and motioned for an opener. They sat down and stared at each other.

"Well," they both said simultaneously and laughed again. "I've missed that," Darren said as he looked down at his beer. "Someone that knows what I'm thinking before I do."

"So, what's up with that wife of yours, buddy? Your dad tells me that she doesn't like us." Paul smirked at his friend.

PACKART'S ORCHARD   57

"That's not true!" Darren said defensively. "It's the thought of being in a small town with nothing to do and none of her family or friends close by. She's scared …" Darren trailed off. "Sorry," he said. He explained that Amy was pregnant and didn't want to leave all that was familiar right now. He hoped if he could get her down here, he'd be able to convince her, but she wouldn't budge. Darren took a long swig from his beer bottle. Darren didn't know what he was going to do if she wasn't willing to move. He'd promised his dad that he'd come back and help with the orchard business, and Albert would be so angry if Darren didn't move back. But Amy wasn't willing to even give it a try. At least not right away. "Damn," he said as he drained his beer. "Got another one?" He pointed at the fridge again.

Paul pulled out another beer and handed it to his friend. "Congrats on the baby, man. But pregnancy does strange things to the woman-folk." He pointed at the picture of his family. "Mary went through this whole nesting thing when she was pregnant with twins. She cleaned and painted everything, even though we'd done all of that before we moved in." Paul drank sparingly from his bottle. He chuckled as he remembered what Mary had been like. "I can't imagine what she would have done if I told her we were moving in the middle of all that. I'm lucky we had both my folks and her mom here with us the whole time. They've been great."

"Not helping, dude." Darren pointed his second bottle at Paul, then took a big swig out of it. "Her family and friends are there. Mine are all here. She doesn't not like you guys; she just doesn't know any of you." He shrugged. "I don't know what to do, man." His words were starting to slur.

Paul laughed and grabbed the rest of the beer away from Darren, informing him he held his beer about as well as he did when they were kids. He handed Darren a cup of coffee; black with just a touch of sugar, assuming his coffee tastes hadn't changed either.

Darren grabbed for the beer but missed. He stared at the coffee cup Paul had set down in front of him and looked at the papers strewn on the desk, and asked what they were as he picked up the cup. "You planning on reinventing our little empire?"

Paul put his and Darren's half-drank beers on the table beside the coffee pot and poured himself a cup of coffee. He turned and looked at his friend. He told Darren he was hoping for a bit more support when Darren came back permanently but that it didn't sound like that was going to happen. The place needed a lot of work if it was going to continue to thrive. He informed

Darren that his dad did lots of hard work around the place every year but didn't want to, or maybe couldn't, put any money into fixing things like irrigation, electricity supply, updated pest control, maybe even some higher-yielding fruit trees – some diversity would be good.

Darren was still staring down at the drawings on the desk. Paul asked if he wanted to take a look at what he was proposing. Darren nodded and grabbed up the drawings, knocking his coffee cup into his lap as he did. "Damn, I really can't drink cheap beer anymore, can I?" he chuckled as he jumped out of the chair and started looking around for something to clean it up with.

Paul threw a roll of paper towels at him and cleaned the desk while Darren dried off his pants the best he could. "Anymore?" Paul chuckled at his friend. "You never could."

They set the drawings back on the desk and stood looking at them for a time, then Paul started to tell Darren about his vision.

It was getting late and starting to get dark when the men climbed out of the treehouse-turned-office. Darren turned to walk back the way he and his dad had come when Paul stopped him. He pointed to the golf cart he'd brought with him that morning and informed Darren he thought he'd give him a break from all the walking just for the day, thinking he'd likely forgotten how much walking got done in an orchard in a day. Looking at the dress shoes Darren had on, he wasn't far off. Paul shook his head and climbed into the golf cart sitting beside the watermill. He looked to see if Darren was coming, but his friend was just staring into the trees beyond the office.

You coming with me?" Paul asked, but Darren didn't respond. "Darren, what are you looking at? You okay?"

Darren looked at Paul with a start. "Yeah, yeah I'm fine. Thought I saw something in the trees over there, but if there was it's gone now. I'm likely just hungry and tired." Darren looked around again and said he hadn't realized they'd been out so long. It was almost dark, and Albert would be pissed if they didn't get back to the house before dinner.

Paul put the cart into gear and headed out toward the mansion. He pulled the cart into the small shed Mr. Packart had erected just for the purpose of putting the carts inside. He'd bought one cart a year after Paul had suggested it would take time off the workers' days if they didn't have to walk the orchard so much. They now had four of them in the shed, and the workers had thanked both Paul and Mr. Packart every spring when they saw a new one sitting with the rest.

"Some things have changed." Darren looked around the shed. "There used to be only one cart that dad wouldn't let anyone else use."

"Yeah, some things have changed.," Paul repeated. "I'm not complaining Darren, honestly," he said in frustration. "I just think the place could do so much more with a little bit of equity and some elbow grease."

Darren nodded in understanding. "I know, I get it. The plans you've drawn up are great Paul, really. I just need to convince dad of that."

They said their good-byes and Darren headed for the house. Paul walked over to his truck and threw his jacket into the back seat. Something caught his eye behind the shed. "Damn, not again!" he exclaimed as he quickly headed for the other side of the truck. "I wish I could tell what it is that's making those shadows come alive," he said as he climbed behind the steering wheel. It was really starting to creep him out.

When Paul got home, he saw Mary pulling weeds from the flower garden and David was chasing Anna with a small garter snake. They were laughing and screaming as they dodged around their mother and her gardening tools.

David ran up to Paul as he got his jacket and briefcase out of the truck, and exclaimed, "Daddy, Daddy, look what I found!" as he excitedly thrust his arm out as far as it would go. "Mom says it's a gardening snake," he said knowingly.

"Garter snake," Paul corrected absently as he turned to look at the small creature wiggling in his son's hand. "And it's not polite to chase your sister with it," Paul admonished lightly.

"I know." David hung his head and shuffled his feet. "But it sure is fun." He giggled as he turned to chase his sister again.

Anna ran past her brother and charged at her father, putting her arms up hopefully. "Up, Daddy. Please!" she pleaded. "Don't let David's snake bite me!" Paul reached down and picked up his curly haired little girl. She may have had her father's colouring, but Paul said she looked more like her mother every day. She snuggled into his shoulder as he walked over to his wife.

Paul informed Anna that garter snakes didn't bite, and it was likely more scared of what David was doing to it than she was of the snake. He set Anna back on the ground beside her mother.

Mary told David and Anna to stop fooling around now and go wash up for dinner. She also told David to put that snake down, as it wasn't going into the house with him. Mary pointed at the front door as she stood up and stretched her back. "You're actually home on time for a change." She leaned

60   WENDY SCOTT-ETTINGER

into Paul's chest and looked up at her handsome husband. Paul brushed a stray blonde curl from Mary's eyes and bent down to kiss her lightly.

"Pew!" Mary waved his kiss away. "You smell like bad beer and coffee. Darren must be home." She chuckled as she grabbed his coat off his arm and put her hand where it had been hanging. "Let's get you washed up too. Supper will be ready in a few minutes, and you can tell me all about what you two have been up to today." They walked amiably up the front steps to the porch and Paul swung the screen door open for Mary.

"It's been an interesting one, all right" he said as he waved his wife into the house ahead of him. "Interesting, indeed."

Paul washed up in the bathroom. He looked around at the small room with water splatters everywhere and wet towels on the floor instead of on the towel rack. He shook his head as he bent down to pick up a towel. He'd have to do something about having only one bathroom in this house once the kids got to be teenagers, he thought as he finished washing his face and brushing his teeth. *Might get my kiss now.* He smiled as he put his toothbrush in its holder and headed for the stairs. He could hear the kids "helping" Mary set the table. *Sometimes she has the patience of Job*, Paul thought as he rounded the corner into the kitchen. He grabbed the plate that was about to fall from David's grasp and set it gently on the end of the table. "Careful there, boy," Paul warned, "you break your mom's good china, she'll have your hide."

"That's not Mom's good china," David corrected, pointing at the plate Paul had just set down. "The good ones don't get used 'cept on special 'cassions," he stated proudly.

"Well, you still need to be careful with them, remember?" Mary said from across the kitchen. She bent down and pulled out a pot roast from the oven. It was covered in potatoes and vegetables and gravy. Paul could smell it from where he stood.

"Man, that smells delicious, Mary! What's the occasion?" You never make pot roast on a weekday," Paul said as he sat in his chair in front of the plate he'd just set on the table.

Mary asked David to get the salt and pepper for his dad as she brought the plated dinner to the table. "This is the last of the root vegetables that were in the cellar," Mary explained. "Thought I'd use them up before the weather gets too hot for such food." She turned to her daughter and asked her to bring the bread over and sit down at the table.

PACKART'S ORCHARD   61

They sat amiably at the table, eating, and chatting. Paul teased his kids about not finishing university yet. They tried to explain why they hadn't even got to go to school yet, and Paul laughed as they became more flustered at their dad. He loved every minute he got to spend with them. Life couldn't get any better than this, he thought as he leaned back in his chair and rubbed what was becoming a belly above his belt. He'd soon need to start wearing overalls like Mr. P's to cover up the belly fat if he wasn't careful. He laughed out loud.

His wife interrupted his musings and leaned down and kissed him. "Finally, I get my kiss today." He chuckled as she walked away from the table. "Here, I'll help you with the dishes and then we can sit down with some tea. I'll tell you about my day with the University Man."

Mary sent the kids out to play in the yard for a while, with strict instructions not to get any more snakes involved and to take turns on the tire swing. As they headed out the back door, Paul sighed and said that old worn-out tire from the Packart's tractor was the best thing he'd ever given the kids.

"So, what's up with Darren and, what's her name again ... Amy, right?" Mary queried. "What's her first impressions of our little town and Mr. and Mrs. Packart?" She sipped on her mint tea.

"She hasn't seen it yet," Paul said, sipping from his own cup. "She won't come down."

"What! Why on earth not?" Mary looked at Paul, concerned. "Does this mean that Darren isn't staying?"

"Don't know." Paul set his teacup on the table and absently watched David push Anna on the swing. "If he can't get her to change her mind, then likely not. She's pregnant right now so that's likely got something to do with it."

"Yeah, no kidding," Mary exclaimed. "How far along is she?"

"What?" Paul looked at her questioningly. "How far along is what?"

"Her pregnancy. How many months is she?"

"Oh. Yeah. Right." Paul sipped his tea, trying to remember what Darren had said. "I think five or six months. Something like that."

"Well, no wonder she doesn't want to move right now. I'll give her a call, introduce myself; let her know she has a friend here in Windsmill. Maybe she'll come for a visit before the baby is due. She can meet everyone and look around without the pressure of having to stay long term right now. Who knows, she might like it here and want to stay."

"Yeah, that might work." Paul was still looking out at the yard. "I'll get the number from Darren tomorrow and make sure he's okay with us getting involved."

"Why wouldn't he be?" Mary asked. "And what are you looking at?"

"Hmm." Paul looked at his wife. "Oh, nothing. Just watching the trees sway in the dusk. They don't look anything like the orchard does this time of day."

"Should they?" Mary asked as she got up from the table with the tea pot and her cup. "You've been far away ever since we sat down for dinner. What's on your mind?"

"Just the strange feelings I've been getting at the orchard these last few days. Like something is out there and watching. I don't know." Paul shrugged. He picked up his own cup and walked it to the sink. He reached over and knocked on the window and shook his finger at the kids.

"What are they doing now?" Mary asked as she rinsed out the cups and put them in their place.

"David has the snake again and won't let Anna anywhere near the swing. Time they came in anyway." Paul walked over to the back door and hollered for the kids to come in. Despite their protests, they headed for the house. Anna swept past her dad and into the kitchen beside her mother. She began to tell the tale of the horrible brother that called snakes at will to torture her, as her mother ushered her up the stairs to the bathroom.

"You can tell me all about it while we wash your hair," her mother commiserated as they walked.

Paul stopped the horrible brother in question at the doorstep and ordered him to drop it. David looked up at his father with a pout. He promised he wouldn't let it escape or anything if he brought it in the house, even suggesting that he could keep it in a box or something in his room. 'Besides, it will get cold if I leave it outside all night by itself." David crossed his fingers on both hands as he held the snake in his palms behind his back.

"I said drop it, David. Your mother said no snakes in the house. That means no snakes in the house." Paul enunciated every word slowly. "Besides, snakes are cold-blooded. The little fellow is not going to freeze to death. He probably wants to get back to his snake family. His mother is probably looking for him right now."

"Okay, Dad. Can we go look for his family and help him get back to his mommy?" David's bright blue eyes twinkled up at his father.

"Fine. Stay right there and I'll go tell your mother that we will be right back. But if we don't find them right away, we leave the snake where you found him, and we come in. Deal?" Paul looked down at his son's excited face.

"Deal" David said. He stood on the steps moving the snake from hand to hand, and his weight from foot to foot, impatiently waiting for his dad to get back so they could go on their adventure.

As Paul and David walked the length and width of the backyard, David became more nervous about being out in the yard as it got dark. He no longer wanted to find the snake family house or any of the snakes that might live in the backyard. He dropped the snake in the garden bed in front of him and looked up at his dad. "That's where I found him, Dad. Can we go in now?" he asked hopefully.

"Sure, bud, if that's what you want to do." Paul was feeling a bit uneasy himself. What if whatever was watching him in the orchard had followed him home? Paul shook his head as if to shake the thoughts out. "Come on, let's go see if Anna is finished with the bathtub." David grabbed his dad's hand and pulled him toward the house. Neither of them wanted to be out there in the dark any longer than they had to be.

"You two are back sooner than I expected," Mary said as Paul and David rushed in the back door. She handed the freshly cleaned Anna a glass of water.

"It's scary out there, Mommy," David said as he hugged his mother. "I don't like the dark anymore!"

Mary looked up at Paul with a question on her face but didn't say anything to him. "How about your dad takes you up and washes all that dirt and snake cooties off you. Then you can come down and have a snack before we put you to bed. Maybe Dad will read you a story if you hurry." Mary pushed David back toward his dad and they walked up the stairs to get cleaned up.

Mary turned back toward her daughter, who was now looking out at the backyard from the dining room window. "What's so scary about the dark, Mommy?" Anna asked as she looked from one side of the yard to the other. "I don't see nothing different than before," she stated.

"Me either, Anna." Mary pulled her daughter onto her lap. "Perhaps we'll ask them when they come back down."

Anna twisted around to hug her mother. "What story should I ask Daddy to read tonight" she asked, forgetting for the moment about the scary dark her brother had mentioned. "Maybe the Princess and the Frog?"

64   WENDY SCOTT-ETTINGER

Mary smiled at her daughter. "You can ask him, but don't be surprised if he and David want something a little less princess and a little more frog." She laughed. "Now let's get the cookies and milk out so they're ready when Daddy and David come back down."

"MAN, I HATE THOSE PRINCESS STORIES," PAUL exclaimed as he plopped himself down on the couch beside his wife. "But I didn't want to read anything that might scare David even more than he seemed to be already."

"What was that all about, anyway?" Mary set her book down on the coffee table and turned toward her husband. "Did you say something to him about there being something in the trees?"

"No. Nothing. We were walking around the backyard looking for the snake's family so David wouldn't keep trying to bring it into the house. I was hoping he'd just get tired of wandering around and leave the snake in the grass or something." Paul put his arm over Mary's shoulders as if to protect her from whatever had scared his son. "The darker it got, the more anxious he seemed to get. I don't know what happened."

"So what did he do with the snake?" Mary asked, hoping it hadn't made it into the house when they'd come back into the kitchen.

"He dropped it in the garden bed at the back fence and said that's where he'd found it. Then he practically ran back into the house like someone was chasing him." Paul looked at his wife again. "I don't know what was out there, but I could feel it too. I hope whatever or whoever has been watching me at the orchard hasn't followed me home, Mary. I'm going to go out in the morning and look around before I head to work. See if there's any sign of someone being out on the other side of the fence."

Paul stood up and walked over to the TV set he'd bought just after they'd moved in. Cable TV was a good distraction after a long day.

Mary picked her book back up. *I guess we're finished talking about this,* she thought as she watched her husband change channels until he found something to watch.

"This looks good." He sat down beside his wife again. "You sure you don't want to watch it with me?" He snuggled closer. Mary put her book back on the coffee table and kissed her husband passionately. "Or we could just do this," he said as he leaned over to his wife.

PAUL CALLED MARY MID-MORNING THE NEXT DAY and gave her the phone number for Amy's parents. He told her that Darren thought it would be a nice gesture for Mary to call. Mary asked Paul if he'd checked the park behind the house before he left, and Paul indicated he didn't have the chance, but not to worry.

"I'm sure it was nothing Mary. David just got spooked about being out after dark and there was likely nothing more to it than that." Paul promised to check back there when he got home that tonight.

"Okay, if you're sure it's safe for the kids to be back there, then I'll believe you." Mary said. She and Paul said their goodbyes, and Mary hung up the phone. After breakfast, she'd take the kids over to visit her mother for a while. That would give her time to chat with Amy without interruption, and hopefully keep David from getting more anxious in the backyard.

CHAPTER 10

"WELL, IF IT ISN'T THE FRIEND WITH the banker's hours," Paul commented as he walked into Mrs. P.'s kitchen and poured himself a cup of coffee.

Darren was sitting at the kitchen table staring out the window. He startled out of his inner thoughts and looked up at his friend. "So what's up for today?" he asked Paul.

"Well, my day is already half over, but for you? I guess you could come out to the irrigation pumps with your dad and me. He's finally agreed to at least look at them and figure out if my plans make any sense or not. I think he figures he can just continue to fix the pumps and that will be that. I could use some moral support right now if you're up for it."

"Yeah, sure. And just so you know, I haven't been sitting around doing nothing this morning. I went into town and bought a new pair of work boots, some work pants, and a few new T-shirts. Thought I should try to dress the part if I'm going to spend any time out here with the rest of you." Darren pointed down to his feet and showed off his new boots. "And how about this jacket?" He held it up to show Paul. "Looks just like yours so I thought it would be okay."

"You finally look like a working man instead of a banker." Paul laughed. "Now if we can just get you to get to work before the lunch bell rings, that would be a start." Paul set his coffee cup down on the counter beside the sink where Mrs. P. had always asked him to put it and headed for the back porch. "You coming?"

Darren hurriedly put his cup beside Paul's, struggling to get his jacket on as he walked out the door to catch up. When he made it to the end of the walkway, Paul was sitting on the golf cart waiting for him. "I'd forgotten how quickly you can move," Darren said to Paul.

"And I forgot how slow you usually are." Paul shook his head and turned the cart toward the back of the orchard. He hit the gas and threw Darren backward. "You might want to hold on." He laughed. "Wouldn't want to lose you out here and make you walk."

"Funny boy." Darren grabbed onto the roll bar. "These things can really move. We should have cart races at the July crew party this year. Could be fun!" he exclaimed as Paul rounded a corner a little too fast and almost ran into a grove of trees. "Or maybe not," Darren said more soberly. "Someone could get killed."

"You are such a wuss," Paul taunted his buddy. "Sitting in a classroom and an office all day has made you soft."

They were both laughing like schoolboys, trading jabs and acting like kids, when Paul pulled up beside another golf cart just across the river from the old homestead. Mr. P. sat quietly looking over the plans Paul had given him before he left to get Darren. His face didn't give away any of his thoughts, but he didn't look up at the boys for a long time.

"It's about time you two showed up for some work today," Albert quipped as he swung himself out of the cart. "These plans are actually very good, Paul. I should have looked at them long before now. I'm sorry."

"No problem, Mr. P," Paul said amiably as he swung out of his own cart. "Mr. University Man here slowed me down with coffee before we left the house." He pointed his thumb at Darren. "He also doesn't move any faster than he did in high school, so …"

"Enough, Paul!" Darren climbed out of the cart, came around to stand with the other two men, and scowled at his friend, hoping he'd cut the banter.

"Yeah, so I looked at Paul's drawings myself yesterday in the treehouse. He's done a good job with them," Darren directed to his father in a business-like tone. "I think it will make things a lot easier irrigation-wise, if we have the cashflow to make it happen Would likely save some money in the long run, on electricity and manpower too—"

"Yes, I see all that," Albert interrupted him. "I think we can come up with the cash to make this happen. I'm just not sure we can get the equipment and manpower in here quick enough to make it happen for this year's growing season. This is everyone's busy time, and we might be too late to get someone out here. Do you have anybody in mind?" Albert asked Paul. "Someone that could get this done, say, in the next month?"

"I think so. Marvin Faulkon has set up his own business in Bellcom City, installing irrigation systems up and down the valley. He has the latest equipment and a good crew. I took the liberty of picking his brain about what might work out here when I was putting these plans together. I think he'd give us a good deal."

"He's a good kid; always liked Marv," Albert mused. "Go talk to him. See if he can work up a cost and time estimate that I can look at. I'd like it on my desk by the end of week." Albert turned toward his golf cart and swung himself back into the driver's seat. "I'll take these plans into my office and sign them off. Then we can get copies made in case Marv or any other contractor needs to take a look at them. I'm assuming that the town inspectors and maybe a lawyer or two will need to have them as well." He looked over at his son for the first time since he and Paul had arrived. "I assume Mr. University Man can look after all that paperwork for us?" He gave Darren a questioning look.

Darren nodded. "I'll need five or six copies of those once you've stamped and signed them, sir," he stated, looking at his father. "Once I have them, I can head into town and see what else the town hall needs for us to get started. Do you have a lawyer's office you use?"

"You can get the names and phone numbers from Paul. He has all those contacts," Albert said as he started to drive away. "I'll get a dozen copies made and bring them around to Paul's office. Then you'll have them if or when we need them." He headed back toward the house without another word.

"You coming up to my office, or you going to work out of your dad's for now?" Paul brought Darren back from whatever he was thinking. He was sitting patiently waiting for Darren to snap out of his thoughts and get into the cart.

"Yeah, I'm coming with you." Darren got back into the cart. "But can you drive like an adult, please?" He grinned.

"Challenge accepted!" Paul grinned back at him. He did a quick donut in the gravel before pointing the golf cart toward the treehouse. He then slowed down so much he thought he might stall the cart out. He could walk faster than they were currently moving. "With a little luck we'll get to the phones before everyone is closed down for the night." Paul chuckled.

"Funny. Really funny." Darren shook his head. He wasn't in the mood for all this craziness. Paul must have understood that Darren was over their

PACKART'S ORCHARD   69

bantering because he sped up to a normal travelling speed and headed quietly to the coolest hideout in the world.

Paul got out of the cart and took the steps up to his office two at a time. He'd make a quick call to Marvin and set up a time for them to come in with the plans and a timeline for an estimate. Then Darren could have the phone to call Town Hall while Paul dug around for the lawyer's name and number. That should get them through the afternoon without any problems.

Darren sat in the cart for a few minutes before he got out and looked around. Nothing was moving. There wasn't even any wind in the trees. The clouds had moved in, and it looked like rain was coming soon. It was so dark in the orchard groves you could have sworn it was midnight instead of early afternoon. Then the rain came. It came so fast and so hard that Darren was soaked to the bone by the time he made it up the stairs. He'd forgotten how quickly the rain moved in, in the spring. It hadn't even cooled off like it did up north before it rained.

"Good thing you don't melt when you get wet," Paul mused as he tossed a towel at him.

"Do I look like the wicked witch of the west?" Darren asked him as he started to wipe water from his face and hair.

"Nope, wicked witch of the north!" Paul laughed, his crystal-blue eyes sparkling like they did when he was up to no good. "You should pay more attention to your surroundings. Have you forgotten what spring in the valley is like already? You haven't been gone that long, have you?"

Darren grunted back at him as he continued towel-drying himself. "Speaking of surroundings," Darren started. "Have you seen or felt anything…" He hesitated.

Paul stopped what he was doing and looked at Darren. "Did you see something?"

Darren shrugged it off. "I don't know. Just a weird feeling, is all," he explained.

Paul told Darren about what had happened the night before with David. He said he thought maybe someone was following him around, but he couldn't catch a good look at who or what it was. He always felt like he was being watched, but thought it was just being out here by himself too much. Darren confirmed that he had seen the shadows moving too and felt like he was being watched. He said when he sat out on the back porch for his morning coffee before heading into town, he couldn't shake the feeling of being under glass. He finally headed out to get some supplies and as soon as he got close to town, the feeling went away.

They compared notes about times, places, and feelings, and Paul began to record it all in his journal. Paul said it couldn't hurt to keep track of what they were both seeing and feeling. He handed a notepad to Darren so he could start doing the same. "I know it sounds crazy, but if both of us have felt it and now my four-year-old son, there might be something to it."

Darren pointed out that he'd noticed that nothing had any locks on it, including the front gate and the office and watermill. He said maybe it was something they should consider until they'd figured out what was out in the orchards.

Paul wondered if he should be having locks put on all the outbuilding doors – how could he talk Albert into having the front gate more secure? Paul had a heck of a time just getting the gate put up in the first place.

"I'll look into the office door, see if I can get someone to put a lock on it and some of the other buildings for when no one's here. But if you want the gate locked, you're going to have to convince your dad yourself. I tried to have a security gate put up, but Mr. P. wasn't having any of it. Said he didn't want people to feel unwelcomed when they came here."

Darren shook his head. "I was afraid you were going to say that." Maybe he could use Amy as the excuse, if he could talk her into coming down. Maybe he could say she didn't feel safe and was used to being in a big city where everything was locked up. That way they could at least get the mansion doors locked at night if nothing else.

"How about you make the calls to Town Hall and the lawyer and see what if anything they need. I'm going to go see if the plans are ready. Marvin says he'll take a look at them and get back to Mr. P. by Friday with a quote, if we can get him the plans today. We can combine stops to the others, and I can introduce you to whoever you might not know or remember, and then we'll head to my place and see what Mary can tell us about that pretty lady of yours." Paul looked out the door to make sure that the rain had stopped, and then headed toward the cart. "I'll be back in fifteen minutes to pick you up. Maybe more if Mr. P. hasn't gotten those plans ready yet. Does that give you enough time to make those calls?"

"Yeah. I should be able to handle a couple of phone calls, thanks!" Darren responded sarcastically as Paul disappeared. He looked around the desk to find the phone numbers. Paul had jotted down the names of the people to talk to along with a short description of who they were and why his dad used

PACKART'S ORCHARD   71

that particular person. The Town Hall contact was Becky Faulkon. "No way!" Darren said out loud.

Darren was hanging up the phone from the lawyer's office when Paul walked back in.

"Have fun talking to all your old girlfriends?" Paul smirked at him.

"You could have at least warned me who I would be talking to," Darren retorted. "Put me off my game a bit." He stood up and grabbed his jacket off the back of the office chair. It was still damp, but not dripping wet anymore. "We need to stop at Town Hall and drop off the plans. I've completed the forms that Becky emailed me to put with them. We don't need to drop anything off at the law office until after Becky has processed the application and it's been signed off. Did you get the copies of the plans from Dad?"

"Yes, he gave me a full envelope of them all stamped and originally signed, so no one will complain about not having an original signature. He asked me to sign them as the plan designer. I'm not sure that's totally legal, but I'll leave it for now." Paul scanned Darren's face for any reaction to his dad's request but didn't see anything. "Shall we go?"

Darren followed Paul down the stairs and they both climbed into the cart.

"I also told Mr. P. that you would be spending the evening at my place and not to expect you for dinner. He said he thought that was a good idea."

"Sounds about right," Darren said nonchalantly. "I guess it's a good thing they don't lock this place up. I might have to sleep in the treehouse tonight."

They put the golf cart in the shed and climbed into Paul's blue truck. They didn't say much else until Paul parked in front of town hall.

"Do you want me to come in with you or shall I give you and Becky some privacy?" Paul chuckled under his breath.

"Funny boy." Darren shook his head as he climbed out of the truck. "I think I can handle this on my own, thanks." He closed the truck door and headed for the steps to the town offices. As he swung open the big wooden doors, he ran into a very tall and muscular man.

"Oh, I'm sorry," Darren exclaimed as he backed up a step. "Didn't see you there."

"That's hard to believe," the very tall man retorted, "but no harm done." The two men stared at each other for a moment before recognition hit both their faces.

"Marv!" "Darren!" they exclaimed at the same time. "Holy man, you've grown a foot since graduation!" Darren said, shaking the massive hand of the black man standing in front of him. "You must be damn near seven feet tall!"

72   WENDY SCOTT-ETTINGER

"Six foot seven, actually," Marvin Faulkon responded, "and yes about a foot taller than high school," he added. "Are you back in Windsmill for good now, or are you just visiting?"

"That depends on the wife and her decision about whether to move down here with me or not. I'm hoping it's permanent. I didn't realize how much I missed this small town and all its people until I got back."

"You here about that irrigation project Paul mentioned earlier today?" Marv inquired.

"Yeah, I am. Have the application right here. Just need to get it into the office before Becky locks up for the day."

"She mentioned she was waiting for a new application package before she could get away for the day. I'll let you go reminisce with my wife for a while. Is Paul dropping off the plans to my place in Bellcom today?"

"He's in the truck waiting for me to get this package delivered, then I think his plan is to head to your place. You can ask him about it if you like, while I finish up here."

The men had another friendly embrace and headed their separate ways.

Marv walked down the steps and over to the bright-blue truck that his buddy sat in. "Hey Paul," he said as he rapped on the driver's window.

Paul jumped and looked around. Spotting Marv, he quickly rolled down the window. "I didn't do it! Never touched her; it was all Darren." He laughed out loud, tongue in cheek and hands in the air. "What are you doing here, anyway? If I'd known you'd be in town today, I wouldn't have brought Darren over to catch up with Becky."

"One born every minute. Do you make those funny remarks so no one will tease you about your baby-blue truck?" Marv laughed, shaking his head. "Thought I'd ask about that package you were going to drop off today. If you have it ready, I can take it now and then neither of us have to drive out to Bellcom City this afternoon."

"Yeah, I got it right here." Paul reached over the back seat and pulled an envelope out from the pile Mr. P. had given him earlier. "And the truck is robin's egg blue, not baby blue." he added. "Let me know if there's anything missing, and I'll get what I can to you right away. Mr. P. really wants to get on this, so the sooner you can get me a quote and a timeframe the better for everyone."

"I'll take a look at it tonight and let you know what my first impressions are." Marv took the package from Paul's hand. "I'm glad Mr. P. is finally getting something new out there. It's long overdue. I kept expecting an emergency call to help fix a break."

"Yeah, I know how you feel. I kept hoping he wouldn't ask me for another patch job. One of these days we're going to have waterfalls out there if we don't get this work done. I think Mr. P. knows it too."

"Talk to you later tonight then. You going to be home or are you heading back out to the orchard?"

"I'll be home. You have my number?"

"I have it somewhere, and if I don't, I'm sure Becky does. I think she spends more time talking to your wife than you do, buddy." Marv smirked as Paul looked embarrassed for not being home more.

"Yeah, you're probably right."

Darren came skipping down the town hall steps and jumped into the truck. "So what have you two fine gentlemen been talking about while I've been in there having an adult conversation with a beautiful lady?" He smirked up at Marv, who was still leaning into the driver's side window.

"Darren, my boy, we really need to get your wife down here PDQ," Marv said. "Maybe she has more control over you than you do of yourself. I'm amazed she even lets you go out by yourself," he teased.

"Okay. Well, I was going to suggest a beer at the bar and grill before heading over to Paul's for the night, but now I don't think I will." Darren turned his head and looked out the passenger-side window, pretending to be offended.

Marv glanced at his watch, and then at Paul. "What do you think? Will Mary be okay with you having a couple before dinner?" he asked.

"I'll drop off the papers at home, let Mary know what we're up to and meet you there," he answered Marv. "That's assuming this knucklehead is paying the tab." He pointed his thumbs toward Darren.

Darren returned to the conversation with a big grin. "Now make sure you get Becky's permission and then you can meet us at Don's place." He stopped and looked at Paul. "Don still owns the Bar and Grill, right?"

"Yeah, Don's still got the place. His son Barry and his wife are running the place now, though. Don's getting up there and much prefers his winters in warmer climates. He might be back by now."

Paul put the truck in gear and headed toward his place. Marv headed back into the town offices to let Becky know he might be late for dinner and not to worry. Darren stared out the window, silently wishing he had Amy here to get permission from. He'd never tell the guys that, though.

CHAPTER 11

MARY AND BECKY SAT AT THE DINING table watching the kids play on the tire swing in the back yard.

"You look tired, Becky. You feeling okay?" Mary asked, concern on her face.

"I'm okay," Becky answered, rubbing her protruding belly. "Baby has been very active today. Did you get hold of Darren's wife; what's her name again? Amy, right?"

"Yes, Amy and I had a very nice, polite conversation. It started off a little rough until she realized I wasn't Darren's mother. Then we had a nice chat."

"She doesn't like Amelia?" Becky tipped her head and smiled impishly. "Imagine that." She laughed.

"Becky, be nice. Amelia means well, even if she's a bit ..."

"Drill-sergeant like?!" Becky chuckled. "I think that's what you were looking for."

"No. Just bossy? Overbearing, maybe."

"Oh, Mary. You are so diplomatic. You should be a politician." Becky laughed at her friend, then picked up her teacup and sipped the hot mint tea gingerly.

"Well, she really is a nice person under all that snootiness. My mother and she have been friends for years. She even bakes everyone those wonderful Christmas cookies every year." Mary thought back to the times that Mrs. Packart and her mother had spent at her own kitchen table, Mother fussing over the wonderful baking Amelia always brought over. *Almost always apple cinnamon something*, Mary mused silently.

"Sure, from all the leftover apples they have from the orchard." Becky sneered, but her mouth watered at the thought of those little turnovers Mrs.

75

Packart always dropped at her parents' place every year. "They really are very good, though," Becky conceded. "So is Amy going to come down for a visit at all?"

"She said she'd think about it, but only if she could fly down and back in a safe manner," Mary answered as she lifted the teapot and poured more into each cup. "I gave her the information for Bellcom Airport and the airlines flying into it, and told her that I could come pick her up any time if Darren wasn't available. I gave her my phone number and told her to call whenever she'd like to. She's a bit like the mother-in-law she isn't fond of, I think," Mary added.

"Well, of course she is. Darren wouldn't marry any other kind now, would he?" Becky chuckled as she reached for a cookie. "Perhaps we should make supper for those men before they decide to eat at Don's Place," she said as she started to stand up.

"You sit and relax. Watch the kids for me. Make sure David is sharing with Anna, will you?" Mary stood up and opened the refrigerator door. "I've got most of supper planned out already. I figured when Paul came home early from the orchard that they'd be up to something stupid. When he told me Marv was going to meet him and Darren at Don's, I added two more to the supper table. We can all sit around tonight after I get the kids to bed and catch up."

Becky nodded and smiled. "I could watch your two play all day. I hope this one is as easygoing and good as they are." She rubbed her baby bump absently. "I wish I had two in here. Then it would be all done and over in one shot."

"Yeah, it was nice that they were one of each. Paul and I wanted a big yard full of kids, but so far, just two" Mary became quiet. She'd had such a hard time with her pregnancy. She'd been so sick and then the twins came early. Too early. But they were healthy and strong, and in no time, they were home. She was grateful every day that they had become the strong, happy children that they are now.

"Oh, I'm so sorry, Mary. I didn't mean to upset you. I know you and Paul have been trying for more." Becky looked out the window again. "Looks like they're on their way in. I'll help you with those veggies." She stood up and walked over to the counter Mary was standing at.

"David is a dummy, Mom!" Anna exclaimed as she flew the back door open, and it hit the wall.

"Anna! Be careful! You break that door, and your father is going to have a fit. And don't call your brother names. It's not nice." Mary looked over at Becky and raised her eyebrows. "You still wish you were having two?" she asked as they continued to peel and cut the potatoes Becky had brought over from her root cellar. Mary set the pot full of water and potatoes on the stove and added a pot of eggs to be boiled.

"Well, he is a poopy head and a dummy and I'm not sorry for saying it!" Anna plopped down in the chair Becky had just vacated. David came storming into the kitchen behind his sister.

"Why'd you have to have her?" he asked his mother, pointing menacingly at his sister. "I hate her!"

"David, that's enough. You do not hate your sister. Now will one of you please tell me what this is all about?" Mary said quietly. They both started talking at once and Mary was having a hard time figuring out what either of them was saying. "Okay, stop!" she said over their chatter. "One at a time would be more helpful."

"He found that stupid snake again and tried to put it down the back of my sweater!" Anna pouted.

Mary raised her hand, palm toward her daughter. "David, is this true?"

"Yes, but ..." David began. Mary raised her hand again. "No excuses, David. I told you no more playing with the garter snakes."

"I told him if he brought it anywhere near me again, I'd put it over the fence and let the bogyman get it!" Anna glared at her brother.

"You said what?" Mary said angrily as David burst into tears. Mary put her arm around her sobbing son as he leaned on her, trying to hide his tears.

"Anna, go to your room right now. I will be up in a minute to talk to you about this." Mary turned to console her son some more. "And no arguing with me, Anna Marie Jackson. Now go!"

Anna stormed out of the room and up the stairs. Mary and Becky held their breath as they waited for the inevitable slamming of the door and smiled at each other as they heard it rattle the windows.

"Now, David, come sit down and have a cookie." Mary guided her son to the table. "You know there's nothing on the other side of the fence out there, don't you?" she asked softly.

"I saw it, Mommy. I saw it last night when everyone was sleeping. I looked out the window and it was there. I know it was!" David tried hard to hold

PACKART'S ORCHARD   77

back the tears as a few more escaped down his cheeks. "Did Daddy look this morning like he promised?"

"No, dear. He didn't have time this morning. But he assured me there was nothing to worry about. I'll mention it to him when he, Darren, and Mr. Faulkon get home for dinner. But I'm sure there's nothing out there." Mary stared out the back door that was still standing open. She reached over and closed it, locking it as she did. Neither she nor Anna had seen anything out there. She had looked herself early this morning before David had gotten out of bed, to make sure there was no signs of any trouble. Anna had caught her out in the park area behind the house and had helped her mother look around. They'd made a game of it, and maybe that was a mistake on Mary's part.

"I'm going to go talk to your sister. You stay here and be polite to Mrs. Faulkon, please. Becky, I won't be long. Can you watch the pots on the stove? I'll make potato salad from them when I get back down, and we can add a tossed salad as well. Paul can cook up some hamburgers on the barbeque when the men get home." Mary walked over to the staircase to go up to her daughter's room when the front door flew open and three tipsy men entered the hallway, giggling like schoolgirls. A police sergeant stood behind them, a wide smile on his face. "Sergeant Harper?" Mary questioned. "Is everything okay?"

"Everything is fine, ma'am." Sergeant Harper removed his hat and smiled at her over her husband's shoulder. "Just thought I should make sure these three got home safe and sound, without driving." He emphasized the last part of his sentence.

"Thanks, Harpy!" Paul slurred as he tried to get his boots off. "Why don't you come in and have a beer with us? I'm sure we have some somewhere. Right, Mary?" He smiled up at her.

"Not tonight, Paul. I'm on duty. You all have a good evening." He turned to Mary. "You might want to get some food into them, Mary." Harpy smiled at her. "Good luck." He chuckled as he left the Jackson house full of people.

"Thanks for bringing them home." Mary laughed as she closed the door behind the sergeant.

"Now, are any of you three sober enough to use the barbeque or am I going to have to figure it out myself?" She put her hands on her hips.

"We'll figure it out," Paul said, waving his hands to indicate his friends would help him. "And we won't burn the place down." The men headed for the back yard, kissing Mary and Becky on their cheeks as they passed them.

78   WENDY SCOTT-ETTINGER

Mary shook her head and smiled. At least it was harmless fun, she thought as she ascended the stairs.

"Anna." She rapped lightly on her daughter's door. "May I come in?" she asked as she turned the doorknob to enter.

Anna was standing in front of her bedroom window staring out into the wooded area behind their house. She turned as her mother entered the room. "I don't see nothing, Mom," she said worriedly. "Just like when we were looking around. Nothing," she said again.

"I know, Anna. I don't see anything out there either. But your brother believes there's something there, and it's not nice to use that against him. Even when he's being a poopy head." Mary smiled as her daughter broke out in a fit of giggles.

"Mommy said poopy head!" Anna giggled and rolled onto her bed, tears of laughter running down her face.

"Now, don't you go repeating that to anyone, young lady," Mary scolded lightheartedly. "Go wash up. Your father and his friends are home. You and David might have to share a room tonight. I don't think Darren will be driving out to the orchard tonight."

"Ah Mommy, do I have to? I'm still mad at him."

"Yes, you have to. Now go wash up." They walked hand in hand out of the bedroom and Mary pointed Anna toward the bathroom. "When you're done in there, I'll send David up to wash up for dinner too, so don't be long." Mary descended the stairs and walked into chaos in the kitchen.

"What in heaven's name is going on in here?" she asked loud enough to be heard over the laughter.

"Oh, Mary!" Darren grabbed her, twirled her around and planted a messy kiss on her cheek. "We're just helpin' Becky make salads," he said as he set her back on her feet. "Meathead can't get the barbeque going so we might have to cook the hamburgers on the stove."

"No, you won't!" Mary headed for the backyard patio, flipping the porch light on as she walked out into silence. "Where is he, anyway?" she questioned over her shoulder. "I don't see him out here."

"Paul?" she yelled out into the darkness. "Paul, are you out here?"

"Go back into the house, Mary," said her husband's disembodied voice. It sounded like he was at the back fence.

"Paul, what are you doing out there? You're supposed to be helping make dinner for all your guests, and the kids are hungry," Mary scolded him.

PACKART'S ORCHARD

"Get back in the house, Mary. Cook the burgers on the stove. We aren't barbequing tonight. And tell Darren to get back out here with that flashlight he was supposed to be bringing me ..." Paul's voice trailed off.

"Darren!" Mary called from where she stood. "Can you bring me a flashlight, please?" She waited a beat to make sure she could hear him rummaging in the drawer for the light. "And Becky, can you show Darren and Marv where the frying pans are? I guess they'll be cooking indoors tonight," she said in a mocking tone. "David, go get washed up, please," she added as she saw Anna's head poke out of the back door.

"Yes, ma'am," David and Darren called together, going in opposite directions.

"What is he doing out there, Darren?" Mary asked as she took the flashlight from his hand.

"We saw something moving out there again, Mary. Honest we did," he added when he saw the look of disbelief on her face.

"Fine." Mary shook her head at the absurdity of the whole thing. "So why aren't you out here looking for whatever it is with him?"

"I ..." Darren hesitated. "I really don't want to go out there right now," he finished.

"Fine, I'll go rescue him myself. Go help with dinner." She walked through her backyard and threw open the gate that Paul had put in when they first moved into the house. It was easier to go for walks in the evenings and made a great shortcut to the downtown shops on a Saturday afternoon. *Hmm, maybe it was just people walking through the park on their way to their own homes that everyone was seeing out here*, Mary thought as she scanned the park with the flashlight.

"Paul, where are you?" Mary called. She couldn't see anything out here in the dark. *The town hall should really consider putting some lights up in the park, so people could use it more safely,* Mary thought as she scanned the tree line. "Paul, are you still out here?"

Paul came running out of the trees toward Mary. "Call Harpy back. There's definitely something out here, Mary," he panted as he reached her. He grabbed her hand and headed back into the yard, making sure the gate was securely locked on their way back in.

Mary and Paul ran back to the house and into the chaos of the kitchen, where all their house guests were preparing dinner.

Darren looked up as the back door opened. "What's up?" he questioned, looking at the fear in his friend's eyes. "What did you find?" he asked.

"Something, I ..." Paul took a deep breath. "Nothing, maybe. I don't know." He plopped down on the chair at the end of the dining table and rubbed his face with his hands. "There's something out there, Darren. I can see it. But I can't see it, either." Paul stared into space. "I was going to call Harpy and have him take a look around, but he'd think I was crazy."

"Yeah, probably. Especially since he had to bring us home from Don's Place not more than an hour ago," Darren confirmed. "Let's wait until morning and have another look around before breakfast." He handed Paul a plate with his dinner on it. "If we still think there's something there in the morning, we'll call Harpy."

"Okay, okay. Let's eat and get everyone calmed down now." Mary took charge of the situation. "I think I'll put a pot of coffee on and save the wine for later. Tea for you, Becky?" she asked as she walked over to the coffee pot and turned it on.

They chatted amiably about just about anything except what was going on outside. They talked about Darren's time in university and the summer jobs he'd had up there. They asked him about his wife and her family and let him know about the conversation Mary had with her earlier that same day. Paul and Marv exchanged stories about their time at Hedley college and the crazy parties they had. They reminisced about how Paul and Mary had met and how long it had been since they'd gotten together with AJ and Jenny.

Becky helped Mary get the kids into their pajamas and into Anna's bed. There were protests all around about the sleeping arrangements, including from Darren, who insisted that he could walk back to the orchard if he had to. He said the couch in the living room looked comfortable. But in the end, Mary won out as she usually did, and Anna and David were tucked comfortably into the big double bed in Anna's room.

Becky stretched her back and yawned. "I think we should be heading home." She looked at Marv for confirmation. "We all have to work in the morning," she said, reminding them that this was not the usual Friday night get together, but a mid-week impromptu one. "Perhaps we could make proper plans next time and invite AJ and Jenny to come in from Allensville." She tried to get her shoes back onto her swollen feet.

Marv got up and helped his wife with her shoes, then put his boots back on and looked around for his jacket. Mary handed it to him from the front closet, and he smiled gingerly. "Thank you for putting up with all of this." Marv smiled at her. He bent down and kissed her on her forehead. "I don't know what Paul would do without you," he said as he ducked to get out of the doorway. Becky hugged Mary good night and followed him out the door.

Mary waved. "Come back any time you'd like to," she called after them. "And be careful driving home," she added as she closed the door. When she returned to the living room, both Paul and Darren were sound asleep. She smiled at them and returned to the kitchen to finish cleaning up the mess. She sat at the dining table with a cup of tea and her book. She stared out the window at the trees. "Nothing there," she said out loud and opened the book she'd been trying to read now for a couple of weeks.

CHAPTER 12

THE NEXT DAY, DARREN AND PAUL PULLED themselves off their respective couches and wiped their faces. Paul ran up the stairs to catch the bathroom before anyone else could get there. By the time they each washed up and found a change of clothes to look respectable for work, Mary was in the kitchen making breakfast. The kids were still sleeping, which was usual in the Jackson house.

"What have you got planned for today?" Mary asked politely as the men sat at the table.

"I don't know about Darren, but I have some more calls to make, and then hopefully Marv will be able to come out and look around at the place, see what needs to be done to get that irrigation system finished before growing season hits full on. Then I'm thinking I'll take another walk around the old Mill House and those old cabins in the back forty. See if there's anything we can do to make them more respectable before we have a new crew come in. If I see anything I like, I'll have Darren here talk to his dad about it." Paul pointed at his friend and winked. "That's why you came back right, to be my defenseman." Paul chuckled.

Darren shook his head. "I really don't know why I came back, to tell you the truth. Dad doesn't seem to need me. You seem to have all the orchard work figured out. I'm just a middleman, and that's not what I want to be doing." He drank the last of his coffee and set the cup in the kitchen sink. "Anyway, we should be going. If we're late, Dad will have our heads, and we have to walk to town to get your pretty truck." Darren grinned. "Love all the exercise I'm getting around here, and I don't even have to pay for a club membership."

Darren and Paul said their goodbyes to Mary and headed out the back door to walk through the park to town. Paul walked slowly, looking through all the trees and on the off-path areas, looking for any signs of anything being back there last night. Nothing. Darren was quiet as he watched his friend inspect the trees and pathways. He knew Paul well enough to understand that he wasn't normally struck by 'flights of fancy', as his mother would say. Paul didn't believe in aliens, or ghosts, or things that go bump in the night. So, when he said something was watching them, Darren believed it.

"Hey, Paul," Darren said, interrupting the silence. "When did Dad start clearing everyone out of the orchard before dark? Is that just to get you to go home to your family, or does he do that all the time now?"

Paul thought about the question and then shrugged. "I don't really know. He's been adamant that no one works past dark for a couple of years now. I assumed it was to keep the overtime costs down, or maybe to keep the crew from partying in the orchard at night. Haven't really talked to him about it, 'cause, well, it works for me." Paul shrugged again. "Why?"

"Don't know. It just struck me as strange. He won't even let me go out in the dark for a walk around the place. Tells me to walk in the morning, or to stay in the quarter acre that the house is on. I don't think he ever used to care if I wanted to go for a walk or play in the back in the treehouse after dark." Darren walked a little faster as he spotted Paul's bright-blue truck in the parking lot beside Don's Place. "Just seems strange, is all," he said again.

Paul hadn't really thought much about it. There were times that Mr. P. would meet him on his way back to the parking area, especially if Paul hadn't taken one of the golf carts that day. He was adamant that he leave the orchard before dark and not come in too early, either. Now that Paul thought about it, it was really strange. He hadn't been that way when Paul had first taken over and now he was curious. Maybe Darren would ask his dad about it today and let Paul know what he said.

THE NEXT COUPLE OF WEEKS WENT BY without any incidents, and Paul and Darren kind of drifted into their own routines. Marvin had come out and inspected everything and given Mr. P. a more than fair quote and timeframe. Paul worried that Marvin had shortchanged himself on the quote and talked to him about it, but he had assured Paul that it was a reasonable price for the work that needed to get done.

A few days into the work, though, Marvin came into Paul's office. "We have a problem," he exclaimed as he ducked into the treehouse. He plopped down in front of Paul, then pointed at the coffee pot. "That smells good. Is it fresh?"

"Yes, go ahead and pour yourself some, and tell me what problem we have now." Paul looked up from his new cabin plans and smiled at his friend. Marvin wasn't smiling back. "What's wrong?"

"Well …" Marvin poured a coffee, took a sip, and sat back down in the visitor chair. "My guys were out in the watermill checking on the electricity connections and making sure everything was going to fit together, you know." Paul nodded. "Anyway," Marvin continued, "they aren't going to fit, which we kind of talked about and knew ahead of time. That's not the problem."

"So what is the problem?" Paul asked, frustrated.

"The guys found a bunch of barrels in the back by where they have to work. They look like really old pesticide barrels, or some kind of chemical, anyway. They said they aren't going back into the watershed to work on the lines until those barrels have either been removed or certified safe by the EPS guys."

Paul sat back and looked directly at Marvin. "Has one of your guys phoned them? The EPS guys, I mean?"

"Don't know. Don't think so. Either way, no more work's getting done until we figure out what to do with them barrels." Marvin shrugged and finished off his coffee. "If it takes too long to get this sorted, I'm going to have to take my equipment to another job site and come back when I can fit it in."

"Don't do anything hasty just yet. Let me talk to Mr. P. and Darren and see if they know what's in those barrels. I'll go in and take a look myself, before I head over to the mansion. See if I can I.D. them. I'll get back to you by this afternoon latest."

Marvin nodded his understanding at his friend. "Let me know. But if we can't deal with this by the end of the week, I have to look after me and my crew. You understand, right?"

"Yeah, I understand. Like I said, I'll give it all I have, Marv, that's all I can do."

Marvin left the treehouse office and headed over to where his men were mulling around murmuring to themselves. When Marvin approached, they became quiet. "What?" Marvin looked at them. "What's up?"

"Nothing," one of the men replied.

"We were just talking about them barrels," another said, then hesitated.

"Okay, and …" Marvin looked at them for more clues.

"Well, we was just wondering if maybe Packart Orchards is still using them restricted pesticides, like DDT or something?"

"Let's not get ourselves all up in arms about those barrels. They're likely just leftover pesticides from when they used to spray. Paul's going to investigate it and let me know the game plan by this afternoon, so you can all head home early." Marvin waved them off. "And don't say anything to anyone about those barrels, at least until we give Paul a chance to figure it out."

They all headed out toward the parking lot in front of the mansion, not saying another word.

Marvin looked over at Paul as he came down the stairs of his office. "You heard that?"

"Yeah, I heard them. I'll get to the bottom of it today one way or the other." Paul walked toward the watermill. "Talk to you soon." He waved at his friend as Marvin headed after his crew.

As Paul approached the watermill, he had that sensation of being watched again. He shook his head and looked over his shoulder, wondering if Marvin had come back for something. But when he looked around there was no one there. *Damn, this is starting to get to me.* Paul pulled out his notepad from his pocket and jotted down the date, time, and location, then stuck it back into his pocket. He opened the shed door and flipped on the lights, but nothing happened. "Damn, did they cut electricity and then leave?" He tried a couple more power switches but nothing. Paul ran up the steps to his office and phoned Darren's office number.

"Hey, bud. I see Marv and his crew are leaving early today. What's happening?"

"Is Marv still in the parking lot? If he is, holler at him for me. I need to talk to him before he leaves."

"Yeah, sure. Anything else?" Darren quipped.

"Now please. I'm heading that way in the cart so will be back to the house shortly." Paul hung up on Darren and headed back out the door. That feeling sent shivers down his spine again, but he didn't have time for it right now, so he tried to ignore it. He leaped into the golf cart and headed toward the mansion.

"Hey, Marv!" Paul waved at Marv and Darren standing beside Marv's truck. "I need to talk to you for a minute."

"What's going on? Darren said you needed to talk to me."

"Just wanted to catch you before you headed out. Thought it would be easier on all of us if you didn't have to come back out here as soon as you got home."

"What's so important it can't wait until tomorrow?" Marvin raised his eyebrows in question.

"The electricity is out in the watermill. If it doesn't work, neither will all the industrial heaters out there. It's still pretty early in the season. We can't risk frost on the trees this time of year." Paul looked at the puzzled look on his friend's face.

"I'm sure we flipped everything back on before we left. Are you sure it's not just a burnt-out bulb or something? The power to your office was still on."

"I don't know." Paul shrugged. "I flipped the switch by the door and nothing. I looked around and flipped another and nothing. No sound coming from the generator either."

Marvin and Paul hopped onto the cart and headed back to the treehouse.

"I'll tell you and your dad what's happening when I get back again," Paul hollered over his shoulder to Darren as they drove away.

They headed out, making record time as they got back to the watermill. Marvin switched some switched and looked around the entrance of the watermill while he waited for Paul to come in with a flashlight.

"Nothing?" Paul asked as he shone the light around. "The service box must be here somewhere." He swung the flashlight around to see if he could spot it.

"Give me that thing." Marvin grabbed the flashlight and headed for the back of the shed. "That's strange," he said almost to himself. "I'm sure we didn't leave this like that." He reached over and flipped a few switches on the breaker box and all the lights in the water house turned on. He flipped the flashlight off and handed it back to Paul. "I don't know what's going on in here, but I know my guys didn't do that." He pointed to the back wall. All the barrels that Marvin had been talking about had been flipped over on their sides. They had been spray painted with big black letters saying "LEAVE THEM ALONE."

"But no one other than us and your crew have been out here all day. I don't understand." Paul looked at Marvin and back at the barrels. "I would have heard something like this happening."

PACKART'S ORCHARD   87

Marvin shrugged. "I don't know, but I know they weren't like that when I told the crew to get out and I came to talk to you about them. I know we didn't leave the breaker box switches turned off, either, and if you didn't do any of this, then you have an intruder. But who?"

"I don't know but I don't like this one bit. Come on, let's go talk to Mr. P. about all of this and see what we should do next. If it were up to me, I'd be calling in the cops to look around."

They headed back to the house and knocked on the office door. Mr. P. looked at the two men standing on his porch and knew something wasn't right. "What's up, boys? Problems with the irrigation system?"

"Not exactly," Paul responded. "It's the water mill. I think you need to come out and look at this."

Albert and Darren grabbed a golf cart from the shed and followed Paul and Marvin back out to the water mill. All the lights were still on and the door was wide open. It looked like they'd left in a hurry. "Did we leave it like that?" Marvin asked, confused. "I was sure I'd at least pulled the door closed."

"All of this is so strange; I don't know any more," Paul responded, then glanced up at the treehouse on his way toward the shed. He stopped abruptly. "What the hell?" He turned around and headed up the stairs. His office door was wide open, and all the equipment had been turned on, including his radio at full blast. Written in red ink across the rough drawings of the cabins was "LEAVE THEM ALONE."

"You seeing this?" Paul asked.

Darren and Marvin both responded "Yeah" in disbelief.

"Same thing that was on the barrels," Marvin commented.

"What barrels?" Darren asked.

"The ones in the watermill," Albert responded at the office door. "What's happened?" he asked Paul as he entered.

"Did you see the message on the barrels?" Paul asked Albert.

"I went in there while you three headed up here. Wanted to know why all the lights had been left on. When I saw them, I knew what you had been in such a hurry for me to see. What have we got up here?" Albert gestured.

"The same message. I know I didn't leave all this on, so whoever wrote those messages also turned everything on up here. Had to have happened after Marvin and I headed back to the mansion to get the two of you. Whoever did this has to still be in the orchard. We need to look around and see if we can find whoever it is."

88   WENDY SCOTT-ETTINGER

"No, we need to call the sheriff's department and let them handle it," Albert responded. "I assume the barrels are the reason your crew left?" he asked Marvin.

"Have a seat." Paul pushed his desk chair out for Albert and handed him the phone. He nodded to Marvin to sit in the other chair as he was having a hard time standing in the cramped office. Paul and Darren leaned against the desk and coffee station respectively. "Why don't we tell you what's been going on the last hour or so, while we wait for the police to get here. Of course," he looked pointedly at Albert, "by that time, whoever has been doing this will be long gone."

Marvin and Paul filled Darren and Albert in on what had been going on in the orchard that day. Albert looked tired at the end of it all. He didn't say a word for a long time, then stood up and looked at his son. "We'll go back to the house and wait for the sheriff to get here." He headed for the door. "You two close up all these buildings and make sure the pumps and generator are all working for the water and heaters out here. We can't afford any more delays, so I'll have those barrels moved out of the watermill after the police have had their look around. Don't be out here too late." He headed down the stairs with Darren right behind him.

"I'll see you at the house in a few?" Darren asked Paul.

"Yeah, we'll be out of here in a few. Just want to make sure everything is secure before we head out. Oh, and Darren," he looked at his friend. "You were right about needing locks on all these buildings. Let's talk to Albert about that tomorrow, okay?"

Darren smiled at him as he practically danced down the stairs. "I was right, I was right." He laughed and waved at the two men at the top of the stairs.

PAUL GOT BACK TO THE ORCHARD EARLY the next morning. The sun was just coming up and the whole valley glowed with a red and orange hue. It was beautiful out here that time of day, and so peaceful. He opened the shed and grabbed a key off the peg board for one of the carts. *We need to get a lock for this building too,* he thought as he pulled the cart out and turned it toward the treehouse. He was going to make sure that nothing else had happened last night before he went in to talk to Albert and Darren about what the police had said and what their next steps were with the irrigation project and the locks.

He hadn't slept at all last night, thinking about who could have done what happened the day before, and how they could do it without Paul seeing them. Maybe the feeling of always being watched was real and there was really someone out there. But why hadn't anyone seen them? Especially with Marvin's crew out there for the better part of a week.

When Paul reached the treehouse, he noticed the watermill door was wide open again. This time, though, there was a golf cart with a pull trailer attached to it, so someone was in there for sure. Paul gingerly approached the door and hollered, "Hello, is there anyone in there?"

"Hey, bud. Glad to see you're here early today. You can help Dad and I get these barrels out of here," Darren called out to him from the back of the watermill.

Paul walked in and saw them trying to lift the barrels. They were obviously heavy, because the two men were having trouble moving them.

"Wouldn't it be easier to just roll them out, since they're already on their sides?" Paul asked as he watched them try to maneuver around the equipment between them and the door.

"Wasn't sure if we could tussle them around too much," Darren answered as he set his end of the barrel down by Paul's feet.

"I'm assuming it's pesticides, not explosives, right Mr. P?" Paul said. As Albert nodded, Paul continued, "Didn't they teach you anything up in that fancy university?" He grinned at Darren.

"Okay, smarty pants, you get to figure out how to get this one in the trailer then." Darren turned back into the watermill toward the remaining barrels.

"Well, that's easy." Paul turned the golf cart around so the trailer attached to it was backed up to the building. He then grabbed a couple of old 2 x 10's that had been left over from building the treehouse stairs and leaned them on the back of the trailer as a ramp. He grabbed a pair of gloves out of the back of his own cart, laid the barrel on its side, and rolled it up the ramp and into the trailer. He then maneuvered the barrel back onto its end and headed toward the door for the next one.

"Okay, so you really are smarter than me," Darren said as he watched his best friend load the second barrel. "On that note, I think I'll leave the rest of this for you and dad. I'm not sure what he's planning on doing with them, but I'm sure the two of you can figure it out." Darren pulled his gloves off and tossed them into the back of the golf cart.

"Where do you think you're going?" Paul asked him. "Leaving when the work gets tough?" Paul laughed as he watched his friend start walking toward the mansion.

"I have to go into Bellcom City this morning. I'll be back in time to see you leave for the day." Darren waved over his head and kept going.

Paul and Albert got the rest of the barrels loaded into the trailer, and Paul moved the boards he'd used for the ramp back around the side of the building. "How did these barrels end up in here to begin with?" Paul asked.

"Oh, I moved them in here last fall. They were out around the back of the cabins and one of the workers mentioned them to me. I wanted to get them out of the elements before winter set in, so I asked Red to help me get them out of there. I'd forgotten I even bought the damn things until they pointed them out to me. Must have been sitting out there for a couple of years or more. Anyway, I put them out here out of the way, thinking we could get rid of them once we figured out how to dispose of them properly, but I guess I just got busy with Darren being here and all, and forgot I'd done that."

"Okay?" Paul looked at him with worry. It wasn't like Albert to do those kinds of things without mentioning it to Paul. And it wasn't like the workers to go directly to Albert with anything to do with the day-to-day orchard work. It was a rather strange little story, but Paul didn't want to question Albert on it.

"So where are you taking them now?" Paul asked.

"Oh, I've got a disposal company coming to get them this afternoon. I phoned them this morning and they said they'd come over from Carson to get them. I'll just park them over by the golf cart shed and they will pick them up whenever they get here."

"Okay." Paul wasn't buying all this, but he wasn't going to push it right now. "What about the locks for all these buildings out here? Did Darren talk to you about any of that last night?"

"No, he didn't mention it. But that's a good idea." Albert climbed into the golf cart and started to slowly move it back around to the pathway toward the mansion. "Why don't you make some calls and see if you can get someone out here to get that done today. Once it's complete, you can pop by the office with the invoice, and I'll make sure it gets paid."

"Will do." Paul waved at him as he drove away. *That was strange,* Paul thought as he ascended the stairs to his office. *This whole spring has been strange out here, come to think about it.*

PACKART'S ORCHARD   91

Paul plugged the coffee pot in and filled it with water. Then he sat down and looked at the mess on his desk. The marked-up plans were still scattered all over the desktop and it looked like fingerprint dust was all over everything. *Guess I'll have to clean all of this up before I get to work this morning.* He pushed all the paperwork together and gingerly walked it to the door. He then proceeded to wipe off all the powder with his sleeve. He shook out the bigger plans and then headed back into the office. He wiped off the desktop with a damp rag and did the same to the telephone, computer, and calculator. *Okay, well that's good enough for now.* Maybe he'd call Mary later and ask her to bring out some cleaning supplies to get the job done properly. They could have a picnic out here with the kids for lunch if he called her now. He called home, but no one answered. He shrugged and didn't think much more about it.

Okay, Marvin first, then I'll look for a locksmith to get this place more secure.

It was around lunchtime when he heard people scurrying around the watermill again. Marvin must be here, he thought, as he pulled his lunch bag out of the fridge and wandered over to the landing at the top of the stairs to make sure that was who he'd heard. Sure enough, Marvin and three crewmen were busy coming in and out of the watermill carrying various pieces of equipment, cables, and piping back and forth between a small truck that they'd driven up the pathway to the watermill. *Sure glad they know what they're doing,* Paul thought as he absentmindedly bit into his sandwich.

Marvin spotted him and approached the staircase. "Hey, you got a minute?" he asked Paul as he started to ascend the staircase.

"Sure, come on up. I think I have coffee left in the pot if you'd like some."

Marvin asked him about what the police had said and done and what happened to the barrels. Paul told him that neither Albert nor Darren had mentioned what happened the night before, but that they moved the barrels out themselves that morning. He also told Marvin about what Albert said about how they got there, and that Albert had called a disposal company in Carson about coming to get them.

"Really?" Marvin questioned. "I don't remember there being a chemical disposal in Carson. I know there's one up the valley past Allensville to the west, and another in Kendall." Marvin scratched his chin thoughtfully. "And doesn't Albert usually leave you to deal with the workers and any issues in the orchard? It just doesn't sound right."

"Yeah, I know. This whole thing doesn't sound right to me either," Paul confirmed. "I'm going to go talk to Mr. P once I finish eating. I've found a guy to put locks on all the outbuildings, so I want to let him know what the guy's going to do and timeframes. Maybe I'll talk to him about all this again this afternoon."

"Okay, well, good luck with that. Doesn't sound like you're going to get much more out of him, though." Marvin finished off his coffee. "By the way, we'll have the electricity shut off for a couple of hours this afternoon, so you won't have power out here for a while. You might want to let Mr. P know in case it affects the house too."

"Will do. How much longer you think your crew will need to get this project completed?"

"Couple of days. Maybe testing the day after that. We'll have you up and running in no time, don't you worry."

"No worries. I trust your work." Paul stood up and threw his lunch wrappers in the trash can, and Marvin headed for the stairs again. "Since I can't use the computer, I might as well wander up to the mansion now then. Talk to you later, Marvin."

They exited the treehouse together and headed their own ways. Paul shook his head, thinking, *at least it's not just me that thinks all of this is weird.* He hopped onto his golf cart and headed toward the mansion.

As he approached the parking area, he spotted an old red pick-up exiting the driveway. It had all six barrels in the back. It didn't appear to have a company name or logo on it that he could see. Paul shrugged. Just one more weird thing to add to the list.

"Paul, what are you doing up this way so early in the day?" Albert asked as he walked over to meet him. "You usually have your head in those drawings or in the computer by now."

"Marvin and his crew are out at the watermill again today. They've turned all the power off so they can get the new connections installed. Told me to let you know in case it affects the mansion too."

"Okay. Better go in and let Amelia know so she doesn't get a surprise when she's doing her housework." Albert waved Paul into the house. "I assume you have other things you want to talk about."

"I do, starting with the locksmith. And I was wondering what the police had to say after they inspected the place. I saw they must have taken fingerprints from my office, since there was powder all over everything when I got in there."

"Sure, come on in and we'll chat for a bit."

PACKART'S ORCHARD   93

PAUL EXITED THE MANSION A COUPLE OF hours later. He wasn't any more in the know about what was going on than he had been before he went in, but at least he had the go ahead to get all the security and locks on the outbuildings that he'd requested. He'd take the cart back out to the watermill and see what the status of the electricity was and then hopefully get a plan together to hire this year's crew and put some calls out around town to see if people knew of anyone looking for work.

"Hey, Marvin." He waved at his friend, who was exiting the watermill. We got any power out here yet?" Paul hollered.

"Not for a while yet. Doesn't look like there's been any work in here for years. We may have to replace a lot of the old wiring too." Marvin shook his head. "Should have listened to you and added some contingency to this project. I'm going to be losing money if I have to replace all of it. Might have to ask Mr. P to hire an electrician and then we'll need inspectors for that as well."

"Damn, it just keeps coming today, doesn't it?" Paul exclaimed. "Maybe whoever wrote that message on the barrels was right. Maybe I should stop trying to fix this old place up."

"Now, don't go starting that," Marvin responded. "It's not your fault this place has been left so long. You've been trying to get it done since you started out here after college. For whatever reasons Mr. P just doesn't want to have anything changed."

"Yeah, I don't get it. He was all gung-ho to get the orchard into this century when he inherited it from his dad. But now he acts like it's a crime to get anything fixed up. If it doesn't start happening soon, he's going to lose the business completely. Anyway, on a happier note, I'm looking to start hiring crew for the summer and fall seasons. If you know of anyone, just give me their names and phone numbers and I can see what I can do. Mr. P said we can start off with a half dozen to help get everything ready for growing and then bring them back in for picking, sorting, and hauling. We can likely put a couple to work on Mrs. P's garden again this year too. She's wanting to expand that again and get the fruit stand moved out to the roadway."

"I've got a couple of cousins that might be looking. They're from up Carson way. Let me know what you're paying and if the cabins will be available or not and I'll get back to you."

"Thanks, Marvin. I'll get you the information you're looking for by the time you leave today. Talk to you later."

Paul headed up to the office to make sure there wasn't anything in the fridge that needed to be taken out while the power was out. Maybe he'd head home and work from there the rest of the day. He gathered everything up that he might need at home, gave Mary a call to make sure him being there wasn't going to cause any issues, and then closed the office door. Hopefully, the locksmith would make it out tomorrow as he'd promised. Paul was getting so he didn't like leaving anything out here at all, but he didn't have much choice. He loaded everything into the golf cart, waved at Marvin, and headed back toward the parking area. He'd put the stuff in his truck and put the cart away, then let Mr. P know what he was planning on doing. He'd also let him know about Marvin's cousins and confirm wages and other benefits would be the same as last year before he gave the information to Marvin.

As he was putting the cart away, he noticed a shadow or something behind the shed. "What the hell was that?" he said out loud as he walked over to the window in the back of the big shed. He looked out through the trees but couldn't see anything. *Fine, I'll just go out there and see what that was* he thought as he closed the shed doors and walked with purpose behind the shed, where he'd seen the shadows. *Nothing. Damn it.* He walked further into the trees. There wasn't really anything out this way except fruit trees, so there wasn't any reason for anyone to be out here at this time of year.

"Hello?" Paull called. "Is there anyone out here?" Still nothing. "Okay, if you are the one that's been messing with the outbuildings and my office, I will find you, and when I do, you'll be sorry! This is private property."

Still nothing.

Paul turned back toward the shed again and decided to walk over to the pathway he'd driven the cart on earlier. It was a bit out of the way, but maybe he'd spot something going the other way. As he reached the edge of the trees and turned onto the pathway, a swarm of what looked like very large black bugs with shiny red eyes came out of the trees and headed straight for him.

"What the hell is that?" He squinted up at the swarm. *I can't tell what they are. Are they wasps?* No, he thought, *too big for wasps or hornets*, but he couldn't tell what they looked like. Suddenly one was in his face and spraying some sort of powder. That couldn't be right. Another one hit him hard on the side of the jaw and then flew away as quickly as it had come at him. He swiped at them to try to catch one, but they were really fast, and Paul was starting to feel dizzy. "What the hell," he muttered and then fell to his knees.

PACKART'S ORCHARD

He looked up again to see where they were, but they were gone. "Bugs," he said out loud. "Have to warn Marvin." Then he passed out.

PAUL WOKE UP IN WHAT LOOKED LIKE a hospital room. *What had happened?* he thought as he looked around slowly. Mary was sitting by the bed. She looked like she hadn't slept in a while. He tried to sit up.

Mary stood up quickly and held his hand. "Paul, it's okay. Don't try to move. You're okay" Concern riddled her face. "I'll call the doctors."

"What ... happened?" he whispered up at her.

"You don't remember?" she asked.

"Bugs. The bugs!" He tried to sit up again but failed. "You have to warn Marvin and his crew. You have to tell Mr. P." He started to panic. *What were those things?* he thought as the hospital room door flung open and a doctor and two nurses came into the room.

"Mr. Jackson, I'm glad to see you're awake again. How are you feeling?" the doctor asked as he checked the monitors on the machines connected to Paul's arms and chest. "Looks like your heart is beating a bit too fast again. You need to calm down. Everything is going to be fine."

"What happened? What was that powder the bugs sprayed at me?" he asked the doctor.

"Bugs, Mr. Jackson? I don't remember anyone mentioning any bugs." The doctor patted Paul on the shoulder. "You came in with signs of a high-stress-related heart attack, Paul, but thank God Mr. Packart brought you in in time for us to deal with it. Your heart is still a bit erratic and your breathing appears to be laboured. Are you feeling dizzy, Paul?"

"No. No. Not a heart attack. A bug attack! Mary, please tell Mr. P he needs to get someone out there to investigate. They could attack someone else!"

"Paul, you need to calm down," the doctor said. "We're going to give you a sedative. Your heart can't take this stress right now." The doctor nodded at the nurse, who injected something into the I.V. bag attached to Paul's arm. "You'll feel better soon," he said as he turned to walk out of the room.

The nurse looked at Mary and patted her shoulder. "He'll be okay, Mary, don't worry. He'll be sleeping again for a few hours. Why don't you go have something to eat and you can come back later?"

Mary shook her head. "I'll stay with him."

When Paul opened his eyes again, the room was dark. A small nightlight shone by what looked like a bathroom door. Mary was still sitting in a chair

96   WENDY SCOTT-ETTINGER

beside his bed, but her head was on the bed beside his hand, and she was sound asleep. Paul looked around. He knew it wasn't a heart attack that put him in this bed. Why was he so weak and dizzy? Something in the powder that bug spewed out at him. But what? Paul couldn't move and he felt really hot, like someone had turned the furnace on full force. He didn't want to wake Mary, but he needed to talk to someone. Someone that could help figure all of this out. He shook his hand beside Mary's head. She stirred but didn't wake up.

"Mary?" he whispered. "Mary, please wake up."

Mary sat up with a start. "Paul? Are you okay?"

"No, Mary, I'm not okay. You need to listen to me."

"I'll call the nurse." Mary reached over to push the call button, but Paul stopped her.

"Mary, no. Listen to me. Please," he pleaded with her.

"Okay, Paul, I'm listening." Mary stared into her husband's face and squeezed his hand.

"You need to tell Mr. P about the bugs. You need to make sure that you and the kids stay out of the orchard. Don't let them go in there until this is all figured out. Don't let David anywhere near the orchard, Mary. He saw it too. They may come after him. Get him out of Windsmill. Please, Mary, promise me you'll have them investigate."

"Okay, Paul. I will. I promise." Mary looked at her husband with tears in his eyes and sweat pouring down his forehead. She reached over and wiped the sweat from his brow with a tissue. "I promise," she said again.

"It's so hot," Paul murmured and passed out again. Suddenly the bells on all the machines started ringing and the lights flashed on as a stat team rushed into the room. They pushed Mary away from the bed and started to work on her husband. Tears poured down her face. She knew she would never hear his voice again. She knew she would never see him alive again. She left the room and headed for the elevators.

As the doors of the elevators opened and Mary tried to enter, Darren and Amy exited into the hallway beside her. "Mary, Darren said softly, "is everything alright?"

"No," Mary said and put her head against Darren's chest. "No, nothing will ever be alright again." She sobbed.

CHAPTER 13

MARY BLINKED RAPIDLY, AS IF TO BRING herself back from the 1990 horrors to her present-day audience. She looked up from the picture album she'd been flipping through while she told her story. Four sets of very wet eyes were staring back at her. Jenny stood up, walked over to her sister, and hugged her tightly. AJ stood and stretched his back, then reached over and grabbed a box of tissues on the back of a side table. He took a couple of tissues from the box and handed it to Anna, who did the same, and handed it over to David.

"Thank you for doing this," Jenny said to her sister. "I'll make some tea." She grabbed a tissue from the box in David's hand and walked into the kitchen.

Mary stared at David. "You were incredibly quiet through all that. I thought you'd have questions."

"Oh, I have a million of them," David replied softly. "But I didn't want to interrupt you. You seemed like you were right there the whole time and I didn't want to break that spell."

Mary smiled at him. "Thank you for listening," she said to him, "and for making me relive all of that. I think it was therapeutic for me to go through all the details again." Mary walked past David and patted him on the shoulder. "Perhaps some tea and cake before we go into your questions," she said.

David nodded and then stood as well. He looked over at Anna, who was still sitting on the loveseat beside him. Tears streamed down her face. He realized that not only was she reliving Paul's death, but most likely her husband Jack's as well. He reached down to try to comfort her, but she waved him away.

"I'll be okay in a bit," she said as she stood up and walked toward the staircase. "I'm just going to check on Johnny."

David nodded at her then walked into the kitchen with the others. This had been a difficult evening for everyone.

They sat quietly at the kitchen table with tea and cake. No one seemed to want to say anything more; all were lost in their own thoughts. AJ and Jenny said their goodbyes and headed for the door. "We'll call you tomorrow, Mary," Jenny said as she pulled on her sweater. "I'm sure you've had enough talking for one night." She smiled at her sister and they hugged each other tightly.

"Good night," Mary said as she turned to hug AJ. "You drive carefully out there, okay?"

"I always do." AJ smiled at her. "And thank you again for the wonderful meal and for putting yourself through all those memories for the kids." They waved at David and Anna and left the house.

"Well," David said quietly as he stretched. "I should probably get going too."

"Why don't you stay here for the night? I can move Johnny into my room with me and you can sleep in your old room," Anna suggested.

"Yes, please," Mary agreed. "Please stay. You can think about what you wanted to ask me, and we can sit down again in the morning and go through anything you'd like. It will save you having to drive back out here in the morning."

"Yes, then you can take me back to Bellcom with you tomorrow and I can finally get my car back!" Anna smiled at him.

"Speaking of your car," David started, "I forgot to tell you what happened before I came out here this afternoon. Now that I've heard about what happened twenty years ago, this is even more curious."

Anna looked at him expectantly. "Well?" she asked impatiently.

"Why don't we help our mother clean up the kitchen and then I can carry Johnny into your room for you. Then we'll sit out on the back deck with a coffee or beer or something, and I'll tell you all about it."

Anna raised her eyebrows at him but didn't say anything. She walked over and started washing the dishes while David headed for the stairs to move Johnny over to Anna's bedroom. This had been a trying day for all of them.

Anna dug around the kitchen and found a bottle of white wine. She found a couple of beers in the back of the fridge that had probably been there awhile too. "We could try these," she said as she heard someone walk into the kitchen behind her, "or we can make coffee or more tea." She turned around

PACKART'S ORCHARD   99

to see her mother standing at the counter. "Mom! I'm sorry, I thought it was David."

"Didn't mean to intrude," her mother said in a sad voice. "I was just going to let you two know I'm going to head up to my room. I think I'll read my book and try to get some sleep. If you're going to open that wine though, I'll take a glass of that up with me." Mary smiled.

"Okay, I'll open it up and see what it's like. Looks like it's been in the cupboard for a while now, though."

Mary chuckled to herself as she remembered the night Darren and Amy had brought that over when they came for dinner. "I'd say it's been in that cupboard for about twenty-two years now."

"Twenty-two years. Well, hopefully it hasn't gone skunky then," David responded from the kitchen entrance. "Mind, it's been in a dark cool cupboard so maybe it's still good."

Anna popped the cork and smelled the wine. "Doesn't smell like vinegar," she said as she reached up and pulled out three wine glasses. "These look like they need dusting too." She smiled. "Did you get Johnny moved okay?"

"He's a very sound sleeper," David replied with a shrug. "Good thing, too, since I wasn't sure what I was doing. I think I got him under all those blankets on your bed."

Anna poured the wine into the freshly cleaned glasses and handed them out. "Mom, you go ahead and taste that, since you've been holding on to it for so long."

Mary took a small sip from her glass and smiled again. "Amy was always a wine connoisseur. Only the best for them."

"Amy? As in Darren's wife Amy?" David asked lightly.

"Yes, they came over for dinner after Paul died. Brought the babies over so I could cuddle them. They were so cute," Mary reminisced. "Anyway," she said before David could ask any more questions. "I'll see you two in the morning. Don't stay up all night."

David reached over and lightly kissed Mary's forehead. "Thanks again," he said to her as she pulled away.

"Tomorrow," Mary repeated as she headed for the stairs with her book in one hand and a full glass of wine in the other. "This is very delicious," she said as she ascended to her room.

"So." Anna looked at David. "Do you want to sit outside or here in the kitchen?"

David looked out into the now-darkened backyard and shivered. He knew there was nothing there, but it all seemed so scary somehow. "It's dark out now. How about we sit in here and I'll tell you about my afternoon before I got here. All in all, a crazy day."

David told Anna about the note and about his college friend from the Bellcom City Police Department. He told her about the building that his office was in, and that he owned the block. He seemed to talk forever, and Anna listened intently. It was like he needed her to know what he'd been doing with his life since they were separated. When he stopped to breathe, he shook his head. "Sorry about that." David looked sheepishly at Anna. "I don't know why I told you my whole life story."

Anna smiled at him lovingly. "Because we both have the feeling that we've missed each other terribly, even though we didn't know it until now."

"Yeah, you're right. This wine is delicious, isn't it?" He emptied his glass. "And of course, the bottle is empty." He laughed.

I could make coffee or something?" Anna offered.

"No, I'm fine." David waved her off. "What do you think about the note? Can you think of who might want to warn you off?"

"The only thing I can think of is someone doesn't like that we're opening up all these deaths again. I can't think of anything else that could have caused someone to put that on my car."

"There are a couple of things I thought of while I was driving out here. Could be a case of mistaken identity. Who in Bellcom City would know you and your car?"

Anna shook her head. She couldn't think of anyone she knew that would be in Bellcom or around the area David's office building was in.

"Or it could be someone warning me off of another case I'd been working on before you got me so busy with this one," David finished. "Although I can't think of that kind of warning coming from them, either."

"What kind of cases do you usually get?" Anna asked curiously.

"Most people see that "paranormal psychology" on my credentials and think about the noises in their attic or the missing things in their house that suddenly show up again. That kind of stuff. Sometimes I get cases similar to this one, where someone has died, and the family thinks the circumstances are strange." He looked over at his sister to see if she was thinking he was crazy, but he only saw interest.

PACKART'S ORCHARD   101

"Anyway, the couple of cases I have right now are simple missing persons cases. I think one is a runaway and the other one I already found. He was hiding out from his dad at a friend's place just outside Bellcom. He figured he was going to be in big shit over something he did. I gave him Mike's phone number and told him that Mike would take him home and talk everything over with his dad."

"Sounds like a good ending," Anna said. "But not what would cause this kind of a note on my car."

"Nope. Already got paid for that one, with a nice thank you from both the kid and his dad."

"So where does that leave us?" Anna asked. "Can I still go get my car tomorrow?"

"I'll call Mike in the morning and make sure, but I don't think it's going to be a problem. Then I have to look into getting proper security on that building so this kind of thing doesn't happen again. Could just be a prank." David put his wine glass in the sink and stretched his back. "I think I'm going to head up to bed now too. I haven't been sleeping too well since I took this case." He smiled over at Anna. "Could be interesting to see how I sleep up there tonight."

"Just don't spend all night staring out the window." She winked at him. When he gave her a "what?" look, she continued, "Like you did for about a month before and then again after Dad died."

David continued to look confused, but he didn't say anything.

"Never mind." Anna shrugged as she got up. "I think I'll watch some TV before I go up. That way I won't wake up Johnny with the lights."

They hugged each other and said their goodnights and David headed up to his room. *My room*, he thought as he entered and flipped on the lights. "Looks like it hasn't been touched much in twenty years, either," he said to himself. He took off his sweater and kicked off his shoes. Then he walked over to the window and peered out through the curtains. A sudden wave of recognition hit him, and his nightmares about the monsters in the trees came rushing back. "Holy shit!" he exclaimed as he backed away from the window. "What the hell was out there?"

He sat hard on the bed and wiped his hands over his face. *I have no idea what caused those nightmares, but I'm going to find out!*

DAVID WOKE WITH A START, NOT SURE where he was at first. Then he realized he'd fallen asleep on the bed still half dressed. He hadn't even gotten under the covers. He looked around to orient himself and saw the sun was shining. He could hear noises coming from downstairs and assumed everyone was up. He tried to remember if he had anything left in the car that would be cleaner than what he was currently wearing. He couldn't even remember the last time he changed his clothes. As he was about to get up to go to the washroom, someone knocked on the bedroom door. "Uncle David?" came a soft, small voice. "Are you awake?"

"Yes," David responded with a smile, "I'm awake."

Johnny flung open the door and came rushing in. He had his arms full of clothing and towels. "Gramma said that you might like to try these on. And the shower is free if you want to have one," he said in a very grown-up voice. "I don't think Gramma ever charges for a shower, though," Johnny scrunched up his nose, "so I don't know why she said that part." He shrugged.

"Thanks." David smiled at him. "Where did these come from?"

Johnny looked at him quizzically. "From Gramma," he repeated.

"I meant who do they belong to," David clarified. He'd forgotten what it was like talking to a six-year-old. They took things so literally sometimes.

"Oh, I don't know. I can go ask," Johnny replied helpfully. "Does it matter?"

"No, it doesn't matter," David responded. "Tell your mom and Gramma thank you. I'll have a quick shower and then be down in a minute."

"Okay, I'll tell them." Johnny bounded back out of the room and down the stairs.

After David showered, he tried on the clothes Johnny had brought him and they fit like they were made for him. *Definitely not his style but they looked okay,* he thought as he pulled on a clean pair of socks. Jeans fit good. Although he didn't usually care for Levis, these ones were nice. And there was a plaid work shirt that was soft cotton and looked like it had been washed a few times. *Comfortable,* David thought as he finished buttoning it up. He combed out his black curls and finger-fluffed them. "That will have to do today," he said as he came out of the bathroom.

Mary gasped as she spotted him at the top of the stairs. She put her hand over her mouth and stepped back.

PACKART'S ORCHARD   103

David bounded down the stairs. "Are you okay?" he asked as she wavered like she was going to pass out.

"Yes. Yes, I'm fine." Mary waved him off. "Sorry." She headed back toward the kitchen. "I'll never get used to how much you look like your father. I've always known it, but with you coming down the stairs with his clothes on, it took me by surprise." She looked back over her shoulder. "Would you like some breakfast?" she asked.

"Just coffee if you have some made." He looked around. "Where's Anna and Johnny?"

"Anna took Johnny to school. She'll be back in a few minutes. We can sit down with some coffee and talk some more, if you'd like to, or we can wait for Anna to get back if you'd rather."

David said coffee and talk would be fine, but maybe they should wait for Anna to get back to get into too much detail, so neither of them had to repeat what was being said. Mary smiled at him. "You know her so well already." He smiled back. Yes, he did seem to know Anna like they'd never been apart. It was a little eerie, actually.

Just as they sat down to have their coffee and the delicious muffins Mary had pulled out of the pantry, Anna came rushing back into the kitchen. "Did I miss anything?" she asked as she plopped herself down.

David and Mary laughed at her, then Mary poured her a coffee. "We decided to wait for you to get back." She smiled at her daughter. *This was the way her whole life should have been*, Mary thought as she looked at her children. So comfortable with each other. Sitting around a table chatting and drinking morning coffee before their busy days took them all away.

"Well," David began, "if you're ready, I have a few questions I've jotted down."

Mary nodded and sat back down. "As ready as I'll ever be. Go ahead." She took a deep breath to settle her emotions.

"Okay." David looked up at his mother. "But if this gets too hard, just let me know. We can always look at it again later if that's easier for you."

Mary knew he was trying to ease her mind a bit and let her know it was up to her, but she really just wanted to get this over with and get back to her life, such as it was. "No, I'm fine, really," she responded. "Let's just get this done, please."

David nodded. "Okay, so how long did Paul work at the orchard before …" He hesitated.

"He worked off and on at the orchard since he was sixteen," Mary responded. "He started full-time when he finished college, so I guess when he was twenty or twenty-one. Mr. P made him foreman when he took him on full-time."

"Okay." David jotted down a few more notes in his book. "So, did they hire different people for crew every year, or did they bring back the same people?"

"I really don't know the details of the hiring," Mary responded. "You should likely talk to Mr. P about that."

"Right." David scanned his notebook again. "So, when did the strange sightings start?" he asked, "you know, the seeing things in the trees and feeling like he was being watched?"

"Never mentioned anything to me until just before Darren came to town. So maybe a couple of months before he died?" Mary seemed to be asking the question instead of answering David's. "At least, that's when he told me about what he was feeling. It was more a feeling than anything."

"You indicated that Mr. P seemed reluctant to do anything to help the orchard business progress. Was that a problem for Paul?"

"Yes and no," Mary said. "Paul wanted the orchard business to grow and thrive. He originally thought Mr. P did too. But every time he'd bring something up to Albert, he'd get shut down. He even talked to Amelia about it one day when he was helping her with putting a bigger garden area in. Asked her how she was able to talk Albert into the garden and orchard stand. She just told him that this was her space and Albert didn't have a say." Mary smiled as she mentioned Amelia. "She is a stubborn one, she is. Don't think Albert would tell her much of anything if she set her mind to something." Mary's smile dropped away. "She did say something funny about the location of the garden one day when I went out to have tea with her. She said it was on the west side of the house, so it didn't bother anyone."

"What did she mean by that?" David questioned, frowning.

"I really don't know," Mary answered. "I forgot all about that until just now. I never asked her what she meant."

"Okay." David made more notes in his book. Maybe he would ask Mr. Packart about that when he got to talk to him. *If,* David thought. *If he got to talk to him.*

"Darren came to town to take over the orchard business?" David asked.

"Well, that was the idea he and Paul had. Albert and Amelia could retire, and Darren would move Amy down and they'd become the main business owners. Of course, I don't think that Darren had talked to his folks much about any of it after he went up to university. I think originally Albert figured that Darren would come back and everything would be the way it was before he'd gone away. When Darren announced he was getting married to a girl he'd met in Kendall, Albert didn't seem so happy. I know Amelia wasn't thrilled after she met Amy, but then the two of them were a lot alike, so that was probably part of it."

"Amy didn't seem too happy about moving down here either by the sounds of it," Anna interrupted.

"No. Amy was pregnant when Darren finally decided he needed to come back and either take over or tell his dad he wasn't staying. I don't know if that conversation ever got to happen. Amy did come down for a visit. Actually, she flew into Bellcom City the day Paul fell ill."

"Yes, you mentioned they had met you in the hospital the day he died," David stated. "Did she stay long?"

"Darren brought her to the hospital hoping that Paul would be feeling better and could meet Amy properly. We'd gone up to the wedding but really never got to talk to her much, and then they stayed up in Kendall so that Darren could finish his studies and wind down a project he'd been working on for Amy's father." Mary had that faraway look in her eyes again. "Amy went back to Kendall about two weeks after Paul died and had her babies up there. She came back down when the twins were less than two months old. I think she was having a hard time with Darren down here and her up there. There was only so much apart time she could take. She was planning on moving down and trying to find a place of their own to live in, but she ended up moving into the mansion with Amelia."

"That must have put a strain on everyone," Anna interjected. "I can't imagine having to live with Mrs. P." Anna smiled.

"I don't think the stay here in Windsmill was a happy one, for sure. I don't think Darren was happy working alongside his dad, and I know Amy and Amelia were not getting along at all. Amy spent a lot of time here with me during the days Darren was working. When he wasn't working, they would head into Bellcom City or spend the weekends up the valley on mini vacations. I don't think it was working for any of them."

"How long after Paul died did Darren die?" David asked. The switch seemed to startle Mary back to the present.

"Well, let me think," Mary said. "The Faulkon twins came down shortly after Paul died, around the end of April or early May. Darren had phoned them and set up a cabin for them to stay in. They were here maybe two or three days, I think, before the first one died. The second twin died a couple of days later." Mary swiped at tears that were starting to trickle down her cheeks. "That whole period was so horrible." She stood up and started to make more coffee. "You'll likely want to talk to Marvin about the twins, anyway," she added as she turned back to the table.

"Darren and Albert had a big fight after the Faulkon boys died with similar symptoms to Paul's. Albert was telling Darren he was being foolish, and Darren was telling Albert he was being blind. I don't think they ever made up before Darren himself was dead."

"And when was that?" David asked gently, not wanting to offend Mary, but trying to wrap this all up.

"Oh, right. Darren was gone before the fall harvest, I think." Mary wiped at her eyes again. "That's when Amelia called us all out to the mansion for a 'family discussion.' I think she had always seen us and the Faulkons as her family too. Marvin, Paul, and Darren were always together." Mary smiled as she remembered the early times. How happy they all were. "Anyway, she got us all together and told us that we needed to get our sons out of Windsmill and make sure we were being cautious about bringing any of the kids out to the orchards. There was a lot of discussion about it. By this time, I'd already sent you to live with Jenny and AJ because of the nightmares you had after Paul died." She looked apologetically at David. "It was so hard to do that, but I knew it was for the best. Whatever it was that killed Paul, you were seeing it too."

"Anyway," she continued before David could interrupt her train of thought. "Amy was more than happy to pack up the boys and head back to Kendall. After Darren died, she'd been looking for any excuse to get away from Windsmill anyway. As you know," she looked up at David again, "Marvin and Becky kept Marty and Matthew here in town with them. Although they did go up to Carson for awhile to help out Marvin's uncle after the twins passed."

"I'll talk to Marvin about all that too, when I have a chance." David looked over at Anna and then back to Mary. "Just a couple more questions, if you're up to it?" She nodded but didn't respond.

PACKART'S ORCHARD   107

"Okay, well, then there were two more deaths after that?"

"No, just one," Mary responded. "At least, only one more that I'm aware of. No one really tied the investigator's death to the others because he wasn't from around here. But I think Albert had called him in to look into everything after Darren died. He was from the Environmental Protection Services or something like that. I think Albert was worried that Paul and Darren were right and that something in the orchard was killing people. I think Albert went to the police after Darren died too, but he got the same response as I had gotten."

"Which was what?" David asked curiously.

"That we were just overwrought with grief and that there was nothing to suggest that any of the deaths were related or suspicious."

"What about the incident with the barrels and the office? Didn't they see any connection with all of that?" David wondered out loud.

"No," Mary said a little too loudly. "Those officers couldn't link together a chain link fence!" Mary stood up again and poured yet another cup of coffee. She offered one to each of her children but they both declined. "Sorry," she said and sat back down. "This whole thing just makes me so mad sometimes."

"What did they find out about that incident?" David asked.

"Nothing. They said there were no other fingerprints in the office or watermill building except what they'd expect to find. Meaning, I suppose, Paul, Darren, Marvin, and Albert." Mary sighed. "Marvin's crew mostly wore gloves, and I don't think any of them had been up in the office. They figured that whoever did that was one of them." She was visibly shaken by now. "Can you imagine one of them did this and then called the cops themselves?" She shook her head. "Anyway, there were so many boot prints in and around the area that they couldn't distinguish between the ones the crew made and anyone else. No other signs of intrusion and no other damage. Bottom line, they did nothing!"

"Okay." David made some more notes and then looked up at the women again. "One more question, then I think that's it for now."

"What is it?" Mary asked her son. He had hesitated and she could tell it was difficult for him.

"Who found Paul in the orchard that day?" David asked quietly. There was a long pause and David didn't think she was going to answer. He looked up at his mother and saw tears running down her cheeks.

108   WENDY SCOTT-ETTINGER

"Marvin did," Mary said quietly. "If Albert or Darren had been paying more attention, they would have realized Paul was still there. Marvin ran into the office and told them to call 9-1-1. He'd come up to the mansion to get the information for the twins that Paul had promised. That's when he found him on the path." Mary took a deep breath and sighed deeply.

David closed his notepad and sighed as well. "I did record last night's session, and I'll be listening to that again in the next day or two. I might think of something else after I've done that. Thanks for putting yourself through all this again today."

Mary stood up and hugged David in his chair. "Thank you for looking into all of this for us. I know this hasn't been easy for you either."

"We'll get to the bottom of all of it, if I have to get the national guard involved," David responded. "Now, I have a couple of phone calls I need to make, and then we should get back to Bellcom City so Anna has her car back in her possession." He stood up from the table for the first time all morning and stretched his back.

"I'd like to talk to you some more about the nightmares I had as a kid," he looked over at Mary to gauge her reaction, "but that can wait for another day too."

"Whenever you're ready, I'm always here for you," Mary said and started to clean up her kitchen.

CHAPTER 14

"SO, WHAT ARE OUR NEXT STEPS?" ANNA asked David as they turned onto the highway toward Bellcom City.

"Your next step is to get your car and go home. I'll put together a game plan and will let you know what I find out," David responded matter-of-factly. He was back to being all business again, Anna thought as she looked at him in surprise.

"So, what? You think I'm going to sit around and do nothing while you 'investigate'?" she said indignantly. "I thought you and I were a team in this?"

"Anna," David began, then shook his head. He knew it was fruitless to try to keep her out of all this. If he tried, they'd just end up tripping over each other. "Okay, okay," he conceded. "We'll go up to my office and put a game plan together. We'll see if it makes more sense to do it together or to take separate tasks and then get back together again and discuss. Okay?" he asked, defeated. He wasn't used to working with anyone else, even though he figured he'd eventually grow his investigation company and add more investigators as things picked up. He hadn't planned on doing it with a sister he didn't know he had.

Anna smiled. "Sounds like a good start." She didn't say anything else as they headed toward David's office. This was going to get solved this time. There would be no more deaths if Anna had anything to say about it. There had been too many now.

As they rounded the corner and pulled into the parking lot, David stopped short. "Oh, come on!" he said, staring at Anna's car. It was covered in red spray paint, and there were three police cruisers parked around it.

"What the hell?" Anna pulled on the door handle to get out, but David stopped her.

"Just let me park the car properly, then we'll both go over and talk to the police," he said as he pulled into his reserved parking space. He was really hoping that it was just typical vandalism that happened around this neighbourhood sometimes, but as he and Anna approached the car and the cruisers, he realized it was far from typical. On the side of Anna's car "STOP INVESTIGATING OR ELSE!" had been sprayed on in big red letters. The whole windshield was covered in red paint dripping down like blood. On the other side of the car, it said "YOUR SON WILL BE NEXT."

David grabbed Anna's arm and pulled her away from that side before she could read the words. *No way was anyone going to get to Johnny. Not now, not ever!* As David did this, Mike walked over to greet them.

"Where have you two been?" Mike asked authoritatively.

"At our mother's house in Windsmill" Anna answered him, not trusting the police officer.

Mike looked from her to David and back again. "You two really do look like twins," he said as he smirked at them. "You really are brother and sister."

"I already told you that," David responded. "What's going on here? Who did this to Anna's car?"

"We got a call about an hour ago. One of the business owners that work in your building noticed the paint when he opened this morning. He said you'd talked to him yesterday about the note and if they'd seen anything. Told me about your questions about security systems and all that." Mike waited for David to interject, but when he didn't Mike continued, "There doesn't appear to be any damage, other than the paint on both sides and on the windshield. It's obviously the same person that wrote the original note. I assume you've spoken to Mrs. Lister about that?"

"Yes, we've discussed it, and neither of us can think of anyone that would write such a thing let alone do something like this!" Anna responded before David could say anything. "Who would do this? And why?" She began to cry.

"Here, let's get you back into my car so you can sit down." David put his arm around Anna and guided her back to his car. Mike followed them over. Anna sat back and closed her eyes. She was finished talking to police officers and hoped it wouldn't be long before she and David could get to work figuring all of this out.

"You have any idea at all who might have done this?" Mike asked David again pointedly.

PACKART'S ORCHARD   111

"No, no one that we've talked to about Mr. Lister's death would do any of this." David wiped his hand over his face and then pushed his hair subconsciously out of his eyes. "I really don't understand why this is happening!"

"Okay, well, let's get a tow truck out here and tow this into the police compound for now. We'll go over it with a fine-tooth comb to see if there's anything we can get off of it. Once that's done, Mrs. Lister can get a new paint job on her car and get on with life."

"Get on with life!" Anna jumped out of the car again and glared at the officer. "Get on with life!" she said again and pointed her finger at him. "If your people had done your jobs twenty years ago when this first started, I wouldn't have to go through it now! Red Lightfeather would still be working in the gardens. My husband would still be alive and playing with his son! Marty Faulkon would still be alive! I had a life until your people decided to ignore the evidence in front of you and not do your jobs!" She was so angry she just wanted to beat on something. She stepped toward the officer and raised her fists. David grabbed her around her waist and pulled her away.

"Whoa!" he said. "That's definitely not going to make anything better!" He sat her back down beside the car. Mike backed up. He knew exactly what she was talking about, but he needed to de-escalate the situation fast.

"If we can just get your car keys," Mike asked tentatively, "I can get my crew to wrap up and get the car out of here," he finished.

Anna rummaged through her purse and found the keys. She didn't look at either of the men as they backed away from her slowly.

"Okay, thank you." Mike reached out and took the keys from Anna's hands. Can we go up into your office and finish this discussion after I get this situation cleared?"

"Sure. Anna and I will go up there now, and you can come on up when you're ready. I'll put a pot of coffee on and order up some sandwiches and maybe some pho?" When Mike nodded agreement and walked away, David turned his attention toward Anna.

"If you can't hold your temper when we're talking to people then I don't think this team thing is going to work. I know you're upset with what the police services in both our towns have or haven't done now and twenty years ago but taking it out on the sergeant who is trying to help us isn't going to get you any further than a jail cell." David looked directly into Anna's eyes to make sure she was hearing what he was saying.

"I know, I know," she responded. "It's just that he made it sound like a minor inconvenience. Like it was just a car. It's not the car that I'm upset about, it's the message and everything it suggests. Someone is madder about us investigating than I am about the police not doing it!"

"I get that. I completely understand the feeling, but you need to control your responses to it. Otherwise, this is not going to work." David pulled his sister out of the car and locked it up. Hopefully it would be safe there for a little while until he had a chance to move it again. "Come on, we'll get some food and while we're doing that I'll talk to the owners and see what they have to say."

They walked into the sandwich shop first and put in an order for three sub sandwiches and some potato chips. Anna smiled, thinking Johnny would love Uncle David's eating habits. The owner served up their order to go then commented on the police activity in the parking lots. "Looks like you've got more trouble with that car," he said as he put the three chip bags in with the sandwiches. "Hope the owner has insurance on it."

"I do," Anna responded. "Was it you that called it in?"

"No, I get here around eleven a.m., just ahead of the lunch crowd. The cops were already here when I arrived. They asked a few questions, but I'm afraid I wasn't much help. It wasn't like that when I left at about nine o'clock last night," he responded. "I'm really sorry this is happening to you."

"Thanks," Anna responded. "I appreciate your help. I know this can't be good for the neighbourhood, or for your business."

"Oh, it will be interesting to see how many people come in today just out of curiosity. They'll be asking about it, I'm sure." He smiled as David swiped his bank card and grabbed the bags.

"Thanks, Joe. Talk to you later." David handed the bag to Anna and headed toward the pho place. "I'll just go in and talk to Phan and thank him for calling this in. I'll be right out." He walked into the restaurant, leaving Anna to stand on the sidewalk alone. She watched as the tow truck hooked up to her car. Someone had pulled a large, tarp-like car cover over it, so she no longer saw the big red letters. She was glad that message wouldn't be dragged through the city as they took her car to the police compound. As the tow truck pulled out, she realized that Mike and his cruiser was still there. He'd parked beside David and was walking toward her. She took a deep breath of air and waved slightly as he crossed the street.

PACKART'S ORCHARD   113

"I'm really sorry about earlier," she said to him as he approached. "It's been an emotional few days, and I'm more than sensitive right now. I'm not normally a violent person." She smiled at him, hoping it would break the ice a little bit.

Mike just smiled back at her. "Where's David?" he asked as he looked around.

"In the pho place," she responded as David came out of the restaurant.

"Awe, food." Mike took the pho bag from David and smiled at him. "After you, my friend." He pointed to the bright-blue door that led up to David's office.

David went to unlock the door but realized it was slightly ajar. "Shit," he muttered under his breath. "Mike, you want to stay back here with Anna, and I'll go up first." He looked over his shoulder at his friend as he pulled the door open. Mike understood immediately.

"We'll stand just inside the door and let you go on up first," Mike responded as he pushed himself in front of Anna. She could feel her anger growing again but pushed it down. Something wasn't quite right, so she let the two men go in ahead of her. Mike stopped at the bottom of the staircase, blocking Anna's approach, but allowing her to get in the door and close it.

"What's going on?" she asked as she watched David climb the stairs two at a time. "What's happened?"

"Oh damn!" David said again, as he gingerly looked around the office without entering. The place had been turned upside down. There was something spray painted on the wall to the left of the door, but David couldn't read it without entering the room. He decided to leave everything the way it was and let Mike take the lead instead. "Mike, you want to put your police hat back on and come look at this?" David said as he descended the staircase again.

"What's up, pal?" Mike smiled at him.

"You might want to glove up and start with my office." David frowned toward the office door again. "Seems I've had a visitor up here, too, while I was in Windsmill."

"Holy crap!" Mike exclaimed as he entered the office area of David's second-floor pad, and David followed him. "Does the rest of the place look this bad?" he asked.

"David, you okay?" Mike asked as he turned toward the wall that David was staring at. STOP LOOKING OR YOU'LL BE NEXT was spray painted in bright red. "Why do they keep saying that? What does that even mean?

Next for what?" Mike questioned as David turned to look at the rest of the walls in case there was more.

"I don't know. Looks like someone doesn't like me looking into the strange deaths in Windsmill." David stared at his friend then started to pick stuff up off the floor.

"Mr. Allen. Please do not touch anything. Leave everything where it is," the sergeant said, sounding more like an official policeman and less like his best friend. "If you can show me the rest of your space in this building, and then I'm going to have to ask you and Mrs. Lister to leave the premises." Sergeant McCall reached for his phone and called for back-up to help process the scene.

David checked the back of the office area, and he was relieved that nothing had been touched in his personal area, at least not that he could see. "Just the office," he commented as they looked around.

"We'll check everything to make sure." Mike put his hand on his friend's shoulder. "Is there a second entrance to this level of the building?"

"Yes, the patio doors act as the private entrance to this space, but it looks closed tight." David reached over to check that the door was locked. When it swung open without turning the knob, he swore under his breath. "Or not," he said as he pushed the door to reveal an easy access and exit.

"Now I'm going to have to ask you to leave. Do you have someplace to stay for the next couple of nights?" Mike asked. David nodded and headed back into the office area where Anna was standing staring at the wall and the mess around her. Thankfully, she hadn't touched anything or moved too far into the space.

"It's going to take us a while to process this" Mike said as he came down the stairs behind David and Anna.

David looked at Anna. "We'll have to find a place to sit and eat our lunch. I can go back and get drinks if you'd like. We can't use the office."

"What's going on, David? Why is this happening?" Anna asked. She was now squeezing the sandwich bag against her chest.

"Well, we won't be eating those now either." David said as he pulled the bag out of Anna's hands. The chip bags inside had been flattened, as had the sandwiches. Anna watched as he looked into the bag, then burst into fits of laughter.

"I'm sure they would have been tasty, but not very healthy," she said between giggles.

PACKART'S ORCHARD   115

David and Anna walked back out of the office stairwell and into the afternoon sunlight. "So what's going on?" Anna asked again.

"Our friendly neighbourhood painter was busy last night," David responded, as the other cruisers showed up to assist Mike. David and Anna got into his car and just stared out the window.

"Damn!" he said out loud as his phone rang. "Now what?"

"Hello?" he answered without looking to see who it was.

"Like the mess?" the voice on the other end asked.

"Who is this? Why are you doing this?" He honked his horn to get the attention of an officer standing by the squad cars and waved him over. By the time the officer got to them, whoever it was had hung up.

"Shit." David tossed the phone on the dash.

The officer knocked on the side window. "You okay?"

"No. Whoever ransacked my office just called me and asked if I 'liked the mess.' Shit! Shit! Shit! Shit!" David exclaimed.

"Okay. Now we're going to need to process your phone too." The officer held out his hand.

"You can't take my phone. I'm expecting calls. I have places to go. Things to get sorted out. Damn it!" He handed his phone over and got back out of the car. "Hopefully I still have that burner in the trunk," he said, then smiled at the officer standing beside him. "You didn't hear that!"

"Hear what?" The officer smiled at him. "You need any numbers out of your contacts before I bag this?"

"No, I have all my contacts programmed into my car. Let me know the minute anything comes up." He wrote the burner's number on a piece of paper from his notepad and handed it to the officer. "Give that to Sergeant McCall when you get upstairs. And don't leave that laying around and don't give that number to anyone else," he said, then jumped back into his car and left.

He pulled up in front of the neighbourhood Starbucks and decided he'd better call his dad to let him know what was happening and to give him his temporary phone number. He made the call as he was walking toward the café. "I'll have a dark with extra sweetener, grandé please," he said, then looked over to see if Anna had followed him. She gave the cashier her order, then headed toward a back table, thinking they could sit and talk about the day's events while they ate. He paid for the order as he talked into his phone. "Hi Dad, it's David again. You can reach me at this number for a while. You'll never guess what happened today!" He hung up and grabbed the order sitting on the counter with his name written on it. He sat down to drink his coffee and figure out what his next steps were going to be when he realized all his videos, recordings, and notes were on his phone. "Damn!" he exclaimed out loud and put his forehead on the table.

"What now?" Anna questioned as she drank from her own cup and unwrapped the sandwich she'd ordered.

"All the recordings I've taken with Mrs. Packart, the Windsmill Police Station, the video of us finding Marty Faulkon, the whole story your mother told us last night. They're all on the phone I just handed over to the Bellcom City Police Department!" David said desperately. "I never had a chance to download any of them to the computer. It's been a crazy few days!"

"Oh no!" Anna exclaimed as she handed her brother half of her sandwich. She didn't know what else to say.

They finished their meal and David finished making yet another call to his dad with no answer. He decided to drive Anna back to Windsmill and was going to come back into Bellcom, but Anna insisted he stay.

"SO, WHAT'S OUR PLAN OF ATTACK?" ANNA asked David as she stared at him from across their mother's kitchen table.

"Is there a laptop or computer or anything around here we can use for a while?" David asked, not answering his sister's question.

"I left my laptop at my place when I came back to stay here, and I never went back to get it. It didn't seem important at the time," Anna replied. "I could go over and get it now."

"There isn't one here?" David asked, then realized what she was saying. "You don't live here?" he asked.

"Yes, well," she hesitated, "no, I don't live here. I sort of moved in here with Johnny after Jack passed away and I haven't really been back to our place since. I only packed enough stuff to stay a week or so, but ..." Her voice drifted away.

"You don't want to go back there because it reminds you too much of Jack," David finished for her.

"Well, yes, and ... once I got back here, Mom and I just sort of fell back into a comfortable relationship. It's been good for her to have Johnny around, and it's been a lot easier for me too." Anna looked over at David. "This whole mess is just so ..." She drifted away again.

PACKART'S ORCHARD   117

"I honestly don't know if Mom has a computer or laptop or anything here. I assume she does, but I've never really noticed one. It could be in her bedroom?"

"That's okay. It would be easier to have someplace to keep notes that's more secure than the notepad in my pocket, or this burner phone, but it will work, I guess."

"I'll go to the house and get my laptop. Maybe it's time I started thinking about getting back into a normal routine again. Johnny could probably use it too." She stood up and started toward the door. "Oh yeah, I don't have any wheels. Could you drive me over there, please?"

"Of course." David stood up and walked toward the door. He bent over to put his boots back on when the front door flung open, narrowly missing his head.

"Hi, Mom. Hi, Uncle David!" Johnny said as he pushed his way past them and headed into the kitchen. Mary followed up the porch stairs and looked at her children, startled that they were there.

"I didn't expect you home until suppertime or later," she said to Anna as she handed her a grocery bag. "And I didn't expect you back here so soon at all!" She handed David another bag.

"It's not been a great day today, Mom," Anna explained as tears started to drip from her eyes. She wiped at her cheeks and then turned back toward the kitchen. "I didn't realize it was so late," she said as an afterthought.

"What's wrong? What's going on?" Mary asked worriedly. "Not another death?"

"No, Mom, nothing like that." Anna pushed the tears away more vigorously now. "Just some more police business and an incident at David's office. He'll need a place to stay for a day or two until it's all sorted out."

David looked at the strain on both women's faces. "I can go back into the city and get a hotel room." He handed the grocery bag back to Mary. "Or better yet, I'll drive into Allensville and stay with Mom and Dad." He pushed past his mother and headed for his car. "I'll give you a call tomorrow sometime, Anna. We'll figure out next steps then."

Mary and Anna waved at him as he drove away. Anna was concerned that all this extra stress was pushing David away. She needed him now more than ever.

"I'm going to go over to the house and start cleaning a few things out. Are you okay to look after Johnny for a bit, or would you like me to take him with me?" Anna pushed her feet back into her shoes.

Mary handed the car keys to her daughter and indicated that Johnny was fine staying there. "You'll tell me what happened to your car when you're ready," she said to Anna. "I won't hold supper for you unless you want me to, but please let me know if you'll be home tonight or if you'll be staying there. Johnny needs to get to school in the morning."

Anna nodded at Mary then kissed her forehead as she'd seen her father do, and the way David did last night. Mary smiled at her and closed the door as Anna walked down the steps toward her mother's car.

CHAPTER 15

A COUPLE OF DAYS LATER, DAVID SAT in Maxine's Café at the back so he wouldn't be disturbed, but it didn't seem to be working. By now most of the townspeople seemed to know who he was and what he was working on. They all wanted to tell him how happy they were that he was back where he belonged, or that they wished him well in getting answers for his family. Many of them asked questions about how it was going, but David couldn't give them much hope at this point. "Lots of leads, but no real answers" was all he would offer.

The bell over the front door dinged and David cringed. *Another local, I'm sure. Maybe if I don't look up, they won't bother me*, he thought as he continued his search. He'd be so glad when he got his equipment back so he could do a proper job of all of this. He had called Mike to see if he could at least get his phone back, but Mike said it would be another twenty-four or so hours before he'd be able to pick it up.

"Hi, David, right?" a deep, booming voice inquired. "Can I join you for a minute?"

David was about to say no, that he was really busy and needed to get some work done, when he looked up and then up again, into the grieving face of a very tall, dark man in his fifties. David remembered him from the park. "Sure, Mr. Faulkon. Please sit down. How are you doing these days?" he asked sympathetically.

"I'll survive," Marvin responded, "and please, call me Marvin."

"Okay. How's your wife doing? She was pretty upset at the park the other day," David inquired. He watched as Marvin's face dropped and he shook his head.

"Becky is having a hard time with all of this. It's like twenty years ago all over again. Not a happy period then or now." Marvin looked down into his coffee. "If we don't get answers soon, I don't think Becky's going to survive this round." He looked back up into David's face. "My god, it's like looking right into Paul's eyes again!"

"Yes, I've heard that a lot these days." David smiled at him. "You knew my father well?" he asked softly.

"Yeah. Paul and Darren and me, we were the three musketeers, you know." Marvin smiled as he thought about the trouble they'd gotten themselves into in high school. "Even in college, Paul and I had fun together when we weren't in class or studying. That's when AJ, your other dad, he joined us. Darren had gone to university in Kendall, so he wasn't around much. The three of us; man, what a time!" Marvin's face lit up for the first time since he'd entered the café. "We were thick as thieves."

"That's cool. Seems our families are all tied up together on every turn," David said, almost to himself.

"Yes, it does, doesn't it?" Marvin looked back into David's face. "That's why I wanted some time to talk to you. First off, to let you know how thankful Becky and I are, that it was you and your sister that found Marty. Most people wouldn't have paid no-never-mind to a bunch of clothes beside the road, let alone stop and investigate. It was good that you found him when you did." Marvin hung his head and tears formed in the corners of his eyes. He closed them tight and wiped his face with his forearm. "Anyway, thank you for what you did."

"It was really nothing. I'm glad we were able to help. If we'd only been a few minutes earlier, maybe …" David's voice trailed off.

"Don't do that! Don't ever do that to yourself, you hear!" Marvin scolded David. "I live with that every minute of every day of my life. If I'd only gone to the mansion with Paul to tell Mr. Packart myself about the damned electricity. If I'd only found Paul a few minutes before I did, maybe he'd still be here with all of us. Maybe, just maybe, none of this would have happened!" Marvin's face became stone cold. His eyes became blacker than coal. "Don't ever do that to yourself!"

"I'm sorry. I didn't mean to bring all that back up. At least, not right now. You need time to grieve. To look after your wife and family." David looked around the café frantically, trying to spot Maxine. He could really

PACKART'S ORCHARD   121

use another shot of caffeine about now. She spotted him looking around and came over with the pot.

"Can I fill you both back up?" Max asked as she poured coffee into David's cup. She looked at Marvin, but he shook his head, and Max left them alone again.

"I want to talk to you about all of this, but not here, not now, as you've said. The funeral is tomorrow and hopefully Becky will be feeling well enough for me to go out for more than a few minutes without her panicking. She's convinced that something is going to happen to me or to Matthew. I keep telling her we're no threat to anyone, but she's not buying it right now." Marvin took a deep breath. "On that note," he continued as he stood up from the table. "I'll leave you to your investigation and we'll talk soon. I promise. I better get home before Becky starts to panic again."

Marvin turned toward the counter and asked Max for two black coffees with sugar and a box of those wonderful cinnamon buns, then waved at David and Max and headed back out to the street. He climbed into an old blue pick-up truck and drove onto the highway and turned toward the orchard side of town. David wondered where exactly Marvin and Becky lived and thought he'd have to ask Anna when he saw her again. As if on queue, Anna rushed into the café.

"Hey, Max, can I get two coffees to go and two cinnamon buns and two muffins, blueberry, if you have them. Maybe ...," Anna hesitated, "yeah, maybe some of that homemade bread of yours if you have any left."

"Sure, anything else?" Max asked as she poured two coffees into the cups and snapped the lids on.

"No, that should do it." Anna looked around for the first time. "David!" she exclaimed, "thank God I've found you. Marvin was looking for you today, and I didn't know what to tell him. Did you happen to see him anywhere?" "You just missed him," David said as he began packing up his equipment and paperwork. He would have to get this laptop back to his dad before the end of day, and he wasn't going to get anything done today anyway. Not without all the recordings and notes from his phone, and definitely not in here with all the interruptions. He smiled to himself as he stood up and put his sports jacket back on. Then he turned to watch his sister try to figure out how she was going to carry everything she just bought. "Need a hand with that?" he asked gentlemanly.

122   WENDY SCOTT-ETTINGER

"Oh yes, please." She picked up the coffees and the box with the buns in it and looked expectantly at David to gather up the rest.

"Where are you heading with all this?"

"Mom just called from Becky's. She's in quite a state. Marvin left the house without saying where he was going or how long he would be. She's panicked that something has happened to him." Anna waved at Max. "Talk to you later, Max." Then she headed toward the door.

David reached around her and opened the door. "Are you driving your mother's car, or did you finally get a loaner from the insurance company?"

"Mom's car. I was at Faulkon's place with her for a bit today, to help set everything up for the reception after the funeral tomorrow. I headed back into town thinking I might get some alone time, but no such luck. I guess Becky suddenly started to panic. She looked all over the house and realized Marvin wasn't there, but his phone was, so she couldn't call. He really needs to remember to take the phone with him when he leaves. Anyway, I really need to find him, so I better get going."

"Marvin was just in Max's a few minutes ago. He stopped in to say hi and to thank us for what we did for Marty." David followed Anna down the sidewalk toward her mother's car. "He wasn't here more than a few minutes. He picked up two coffees and some cinnamon buns and said he needed to get home."

"Oh, thank God!" Anna exclaimed as she put the coffees and box on the roof of the car to search for her keys. "He'd said he wanted to talk to you, but I didn't think he meant right this minute." She shook her head. "Maybe he just wanted to get out of the house and away from all the women for awhile. There's not many of his male friends or family left anymore."

"What about ... Matthew, is it? I assume he's Marty's brother," David asked.

"Yes. Matthew is about a year younger than Marty is ... was," Anna said. "I think he's going to university up in Kendall this year. I assume he'll be down tomorrow for the funeral."

"By the way," David started as Anna finished putting everything onto the passenger seat of the car. "Where exactly do the Faulkons live, anyway?"

"Oh, yeah." Anna looked over her shoulder at her brother. "I keep forgetting you aren't really from around here." She looked at the highway. "You go out to the highway and turn right. There's a dirt road off to the left of the highway about a mile and a half. Just before that rest area where we found Marty."

PACKART'S ORCHARD   123

"So you go up the dirt road by the rest area and then what?" David asked.

"That's it. You go up the dirt road about a mile, which is really the Faulkon Farm driveway. Park on the far side away from the house and walk the rest of the way." Anna shrugged as if everyone knew that part.

"So," David frowned, "Marty was almost home when he …"

"Yeah," Anna replied. "That's almost worse than if he'd been found somewhere else. Marvin's glad that we found him instead of Becky spotting him on her way to work the next morning." She started to get back into the car. "We'll see you later then?"

"I think I'm going to go back into Bellcom City for awhile. See if Mike's crew has finished with my office equipment and phone and your car. Maybe, if I can get back into my apartment, I can actually wear some of my own clothes to the funeral tomorrow." He gestured to the jeans he was still wearing that their mother had given him.

"Okay. I'll call you later to let you know what time and where to meet us tomorrow." She closed the car door and took off toward the highway.

David turned back into Max's Café to gather up his stuff. He'd get a coffee to-go too. Maxine's coffee was the best he'd ever had. It was worth driving out this far just to get a cup. He smiled as he watched Max look up and come over to the counter area.

"There you are," she said with a smile. "I wasn't sure if you'd forgotten your stuff or if Anna just talked your ear off for too long like she does with everyone." She laughed.

"I didn't forget." David smiled back at her. "Can I get a coffee to go, and a six pack of those cinnamon buns that everyone keeps raving about."

Max set his coffee and buns on the counter and told him the total. "What about the coffee I've drank all day? Did you include that?" David asked as he pulled out his debit card.

"Oh, you already paid for the first one, and refills are free." Max explained.

"I've been sitting here drinking all your coffee all morning and into the afternoon. You can't really give that many free refills!" David exclaimed.

"Don't be silly" she waved it off. "If you didn't drink it, I would have had to throw it away every ½ hour to make sure it was always fresh for the next customer. You being here just helped me not waste as much." She smiled and winked at him. "You're welcome to come work here any day you'd like to."

"Thank you," he added a significant tip and grabbed his coffee and briefcase and headed for the door. "See you soon Max" he called as he left the café.

He'd have to remember not to mention this place to anyone in Bellcom City. They'd overrun the place with that kind of service policy. He hopped into his car and was about to drive away, when he noticed Max hurriedly coming out of the café, carrying a box and waving her hands. He stopped and rolled down the passenger window. "What's up?"

"You forgot your buns" she explained, out of breath. "Can't brag about my cinnamon buns to all your friends in the City if you haven't even tried them", she set the box on the passenger seat. "See you tomorrow!" she waved and headed back into the café.

"That's the prettiest damn smile I've ever seen," David said out loud as he turned onto the highway and headed back into Bellcom.

As he was driving the highway back to the city, it suddenly dawned on David that everyone in Windsmill seemed to know that he and Anna were investigating the deaths of Jack and Paul again. Everyone in and around the small town was now a suspect in the case of the red paint!

CHAPTER 16

DAVID HATED FUNERALS. HE'D ONLY EVER BEEN to two others, at least that he could remember. One was for a grandparent that he couldn't remember ever seeing before, and the other was a college friend that had been in a deadly car accident. That one really hit David hard. He was likely at Paul's funeral, but he couldn't remember much from that time.

He loosened his tie and unbuttoned the top button of his dress shirt. He'd taken his suit jacket off awhile ago and was using the excuse of putting it into his car to get out of the house for a bit. It was hotter out here than in there with all the people but at least David didn't have to listen to anyone else tell him how shockingly similar he was to his father, and all the stories of fun, joking around, and serious work that his father had gotten into over the few years he'd lived. David really wished he could remember something about him. Anything that would give him an inkling about what he was like. So far, nothing was coming. Maybe he'd just been too young to remember anything when he was sent away.

He flipped open the car trunk and tossed his jacket into the mess. He really needed to clean that out once he could get back into his apartment. As he was about to close the trunk, he heard a deep voice call after him. "Shit!" he said under his breath. "Just a minute alone would be nice." He turned to find Marvin walking toward him and waving.

"You aren't leaving already, are you?" Marvin asked as he came up to David's car.

"No, just getting a breath of fresh air before heading back in." He smiled at Marvin. "How about you? What are you doing out here?"

"Same thing you are." Marvin chuckled. "Trying to get away from all the clucking and flapping going on in there. It's nice to see Jenny and AJ again. Did they come with you?"

126

"No." David smiled, realizing it was likely the first time Mom and Dad had come out this way in over twenty years. "They drove themselves out so that they could stay as long as they'd like and not have to worry about what I was up to." He pointed a thumb behind him at his car. "Besides, this isn't very comfortable for more than two people, and I hate Dad's driving. Don't tell him that," he said as an afterthought, forgetting for a minute that Marvin and his dad were friends.

"Mum's the word." Marvin laughed. "AJ never was a very good driver. Did he tell you about the sports car his dad bought him for a graduation present back in the day?"

"No, he didn't." David looked up at Marvin with curiosity. "Pray tell." He smiled conspiratorially.

"Well," Marvin looked around to make sure no one was listening, and that AJ hadn't seen them out here. "He got this shiny red convertible from his dad. It was a beauty!" Marvin exaggerated his voice. "We were all going to go out to a college party that night and AJ wanted to show it off to all the ladies. That was before he'd met Jenny, of course." Marvin winked. "Anyways, we put the roof down, 'cause, well, I don't fit in them little cars and all." He pointed at David's car. "So, Paul jumps into the passenger seat and I kind of fold myself half in the back and half out of the car, see." He bends down in a squatting position and wraps his long arms around his knees to demonstrate his position in the vehicle.

"I darn near fall out going around a corner between Bellcom and Allensville, and that caught the attention of the policeman hiding in the bushes. He was sure we'd all been drinking and wanted us all to do those tests, you know." Marvin stood up and put his arms straight out at his sides, shoulder high. He reached his right arm back and touched his nose, and then stood on one leg. He was laughing so hard by this point he almost fell over. David reached over to steady him, and that made Marvin laugh harder. "See," he said between giggles. "That's exactly what that cop did when I was trying to do this on the side of the road." Marvin wiped tears of his cheeks. That's when both of them realized they had an audience. The women stood at the top of the steps looking down at them. AJ came down the front steps two at a time.

"David, don't try to catch him if he falls." AJ laughed. "He'll squish you too!" Marvin wrapped his arms around AJ's shoulders and the two of them laughed until their sides were sore.

"Man, what a night that was!" AJ said after they'd calmed down. "Your grandfather near took my head off that night when I phoned him to ask for money to bail us out and get the car out of impound," he said to David and then started to laugh again. "Remember what Paul said to my dad that night, Marv?"

"Sure do!" he said, and they both said together, "But Mr. Allen, it's actually your fault, sir. You bought him a car that's too small for all of us!"

"I thought Dad was going to kill us all that night. But Paul had him stopped in his tracks, and he started to laugh too. I don't think I'd ever seen Dad laugh before that night" AJ smiled so widely David was sure his face was going to split right open. "Man, those were the days." AJ and Marvin started back toward the house. "Come on, David, a little more people and a little less work would be good for you."

By the time they reached the top of the stairs, Becky, Mary, and Jenny were laughing too. "Thank you, David," Becky said as she hugged him when he got to the door. "Marv hasn't laughed like that in years!"

"I didn't do anything! Really!" he tried to explain. "I just went out for some fresh air!"

CHAPTER 17

DAVID WAS SO GLAD TO BE SITTING in his own office chair, with his own computer equipment. He was also glad that he got his phone back completely intact, although he was sure the police had taken a complete copy of all his current files. He'd asked Mike about that when he signed everything to get them out of the police evidence room, but Mike just stared at him with that cop stare of his and never said anything. Anyway, he had it all back, and his own coffee pot too; although the coffee wasn't as good as Max's, David thought as he put his feet up on the desk and leaned back to drink his sludge. He'd have to ask her what her secret was. He smiled. He stared at the wall that up until this morning had red paint scrawled all over it. He was also glad that Mom had a designer on speed dial, and they knew a professional painter that just happened to be in Bellcom City and looking for work. It wasn't much work, but the guy did an excellent job.

The office phone rang, bringing him back to reality. "Allen and Associates Investigations, David Allen speaking. How can I help you?"

"Hi David," Marvin said at the other end. "How's your schedule today?"

"Not bad, I could make room," he answered. "What's up?"

"Well, I came into Bellcom City for a bit this morning to make sure my business hasn't suffered too badly these last few weeks. I thought I'd swing by your office or take you someplace we can talk for awhile. I can tell you about my cousins, and about my suspicions about Marty's death. If you have the time and want to hear it, that is," Marvin finished.

"Of course, I want to hear all about all it, if you don't mind telling me." David tried to tamp down his excitement. He hadn't contacted Marvin yet because it had only been a week since the funeral, and he was worried about

129

it being too soon. Obviously, Marvin wanted to get it all done and over with. "What time were you thinking of swinging around?"

"I'm just leaving my office now. You back in your office or should I be looking for you somewhere else?"

"I'm back up and running in my office," David answered with a smile. He gave Marvin the street address and told him that he'd have coffee on when he got here.

"By the look of my GPS, I should be there in about forty-five minutes, assuming traffic isn't too bad this time of day. Does that work?"

"Sure, come on up. It's the blue door to the right of the sandwich place. I'll leave both doors unlocked so just come on up." David ended the call and then realized he'd better download the recordings and videos he had on his phone and clear some space for this meeting. He was sure that Marvin wouldn't mind him recording their conversation and he was also sure Anna would want to hear it.

True to his word, Marvin arrived almost exactly forty-five minutes later. He tentatively knocked on the office door then pushed it open. "Hello?" he called out. "David?"

"Hi, Marvin," David called from the kitchen in his apartment. "I'll be right there. Would you like a coffee?" he asked as he entered the office holding two cups and a new carton of cream.

"No, thanks. Too much coffee this time of day will have me up all night." Marvin reached out to shake David's hand then realized he still had his hands full. "I'll let you get your own coffee though before we get started."

David smiled at him and put down the items, then reached out and shook Marvin's hand. "Thanks for coming in to meet with me. I really appreciate it."

"No problem. I mentioned to my aunt that you were investigating all this again, and she was pleased that someone was finally taking it seriously. My uncle died a broken man after losing both his sons to something no one knew anything about. He didn't think any of the police took it seriously, and none of them did anything to help. Aunt Agnes asked me what I meant by 'again,' since no one else ever did any real investigating." Marvin smiled at David. "I think there's a lot of people that seem to be happy that someone is looking into it finally. Especially now that Jack and Marty have died in similar ways."

"Really?" David asked. "I mean, I'm glad so many are happy about it, but at the same time, I can't imagine any of this is easy on the townspeople. Dredging up old memories and long-past deaths can make some people a little jumpy." David didn't mention anything that had been happening at and around his office over the last couple of weeks and wondered if Marvin had heard about it.

"Yes, I can imagine you're a little jumpy with everything that's happened here too." Marvin looked at him with sympathy. "I can't think of anyone that would want to stop this investigation. At least, no one in Windsmill."

"Well, that answers that question," David said quietly to himself. "I was wondering if that had gotten around."

"I don't know about 'around,' exactly, but Mary told Becky who told me. I don't imagine either of them have said anything to anyone else, and I know I haven't." Marvin sounded a little put off by David's remarks.

"I didn't mean any offense and wasn't accusing anyone of anything. I was just wondering who would have told anyone that we were investigating in the first place. As far as I was aware, only a handful of people should know about it. But I realized the day before the funeral, when I was trying to get some work done in Maxine's café, that all the townspeople seemed to know what I was working on. News travels fast in small towns, I suppose."

"That it does for sure. I think people saw you around town and immediately knew who you where. It's hard to hide your resemblance to your father. I'm sure they had wondered what had brought you back to town and if it had anything to do with Jack's death. You know, most of the townspeople had been to his funeral, and Anna was not quiet about what she believed happened to him. Then when they heard about Marty, they started bringing up the similarities between now and twenty-two years ago. A lot of what they knew and know now is mostly just conjecture and gossip."

David thought about what Marvin had just said. He was likely right. Small towns and gossip seem to go hand in hand. He'd seen similar grapevine news happen in Allensville after his friend's car accident. It was off-putting to be part of that, and it was one of the reasons he'd moved to the city. Now that same kind of gossip could be responsible for someone threatening his and his sister's lives.

"Anyway, that's not what you came here to tell me. Shall we get started?" David pulled out his phone and set it on the desk. "I'd like to record our conversation, if that's okay with you. It won't be shared with anyone other than Anna, and it's simply so that I can pay attention to what you're saying and not have to make copious notes while we talk."

PACKART'S ORCHARD 131

"No problem," Marvin agreed as he watched David turn on the recording app. "We'll start with Malcolm and Manny, if that's okay. As I said, I mentioned your investigation to Aunt Agnes, mostly to make sure she was okay with me telling you about the twins. I assume you'll want the toxicology and autopsy reports from back then. Aunt Agnes is looking to see if Uncle Mo kept a copy in his filing cabinet. If not, the coroner's office in Carson should still have copies since it's considered an open case still."

"Open case?" David looked interested. "The Carson Police opened a file on them?"

"Yes, the coroner recommended an investigation take place into where the drugs that were in their system came from. I don't think they got too far when they tried to talk to the sheriff's department in Windsmill, but you can decide if you want to talk to them after I tell you everything I know about it. I think the Carson P.D. also talked to the police here in Bellcom back then, but I'm not a hundred percent sure about that."

"Sure, that'll work." David wrote down a note in his book to talk to the police stations involved and made sure his phone was on record.

"So, let's get started ..." Marvin looked up in deep thought. He pulled out an old photograph of his cousins and set it on the desk in front of him. They looked to be in their late teens, and if you didn't know there were two of them, you'd think it was a double-exposure photo of only one person. They definitely were identical twins. They smiled at the camera with a twinkle in their eyes. "They had just celebrated their twentieth birthday the week before they died," Marvin began. "They were a handful even at that age, and Uncle Mo had finally talked them into getting some kind of education that would give them a career instead of hopping from one job to another." Marvin shook his head as he remembered Mo's temper.

MANNY'S STORY — APRIL 1990:

Uncle Mo was a good man, but sometimes he let his temper get the best of him. Especially when he thought the twins were doing something they shouldn't be or not doing something he thought they should be. It was March, and the twins were between jobs again. It had been that way since they'd finished high school.

Manny was sitting in the TV room trying to decompress from what he and his mother had been working on at the kitchen computer. They had gone through the Hedley College calendar and found the courses he would need to take to eventually be able to transfer to Northern University in Kendall to become the architect he always wanted to be. Manny was excited but wasn't sure how to tell his brother that he would be leaving Carson in the fall. They'd always done everything together, so this would be different for them both.

Malcolm came storming into the room with Mo right behind them. They'd been arguing about something all afternoon. Mo wanted the twins to start thinking about what they were going to do with the rest of their lives, and Malcolm wasn't having any of it. He'd hated high school because it was so boring and didn't hold his interest. While Manny was the studious one, Malcolm had always been the class clown and the troublemaker.

Manny sat with his feet up on the coffee table, watching the fireworks, when Mo reached over and hit Manny's feet off the table, exclaiming that it was both their futures he was trying to get them to sit up and pay attention to. He scolded them for not wanting anything more than sitting there doing nothing! Manny tried to interject that he'd already done this, but Malcolm cut him off, telling him not to try to explain himself since their father wasn't interested in what they wanted anyway.

Manny didn't move. He was stuck between his father and brother again. Seemed to be the story of his life since he could remember. Mo and Malcolm fought all the time, and they both dragged Manny into the middle. It never really mattered to either of them what Manny wanted or what he did or didn't say or do.

Malcolm tried to get out the back door, but Mo stopped him, asking where he thought he was going when they weren't finish talking about this. Malcolm informed him that he was done with all of this and turned to ask Manny if he was coming with him, but Manny had already snuck out of the house without them noticing.

When Malcolm got out to the car the twins shared, Manny was already sitting in the passenger seat waiting for his brother. Malcolm hopped in the driver's seat and spun the car out of the long-hilled driveway, shooting gravel all over the other vehicles in the parking area. He headed north through Caron and up toward Kendall at record speed.

That night Mo sat at the dinner table deep in thought. If only Malcolm would put as much energy into his future as he did trying to get under his father's skin, he'd be going places. He hoped the boys would be home for supper so he could talk to them about the job offer Marvin called him about this afternoon. Maybe getting them out of Carson for the summer would do all of them some good. It didn't look like they'd be here to eat again tonight.

Agnes looked over at Mo. She worried about how hard he pushed the boys. Mo and Agnes had talked about her conversation with Manny and what had gotten him to change his mind about college and university. Agnes tried to explain to Mo that Manny had always been the more studious of the two boys, and she and Manny had talked a lot about what he'd like to do with his life. Manny spent most of his high school years following his brother from party to party and had failed to meet university requirements for the courses he'd wanted to take. He'd talked to the guidance counsellor at the university about what it would take to get in, and he'd suggested that upgrading at Hedley for a year would be a good start. Manny and Agnes had looked into it, and he'd enrolled in the upgrade courses without telling his brother, and without Agnes telling Mo what was going on. She'd hoped that when Malcolm found out he might want to go too.

Agnes interrupted Mo's quiet thinking time by asking him what Malcolm said when he found out what Manny was going to school in the fall. Mo looked at her blankly and said he didn't think Manny had said anything and even if he did, Malcolm wouldn't have been listening. Mo told Anges that all that boy did was spout off about how he was always being blamed for everything, and that Manny wasn't an angel. The usual bull. Mo looked up at his wife and said he wished Malcolm would just sit down and talk about it in a reasonable manner.

Agnes shook her head. That's what both of them needed to do. Sit down and talk to each other instead of always yelling and fighting. Malcolm was so much like this father, she thought. Agnes stood up and started clearing the table. She'd put the leftovers in the fridge in case they come home hungry.

Agnes prayed that the boys would agree to work in the orchard at Windsmill if for no other reason than to separate them from their father for a couple of months. Maybe everyone would settle down and start thinking like the adults they were, instead of being so busy trying to one-up one another.

Meanwhile, the boys had driven up to Kendall but there wasn't anything going on up there. They'd driven back to Carson and then decided to head west to Windsmill. By the time they'd gotten there, everything was closed tight, and the town was sleeping. *Small towns suck,* Malcolm thought.

Malcolm turned the car around and headed back toward Carson, as Manny talked to him about registering at Hedley. Malcolm asked a lot of questions about why Hedley and not the other colleges in the area, and why Manny wanted to be an architect all of a sudden. Manny told him about the research he and their mom had done, and Hedley was the only one offering an architectural technology diploma, that would give Manny a head start to get into the Northern University degree program. The colleges in Carson and Kendall don't offer that specific program. Manny had told Malcolm many times about wanting to be an architect, but he never listened.

It was late when they returned home, and they'd missed supper, Malcolm had calmed down enough after his fight with their dad to want to know more about what his brother was thinking about doing and how Malcolm might get into something too.

Manny opened the fridge and took out the containers of leftovers his mother had put there after supper. He popped open a corner of the lid to see what they'd missed. He set the containers on the counter and pulled out a plate to scoop it on to. He asked his brother if he wanted some.

Just then Malcolm's stomach growled. He'd been so angry at their father he couldn't think of anything but getting as far away from the house as possible. He looked over at his brother's plate coming out of the microwave and finally said he'd have that. Manny handed him the plate of food and then made another one for himself.

They finished eating all the leftovers and were looking in the fridge for whatever else might be in there, when their parents entered the kitchen.

"What do you two think you're doing?" Mo growled at the boys. "Look at this mess! Do you know what time it is?"

"We'll clean it up," Manny said as he started loading everything into the dishwasher.

"And just where have you been all night?" Mo accused.

"I'm sure they were doing what young men do." Agnes gave her husband a stop-it look as she went over and helped Manny clean up.

"We were just up in Kendall looking at the college up there. Isn't that what you wanted us to do?" Malcolm glared at his father. Mo didn't respond. He could tell Malcolm was lying but didn't want to argue with him about it. Malcolm took his plate over to the counter and set it down. He grabbed a wet towel to wipe up the gravy they'd spilled on the table.

"I spoke to Marvin this afternoon. He found some work for the two of you," Mo stated as he pulled out a beer from the fridge and sat down at the table.

"Work? I thought you wanted us in school again instead of work?" Malcolm mocked. "Which is it?"

Mo held his breath and counted to ten, then looked at Agnes for some support, but she wasn't paying attention to them. "This is summer work. Just until the fall season at college starts. You could start next week, and they even have cabins for the workers, so you could live on your own." Mo stared at Malcolm. "Isn't that what you wanted?" He emphasized every word.

"What kind of work?"

"Packart's Orchard is hiring their spring and summer crews."

"What's the wage?"

"Minimum wage, plus a cabin and two meals a day."

"Minimum wage?" Malcolm baulked. "You ain't paying college tuition with that kind of wages!"

"If you'd make up your mind what you wanted to do with your life, you wouldn't have to work for minimum wage. Get an education, get a real career," Mo snarked back.

"Okay, you two, that's enough!" Agnes raised her voice. "If you work the full summer, you'll have pocket money for college. I'll pay your tuition, but you have to be serious about it!" She pointed at Malcolm. She asked him if he had something specific in mind that he'd like to do and told him she would help him look up where to start in the morning and see where they went from there. In the meantime, she asked them both to think about the job. If they were interested, Marvin would need to let Mr. Packart know by the end of this week so he could make sure he's got a full crew.

Both boys hugged their mother and thanked her for everything she'd done for them. Manny patted Mo on the back and headed for their room. Malcolm went to say something just to get the last word but saw the don't-you-dare look on his mother's face and decided against it. Agnes looked over at her husband, who did exactly the same thing. She smiled at them and told them to go to bed. They'd talk more in the morning. As her family exited the kitchen, Agnes checked the back door to make sure it was locked, turned off all the lights, closed the microwave door that had been left ajar, and smiled at herself as she headed upstairs to her own bedroom.

MALCOLM AND AGNES SAT STARING AT THE computer screen in the kitchen. There was room left in the courses he had decided on, so Malcolm was trying to put a schedule together that wouldn't be too heavy. He couldn't believe he'd let his mother talk him into this. He also couldn't believe he didn't have to take any upgrade courses to get into the criminology program he needed to become a police officer. This was way too easy, and nothing in his life had been easy.

"So, what do you think?" Agnes asked as he picked the last course for the semester. "Do you really want to go down this road?"

"Yes, I really do, Mom. Thank you for pushing me to do this. I didn't think I'd ever get in with the crap I learned in high school!" He smiled as his mother hugged him.

"I always knew you had some good stuff locked under all that anger," Agnes said as she stood up to get her purse. "Is your brother around? We could all drive into Bellcom City and get all of this paid for and the paperwork all finished up this afternoon."

Just as they were shutting off the computer, Manny came wondering in, an apple in one hand and a soda in the other. "Did I hear road trip?" He smiled. "I'll drive!"

They drove into Bellcom City and got everything finalized at Hedley College. They called Mo from a pay phone by the entrance of the bookstore. They'd have to pick books up at the end of summer, but it didn't need to be done today. Maybe they could pay for some of those themselves and give their mother a break. Agnes told Mo he'd be on his own for supper as they would be stopping somewhere for dinner to celebrate the day. It was late when they were passing through Windsmill. Most of the town's shops and restaurants were closed for the evening, but Don's Place was still open. They stopped in and had burgers and a beer as their celebration.

They finished their meal and headed back onto the highway toward Carson. As they passed the orchard, Malcolm noticed lights on in a row of cabins by the highway. A small dirt road went off the highway in front of them. He hollered at his brother to stop so they could see what their new accommodation would be like for the summer.

Manny pulled onto the road and bumped his way over to the cabins. "I wonder which one is ours?" he said as he stopped the car and looked out the window.

Malcolm jumped out of the car and started over to the first cabin. The lights were on, so someone must have lived there already. He knocked. No answer. He knocked louder; still nothing. Maybe they were sleeping already or something. He looked around and spotted lights on at the far end of the

PACKART'S ORCHARD   137

dirt road. It looked like it was on the other side of the river, away from everything else. He hollered at Manny again to drive over to the end so he could see if someone lived there.

"No! I'm not driving over there tonight. This road isn't in good shape, who knows what that bridge is like. Maybe we can look around in the daylight after we move in." Manny watched as Malcolm started walking down the road. "Come on, man, let's get out of here," Manny pleaded.

Agnes got out of the car. "Malcolm James Faulkon, get back over here right now!" she scolded her son. "What are you thinking? Do you want to get arrested for trespassing just before you're aiming to join the police force?"

Malcolm strolled back over to the car and got in. "Fine, okay, we can go now." He pouted. "And for your information, this looks like a standard access road and therefore is public domain. I'm not trespassing!"

ON SUNDAY, MANNY AND MALCOLM PACKED UP their car to get ready for the drive back to Windsmill. It was about seventy-five or so miles, so it didn't take them long to get there. They were scheduled to meet up with Marvin right after lunch and he'd take them over to Mr. Packart's office to get everything settled and get the keys for their cabin. Malcolm hoped they'd have some time to look around town in the daylight when everything was open. Maybe see what kind of shops they had and where they might be able to get some food and drinks and stuff for the cabin kitchen. He hoped there was a kitchen, he thought, as he finished putting his suitcases in the trunk.

Manny came out with a cooler full of drinks and snacks their mother had packed for them. Malcolm asked if there was any beer in it, but Manny told him it wasn't likely since their mom had packed it. They'd have food so they didn't starve to death, but they weren't going to be partying with what she'd put in there.

Agnes and Mo came out to the parking area to say goodbye and tell them that they were always welcome to come home for a meal, or whatever they needed, any time. After all, they weren't going to be that far away. Both boys hugged their mother and said their goodbyes to their father, and they were off. Agnes and Mo waved as the brothers drove down the driveway and headed west on the highway.

"They'll be fine." Mo put his arm over Agnes's shoulders and hugged her lightly. "This will be good for them both. I'm going to go let Marvin know they're on their way." He kissed Agnes lightly on her forehead and headed into the house. Agnes watched the highway for a while longer, knowing her boys would be just fine. She smiled to herself, thinking this separation would be good for Mo too.

AS THEY APPROACHED THE ENTRANCE TO MARVIN and Becky's house, they spotted Marvin's work truck coming down the driveway. They pulled over into the rest area, wondering what was going on. Marvin pulled in and parked beside the boys.

"Hey guys," Marvin said as Manny rolled down the driver's window. "I'm glad I caught you. I have to get Becky into the doctor's office. She's having contractions and we don't know if we need to get to the hospital in Bellcom right away or not. You can wait up at the house, or you can go into Packart's place on your own if you'd like. I'll be back as soon as I can." Without waiting for them to respond, he turned his truck around and headed toward town.

Manny asked his brother which way he wanted to go as he rolled up the window again. Malcolm indicated that they might just as well go to Packart's and get it over with. They could sign whatever papers Mr. Packart had for them and then maybe get into the cabin and see what they'd be living in the next couple of months. They would have time to unpack the car and then maybe go into town to get more supplies.

Manny turned the car back toward the Packarts' driveway. Manny pushed the button on a post beside the big black gate and announced they were there to see Mr. Packart. They heard a click like the gate had unlocked, but it didn't move. Malcolm got out and pushed the gate open. Once Manny had driven through the gate opening, Malcolm closed it again, and they drove up toward the Packarts' mansion.

"Wow!" Manny said as he exited the car. "Now this is a house!" He loved the architectural design of old Southern plantations, even if he wasn't thrilled with the history that it raised, that made his blood boil. This house had that Southern charm to it.

"Yeah, it's okay," Malcolm said as he heard the big wooden door slide open. A man about the same age as their dad came down the stairs. He was stout, with denim overalls over a plaid shirt and salt and pepper hair. He smiled at the boys and stuck out his hand to shake theirs.

"The Faulkon boys, I presume," Albert said as he shook their hands. "The Faulkons don't believe in creating small people do they?" Albert chuckled.

PACKART'S ORCHARD   139

"No, sir, we don't." Malcolm smiled at him and shook his hand. "I'm Malcolm, and this," he pointed his thumb over his shoulder, "is my brother Manny."

"Good to meet you, sir." Manny shook Albert's hand. "Thank you for this opportunity," he added.

"Oh, not so much an opportunity for you as it is a blessing for me," Albert said. "I'm short on workers this season, so it's nice to have two hard working boys like yourselves come on board. Come on in and we'll get the paperwork all sorted out. Then I'll take you over to the cabins and show you your accommodation for the season. They aren't much but they'll keep the rain off your head and the mosquitos out of your bed." He smiled at them again.

About an hour later they were coming back out of the house and getting ready to get back into their car. "I'll meet you over by the cabins. Just head east 'til you get to the end of the orchard, then turn right onto a dirt road. There's a row of cedars between the cabins and the orchard, so it shouldn't be hard to spot. I'll put you two boys in the second cabin from the highway. Beside old Red's place there." They watched as Albert unlocked a big shed and pulled out a golf cart. "The gate's opened so just go on through," Albert said as he headed into the orchard.

Cool cart, Malcolm thought as they watched Albert go. Maybe he could borrow one to look around the area. Manny pulled him back to the present by getting into the car and starting it. As he started to back out, Malcolm hopped in, and they headed out toward the cabin road.

As they went through the gate, Manny pulled to a stop and waited. After a few seconds Malcolm asked Manny why he'd stopped.

"Get out and close the gate."

"Why? Mr. Packart didn't say anything about closing it up."

"Just get out and close the damned gate," Manny said.

Malcolm jumped out and did as his brother had asked. As he did, he thought he saw someone in the shadows of the cedar trees. "Hello?" Malcolm hollered at the trees. "Can we help you with something?" No answer. That was strange, Malcolm thought as he got back into the car.

"What was that all about?" Manny asked as he turned onto the highway again.

"There was someone there," Malcolm shook his head, "or at least I thought there was." He couldn't shake the feeling of being watched.

"Okay, have you been drinking already today?" Manny laughed. He turned onto the gravel road and drove up to the second cabin. Mr. Packart was standing on the porch talking to a tall, red-headed man about the same age as he was. The boys got out and walked over to the men.

"There you are," Albert said and then turned back to the man. "This is Hector Lightfeather. He is the only permanent resident over here in the cabins. If you need any information or assistance, he knows everything about this part of the orchard."

The man nodded at the boys. "Please call me Red. Everybody does," he said.

"Great, nice to meet you, sir," Manny said and nodded back at him. Malcolm stood back, looking at the exchange. It definitely wasn't this man in the trees back there, he thought. Too small. In fact, the shadow was about the same size as Mr. Packart.

"So, is there anyone else living over here in the cabins yet?" Malcolm asked as Mr. Packart handed each of them a key.

"Not yet," Albert responded as he swung open the door. "After you." He stood aside to let the boys enter first.

"Nice," Manny said as he looked around. "This is better than expected."

"Glad you like it. The electricity has been turned on and the plumbing should be working. As I said, if anything is missing just let Red know and he'll help you out. If he's not around, then just come to the main house and myself or my son Darren or my wife Amelia should be around to help out. You'll be meeting them tomorrow at breakfast."

"Thank you," Manny said as he headed back out to the car and popped the trunk open. "I'm sure everything will be just fine." Albert and Malcolm walked back out to the car with Manny.

"What about the house at the end of the road there? The one on the other side of the river?" Malcolm asked curiously.

"That's the old homestead that my grandfather built when they started the orchard. No one has lived over there in years now," Albert said. "It's very unstable. I'm thinking of having it torn down before it falls over and causes a bigger mess. I'd stay away from that old building if I were you."

"Hmm. I'm sure I saw lights on over there when we stopped by this way on Friday night." Malcolm watched Albert for any reaction.

"No electricity over there anymore, so no lights could have been on. Maybe you just saw a car passing on the road over there. There's a number of other farms and acreages out that way. Maybe it was one of them." Albert dismissed the conversation. "Breakfast will be at the main house at eight a.m. sharp. If you're late, you won't eat again until suppertime." He waved at them and nodded at Red, then headed around the side of the cabin and back to the house on his golf cart.

"If you're smart, you'll heed what Mr. P told you and stay away from the homestead," Red said to Malcolm. "Strange things happen out here at night." Red headed into his own cabin and shut the door before Malcolm could question him further.

"Well, that was strange," Malcolm said as his brother passed him with a handful of stuff from the car.

"I'm calling the big bedroom," Manny called back to Malcolm, ignoring his ramblings. "If you don't get your stuff out of the car, you can unpack tonight. I'm going into town before everything is closed down for the day."

Malcolm ignored what Manny was saying. "Do you feel that?" he asked as his brother came back outside.

"Feel what?" Manny said as he pulled the back door of the car open and hauled out the cooler.

"Like someone is watching us," Malcolm said as he pulled his suitcase and duffle bag out of the trunk. He walked over to the steps of the cabin, set everything down, and started to look around. There was no one around but the two of them. Malcolm couldn't see anything through the cedar groves, but he was sure there was something there. He grabbed his luggage and headed into the cabin. "Hey, how come you get the big bedroom?" he complained to his brother.

"I told you I was taking it, and you didn't say anything. You snooze, you lose." Manny chuckled. "Besides, the other room isn't that much smaller. I'm putting all the stuff Mom sent with us into the fridge. This kitchen has everything. A toaster, a microwave, a coffee pot, yew!" Manny backed away from the cabinet he'd just opened. "And old boxes of stuff that look like they've been here since the last time someone lived here." Manny poked around and a mouse ran across the cabinet, down onto the next shelf and disappeared. "Crap! And mice!" Manny headed for the door.

"What, you scared of a little mouse?" Malcolm called after his brother as he left the cabin. Manny didn't answer. He went over to Red's cabin and knocked on the door.

142   WENDY SCOTT-ETTINGER

"Sorry to bother you already, sir," he said when Red opened the door. "I was hoping we could borrow a garbage bag. It looks like the last tenants left some food in there, and it's attracted mice."

Without saying anything, Red turned back into his cabin and came back out a few minutes later with two black garbage bags, three mouse traps, and a package of cheese. He handed the items to Manny, and just before he closed the door, he said, "Garbage bins are in the back behind cabin number five."

"Okay then," Manny said as he headed back into the cabin. Malcolm was already unpacking his luggage and putting his clothes in the dresser drawers. He carried a handful of toiletries to the bathroom then came back out to the kitchen.

"Where did you disappear to?" Malcolm asked. "And what do you have there?" He walked over to his brother and peered over his shoulder to see what he was doing. "Are those mouse traps?"

"Yes." Manny handed Malcolm a garbage bag. "You can clean up the cupboards while I get these set. I'm hoping there's some cleaning supplies in here somewhere."

The boys got the cabin cleaned as much as possible. At least the vacuum worked, and they were able to get most of the mouse droppings out of the cabinets. Manny looked at his watch. It was almost three o'clock and they hadn't eaten anything all day. "I'm going to head into town and see if there's anything opened. We could use some more supplies in here, and I'm starving. Maybe that pub is opened today, what was it called? Don's Place, right?"

"I'll come with you." Malcolm pulled his work gloves off and laid them on the counter. "I could use a beer or two after all this."

When they got into town, they realized there was nothing open at all. Small towns didn't believe in commerce on a Sunday. Maybe they could drive into Bellcom City. Surely something would be open in the bigger centres. Especially around the college area where most of the people were temporarily living while they attended school. They drove around and finally found a place that looked like it was open. They wandered into what looked like a full-blown college party. They smiled and found a seat at the bar.

"Which house you in?" asked the bartender as he set a coaster in front of each of them.

"House?" Manny asked. "Is this a private party?"

PACKART'S ORCHARD   143

"Nah," the bartender smiled, "not really. But if the cops show up and ask you that question, you'd better have an answer for them, or we all get hauled away. What would you like?"

"Two beers, whatever's on tap, and do you have a menu? Any food at all? We're starving!" Malcolm said as he pulled out his wallet.

"Two beers, two burgers with fries, and a list of houses to choose from," the bartender said. "I'll have that right out for you." He came back a couple of minutes later with the beers and a long list of college houses. "It'll take awhile for the food, but these should tide you over."

"What do we owe you?" Malcolm asked as he laid a twenty-dollar bill on the bar.

"That'll do for what you ordered, plus another round." The bartender looked from one brother to the other. "Good thing I don't drink. Otherwise, I'd swear I was seeing double."

"Yeah, yeah. What is this place anyway? Why's there so many people in here tonight?" Malcolm asked as he turned his stool to look around.

"Oh, this is one of the few places open on a Sunday night. Private college functions only, of course." The bartender winked. "Bellcom ain't like Kendall. They haven't decided that money is worth more than Sundays off yet."

"Man, that sucks. We should have registered at Kendall College, bro." Malcolm chuckled and patted Manny on the back.

"So, you're registered at Hedley?" the bartender asked. "What you taking?"

"Don't start 'til fall. We're working in Windsmill for the summer and then moving over here at the beginning of September. Looks like they have fun here, anyway."

A small blonde that looked like she wasn't old enough to be in college, let alone in a bar, came walking up to them and plopped down two plates. "Hope this is enough food to fill you two up." She smiled at them. "Anyone tell you, you two look exactly alike?" she asked as she looked from one to the other and back again. "And god, you must be seven feet tall!" she exclaimed.

"Only about a thousand times a day, every day of my life," Manny said, speaking up for the first time since they'd sat down. "And I'm only six-six. He's six-eight." He pointed at his brother.

"You twins or something?" the blonde asked.

"Yeah, you think?" Malcolm said sarcastically. The blonde walked away.

"You could try to be a little nice, bro," Manny berated Malcolm. "Some of these people might be your classmates in the fall."

They ate and drank their beers, then headed for the door. "Thanks, man, for the food and drink. Hope the cops leave you alone tonight." Malcolm waved at the bartender as they walked toward the door. Everyone turned to look at the two very tall, dark men and separated the crowd like a walkway through to the door. No one bothered them.

"That was a little weird," Manny said as he unlocked the car doors.

"Yeah, a little weird. Did you notice not one other Black person in the whole crowd?" Malcolm asked as they started to drive away.

"Yeah, a little weird," Manny repeated.

As they drove back to Windsmill they were quietly thinking about whether Hedley was actually the right college for them after all. They were hard enough to miss, being so big and tall, but if they were the only ones of colour in the college, that was going to be a problem.

"Maybe we should reconsider all this," Malcolm said finally. "That felt really strange."

"Let's talk to Marvin about it tomorrow," Manny suggested. "I wonder if he's a father right now."

"Yeah, probably," Malcolm answered, not really thinking about what he was saying. How had he let his family talk him into all this, anyway? he thought. What the hell was he doing out here in the middle of nowhere?

"Pull over!" he snapped at Manny as they passed Marvin's driveway. "Now!"

Manny pulled the car into the rest area. "What the hell is wrong with you?" he asked as Malcolm jumped out of the car.

"Manny, come out here for a minute," Malcolm demanded as he started looking around in the trees. "Do you see that?" he pointed into the trees up the side of the hill. "See what?" Manny asked as he looked where his brother was pointing. "There's nothing there, Malcolm. Can we go now?"

"No, you stay here and keep watch. I'm going to go get my camera and a flashlight. I'll be right back." Before Manny could respond, Malcolm jumped into the car and took off.

"Shit!" Manny said as he watched him drive away. "What the hell am I supposed to do out here now?"

He stood there looking around for a few minutes. *Maybe I should walk up and see if Marvin's back yet,* he said as he spotted the driveway up to their house. *Malcolm can just go straight to hell with all this craziness.* Manny started to walk toward Marvin's drive when he heard something behind him. *Just my imagination,* he thought as he kept walking. He turned up the gravel road

PACKART'S ORCHARD 145

and walked about a hundred yards when he heard the same noise. He turned around to look, expecting to see Malcolm coming up the driveway, but it wasn't a vehicle. Manny squinted out in the darkness. "Hello?" he said. "Is there anyone there?" He heard laughter. "Malcolm, so help me god, if that's you I'm going to kill you!" he hollered and turned back up the hill.

"No, but I'm going to kill you!" the disembodied voice came booming back. "You should mind your own business."

Manny turned back toward the voice. "Who are you and what are you talking about?" No answer. "Hello?" Manny saw what looked like a small bird come out of the bushes beside the road. "What the hell is that?" he said as he squinted into the darkness. "Is that a bird? No, bugs of some sort. Big ones!" He swung his long arms out to try to hit whatever it was, but he missed. It spit out a powder into his face, and Manny wiped at it. He waved his arms again and tried to turn around to walk up the hill. Marvin would help him. The bug hit him in the side of the neck, and Manny spun around, waving his arms frantically. "Swarms of them," he said to himself and fell to his knees. The birds or bugs or whatever those things were flew back to where they'd come from, and the bushes became quiet.

Manny lay face down in the gravel on the right side of the road. He didn't move.

MALCOLM GOT BACK TO THE REST AREA about ten minutes after he left. Manny was nowhere to be seen. He hadn't passed him on his way back, so he had to have gone the other way. Malcolm got out of the car and looked around.

"Manny? You out here?" he hollered in the direction of the trees. "Manny! Damn it, where are you?" No answer. No sound. Nothing. Malcolm started to panic. Something wasn't right. Manny wouldn't just disappear.

Why did he leave him out here by himself, especially when Malcolm had seen something in the trees? "Damn it, Manny, come on. I'm sorry. I shouldn't have left you out here like that. Manny?" Malcolm was starting to panic. He'd never had this feeling of pure emptiness before. Something was wrong, but he couldn't put his finger on it. It was suddenly too quiet. He spotted the driveway up to Marvin's place and decided that must be where Manny went. He hopped back into the car and spit gravel when he headed up to Marvin's. As he turned the first corner going up the road, he spotted something on the road. What was that? He stopped and got out of the car.

146   WENDY SCOTT-ETTINGER

He walked cautiously toward the lump of clothing, then ran the rest of the way when he realized it was Manny.

"Manny? Manny! Wake up. What happened? Come on, Manny, please!" Tears started to roll down his cheeks as he frantically tried to wake him up. He felt for a pulse but couldn't find one. He looked around from side to side and back at his brother. "Manny, please come back." Malcolm started to sob. He yelled for help, but no one was there to hear him. He dropped his brother back where he'd found him and ran as fast as he could to Marvin and Becky's house. He pounded on the door, but there was no answer. A note hung on the door from Marvin. It read "KEY UNDER THE MAT, HELP YOURSELF. I'LL BE BACK WHEN I CAN." Malcolm pulled the mat up and threw it into the rose bush beside the porch. He flung open the door and searched frantically for a phone. He flipped every light on in the house. When he spotted the phone sitting on the kitchen counter, he practically tripped over the table to grab it. He dialled 9-1-1.

"Dispatch, how can I help you?"

"Yes, send an ambulance, a doctor, something, hurry, please!" Malcolm screamed into the phone. "My brother, he's injured, he's maybe dead, help me please," he sobbed.

"Calm down, sir. Where are you?"

"I'm at my cousin's place. My brother is on the road by my car. Please hurry."

"What is your cousin's name please, and what is his address?"

"His name is Marvin. Marvin Faulkon. I don't know the address. Just outside of Windsmill. Between Windsmill and Packart's Orchard. Please hurry!" Malcolm folded onto the floor and openly wept.

"Please do not hang up sir. Sir? Are you still there?" When the dispatcher didn't get an answer, she added, "I'm sending help right now! Please do not hang up the phone until emergency services get there."

Malcolm picked himself off the floor and ran back down the dirt road. As he rounded the corner where he'd left Manny, he heard sirens and lots of tires hit the gravel. He reached down and picked up Manny's head again. "They're coming, Manny, just hold on. Don't leave me, man." He started to cry again.

CHAPTER 18

SERGEANT HARPER ESCORTED MALCOLM INTO MARVIN'S HOUSE and told him to sit in a chair by the kitchen table. He handcuffed him to the kitchen table leg and picked up the phone receiver that was dangling down the side of the counter and said, "Hello?"

"Hello. Did the emergency services get there, sir?" the dispatcher asked.

"Hi, Mavis. This is Harpy. We have the scene cleared. The body is on its way to the medical examiner's office. I have the suspect in custody and will be questioning him now. Can you please try to get hold of Marvin Faulkon for me? He's likely at Bellcom General with his wife. Seems to me someone told me they headed that way earlier today."

"Will do, Harpy. I'll let you know." Harpy hung up the phone and turned to look at the identical twin of the man they'd just sent to the morgue. "Okay, now, can you tell me what went down here tonight?"

"Don't say anything, Malcolm," came a booming voice from the front entrance. "What the hell do you think you're doing, Harper?" Marvin came marching into his own kitchen.

Harper looked up at Marvin. "I'm trying to get that out of him!" He pointed at the young man sitting at the table. "He won't say anything except he's sorry and he didn't mean for anything to happen. What the hell does that even mean?" he said in frustration.

"Have you checked the security system to see if the cameras up and down the driveway picked anything up?" Marvin asked. "Do you even know what you're doing, Sergeant?"

"Now just wait one minute," Harpy started.

"No, you wait!" Marvin yelled at him. "I come up my drive after passing a cruiser, a fire truck, and an ambulance heading none too slowly into

148

Windsmill. I find a car parked crooked like it had been abandoned on the road coming up to my place and a cruiser parked haphazardly in my parking area. The front door is wide open, and you have my cousin handcuffed to my kitchen table and his twin is nowhere to be seen." Marvin glared at the officer. "If I didn't know you better, I would have you charged with harassment and discrimination! I didn't pin you for a racist, Harpy, but this sure doesn't look good. Did you even read him his rights before handcuffing him to my table?"

Marvin sat down in the chair beside Malcolm. "You okay?"

Malcolm looked up at his cousin, and he started to sob again. "Manny's gone, Marv. He's dead. I don't know what happened to him. I shouldn't have left him at the rest area. I was only gone a few minutes, honest. I didn't do this." Malcolm put his head down on his free arm and sobbed.

Marvin looked back up at Harpy, anger and sadness in his eyes. "Uncuff him, Harpy. Now!" he demanded when Harpy was about to disagree. The sergeant took his key ring out of his pocket and unlocked the cuffs. Malcolm threw his arms around Marvin. "I didn't think," he said to his cousin. "I shouldn't have left him there."

"It's okay, Malcolm. This isn't your fault. Do you have the car keys?" he asked softly. Malcolm stood up and dug the car keys out of his jean pocket. He handed them to Marvin, who immediately threw them at Harpy. "Move the car up to the parking area before you leave, will you?" He turned back to his cousin. "Sit down. You'll stay here tonight. We'll go down tomorrow and talk to Mr. P about what happened, then we'll clear everything out of the cabin. I assume you got moved in today?"

"Yeah, we did. Sort of, at least. Manny found mice in the cupboards when he was looking through the kitchen to take stock of what was there. He didn't get some of his stuff unpacked. We headed into town thinking we'd get something to eat and pick up supplies but nothing's open here on Sundays. We went into Bellcom City and got something to eat then came back. We were going to go finish up in the cabin when I spotted something on the side of the road. I told Manny to pull over, but I'd taken my camera and flashlight out of the car when we were unloading. I jumped into the car and headed for the cabin. I wasn't thinking!" Malcolm wiped at his tears again. "I shouldn't have left him out there. I should have stopped to think about what I was doing."

"Okay, Malcolm. It'll all be okay." Marvin hugged him again, then looked back up to see Harpy still standing in the kitchen. "What the hell are you still doing here? Didn't I just tell you to leave?"

PACKART'S ORCHARD   149

"I suppose you're going to tell me that whatever killed that kid is the same thing that Paul died of?" Harpy said to Marvin. "You know that was a heart attack. This wasn't some monster bugs or anything."

"Yes, I am going to tell you that this is connected. I'm also going to look at my security feed to see what really went down tonight. Something the Windsmill Sheriff's Department seems unable or unwilling to do – investigate a suspicious death. It's just easier for you to blame the person that called 911 than to actually do something useful. Now get the hell out of my house and move that damned car before it causes an accident!"

Harpy glared back at Marvin. He didn't like being talked down to like that and he sure as hell was not used to taking orders from civilians, but this was not the time to take it up with Marvin. "Fine, Mr. Faulkon. I'll be clearing the scene and securing the vehicle. I will also leave your premises as you've requested. I will expect you and your cousin at the precinct tomorrow morning for further statements and questioning." He turned to leave the house, then turned back to Marvin. "Oh, and Mr. Faulkon. You may wish to find a lawyer before you come in tomorrow." The sergeant strolled out the door, closing it soundly as he left.

Marvin picked up the phone. This was not a call he wanted to make, but he had to do it before the damned sheriff's department screwed that up too. He dialled his uncle's number and waited for an answer.

"Hello?" Mo groggily answered. "Who the hell is calling at this time of night?"

"Hello, Uncle Mo. It's Marvin."

"Marvin. Oh hi! Did Becky have the baby? Is everyone okay?" Mo sounded wide awake and happy. It killed Marvin just a little bit to have to take that away from him too.

"Well, yes, Becky had a baby boy this afternoon at about four-thirty p.m. Everyone is healthy. But unfortunately, that's not what I'm calling about so late." Marvin took a deep breath. "There's been a situation." Marvin didn't know what else to call it.

"A situation?" Mo said, more alert than before. "What kind of situation?" he asked quietly.

"Uncle Mo, Manny was killed tonight," Marvin said quietly. "We don't know exactly what happened at this point, but the sheriff's department has taken him to the medical examiner's office in Windsmill. They've informed me that Malcolm and I have to report to them in the morning."

"What the hell happened? Where's Malcolm? What did he do now?" Mo was up and pacing the floor. Marvin could hear Agnes in the background asking what was happening.

"Malcolm is right here with me Uncle. He didn't do anything wrong. The cops were being assholes, is all." Marvin was frustrated all over again. What a messed-up, crazy situation this was.

"I'm coming out there right now. I want to talk to Malcolm. I want to know what's going on over there," Mo said as he walked into the closet to get some clothes on.

"There's no use you coming here tonight. Everyone is tired and stressed and the sheriff's office and the coroner's office aren't going to tell anyone anything tonight anyway. I shouldn't have called you tonight, but I wanted you to hear this from me and not those screwed-up idiots from town."

Marvin could hear Mo breathe in deeply. "Malcolm's alright, though, right?" he asked softly.

"Malcolm is right here beside me. He's obviously very upset and visibly shaken. He's the one that found Manny. It's been a hell of a day, Mo. Let's try to get some rest and we'll talk in the morning." Marvin was so tired now. This should have been the happiest day of his life and instead it was one of the saddest. How could he tell Becky about all of this when he picked her up tomorrow? This was all so screwed up. He said goodnight to his uncle and hung up the phone.

"How about a beer?" he asked Malcolm and pulled open the fridge.

The next day, Marvin and Malcolm hopped into Marvin's work truck and headed over to talk to Mr. P. Marvin wasn't exactly sure what he was going to tell him about what happened to Manny, because he really didn't know. And Malcolm didn't look like he'd slept at all last night, so he was in no shape to answer any questions.

"Hey, Marv." Darren waved at him. "Where are those cousins of yours? They didn't show up for breakfast and they aren't in their cabin." Just as he finished his sentence, he spotted the very tall young man that looked a lot like Marvin, except bigger.

"Oh, hi!" Darren waved at him. "Everything all right?" he inquired when he realized the young man looked like he was going to burst into tears.

"No, sir. Nothing is okay." Malcolm hung his head.

"It's okay, Malcolm. Get back into the truck. I'll talk to Darren and his dad, and then we'll go into town and see what the police have to say." Marvin

PACKART'S ORCHARD   151

turned away from his cousin and headed toward the steps where Darren was standing. They went into the house office and Darren handed him a hot cup of coffee.

"You look like you could use this," Darren said as he offered the cup to Marvin. "What's going on, anyway?"

"Manny was killed last night." Marvin took a tentative sip of the hot coffee.

"Killed? What are you talking about? At the cabin here at the orchard?"

"No, not exactly. Malcolm left him at the rest area by our driveway. I'm not exactly sure what went down, but Malcolm came over here to get something he'd left at the cabin and before he got back to the rest area, Manny had started to walk up to my place. Malcolm found him on the side of the road." Marvin set the coffee down on the office desk. "We'll be back later to clear the stuff out of the cabin. Malcolm's in no shape mentally to do anything right now, let alone start a whole new job out here."

"Understood," Darren said. "I'll let Dad know what's happening and talk to him about what, if anything, we can do to help you with all of this."

"Thanks, Darren, I appreciate it. I'm really sorry for leaving you hanging like this." Marvin patted Darren on his back and walked back toward the door. "Oh, by the way, you can tell Amy that Becky had the baby yesterday afternoon. A big, tall baby boy." Marvin smiled at the thought of his beautiful son. What a shitty way to start his life with all this going on in the family.

"Congrats! Man. I'll let her and Mom know right away. And Marv," Darren looked over at his friend, "I'm really sorry for your loss. That boy out in your truck is going to need some support in the next while. I hope your family can give it to him."

"Yeah, me too." Marvin waved at Darren and headed down the steps. Just as he was getting into his truck, he heard Albert calling after him. He turned to see Albert coming down the steps two at a time and rushing over toward Marvin.

"Hey Marvin," Albert said. "What's this about one of those boys being dead?"

"That's right. Manny was found dead on his way to my place last night. I'm not sure of all the details, but if there's anything to tell after I get back from the sheriff's office today, I'll be sure to let you know."

"Sorry about all this. Those two boys seemed like nice folks," Albert said. "The one was real curious, you know. Asked a lot of questions and looked around at where he was. The other one was real quiet like. Kind of the thinker

152   WENDY SCOTT-ETTINGER

of the two. Got down to business unpacking the car while the other stood and talked to me and Red."

"Yes, Manny was a lot quieter than Malcolm. He was the thinker and Malcolm does stuff and then thinks about it afterward." Marvin turned back toward the truck. "I really have to get into town now," he said as he opened the truck door. "We'll be back to clean out of the boys' personal belonging from the cabin after we're done." He closed the door without waiting for Albert to respond. He put the truck in gear and headed back out to the highway.

Malcolm hung his head and didn't say a word all the way into town. When Marvin parked his truck outside the sheriff's office, he noticed a ruckus just outside the door. He sat and watched for awhile, trying to figure out if he wanted to get into the fray of it or wait until it was over. It appeared as if two police officers and a guy in a coroner's uniform were arguing with the sheriff about something. When Marvin looked closer, he realized that, on the other side of the two officers, was his Uncle Mo. "Oh shit, now what?" Marvin said as he climbed out of the truck. "You might want to stay here for a bit." He pointed at Malcolm as he closed his door, then locked the truck up.

Malcolm looked out the window for the first time, and the first person he spotted was his dad. "What the hell is he getting us into now?" Malcolm said out loud. He went to open the door and realized Marvin had locked him in. "The hell with this!" he said as he pulled open the lock and got out. "Dad?" he called across the parking area, "You okay?"

"Malcolm, stay out of this," Mo answered without looking at his son. If he looked at him now, he'd break down and that wasn't going to help anyone. He turned back to the sheriff, who was standing at the top of the steps with his arms crossed in front of him and his feet shoulder width apart. Typical cop stance, Mo thought as he scowled at the man. "We are taking my boy to a real police department. One that will actually look into what really happened to him. No one is going to accuse my sons of being drug users, you hear me!" Mo pointed his finger at the man. "No one!"

Malcolm was confused. What were they talking about? But he didn't say anything and stood back like his father had requested. *Who was accusing them of using drugs?* Malcolm wondered. Marvin walked back and stood beside Malcolm. They looked at each other, then took the same stance as the sheriff; arms crossed and feet apart. Good luck getting through them if it came to it. After a few minutes of arguing and huffing at each other, it became real quiet.

PACKART'S ORCHARD   153

Dr. Redford came out of the office door with a stack of papers in his hand. He handed the stack to the coroner's office rep.

"Here you go, John. Sorry for the wait. If you drive around to the back of the building, I'll help you load the body into the van."

"Thanks, Tony. Are these just the release papers, or do you have a preliminary for me to look at?"

"There's a very rough start to my report. After I got your call, I decided against doing the full autopsy we discussed last night. The tox screen hasn't come back from the lab yet, although I did a quick look last night and my findings are there. I'll have the lab forward the results directly to you."

"Thanks again, Tony. We'll talk later when we've all had a chance to calm down."

Dr. Redford put his hand on the sheriff's shoulder. "It's not worth the heart attack, Hartford," he said and then opened the door and waved at the other officers to come on in. The two men went into the office, closing the door behind them.

"I guess we won't be going in after all," Marvin said to Malcolm as the crowd started to disperse and Uncle Mo headed in their direction.

Malcolm braced himself for the onslaught of angry questions and accusations he was expecting from his father. Instead, Mo walked right up to him, hugging him so tight Malcolm could hardly breathe, and started to cry.

MARVIN DROVE INTO BELLCOM CITY TO PICK up Becky. What the hell was he going to tell her? She'd just given him the most incredible baby boy, and he was giving her a house full of grieving relatives. This was not going to be the homecoming she was expecting. Maybe he should offer to drop her off with Mary, or better yet with Jenny and AJ in Allensville. As far away from all of this as he could get her. Maybe her and the baby could go visit her mother on the coast for a while. Just until they got all this craziness sorted out and it was quiet again.

Marvin pulled into the parking lot at the hospital and pulled the pay ticket out of the machine. He usually just parked across the street at the mall and walked over, but Becky and the baby probably didn't feel like a lot of exercise just now. He pulled into an oversized spot and got out.

He didn't feel like the happy father who should be bouncing up the steps and into the elevator in high spirits. He dragged his butt into the hospital. The more he thought about what he had to talk to Becky about, the worse he

154   WENDY SCOTT-ETTINGER

felt. He rounded the corner into the maternity ward waiting area, expecting to have to ask the nurse what room Becky was in. Instead, there sat Becky, fully dressed and holding a bundle of blue blankets.

"It's about time you got here." She smiled up and started to stand before sitting back down again quickly. "What's wrong?" Becky asked him.

"Everything. Nothing. I don't know," Marvin stammered. "I'll tell you in the truck."

"Did you at least remember the car seat?" she asked. "They won't let us leave without it."

"Shit, it's in the truck." Marvin headed for the door and back outside. A few minutes later he returned with the box with the car seat in it.

"We have to set it up and put Martin Bentley into it and secure it or we can't leave" Becky handed Marvin the baby. "Here, hold him and I'll do it," she said with a huff.

Marvin held the baby out away from his body and stared at it. A nurse came over and gently rearranged the baby in Marvin's arms, pushing him closer to Marvin's chest. "Like this," the nurse said. "You need to support his back and neck until he gets strong enough to hold it up on his own."

Marvin tried to smile at the nurse, but he was afraid it was coming out as a grimace. "Thank you," he said and then watched as his wife put the baby seat together. Becky stood up and set the carrier on a chair. She looked around and finally asked the nurse if there was somewhere she could leave the box and packaging the seat had just come out of. The nurse looked inside the box, handed Marvin a strap that had been left in the bottom, and gave Becky the instruction manual. She took the box and disappeared.

"Marvin, for heaven sakes." Becky took the baby and laid him gently into the seat. She buckled him in and made sure he was covered before looking back at her husband. "What is going on with you?"

Marvin sat down beside the car seat, making sure it was secure on the chair and wouldn't fall down. He picked it up and set it on the floor in front of him and stared at the baby. He was so beautiful! Marvin thought. "He looks just like his mother," he said out loud.

"Marvin." Becky sat down awkwardly on a chair beside her husband. "You're acting very strange. Please tell me what's going on."

Marvin stared into her face. "I'm so sorry, Becky. It's just so crazy. Everything is just so crazy right now."

PACKART'S ORCHARD   155

Becky took his face with her hands and stared into his eyes. "Marvin, please tell me what you are talking about." And he did. He told her about getting home to the police in the house. He told her about Manny being killed in the driveway coming up to their place. He told her how Malcolm had found his brother, and how Harpy blamed him for the murder. He told her about Mo taking the body out of the Windsmill morgue and the investigation away from the sheriff's department. He told her everything. When he was done, he looked over at her as she stared at the baby on the floor. "I'm so sorry, Beck. This should be your time, your happy time with your baby, and I've got a house full of relatives and a murder investigation going on at the house. I don't know what to do." He wiped at the tears that had trickled down his cheeks.

Becky reached over and hugged him. "We'll get through this together, Marv. We always do. Now take me home so I can put my baby in his own crib, and we can deal with all this crazy together."

"You sure, Beck? I can take you someplace else until this thing blows over. Maybe to Jenny and AJ's place, or out to the coast to visit your family. You don't need all the extra stress while trying to deal with a new baby." Marvin looked at her with worried eyes.

"We'll deal with this together, Marvin. Now please, take me home." Becky stood up and picked up her suitcase. "Can you carry the baby in his seat?" she asked as she walked over to the nurse's station to sign off her formal release papers.

"Heading home, Mrs. Faulkon?" the nurse asked as she came up to the counter. She leaned closer to Becky and whispered quietly, "Is everything alright? Your husband looks very upset."

"Everything will be just fine." Becky smiled at the nurse. "Just a bit of family problems that we'll need to deal with when we get home. Nothing we can't handle."

CHAPTER 19

MARVIN PAUSED AND BLINKED RAPIDLY, AS IF to bring himself out of a trance. He looked over at David. "I'll take that coffee now, if you don't mind. My throat is a little dry." Marvin stood to stretch his back while David reached over and paused the recording on his phone.

"Cream or sugar?" David asked as he poured coffee into a mug.

"Just a touch of sugar, please," Marvin responded.

David handed him the coffee and sat back down. "Would you like to continue with telling me about Malcolm or have you had enough for today?" David hoped he'd continue but wasn't going to push him. Marvin had gone through a lot in the last few days, and David understood the emotional turmoil telling these past stories were taking on everyone.

"No, I'm good to get back to it. I think I was getting sidetracked with Becky and the baby. It's part of the story, but not completely relevant," Marvin said apologetically. "Can I use your phone for a minute? I just need to call Becky and let her know I'll be later than expected. Then, if you have any questions before I get to part two of this story, we can go from there."

"Sure, go ahead and use the office phone. You really should start remembering to carry your cell." David chuckled at him and walked back to his apartment to give Marvin and Becky a minute to talk. He had a dozen or more questions brewing in his head, but the second part may answer some of them, so he hoped they could just get back to it. After a few minutes he re-entered the office area. David reached over and turned the recording back on. "You ready to get back at it?" he asked Marvin.

Marvin took a deep breath. "Now, where were we?" He looked back down at the picture of Malcolm and Manny. "Oh, yes, just about the time Becky

157

and I walked into the house to Mo and Malcolm arguing." He shook his head and continued …

MALCOLM'S STORY — APRIL 1990:

"Malcolm, don't be ridiculous! You are not staying here in Windsmill, and you're in no condition to be going to work in the orchards right now!" Mo was pacing back and forth between the front door of Marvin and Becky's house and the kitchen, where Malcolm had sat down. "You are coming home with me and that's final!"

"No, I'm not, Dad." Malcolm stood up and glared at his father. "First of all, I'm not a kid anymore and you can't order me to do anything! Secondly, the Carson P.D. will need someone to keep a lookout around here in case the monster that killed Manny is still hanging around. I have a few things I want to look into myself before this thing is finished, and I can't do that with you breathing down my neck."

Mo turned to pace back to the front door when he saw Becky and Marvin enter their home. "Awe, the baby is here," Mo smiled at them, "with his beautiful mother!" Mo reached down and kissed Becky's forehead. "Awe, let me help you with all that." He reached over and took the car seat out of Marvin's hand.

Malcolm walked into the front room. "Oh, thank god! Level heads have arrived!" He smiled at Marvin and hugged Becky tight. "How's the little mother feeling?" he asked with a smile.

"I'm fine. Sounds like the two of you are having a little disagreement about something, though." She looked from father to son and back again. She raised her eyebrows at them. "And what does Aunt Agnes say about all this?"

"She doesn't know," they both said together. "And let's keep it that way!" Mo added.

"I need to get baby changed and fed and put back down. I'll be down as soon as I'm finished. Marvin," she looked over her shoulder, "can you please bring the baby and my suitcase up to our room for me?"

Marvin picked up the suitcase and reached over for the car seat. "Awe, do you have to take him?" Mo asked as Marvin reached down to pick him up.

"Becky says she needs him upstairs, so yes I have to take him," Marvin reminded him. "I'm sure you'll see him again very soon."

Mo stood back up and headed back into the kitchen. "I'll put on some coffee and you and I can have a little talk," Mo said to Marvin. "Maybe you can talk some sense into him."

Marvin ignored his uncle and headed up the stairs with the baby. After Becky had a shower and Marvin figured out how to change his first diaper, he handed the baby back to his mother and stated that he needed to get back down to whatever Uncle Mo and Malcolm were arguing about now. He shut the door before Becky could talk him out of it and headed down the stairs.

"Malcolm, you are not staying here!" Mo said for the hundredth time.

Malcolm headed for the front door. "Tell Marvin I'm going to go back over to the Packarts' place. I'm going to let Mr. Packart know that I'd still like to work at the orchard if he'll have me. My stuff is still in the cabin, so I'll just stay there the night and work in the morning." Malcolm opened the door to leave.

"Hey, Malcolm, hold up a minute will you," Marvin said as he came down the stairs. "Let's make something to eat first, then I'll go with you to the Packarts' place." He looked over at Mo, who just held up his hands in frustration and turned back into the kitchen.

Malcolm looked at his cousin. "You sure you want to get into the middle of all of this?" he asked as he closed the front door again. "You have your plate full with your own stuff right now. You don't need Dad's crap too."

"I know Uncle Mo has a temper sometimes, but he is only trying to protect you. You do get that, right?" Marvin put his arm over Malcolm's shoulders and walked him into the kitchen. "Sit down, have a coffee or beer or something and relax. I'll scare up some food and we can all sit down like the civilized people we are."

Marvin looked over at his uncle. "What would you like to drink, Uncle?" he asked as he steered Malcolm to the far side of the table.

"Nothing. I'm fine. I don't need anything." Mo pouted at his nephew.

"Sit down anyway," Marvin instructed as he reached into the fridge and set three cold beer on the table. "Open these will you, Malcolm?"

Malcolm opened the beer and Marvin made soup and sandwiches. The two men hadn't said a word to each other the whole time Marvin was working in the kitchen. They sat across from each other and glared, but neither spoke. They both managed to finish their beer, though.

"Okay," Marvin started as he sat down between the two men. "Have a sandwich and some soup. Here's more beer if either of you want it." Marvin grabbed the beer Malcolm had opened for him earlier. "That sure does taste good," he said, looking at them and then reaching for his own sandwich.

The two men each waited for the other to start first. When neither of them took any food and didn't say anything, Marvin let his frustrations show. "Oh, for Christ's sake, you two are acting like children!" Marvin reached over and ladled soup into each of their bowls. He handed them each a sandwich and then asked if he needed to crush their soup crackers too!

"No, that's good thank you," Malcolm said quietly.

"I'm fine too," Mo agreed.

"Okay, so what's this about you staying to work at the orchard?" he asked Malcolm in what he hoped was a nonconfrontational tone.

Malcolm looked across the table at his father, then looked at Marvin, and back at his father again. "Okay, let's start there." He took a deep breath. This was usually when his father would jump in, but he didn't. "I think it would be a good idea for me to stay here in Windsmill for awhile. I think I could help the Carson P.D. with whatever information they might need. I know that the Windsmill Sheriff's Department is not going to be cooperative after what went down this morning, and I just think having a man here to help out would be a good idea."

"Okay, sounds reasonable," Marvin said, "but what makes you think the Carson Police are going to let you help them?"

"Exactly!" Mo pounded his fist on the table and went to stand up.

"Hold it a minute, Uncle Mo." Marvin lifted his hand in a motion for the older man to sit back down. "I want to hear Malcolm's response first, please."

Mo sat back in his chair with his arms crossed like an insolent child. Malcolm stared at his cousin. He didn't think anyone other than his own mother had ever spoken to his father like that before. "Really?" he said quietly.

"Yes, really." Marvin looked at Malcolm intently. "So?"

"Well, I figured you and I could go through the security tapes from last night and see what, if anything, is there. If there's any indication of what happened to Manny, I could take a copy into the Carson station and give it to them. I could tell them what I know about what happened last night and then offer to look out for any signs from here. They'd know I was here and willing to cooperate and they could use me as their eyes and ears. I'm sure Mr. Packart could use the extra hands around the orchard, and if I stay at the cabin, it will give me a chance to look around a bit." Malcolm took a deep breath and waited for the onslaught of 'how-stupids' and 'you-can't-do-its'

160   WENDY SCOTT-ETTINGER

but none came. He looked at his father and then over to Marvin. "So?" he asked tentatively. "What do you think, Marvin?"

"I think it all sounds good from this end. What do you think, Uncle?" Marvin asked. He waited for Uncle Mo to huff and puff and tell Malcolm it wasn't safe, but it didn't come. "Well?"

Mo looked at his son. "You really think you can make a difference with all this mess?" he asked Malcolm.

"Yes, I really do," Malcolm said sincerely.

"And if the Carson P.D. tells you to stay out of it? What then?" Mo asked reasonably.

"If they tell me they don't need my help, or if Mr. Packart tells me to pack up and leave, I come back home," Malcolm conceded.

"Okay then," Mo said. He hadn't realized how hungry he was until now. "This is really good soup, Marvin," he said as he took the last spoonful and had a bite of his sandwich.

Malcolm opened up a beer and took a big sip. "This really is good," he said to Marvin as he finished up his soup and sandwich. "I don't suppose you have any dessert, do you?" He grinned at his cousin.

"I have chocolate chip cookies that one of Becky's friends brought over the other day. Will that work?" he asked as he stood to get them out of the cupboard.

"Sounds delicious!" Malcolm smiled widely.

After they'd finished their meal and cleaned up the kitchen together, Marvin showed them into a small room off the back door mudroom. "This used to be a storage closet, but I had the security company put all the equipment in here," he explained as they entered the cramped room. "It's the latest technology!" He sat down in front of the computer screen and started to scan the camera videos for the day before. "Here we go," Marvin said to the men behind him as he started the feed. "This is from about 8:25 p.m. last night; if you watch closely, you'll see Manny setting off the camera as he starts up the driveway."

"So about five minutes after I went back to the cabin," Malcolm said matter-of-factly.

"That's funny …" Marvin squinted at the screen in front of him. "How come the lights didn't go on?"

"Lights?" Mo asked curiously.

"Yeah. I had the security people put up motion detection lights about every hundred feet going up and down the drive. They didn't come on."

Marvin watched some more, and he saw his cousin turn back toward the highway and started waving his arms. "What is that, there?" He pointed at the screen. "Just a minute, let me back that up a bit." He did so, then stopped the feed. "There, see?" He pointed again.

Malcolm and Mo leaned into the screen and squinted at it. "There's definitely something, but I can't make it out. What the hell?"

"I don't see anything, what are you looking at?" Mo leaned in closer.

"There." Marvin and Malcolm pointed at the screen together. "In the bushes just down from where Manny is standing. It looks like something or someone is standing there," Malcolm said to his father. To Marvin, he said "Continue the feed, let's see what happens." They watched the video as Manny waved his arms around in front of him. They could clearly see what looked like a bird or large bug in front of him, but it didn't look real somehow. Then they watched as Manny turned back toward the house and fell to his knees. His face was covered in a white powder and the bird, or whatever it was, was gone.

Mo gasped and put his hand up to his mouth. He backed out of the room. "Oh god, oh god," he said. Malcolm turned around to grab his father as he slid to the floor and started to sob.

Marvin stopped the video feed and hit a few buttons to make a copy of the video from 8:15 p.m. until he had gotten home around 10:30 p.m. He saved it to a disc and popped it out of the machine. He put a label on it and marked the date, times, and location on the front. He handed it to Malcolm as he came out of the security room. "I'm so sorry, Uncle Mo, I wasn't thinking. Both Malcolm and I had an inkling of what happened last night, so it wasn't as big a shock to us. I'm sorry."

The two young men helped Mo to his feet and took him back to the kitchen. Marvin pulled out a bottle of bourbon from a cupboard. He poured a small amount into a tumbler glass and handed it to Mo. "Here, drink this. Then I'll show you to the spare room and you can lay down for awhile. Do you want to phone Agnes now?"

"Thank you." Mo reached for the tumbler and took a deep swallow. "Yes, I will call Agnes and let her know what's going on. And then I'd like to lay down for awhile." He reached over to the phone on the counter beside him and dialed his home number. As he started talking to his wife, Malcolm and Marvin went into the living room.

"Have a seat for a minute, I'm just going to go up and let Becky know that you and I are going over to Packart's place for a bit. I'll show your dad upstairs before we leave." Marvin took the steps two at a time and headed to the end of the hall. When he opened the door, his wife was lying on the bed with the baby wrapped in her arms. They were both sound asleep. He quietly put a blanket over them and closed the door again. He went back downstairs, wrote a note for Becky, and left it in the kitchen in 'their spot' then asked Mo if he was ready to lie down for a bit. Mo nodded and followed Marvin back up the stairs. "There's a few blankets and comforters in the closet, and a couple of extra pillows if you need them. You know where the bathroom up here is. Malcolm and I will be back in about an hour, I think. Mr. P likes to talk when he gets the chance."

Mo nodded again but didn't say anything. Marvin walked out of the room and closed the door behind him.

"You ready to go talk to Mr. P?'" Marvin asked Malcolm as he got to the bottom of the stairs. He watched Malcolm as he stared at some family pictures on the mantel.

"Yeah, sure. Let's get it over with," Malcolm replied as he turned around to face his cousin. "Do you think he'll let me come back?" he asked. He wasn't so sure about his plan now that he was able to put it into place. What if it didn't go as he'd planned in his head?

"Only one way to find out," Marvin said as he opened the front door and proceeded down the porch stairs. "Let's go talk to him. I'm sure he's dying to find out what went down today at the police station anyway." Marvin smiled back at Malcolm as he unlocked his truck. "Remind me to check those lights when we get back," he said mostly to himself. They climbed into the truck and headed toward the highway.

Five minutes later they were driving up to the parking area in front of Packart's mansion. Mr. Packart and Darren were standing on the porch at the top of the stairs. As they saw Marvin and Malcolm get out of the truck, they came down to greet them.

"How are you doing, young man?" Mr. Packart asked Malcolm as he shook his hand with one hand and squeezed his shoulder with the other.

"I'm doing okay, I guess," Malcolm said, looking down at the ground. "It's been a long, hard day."

"I can't imagine," Albert said as he turned toward Marvin to greet him as well. "Hell of a thing, this whole mess," he said as they shook hands.

PACKART'S ORCHARD   163

"Yes, it is that," Marvin responded. He turned to look at his friend. "Is there somewhere we can sit down and have a talk?" he asked Darren.

"Sure. Mom put on some coffee. I think we have some cold drinks too, if you'd rather. We can sit in the kitchen and chat without being bothered." He looked back at Marvin. "Mom took Amy and the babies out to do some shopping in the city, so they'll be gone for awhile." Darren laughed at the thought of his mother and his wife buying up all the baby stuff in Bellcom. "Hopefully they leave enough for you and Becky when you get a chance to shop for that baby boy of yours."

"That would be nice." Marvin smiled as they ascended the steps into the mansion and walked the long hallway to the kitchen. He'd made sure to walk between Malcolm and Albert so they didn't get waylaid with Albert's talking.

After more than an hour and a half, they finally got everything all sorted out. Mr. Packart agreed that Malcolm could stay on as a crew member. He also agreed that for the next week, Malcolm could take as much time as he needed to talk to the police, both here and in Carson, and that he could have the day of the funeral off to be with his family. He asked Malcolm if he was sure he wanted to stay in the cabin by himself a number of times throughout their discussion, and Malcolm finally conceded that if he found it too difficult to be there by himself, he'd move up with Becky and Marvin. He really hoped he didn't have to do that, but they'd play it by ear.

"Thank you, Mr. Packart. I really appreciate all this. I'll be a good worker for you, I promise." Malcolm shook his hand as they went to leave the house.

"I'm sure you will be." Albert smiled at the boy. "Please let Darren know when you get back from Carson tomorrow. He'll be able to set everything in motion as far as the work goes. We'll see you tomorrow some time." Albert waved at them and headed back into the house.

"I'll be here when you get here tomorrow, Malcolm." Darren shook his hand again. "I'm sure everything will work out for the best," he added. "Will you be staying in the cabin tonight?"

"Yes, I think so. I'll have supper up with Dad and Marvin, then come back down and get settled into the cabin properly," Malcolm responded.

Darren nodded. "We'll talk soon." He waved at Marvin. "I'm sure Amy will want to see that baby of yours after everything settles down a bit."

"Of course. And I'm sure Becky will want to show him off too." Marvin waved back at him. "We'll set something up, for sure."

164   WENDY SCOTT-ETTINGER

As they were heading back to Marvin's, Malcolm remembered that Sergeant Harper hadn't given him back his car keys. "Hey, Marv, can we drive into town and see if that sergeant is around? I need my car keys if I'm going to go back to the cabin tonight. I'm not crazy about having to walk around in the dark, at least not until I get my bearings back."

Marvin drove past his driveway and headed directly to the sheriff's office. "I'll come in with you," he said to Malcolm as they got out of the truck. "I don't trust any of them to be civil right now."

As it turned out, the young rookie at the counter was more than pleasant. He searched around and found the keys in question, asked Malcolm to sign for them to ensure they were properly returned, and told the men to have a good evening.

"Wow!" Malcolm smiled at his cousin as they descended the stairs from the sheriff's department. "That was almost too easy."

"Yeah, I was thinking the same thing. Do you suppose Harpy got a talking-to from the sheriff over what went down last night and again this morning? That whole scene can't be good for PR." Marvin laughed as he got back into his truck. He looked at his watch and realized it was almost suppertime already. "How about we splurge and get some take-out from Don's Place to take home with us?" he asked Malcolm as they headed toward Main Street.

AS THEY ENTERED THE HOUSE, THEY SAW Mo sitting on the couch in the living room. The TV was on but no one was watching it. Mo was sitting in the big easy-boy chair holding the baby. He made cooing sounds and funny faces and Marty stared up at him. "Where's Becky?" Marvin asked as he kicked off his shoes.

"In the kitchen, I think," he said without looking up at the men.

"Did you sleep at all this afternoon?" Marvin asked his uncle.

"Oh, I did have a nice little sleep. Then I heard the baby crying and thought I should investigate. Becky told me to go on down and put on some coffee while she fed this wonderful little boy. Then I got to hold him." Mo smiled lovingly at the baby.

"A baby seems to be the best medicine to kill the sad," Becky said as she entered the living room and reached up to kiss her husband. "What is that wonderful aroma I'm smelling?" she asked, looking down at the bags in Marvin's and Malcolm's hands.

PACKART'S ORCHARD   165

"Supper," Marvin said, as he led his family into the kitchen. Becky took the baby and Mo helped Marvin set the table, while Malcolm pulled all the food out of the bags. *A little normalcy in the middle of hell*, Marvin thought as he sat down with his family to break bread.

The next couple of days seemed to fly by. Malcolm had gone back to the cabin after dinner that night and got settled in. Mo left to drive back to Carson about the same time as Malcolm had. The two men had hugged each other and promised to stay in touch with anything that might come up as they parted ways.

"They really are so much alike, aren't they?" Becky commented to Marvin as they drove away. They went into the house and spent the evening cooing and staring at the baby.

"He really is good medicine for what ails you," Marvin said, as they tried to figure out what their own normal was going to look like now.

"SO, WHAT DID THE CARSON POLICE HAVE to say to you this morning?" Darren asked Malcolm as they walked from the cabins into the orchard.

"Not much." Malcolm shrugged. "They thanked me for giving them the disc from the security feed and said they'd opened a file." He hung his head as they walked. He really wasn't in much of a mood to work today, but he'd promised he'd do his best and that's what he was going to try to do. "They wouldn't tell me anything about the autopsy or the tox screen, but they sure asked a lot of questions about our trip to Bellcom City; why we went up there and what we'd done once we got there. I hope I didn't get that bartender into any trouble."

Darren chuckled. "Those pop-up Sunday bars have been in and around the college for years. I don't think the police really care about them most of the time. They may ask around a bit and see if anything weird went down, well, weirder than normal, anyway. That's about all that will come of it unless they find drugs or something illegal." Darren looked over at Malcolm for the first time since he'd started walking the orchard. "You sure you're okay to work today?"

"Yeah, I'll be okay. Once I have something different to think about, I'll be fine." Malcolm looked over at Darren and tried to smile. "What is that?" he asked as they got closer.

"That's the treehouse." Darren smiled. "At least, that's what it was when I left for college. When I got back, my best friend and the foreman for the orchard, turned it into his office. Cool, isn't it?"

"Cool doesn't even cover it," Malcolm said as he tried to take in the house in the trees. "That's not what I'd call a treehouse. It's more like an apartment in the trees! Manny would have loved this!" Malcolm stopped himself and shook his head.

"Well, now it's my office," Darren said as he pulled his key ring out of his pocket and unlocked the office door. His face fell as he thought of the day the locksmith came to put locks on all the outbuildings, including this one. It was the day after Paul had been found in the orchard. It was the last thing Paul ever did for them, before ...

He turned back to Malcolm. "Come on in, I'll show you the drawings of what we need to have happen before the rest of the crew gets here, then I'll walk you around to the mansion so you can meet Mom, I mean, Mrs. Packart. She has some prep work for you today in her garden."

"Garden?" Malcolm asked. "I'm not much for planting flowers and such."

"Oh, mom's garden is much more than some posies." Darren smiled at him. "You and Red will be helping her rototill the whole acre and get the fertilizer spread, and the seed rows planted, and whatever else it is she gets done to it this time of year. I think your cousin is coming down in the next day or two to show everyone how the sprinkler system he installed works too."

"Okay, sounds like more than a garden then." Malcolm smiled. "That should keep me busy for a while."

They went over all the plans for the changes that Paul had drawn up for the cabins, the watermill, and even some possible uses for the old homestead, although Darren didn't think his dad would actually let anyone over there let alone do anything to the property. Malcolm soaked it all in. He asked questions about Paul and what had happened to him. He asked about why Mr. P was so against anyone asking about, let alone doing, anything with the old homestead. He had a long talk about all the old pictures and architectural drawings on the walls. Malcolm told Darren that Manny had planned on becoming an architect and that cooled the conversation even further.

"Wow! Look at the time," Darren said as he looked quickly at his watch. "We better get you over to the garden before Mom thinks we've both gone AWOL."

PACKART'S ORCHARD   167

Mrs. Packart introduced herself to Malcolm and he said hello to Red again. They got to work, each with their own rototiller pulled by one of the carts.

Albert came out of the mansion and stood, surveying the progress the two men had made with the garden area. At this rate, they'd have it finished before the week was over, and then he'd have to make a decision on the changes Darren was pushing for. He looked up in the sky. A beautiful, cloudless day, and the spring was turning into summer more quickly than in the past. It was hot out here. He carried the large pitcher of water over to the men and handed them each a glass. "Amelia asked me to bring this out to you all," Albert said to them. "And to remind you that dinner will be served in about half an hour. You might want to take a cart back to your cabins and wash up before we eat."

Both men drank the water quickly. Red said he'd be passing on dinner tonight as he had other plans but handed the keys to the cart he usually drove to Malcolm. Malcolm took them eagerly and thanked Mr. P for the water. He asked if they should be putting any of the equipment or tools away before they left and was told to leave them where they sat, as they'd just need them all in the morning anyway.

Malcolm figured he'd drive to the cabin, shower, change, come back for dinner, and maybe head into town and see if everything closed up early every day or if he could talk to some of the locals for a bit. He was able to do the first part of his plan, but when he drove back to the cabin, he found himself too tired after a hard days' work do think about anything else. He sat down, turned on the old TV, and promptly fell asleep. He woke with a start when he heard banging coming from outside. He looked out the front window to see Red standing on his porch, pounding on the door.

Malcolm opened the door. "Sorry to bother ya so late. But you got my keys and I kinn't get into me cabin," Red said.

"Oh sorry, I didn't realize." Malcolm dug into his pocket and handed the keys to Red, who took them with a swipe,

"I'll see you in the morn then," Red said. "You can catch a ride with me, or you can walk, whichever ya like." Before Malcolm could ask what time he'd be leaving, Red opened his own cabin door and closed it again.

"Okay, then." Malcolm turned the TV and all the lights off. He locked the cabin door and headed for his room. He hadn't packed Manny's stuff up yet and didn't have the heart to sleep in the big room at the front of the cabin. He just couldn't do it. He'd maybe take all Manny's stuff up to Mom on the weekend.

He went to bed and tossed most of the night. The sleep he did have was full of nightmares and he found himself waking up in a sweat, terrified of the monsters in the trees. He'd really need to find some time to figure out what those are he thought to himself as he rolled out of bed and headed for the shower again. He'd be the cleanest worker in these parts if he showered 2 and 3 times every day.

He was just coming out of the cabin when Red started the golf cart. "About time you got out here. I was just about to leave without ya." Red said as he stopped the cart just long enough to let Malcolm jump in, then they were off. It was going to be another hot and hardworking day.

CHAPTER 20

WEDNESDAY AFTERNOON, MARVIN PULLED HIS WORK TRUCK into the mansion parking lot. He watched Malcolm and Red as they worked seeding the rows and planted god-only-knows what in each one. They hoed, seeded and covered each them, then marked the end of each row with a seed box with the name of the fruit or vegetable. They seemed to have a real rhythm going, so Marvin didn't interrupt. He just watched.

"I've never seen Red work so well with anyone before," Albert said as he came up beside Marvin, startling him out of his own thoughts.

"Good afternoon, Mr. P," Marvin responded. "They look like they've got it worked out."

"Sure does, doesn't it," Darren responded as he walked over and stood beside his friend. "Hate to interrupt all that good work." They chuckled.

"Is Mrs. P around? She wanted me to show her and the crew how to use the sprinkler system I installed with the irrigation pumps. Said I'd come out but wasn't sure when she wanted to do that. I was in the neighbourhood, so thought I'd come over and see how Malcolm was holding up."

"Between you and me, we are the neighbourhood!" Darren laughed. "How's Becky and the baby doing?"

"Good. Tired. Grumpy, both of them. But good." Marvin yawned. "We'll get into a routine soon, I'm sure."

Darren laughed again. "Well, if you do, you'll have to share your secret!" He looked over at Marvin as his face dropped. "We'll all work it out eventually." Darren patted Marvin on the back. "At least that's what Dad tells me."

Amelia came out of the house and rang a large bell. The two men stopped working and pulled off their gloves. They looked around and realized they had an audience. Amelia held up a large pitcher of what looked like lemon water and a plate of baking. "Come on in for a bit. Marvin is here to show us how to use the sprinkler system and give us any special instructions he might have for us. I've baked some apple cookies and a crumble with some ice cream. We can have a sit down for a while."

Both men sauntered over to the table Mrs. P had set up beside the house. There was a big apple tree on the far side that provided shade and it was covered in blooms now, so it filled the air with fragrance.

"Come on over, I'll see if Amelia has enough for all of us." Albert smiled as they joined Red and Malcolm.

After they were done with their break, Marvin showed them how the sprinkler system was turned on and off, how they could roll the sprinklers themselves from row to row using the remote that was in the shed, and how to change the water pressure, direction, and stream using the same remote. When he'd finished answering all of Mr. and Mrs. P's questions about the system, he asked Malcom if he could talk to him before he got back at his seeding. They walked to the far side of the mansion, away from the others.

"I've been meaning to come see how you're doing." Marvin looked pointedly at Malcolm to make sure his cousin was okay. "How'd it go with Carson P.D. on Monday?"

"Not as good as I'd expected. I was hoping they might come out this way and want more information, not that I'd have any, but you know." Malcolm shrugged.

"Yeah. Did they say anything about the security disc?"

"No. Just thanked me for dropping it off and coming in to talk to them. Asked me a lot of questions about that night, but no information from them." Malcolm kicked at a lump of grass at his feet. "I'm thinking of heading up there after work tonight. Maybe I can bow out of dinner here and head up right away. See if they can tell me anymore about it. I'll stop in and see Mom and Dad and find out what's going on with the funeral and all that." Malcolm looked up at Marvin. "This not having a phone in the cabin is a pain."

"I haven't heard from them either, so I'm not any help. If I do, I'll be sure to let you know right away."

"Yeah, I know. I better get back to work." Malcolm strolled toward Red, who was already back at it. He handed the hoe to Malcolm when he got there, and they were back into their groove in no time. Marvin smiled as he watched them. It was really good to see his cousin enjoying a good day's work.

PACKART'S ORCHARD   171

He waved at the Packarts as he drove back down the driveway. Hopefully Malcolm would find out something about Manny's death and they could start putting all of it behind them.

THAT NIGHT, MALCOLM TOLD THE PACKARTS AND Red that he would be heading to Carson that evening and wouldn't be around for dinner. He hopped a ride back to the cabins with Red, showered, and changed quickly. He wanted to catch the Carson police before they went into night mode and no one would be around to talk to him. He got into his car, checked to make sure he'd make it there without getting gas first, and headed northeast. It actually felt good to be heading back home for a few hours, knowing he didn't have to make excuses to get away from his dad. He could just head out to the cabin whenever it felt it was right to do so. Maybe Mom had been right. Maybe everything would have been different if Manny and he had moved out on their own right after high school. Malcolm shook his head. He couldn't think about the what ifs and maybes right now. He needed to figure out the here and now first.

As he parked his car in the police parking lot and got out, the sergeant he talked to on Monday was coming down the stairs.

"Hi, Malcolm. You got more information for us?" the sergeant asked.

"Hi, Sergeant." Malcolm waved as he locked up his car. "No, but I was kind of hoping you'd have more information for me. Has the tox reports got back yet? Do you know anything more about the security disc I dropped off earlier?"

"Malcolm, you know I can't give you any information on an open investigation." The sergeant shook his head. "Look, I'm off duty now, so how about I go home and change, and we can meet up somewhere. Maybe over at the Local Hole?"

"That the new name for the Windsor?" Malcolm asked.

"Yeah, that's the one. Give me half an hour." The sergeant climbed into his car and headed out of the lot. Malcolm looked at his watch. If he went to his parents' place now, Mom would insist he stay for supper. He really didn't want to do that now. He looked over at the police station. *Maybe I'll just go in and see if there's someone else that will give me anything,* he thought as he swung open the door.

Malcolm waited at the station's reception desk for about ten minutes before he rang the bell on the counter Still no response. *Someone must still be here*, he thought as he looked around the corner to see if he could spot someone. An elderly man came down the hallway with a mop and bucket. "Hello?" Malcolm called out. The man turned with a start.

"How'd you get in here?" the man asked as he left his mop in the bucket and sauntered over to talk to Malcolm. "There ain't no cops around here this time of night."

"Why is the door still unlocked?" Malcolm asked, "and who are you, exactly?"

The man looked up at him. "You're one of them Faulkon boys, ain't ya?" he said as he pointed his bony finger at him. "Ya ain't the one in the morgue, but you look just like him."

"Is my brother still in the morgue?"

"Yeah, seen him there earlier. Think the medical guy is still working on him, though."

"Okay, well, is there anyone still in the morgue I could talk to about my brother?"

"Nobody down there. Now if you'll excuse me, this floor ain't gonna clean itself." The old man waited for Malcolm to exit, then locked the door behind him.

That was strange, Malcolm thought when he left the parking lot. Who was that old man? He knew almost everyone in and around Carson, but he'd never seen him before. He looked familiar, but Malcolm couldn't figure out why.

Malcolm pulled up in front of the Local Hole just as the sergeant pulled in behind him.

"Hi, Malcolm. Good timing," the sergeant said as he got out of his car.

"Thanks, ah … I'm sorry, I don't know what to call you." Malcolm waited for the police officer to give him a name, but it didn't come.

"Sarge is fine," the man answered. "That's pretty much what everyone around these parts calls me."

To prove his point, as they walked into the bar, the waitress called out, "Hi, Sarge. You've brought us company tonight, I see." She smiled at them. "Hi, Malcolm. How are you?" she said sympathetically.

"I'm good, Carla. Thanks for asking."

"Usual table, Sarge?" Carla asked.

"That would be great. More privacy back there anyway." They continued into the far corner at the back of the bar and Carla put two coasters on the table. "What can I get you two?"

PACKART'S ORCHARD   173

"The usual for me please, and …?" Sarge looked over at Malcolm. "On me."

Malcolm looked from the police officer to Carla and back again. He didn't want to be ungrateful, but he had to drive back to Windsmill tonight and didn't want to be caught drinking and driving. "Just a Coke for now, thanks," he responded. When both people gave him a "really?" look, he added, "I'm driving back west tonight." That seemed to satisfy them both.

"So," Malcolm started when Carla disappeared from earshot. "Who's the new cleaner at the station?" he asked casually.

"New cleaner?" Sarge looked at him questioningly. "There's no cleaners in tonight at all."

"Well, I went into the station after you left, just to see if I could get any information on my brother, or what's going on as far as releasing the body to my parents. There was this old man pushing a bucket and mop around in the hallway. He came and told me there wasn't anyone around and that I should leave. Then he said I looked just like the guy in the morgue and asked if it was my brother. He gave me a really weird vibe. Something seemed off, but since no one seemed to be there, I left."

"There are no cleaners at the station, and there should have been a whole bunch of night-shift guys in there going over the day's logs and figuring out their next steps." Sarge got up and hollered at Carla to hold the beer. He looked over at Malcolm, who hadn't moved. "You coming?"

They headed for the door as fast as they could get out, and Sarge pulled a magnetic light out from under the passenger seat and placed it on the roof as they sped out of the parking lot and headed back to the station. When they arrived, the door was wide open, and the place was on fire. "Shit!" Sarge tossed the radio mike at Malcolm. "Get the fire department over here, NOW!" he hollered at him.

Malcolm did as he was asked, and then followed Sarge up the steps. The black smoke was thick, and they could hear faint coughing coming from the back. "Go around to the morgue entrance and see if we can get in that way. I'll keep trying this entrance." He looked behind him to make sure Malcolm had headed around back, then started to pull at the debris from around the door. "Hello, anyone in there?" he called as he worked. He heard more coughing, then a faint voice saying, "Get us out of here!"

"We're trying!" Sarge called back as he heard the fire trucks barrelling down the highway toward them. "Help is on the way!"

"Oh, thank god," he heard the voice say, "who are you?"

"Malcolm Faulkon, sir," Sarge heard over the sirens. "I'm going to do everything I can to get you out of here. Is there anyone else in here?" Malcolm said as the voices became fainter.

The fire chief came up behind Sarge. "What's happening here, Sergeant? Any people in there?"

"There's at least one guy in there and a civilian, Malcolm Faulkon. He went in through the morgue entrance and has been able to make it in behind this mess," Sarge informed the fire chief as the fire fighters pulled out their hoses.

"Okay, stand back." The firefighter turned on the hose and blasted the front entrance of the building. As they were about to enter the building to see if they could find anyone, Malcolm and four police officers came around the corner from behind the building. Two of them were being helped up the side stairs by the others and looked like they were in pretty bad shape. The rest seemed to be okay. "Paramedics!" the chief hollered over his shoulder and pointed toward the men to his left as the fire crew continued to blast the flames. "Is there anyone else in there?" he asked what appeared to be the lead officer.

"No, I think we have everyone. Two of my men left the building just before this took off. There's only six on at night." He coughed again and a paramedic pulled an oxygen mask over his face.

"Malcolm, what are you doing here?" the chief asked as he looked over at his nephew. "Aren't you working in Windsmill this summer?"

"Yes, sir, I am," Malcolm said to his uncle. "Marvin got me a job at Packarts for a few months."

"Right. Your dad told me about that; said you were staying over there, though, so what are you doing in Carson? You holding up okay with everything going on and all?"

"I'm fine, sir, just came to town after work today to talk to the sergeant. He pointed over at the policeman still trying his best to help the firefighters get the hot spots out at the front door.

"Okay, well, go over and see if you need anything from the medics. Looks like you've burned your arm pretty good." His uncle pointed at his arm and then headed over to the building to try to get the sergeant out of the way before he got hurt too.

Malcolm hadn't even noticed the hole in his jacket or the burn up his forearm until his uncle pointed it out. He looked at it for a few seconds

PACKART'S ORCHARD   175

before the pain hit him and he sprinted over to the paramedics, climbing into the back of the ambulance. "Hey, before you go, do you have anything I can put on this?" Malcolm held up his arm.

The medic jumped back down, looked around, and then hollered at another medic who was tending to the officer in charge. "Hey Chuck, can you help this guy with his arm?" When Chuck nodded and waved Malcolm over to where he was standing, the other medic jumped back into the ambulance, and they took off. They had two men in the back, Malcolm observed as he moved over to the other group of people standing to the left. "Hope they're going to be okay," he said as he reached Chuck.

"Yeah, me too," the paramedic answered. "Mike never regained consciousness and John's been in and out. What are you doing here, anyway?"

"Sarge and I were in the bar a few minutes ago. I asked him who the new cleaner was that told me no one was here around five-thirty or so. Sarge said that you didn't have cleaners in this time of day, and there weren't any new ones that he knew of."

The Police Captain Chuck was tending to held up his hand to stop Malcolm. "This new cleaner, do you think you could identify him if you saw him again?"

"Sure, I think so," Malcolm replied. "Why?"

"Because Mike was talking to someone in the hallway just before," the captain hesitated, "just before the fire started."

"Okay." Malcolm waited for him to continue. "So do you want me to give you a description or anything so you can catch this guy?" he asked.

"Yeah, yeah, that would be good. I'm hoping that the security cameras picked something up. But if we need more of a description, we'll definitely be in touch. And Malcolm," the captain continued, "thank you for helping us out of there. You may have just saved all our lives, and I can't thank you enough for that."

The paramedic put the oxygen mask back on the officer's face and loaded him into the back of the ambulance, then waved Malcolm over to get his arm taken care of. "I'll get you wrapped up while this other guy loads himself into the back with his oxygen tank." He smiled at the other officer who had been standing quietly listening to what Malcolm had said.

"Thank you, Malcolm, for helping us out of there. The captain is right, you likely saved us all. This older gentleman that you saw; what did you call him? A cleaner?" the young officer asked as he held his own mask away from his face.

"Because he was dressed in a lab coat and blue work pants with sensible walking shoes on, and he was pushing a mop and bucket around in the hallway when I stuck my head around the corner."

"Okay, did he say much else to you except that no one was there?"

"Just that I looked like the body in the morgue and I must be his brother. When I asked if there was anyone down there, he said the doctor was gone for the day, or something like that."

"You didn't see Dr. Daniels down there, did you?"

"You mean when I came through there a few minutes ago? No, no one was in there when I went through to the stairway. Why?"

The officer called over to Sarge, who was pacing in front of the door waiting for the all-clear from the firefighters so he could go in and get the investigation started. "Hey Sarge, come here for a minute, will you?"

Sarg trotted over to them. "How you feeling, Bill?" he asked the young officer.

"I'm good, but I'm a bit perplexed. Your friend here says that no one was in the morgue or coroner's office area when he went through to get upstairs. But I had just come up myself from talking to Dr. Daniels before all this shit hit. Can you go down and see if anything is out of place?"

"Yeah sure, but how would I know? I don't go down there unless I absolutely have to, so I wouldn't notice anything out of place." Sarge looked a little fearful of the whole idea.

"You still scared of ghosts?" Bill laughed as he turned his attention to the medic. "Hey Chuck, can you take my blood sample from here and check my oxygen levels? I promise if I feel worse during my shift, I'll get someone to bring me to the hospital."

Chuck raised his eyebrows but understood why the officer wanted to hang back. "Sure, I'll do that now, but if you pass out because of all this and something happens, it's going to be my neck on the line too, you know." He took out the syringe and vials as he patted Malcolm on the shoulder. "I think that should do it for you. Keep that dry and clean and if there's any sign of infection, go to your doctor, got it?"

"Yes, sir!" Malcolm rolled his sleeve down as best he could and stepped away.

"You heading out?" Sarge asked Malcolm as he started to head over to Sarge's car to gather up anything he might have left in it.

"I was thinking I could just walk over to the bar and get my car if you don't need me around here," Malcolm replied.

"Stick around for a few more minutes and I'll drive you back." Sarge turned toward Bill and asked Chuck how much longer they were going to be before he could unleash his friend. Chuck laughed and said five minutes max. "Okay, I'll be back before you leave. I'm just going to take Malcolm back to his car, and I'll be right back."

Sarge headed toward Malcolm and they climbed into the car. "Sorry about all this craziness. We'll get to the bottom of what's going on. Hopefully the security system will give us something." Sarge was rambling; he was so hyped up on adrenaline. He pulled into the parking lot of the local bar and parked beside Malcolm's car. "You okay to get yourself home, or wherever it is you're heading tonight?" Sarge asked.

"Yeah, I'm good. I wish I could figure out what's happening around here these days. Do you think this fire and stuff has anything to do with Manny's death?" he asked, without expecting to get an answer.

"It's possible," Sarge said. "This whole cleaner thing has me thinking that someone doesn't want us involved in what's going on. The powder on all the guys' faces was apparently blown through the vents somehow. Whatever it was wasn't enough to kill them, just knock them out. But the similarities to that and what was on your security tape at Manny's scene was interesting. I need to get back," Sarge said suddenly. "Is there a number I can reach you at if we need to?"

"I don't have a phone, and there isn't one in the cabin I'm staying at. You can call Marvin, my cousin in Windsmill, and he'll get a message to me. If its urgent you can call the Packarts. I'm sure they would let me know." Malcolm wrote the phone numbers on a piece of paper that Sarge handed him, then climbed out of the car.

"Thanks again for all your help, Malcolm. Take care of that arm." Sarge drove out of the parking lot and quickly headed back toward the station. Malcolm watched him go before getting into his own car and starting it up. He turned on the radio and sat there for a few minutes, thinking about what Sarge had just revealed. What if they hadn't gone back to the station when they did? Would those officers have all burned to death? Were they knocked out and left there to die? And were Sarge and Bill now in danger because they were poking around trying to figure out what went down? And just how would this have anything to do with Manny's death? Malcolm shook his head. He seemed to have more and more questions and no answers. Maybe he'd drive back to Windsmill and talk everything over with Marvin before heading back to the orchard.

Malcolm drove up the driveway to Marvin's house and parked. He walked across the parking area and up the steps to the front door. Marvin swung the door open just before Malcolm could ring that bell. "Don't even think about ringing that bell!" Marvin exclaimed as he pushed his way out of the house. "It took Becky three hours to get that baby to sleep and you are not going to wake him now!"

Malcolm backed up until he was standing on his toes at the edge of the porch. "Okay, fine, sorry," he said as he started to descend the stairs again. "I was just going to talk to you about the fire and the cops and seeing Uncle Mason, and all the shit that's going on. But we can talk some other time."

He headed back toward his car when Marvin spun him around. "What fire? Why were you talking to Dad? Is he okay?"

"Yes. Uncle Mason and his crew where at the police station putting out the fire. He asked me why I was there and if I needed medical attention for my burnt arm." He looked down where Marvin's hand was squeezing his forearm. "Could you please let go now?" Malcolm said as he winced in pain.

"Oh man. I'm so sorry. Are you okay?" Marvin asked as he quickly pulled his hand away from Malcolm's arm.

"I'll live." Malcolm unlocked his car and opened the door.

"Hey, Malcolm. I really am sorry," Marvin said more quietly. "Becky and I haven't slept more than a couple of hours every night since Marty was born. They're both sleeping now, so can we get together tomorrow?"

"Yeah, sure." Malcolm climbed into his car. "I just was hoping to talk to you about what went down tonight. I used to talk to Manny when I needed to clear my head. Tomorrow will be fine." Malcolm closed his door and drove back down the hill.

As he looked east to make sure it was safe to cross the highway toward the cabins, he spotted something in the trees. He pulled into the rest area and grabbed the flashlight off the passenger seat. He got out of his car and flashed the light through the trees. "Whoever you are, we're going to catch you, you son of a bitch!" he yelled at the trees. He looked again, but everything had gone quiet. *Maybe too quiet*, Malcolm thought as he climbed back into his car.

Whatever, or whoever, it was out there, they moved with stealth and seemed to know the area pretty well. How was he getting from place to place so quickly?

Malcolm pulled up in front of his cabin and grabbed the flashlight again. He pulled his camera out of the backseat, locked the car, and stuffed his keys into his pocket. "I'll just take a little walk around the place and see what's up at night in the area," he said out loud. He felt like he was being watched and he was just angry enough about everything that had happened tonight that he was hoping his walk would draw out whoever it was that was out there. Malcolm was big and tall and strong. If the predator was the old man that had disguised himself as the cleaner, then Malcolm wasn't scared of him at all.

He walked slowly and quietly down the gravel road. "You still following me, you coward?" he hollered out into the trees. "You're nothing but a coward and a murderer and a snivelling liar!" Malcolm continued to goad the shadows. "Have to drug people to take them down? Is that your M.O.?"

Malcolm shone the light into the field to the north of the orchard. There didn't seem to be any lights for miles. He remembered what Mr. P had said the first time they'd met: "Lots of other farms in the area, the lights were likely from them." But tonight, Malcolm wasn't seeing any other farmyards or lights. There did seem to be a light shining from the upper level of the old homestead, though. He continued to walk toward it, but something caught his eye in the orchard.

"Hello? Is there someone over there?" he called as a light went on in the treehouse office.

"Who's out there?" Darren called back.

"It's Malcolm. It that you, Darren?" he asked.

"Yeah." Darren started walking toward him. "What are you doing out here so late?"

"I was just taking a late-night walk. It's been a crazy few hours," Malcolm responded. "How about you?"

"Oh, just trying to get some quiet time of my own," Darren responded. "You should really try to stay close to the cabins this time of night. Dad says there's coyotes out this way this time of year. They'll be looking after their dens and that makes them more protective of their area."

"Sounds like a plan," Malcolm said as he turned back toward the cabins. "I should probably try to get some sleep anyway."

"Good night, then," Darren said as he waved at Malcolm. "See you in the morning."

Malcolm got almost to his cabin door when he heard something snap behind him. He turned around to see a large black bird-like object flying straight for his head. He tried to duck but it was fast. It hit him in the forehead and Malcolm felt what seemed like a stinger or a needle go into his head. Then he heard a voice. "I'm not a coward!" the voice said. "You are, however, a problem. You should really mind your own business." Then Malcolm passed out.

THE NEXT MORNING RED CAME OUT OF his cabin and looked around. He hadn't heard Malcolm come back home last night but was glad when he saw his car parked in front of the cabin. *Wonder where the boy's gotten to*, Red thought as he pulled out the keys for the golf cart and brought it out to the road. When he looked toward Malcolm's cabin, he saw him lying on the grass beside the building. "Whatcha doing over there, Malcolm?" Red asked as he got out of the cart and walked over to his friend. Malcolm was his friend. He'd accepted Red as he was and didn't judge him like so many others had. He really liked this boy.

"Malcolm, you okay, boy? You out drinking last night, were you?" Red chuckled. When he got closer, he realized that Malcolm wasn't just passed out or too hungover to stand. Those things Red could understand. Malcolm was lying on his back, his eyes wide open and his face all swollen and pale. Red backed up slowly and, jumped into his cart, and headed as quickly as he could into the orchard.

He was out of breath and scared when he reached the treehouse office door. He banged on it with both hands, knowing that Darren had been spending his nights out there by himself.

Darren pulled open the door. "Red, what's wrong? You look like you've seen a ghost!

"The boy," Red huffed out. "Call the cops, call a doctor, call the morgue. Someone needs to help!" Tears started rolling down his face. He swiped at them and stared at Darren.

"Red, slow down. What are you talking about?" Darren wasn't understanding what was going on, but he knew something was wrong. He'd never seen Red this upset about anything before.

Red headed back out to the golf cart and continued all the way to the mansion. He almost ran Albert over in the driveway. "Where are you going in such a hurry?" Albert asked as Red climbed out of the cart.

"Call the cops!" Red yelled at him. "The boy, Malcolm, he's dead!"

PACKART'S ORCHARD   181

"Dead? What are you talking about, Red?" Albert asked as they both headed for the house. Albert picked up the phone in the foray and dialed 9-1-1. He told the operator that they'd had an accident at the cabins on the east end of the orchard. No, he said, he didn't know the exact nature of the situation, but there was apparently a dead body. The dispatcher asked him to hold the line and said that emergency vehicles would be there shortly.

By the time Albert got to the cabins, Red and Darren were both there. Darren had headed over to the cabins when Red left the treehouse and had run back to the office to phone 9-1-1. The operator told him that Albert had already called it in, so Darren had hung up and phoned Carson P.D. to let them know what was going on. He then made the hardest call he'd ever made in his life, to his friend Marvin. Marvin made it to the cabins about the same time Albert did.

Malcolm's body was taken to the coroner's office in Windsmill because the Carson building was still under investigation due to the fire. The two police stations decided that cooperating with each other would be a better approach than fighting each other on the situation. They'd shared as much as they could and then headed out.

Marvin asked the Carson P.D. to stop by his uncle's place and let them know what was happening. Marvin asked the Windsmill Sheriff's department if they'd need to search the cabins or Malcolm's car before he could clear them all out, and they informed him they'd let him know as soon as they were finished investigating the scene.

Marvin stood staring out into the field to the east of the cabins. Darren came over and put his arm around Marvin's shoulder and gave him a hug. "I saw him last night," Darren said as he too stared out into the field. "He was out walking the gravel road at about ten-thirty. I heard him hollering out into the field, like Paul did, remember?" he asked Marvin.

"Yeah, I remember," Marvin said quietly. "There's something out there, Darren. Even if we can't see it, there's something there. I've seen it on the cameras where Manny died."

"Yeah," Darren agreed. "There's definitely something out there. I think I know who it is, but I can't quite figure out how. Or why."

CHAPTER 21

MARVIN STRETCHED HIS BACK AGAIN AND LOOKED up at David. "Malcolm's autopsy and tox screens were rushed through and the body was released quickly. Uncle Mo and Aunt Agnes held a single service for both boys and buried them in the Carson cemetery. Uncle Mo went from being angry to being inconsolably sad and depressed. He pushed hard to get the police investigation to find something, but they hit dead end after dead end. The Carson police pushed hard too, and we thought it was going to be solved, but then ..."

Marvin looked away from David. "But then Darren died, and Albert was the one pushing to get this solved. The orchard, and Mrs. P's garden, were left to nature, and none of the crops were taken off or sent in to Allensville that year. The next year, Albert and Amelia went away for a holiday somewhere. They were gone quite awhile, five or six months, I think. They didn't plant the garden or hire a crew for the orchard for more than three years after that. It was such a mess, the whole situation." Marvin took a deep breath and exhaled slowly.

"I'm sorry, David, but I don't think I can take any more of this today. Can we meet up tomorrow sometime and finish up? I'm sure you have a million questions, but I just can't rehash this anymore." Marvin bent back to stretch his back out again.

David reached over and turned off the recorder. "Yeah, we can stop for now. It's been a long and difficult afternoon. You can call me whenever you'd like to finish up. That will give me time to review the recording and jot down my questions. That will be smoother anyway."

Marvin shook David's hand and smiled at him. "I don't know if you'll be able to solve all of this or not. A lot of police officers and investigators from Bellcom City to Kendall were involved in one way or another. There's

183

definitely someone out there that knows what's going on, but I honestly don't know who it is."

"Thanks for giving me all this information, Marvin. I know this can't be easy. We'll talk again soon. In the meantime, I think it's time I talked to the sheriff's office again, and the Windsmill coroner's office."

"Speaking of the coroner's office," Marvin said quietly, "I've given them my okay for you to get Marty's autopsy reports. They might help you sort all this craziness out once and for all."

"Thanks. That will give me the excuse I need to go talk to him again." David walked Marvin out to the front of the building and watched as he climbed into his truck and headed east toward Windsmill. He really needed to look into a good security system for out here soon, David thought as he walked back in and locked the doors.

David poured himself another cup of coffee and took a sip. *Definitely not as good as Max's coffee*, he thought as he set the cup back onto his desk. He'd need to review the recording he'd made of Marvin's story and make notes about anything that seemed out of place or that he needed more details on. He'd also have to let Anna listen to it or she'd have his head, he thought, and chuckled at how quickly they'd gotten used to having each other around. As if on queue, his burner phone rang. When he glanced down at it, it was his sister's number.

"Hi, what's up?" he asked. "By the way, I've got my own phone back, so you can use that number now to get hold of me instead of this one."

"Yeah, okay," Anna answered. "Have you seen or spoken to Marvin today?"

"Yeah, he was here most of the afternoon. Left about half an hour ago. Why?"

"Oh, Becky is still fussed about him being away from the house for so long. He left early this morning to go into Bellcom for some work of some sort, and she says he didn't take his phone with him again."

David chuckled. He'd reminded Marvin to start carrying his cell, but with everything else going on, Marvin would likely forget again. "He did phone Becky just after lunch and told her he was here. He used my office phone." David remembered that Anna didn't know he'd been able to get back in. "Oh, and I got the go ahead to move back into my office and apartment building this morning from Bellcom City PD. You should call Mike and see if you can have your car towed to a body shop for repainting."

"Yeah, I'll do that. So, what was Marvin doing at your office all afternoon?" Anna sounded a little curious and a lot ticked off that she hadn't been invited.

184   WENDY SCOTT-ETTINGER

"He phoned me from his office and asked if he could come over for a bit. It was completely impromptu. I think he wanted to get everything out about his cousins' deaths. With everything going on in his life right now, it's brought back a lot of memories about what went on back then. It was completely unplanned, but he was here for at least a couple of hours or more."

"Mmmhmm," Anna grunted into the phone. "Did you record it like the others?"

"He gave me just enough notice that I downloaded all the recordings and videos I'd taken earlier onto my office computer, and then I recorded the whole conversation with Marvin on my phone." David put his feet up on his desk. "I was just thinking of giving you a call to see when you'd like to get together and where. We still need to put a plan together so that we can both be more productive." David's mind was going a mile a minute, and his mind wandered into all the things he had to accomplish in a short period of time. He would need to jot them all down before Anna came to help so they didn't forget anything important.

"David, are you still there?" Anna said into the phone. "Did I get disconnected?" she asked, mostly to herself.

"No, I'm still here, sorry. I just have a lot going on in my head right now. We have a whole list of people we need to talk to and I'm not sure how we're going to do that." David paused. "By the way, do you have a job or anything that's going to want you back to work some day?"

"After Johnny was born, I quit work in the city and he became my job. I had been talking to Jack about getting back to work now that Johnny is in school full time, but it just never seemed like the right time." Anna paused. "Well, now I really don't think it's the right time to leave Johnny with someone else while I work outside the home."

"But you've kind of been leaving him with Mary while you've been helping me out, right?" David said gently.

"Yeah, I guess I have been." Anna sighed. "What are you getting at?"

"Well, I was just thinking that this job is becoming bigger than I'd expected. It would be nice to have an associate around to help with the planning, making phone calls, and attending some of the meetings without me. That kind of thing ..." He trailed off.

"What are the hours?" she asked.

"Flexible, I suppose. We'd need to get together for the first few days here, but after that the schedule would be your own. We could talk about it."

"Wages?" Anna asked tentatively.

"A percentage of the net, depending on what the client is paying." David chuckled. "Oh, of course, the current client is a bit tardy with the retainer."

Anna laughed out loud for the first time in a long time. "Yeah, guess I'll have to have a chat with her about that."

"Let me think this over and get back to you," Anna said. "Are you coming out this way so I can hear what Marvin had to say, or did you need me to come that way?"

"I'm not sure yet. Let me get my head back on straight. After listening to Marvin all afternoon, I need some thinking time. I'll let you know when and where later."

"Okay, call me," Anna demanded. "Oh, and by the way, Max says hi!" She hung up.

David stared at the phone. Maybe he should drive out to Windsmill now and get a descent cup of coffee and one of those made-to-order sandwiches Max loved to serve. He smiled at the thought, then shook his head.

Too much to do right now, especially now that he was back in his own office. He turned his chair, so he was facing his computer. Where to start, he thought as he turned sleep mode off and his screen came to life.

He jotted down a few questions for Marvin and made a note to give him a call in a day or two if he hadn't heard from him before that. With all the information Marvin had given him, they'd have to go up and talk to Carson Police Department and see if any of the police that were there twenty years ago were still around. If not, maybe they'd give David a copy of the case files. He'd ask Mike about his dad's files on Darren's case too and see if he could get those. He'd need to talk to the coroner's office about all of the deaths, both from twenty years ago and the ones from recently. He has Marvin's consent to give them Marty's reports now, so that should speed things up a bit. He hadn't really read through Jack's file yet and he wondered if there was anyone that could give consent for Red's file. He'd also see if he could get in to talk to Albert in the hospital and see where that would lead him. That conversation might be a little easier if he took Anna with him, he thought, as he made more notes. He might go back and talk to Amelia again too, but he'd have to think about that one.

He spent the rest of the afternoon and evening reviewing all the recordings and videos he had taken for this case. He even went over the video of the orchard at least three times, trying to figure out if the shadows were something more, but couldn't see anything that looked out of place.

He'd sure like to find out what Deputy Carter had found at Marty's scene too. Maybe he could bring it up when he talked to the sheriff. Man, a lot of people to talk to and a lot of running around to do. He really hoped Anna would come work with him on a full-time basis, at least until they could get this case wrapped up.

He walked into his apartment and looked around. *Now what had he done with the case files from before he started all this craziness* he wondered. He needed to call the clients back and ask if they would like him to find another investigator for them, since this case was taking up all of his time. *They must be here somewhere,* he said to himself as he walked back into his office to see if he'd put them away for a change. He rifled through his desk drawers and the filing cabinet. *Nothing. That was strange. Where could they be?*

David flipped through his phone to find the numbers for the two clients he had just gotten before his meeting with Anna. He called the first one, and after the third ring a soft voice answered.

"Hello?" the young women answered tentatively,

"Hi, Miss Colins? This is David Allen from Allen and Associates Investigations."

"Oh, hello, Mr. Allen. I wasn't expecting your call."

"Oh? I know it has been a couple of weeks, but I just wanted to touch base and let you know I haven't forgotten about you."

"I see." She sounded annoyed. "Your associate told me that you had a family emergency and wouldn't be able to look after my case any further. They said I'd be better off finding someone else to handle it."

"My associate?" David was perplexed. "Did they give you a name?"

"No, just said you would no longer be in business and that I should find someone else. Is there a problem, Mr. Allen?"

"Yes, as a matter of fact, there is. I don't have an associate, at least not yet, so I have no idea who would have called you and said those things."

"That's very strange. When I called my current investigation company, they said I was the third person who had been left hanging by your company. I have the feeling you have someone out to ruin your reputation, sir."

"I'd say so. Could you give me the name of your current investigator? I'd like to talk to them about the other cases they've taken on."

Miss Colins told David she was now dealing with Line of Sight. "If you don't mind me asking, why has it taken you so long to get back to me?"

PACKART'S ORCHARD   187

"I did have some family issues to take care of and a number of issues at my office that involved police investigation. I've just today been able to get back into my building to get things sorted out and back to normal. I'm really sorry I've left you hanging. It wasn't intentional."

"That would explain the 'Closed for Business' sign I found on your office door when I went over there the other day. You didn't answer either phone number you gave me, so I drove to your office building. The sign seemed to confirm what the caller told me. I'm sorry we weren't able to work together. I think your company sounded more in line with the issues I'm having, but I've now committed to Line of Sight Investigations. Good luck in getting it sorted out."

They ended their conversation and David went back to his computer to look up Line of Sight. He punched the number into his phone and got a recording saying they would be open again in the morning. David looked at the clock hanging above his desk and realized it was after 9:00 p.m. No wonder he was tired and hungry. He'd grab something to eat and then try to get some rest. He needed to talk to Mike and find out why they'd put the sign on his door. He hoped Anna would show up in the morning and they could get some of this sorted out quickly.

He hit Mike's personal number on his phone to see if they could meet up somewhere and have a beer. He would ask him about the sign and his father's availability and get those two to-dos off his list right away.

When Mike answered, he sounded like he wasn't quite awake. "What?" he said into the phone.

"Well, hello to you, too." David chuckled. "Did I wake you?"

"I have to be at work at midnight. Whadaya want?"

"Well, I was hoping we could go out for a few beers and chat." David was disappointed. "We haven't done that for awhile. Guess I'll call some other time when you're in a better mood." They hung up and David rubbed his face. "Guess I'm on my own tonight."

He grabbed his keys off the desk, pulled his jacket off the coat rack at the door, and was about to leave when he decided he'd better double-check all the doors and windows before he left. When he was sure everything was as secure as possible, he headed back into the office, jotted another note on his do-to list about a better security system, and headed out to his car. He'd drive over to that hole-in-the-wall taco place in the strip mall. Hopefully they were still open this time of night.

CHAPTER 22

ANNA PULLED INTO THE PARKING LOT BY David's office building and parked beside his car. Hopefully it was safe here while she was in the office. If anything happened to the rental car, she'd be getting a room in the psych ward beside Mr. Packart in the hospital. She locked the doors and looked around to make sure no one was watching her before she opened the trunk and took out a briefcase. She'd gone to her own house the night before to try to find the resume Jack helped her put together just before he died. She also had a notepad and pen, and the laptop Jack used when he wasn't in the treehouse office at work. She wanted to look professional in the hopes that David would stop treating her as just another client.

When she got to the blue door, she found it was locked. She pulled out her phone.

"Hello." David answered his cell on the fourth buzz. He'd gotten in late last night and forgot to set his alarm. "What time is it?" he asked, not really knowing who he was talking to.

"David, are you alright?" Anna asked. "Are you still sleeping?"

David sat up in bed and looked around. He felt like he'd been on an all-nighter but hadn't had anything to drink last night. "Yeah, I guess I am," he answered. "Where are you?"

"I'm outside your office door. It's locked and there's a sign on it that says 'Closed for Business.' What's going on?" Anna asked worriedly. "Are you sure you're okay?"

"I'll be right down!" David hung up and threw on a pair of jeans. He stumbled through his office, down the staircase, and flung open the door.

"Anna! What are you all dressed up for?" He looked at her questioningly. "And where is this sign?"

189

Anna didn't answer him about her attire. She pointed at the door where the sign hung and raised her eyebrows. "What's going on, David?" she asked again as she pushed passed him and walked up the staircase. She set her briefcase beside the desk and sat down in the visitor chair. "Well?" she said as David came into the office and closed the door. He was holding the sign from the door in his hand, and he was visibly shaking.

"I don't know where this sign came from or who put it up. It wasn't there last night when I came home." He felt dizzy, so pulled out his office chair and sat down. He told Anna about the phone call he'd had with his now ex client and about the sign she had also found on the door. "The same sign, by the sounds of it," he continued. He started to sweat and shiver at the same time. He stood up and headed for the washroom and was violently ill. He pulled a sweatshirt on and walked slowly back to his desk. "I don't know what I got into last night, but I'm not feeling good. Must have been something from the taco place, but they're usually really good." He sat down on his office chair again and looked at his sister. "Or it could have been the milk in the fridge. I wondered how old it was when I poured it into the glass last night, but it smelled okay."

Anna picked up the phone and called for an ambulance. The symptoms David was showing were the same that Jack had before he died. She went into David's kitchen and pulled a cloth out of a drawer, put cold water on it, then placed it on her brother's forehead. She helped him into his shoes and jacket, stuck his phone in his pocket in case he needed it, and walked him slowly down the stairs to the front door. By the time they got to the bottom, the ambulance was there. They told her they would be taking him to Bellcom General and she said she would meet them there. She ran back up the stairs, put the carton of milk from his fridge in a plastic Ziploc bag, locked everything up, put his keys in her own purse, and headed back out the door to her car. She punched in the Bellcom City Hospital address into the car's GPS and headed as quickly as she could to get there.

When she got to the emergency room, she was told that they couldn't do anything to help her. Since she was not a direct relative of Mr. Allen's, they would not give her any information on David's condition. After arguing with the triage nurse for what seemed like forever, Anna backed away from the counter. She phoned her mother, who gave her Aunt Jenny's phone number and Anna called her. When Aunt Jenny answered her phone, Anna told her where she was and what was going on. She said she couldn't get any information on David since she wasn't a direct relative. Aunt Jenny told her not to worry about it, that she was going to get there in about a half hour and in the meantime, she'd make sure Anna was given full access.

Anna found a corner to sit in away from the patients to wait for Aunt Jenny to get there. Just as she was about to thumb through an old magazine, her name was called over the intercom. She walked quickly to the counter and was greeted by an older nurse she hadn't seen before.

"Mrs. Lister?" the nurse asked as she opened the emergency room doors and escorted her in. "Please follow me. I'll take you to your brother now."

"But how did you know?" Anna asked, confused about the about-face.

"Mrs. Allen phoned and asked me to look after you. She'll be here shortly." The nurse smiled. "Jenny and I went to nursing school together," she explained when she saw Anna's confused look. "I was one of the only ones Jenny ever told about David's story."

"Oh, okay. So you knew he had a twin sister and all that?" Anna said as she processed what the nurse had just told her.

"Yes." The nurse nodded as they rounded a corner and Anna spotted David on a gurney. "They're still working on him, so you'll have to wait here for a bit. What's in the bag?" she asked as Anna went to set it down beside her chair.

"Oh, I almost forgot. This is the milk from David's fridge. This was the last thing he drank last night before bed. He said he'd had Mexican food at a taco place last night then came home and drank this milk. He didn't have any alcohol last night. When I got there this morning, he was really groggy and dizzy and not well at all. He threw up and then began to sweat and shiver. I think maybe something was added to the milk that made him sick."

"Okay, I'll take it to our lab and have it analyzed. I'll let the doctors know what you've said about David's symptoms. Is there anything else?"

"Only that both my husband and my father died shortly after having these same symptoms." Anna took a deep breath and closed her eyes, so she wouldn't start to cry. "Their deaths are still under investigation."

The nurse hurried away and left Anna in the hallway to wait. She hated waiting. She leaned her head back and closed her eyes, hoping it wouldn't be too much longer before Aunt Jenny showed up.

"Anna?" Someone touched her arm and startling her. She opened her eyes and turned her head in the direction of the voice.

"Aunt Jenny!" Anna jumped to her feet and hugged her aunt.

"Are you alright, Anna?" Jenny looked at her with worried eyes. Before she could respond Jenny turned away as her friend walked by. "Martha." Jenny turned to the nurse. "How's David?"

"Oh Jenny." The nurse gave her a big hug. "I'm so glad to see you. I'm just heading in to check on him now. Anna, I see you're back with us. Are you feeling alright?"

"Yes, I'm fine." Anna blushed. "Just please look after David."

A few minutes later Martha returned with a doctor. "Good morning, ladies." He shook their hands. "You're the one that brought the milk carton into us?" he asked Anna as he held her hand in his.

"Yes, why?" she asked.

"Well, doing that just saved your brother's life. That was quick thinking on your part." He let go of her hand and pointed to a "quiet room" next to where David was still laying. "Can we please have a chat in a more private area?" he said as he proceeded into a small room with a table and chairs in it. "Please, have a seat."

Martha came into the doorway behind Jenny and Anna as they sat down. "Would you like me to stay, Doctor?" Martha asked.

"Yes and close the door please, Martha." She came in and sat down.

The doctor questioned Anna about the symptoms David had shown before she'd called the ambulance. He asked her to explain how she knew about the milk and why the symptoms were so serious to her.

Anna told the doctor about Jack's death and about what her mother had told her about their father. She said that it seemed as if all the deaths started with the same symptoms, and when David had mentioned the milk he'd drank the night before it just seemed to be suspicious, since he hadn't been able to use his office apartment for a couple of weeks, yet there was milk in the fridge that 'didn't smell bad' as David had said.

The doctor indicated that they would have to keep David overnight, and that the hospital would be calling the police to advise of their findings. He asked both women if they had any other questions.

"So what exactly was in the milk?" Anna asked curiously. This would be the first time they'd get a lead on the causes of all the deaths.

"An interesting mixture of phencyclidine and cyanide. In this case, it doesn't look like there was enough to kill, but it can definitely be a lethal combination."

"Phencyclidine, as in PCP?" Jenny asked. "Where in god's name would that come from?"

"Yes, PCP," the doctor responded. "The cyanide is industrial strength; the kind you'd find in large amounts in some mining operations. Usually in liquid form. The PCP could have come from pretty much anywhere these days. There's a lot of it on the streets and seems easier to come by than almost any other type of street drug. The analysis suggests a variant called Angel Dust that's commonly found on the coast and in some of the valley resort towns. More prevalent in the nineties but still widely available."

"Wow! That sounds seriously scary," Anna said. "Is there any way the police will be able to trace any of that?"

"I don't know. The technology in the police departments these days is amazing. It's hard to say what might provide them with a lead." The doctor stood up to leave. "I'm going to have to get back to the ER now. Lots of people out there today. I'm sure Martha can help you find your way out of this maze." He smiled at them and then hurried out to the hallway.

"Can we see David?" Jenny asked Martha as they all got up to leave. "I just need to know that he's safe." Jenny smiled at her friend.

"Sure, I'll take you both down to where he's currently being looked after. I assume they'll be moving him up to a ward soon, so I'll let you know when that happens. In the meantime, follow me."

As the curtain was drawn back to allow Anna and Jenny to enter the area, David turned his head. "Anna is that you?" he asked weakly.

"Yes." Anna hurried over to him and picked up his hand. "I'm here and so is your mother."

"Aunt Mary?" David questioned. "Why is she here?"

"No, not my mom, yours, David. Aunt Jenny is here."

"Oh, Mom!" David tried to sit up so he could see his mom. "I'm sorry to worry you," he said over Anna's shoulder.

"No problem. Anna phoned me to let me know what was going on and the doctor just briefed us. I assume he told you about the analysis of the milk?"

"No, what analysis? What milk?" David sounded confused and afraid. "What's going on?"

Jenny and Anna explained what had happened and how he got to the hospital. Anna told him about grabbing the milk carton before leaving his office and that she locked up before leaving. They told him the police would be investigating.

PACKART'S ORCHARD   193

"Anna, call Mike, please. His number is in my cell. He's the only one I want on this. And tell him they must have missed something when they cleaned up from the first mess. Tell him about the sign and make sure they dust it for prints. And Anna," he looked up at her and squeezed her hand, "thanks!"

"No problem. I'll need your cell to get Mike's number. Do you have the name of the client that told you about the first sign? I'll need to let Mike know about that as well. Anything else I need to be aware of before I head back to your office?"

"No, I can't think of anything. I think my cell is in with my clothes." David started to look around but became dizzy again.

"I'll look. I put it in your jacket pocket when we left this morning." Anna found the closet with his clothing and searched his pockets for the phone. When she found it, she brought it back to him so that he could unlock it and then she searched for Mike's phone numbers. She copied them into her own phone, made a note of Ms. Colins's name and phone number and then handed it back to him. "Let me know if you need me for anything else. I'll head out and let you and your mom catch up." Anna hugged David and Jenny and headed down the hallway.

"You leaving Mrs. Lister?" Martha asked as she saw Anna looking around to try to figure out where the exit was.

"Yes, at least I'm trying to." She chuckled. "I don't suppose you could point me in the right direction?"

"Sure, I'll walk you out." Martha took her by her arm and they walked down the hallway in the opposite direction that they'd come in. "This place is like a little maze back here. It's easy once you get used to it, and it really does make sense for an emergency area, but most people get turned around." She smiled at Anna. "I'm so glad you and David have found each other again. Sounds like you're getting on real well."

"Yes, surprisingly, we really are. Like we've known each other all our lives." Anna smiled back at her. It really did seem like they could read each other's mind sometimes.

Anna thanked Martha and waved goodbye. When she got back to the parking lot, she sat and stared at her phone for a few minutes. Mike first, then she'd better call Mom again and let her know what was going on. *I'm sure she'll be worried too*, Anna thought as she pulled up Mike's work number and hit call.

"Bellcom Police Station, Precinct 5, Sergeant McCall speaking," Mike answered.

"Hi, Mike?"

Yes," Mike responded tentatively.

"This is Anna, David's sister," she began. "David asked that I give you a call and let you know what's been going on this morning. I don't know if you have been told about the incident at his apartment or the fact that he's in hospital, but he wanted you to lead the case for him."

"I have heard rumours that something new has come up at his place. Don't have any details, though. What can you tell me?" Mike answered formally.

"Can we meet somewhere in person, preferably at David's office? Then we can go over everything that took place and where we're at right now," Anna responded as formally and professionally as he had.

"Yes, of course. I can be there in fifteen minutes, if that works," Mike said more urgently.

"I'm at Bellcom General in the parkade right now. I'm not sure how long it will take me to get back there. The doors will all be locked unless someone from your work has already gotten in, or…." She hesitated.

"Or the culprit that has been doing all the messing around has returned," Mike finished for her. "I'll wait in the parking lot at David's office for you to get here. What are you driving these days?"

Anna told Mike about the rental car she was currently driving, and that she had to make one more call and then would be heading back to the office. He confirmed he'd be waiting for her, and they hung up.

Anna called her mother, then punched David's address into the GPS and headed back there. When she pulled into the parking area, a cruiser was there waiting for her. Mike jumped out of the car when he saw her pull up and pulled her door open when she finished parking. Anna thanked him, and they walked over to the building while she was digging in her purse for David's keys. As she reached for the door, it swung open. A young police officer stood just inside.

"I'm sorry, no one is allowed to enter this area until further notice," said the officer. He stood with his feet placed firmly on the floor, shoulder wide, and his hands at the ready beside him. Mike pushed in front of Anna and looked at the rookie.

"No problem, Officer," Mike responded. "I'm Sergeant Mike McCall from precinct number five downtown. I've been requested to take over this case. Who sent you over here and when?"

"The chief asked me to come over about half an hour ago. He said I wasn't to let anyone on the premises until he called me. I have not received that call." The officer looked stoically at Mike.

"Fine." Mike turned around and pulled out his phone. He pushed a couple of buttons, waited, then said, "Good afternoon, sir, this is Sergeant Mike McCall from precinct five. I'm in front of 2012, 2nd street. There's a young officer here that says you've asked him to guard the premises until he hears from you directly?" There was another pause, then he said, "Yes, sir, Mr. Allen has requested that I specifically look after this case. I was the lead on the recent incident at this same building and this may be a continuation of that same harassment, sir." After a pause, Mike said, "Thank you, sir, I will," and hung up.

As he turned back to Anna and the officer, the young rookie's phone rang. He answered the call, said, "Yes sir," and handed the phone back to Mike. Mike and the chief exchanged quick greetings to confirm Mike's presents at the scene, and then Mike handed the phone back to the officer.

"That will be all for now, Brent. If I need help on this situation, I'll give you a call." The rookie left and Mike and Anna headed up the stairs.

"At least we don't have to worry about anyone else being in here," Anna said as she unlocked the office door and pushed it open. As she did so, they heard a rush of footsteps and a bang coming from the apartment side of the floor. Mike pushed passed Anna and ran into David's apartment. The cupboard doors were all open, as was the refrigerator door. The trash can had been turned upside down like someone was looking for something in it, and the patio doors leading to the outside staircase to the alley were wide open.

Mike rushed down the stairs and looked up and down the alley but saw nothing moving. He waited quietly for a few minutes to make sure someone wasn't hiding behind a car or trash bin or something, but still nothing. "Damn!" he exclaimed as he dialed his phone again. Then he said, "Hey Brent, you still in the vicinity? Yeah okay, can you take a quick drive around the block in front of and behind the building? Someone just headed out the back door when we came in … no, its not your fault. They should have had both entrances manned… okay, call me back." Mike hung up and headed back up the stairs. Hopefully Anna hadn't touched anything.

As he re-entered the apartment, he spotted Anna, camera in hand. She'd pulled on a pair of gloves and was taking pictures of the scene. Mike shook his head. "You really are related to David, aren't you?" He laughed as he closed the door behind him. He told her about his conversation with the rookie and said that he didn't see anything in the alley. "Whoever it was must know the area well and must be in good shape to move that quickly," he finished as he began to look around.

They sat down and Anna told him about that morning's events and what the doctor had told her. She told him about the milk and David's condition. She looked around the office for the sign that had been placed on the front door, but it was nowhere to be found. Whoever had been in there while they were trying to gain access much have taken it. She told him what David had said about his telephone conversation with Ms. Colins the night before and the sign she had seen on his front door when she came to check on him. She gave him Ms. Colins's phone number from the information she had taken from David's cell.

"So, what's next?" she asked Mike as he looked up from his notepad when she stopped talking.

"I'll be calling the precinct to get a couple of sweepers up here. I don't expect there to be anything left after our intruder was here, but we'll look. I don't suppose you took a picture of the sign, did you?" He looked at her inquisitively.

"As a matter of fact," Anna scrolled through her phone, "here it is. Not the best pic, but better than nothing, I suppose." Mike asked her to text it to him and then asked if she could send him the pictures off her camera that she'd just taken. She reached down to pick up the briefcase she'd set beside the desk before they'd gone to the hospital, but it wasn't there.

"Damn it!" she exclaimed as she looked around the office and under the desk to make sure it hadn't been misplaced or kicked somewhere in all the rush.

"What's wrong?" Mike asked as he stood up from his chair. "What are you looking for?"

"I brought a laptop and a few papers with me this morning in my husband's briefcase. I set it right here." She pointed to the floor beside the desk. "It's gone." She plopped down on her chair again, willing herself not to cry.

Mike answered his cell on the first ring. It was Brent, telling him he found something and if it was related to the break-in, it wasn't good news. "Okay, don't touch anything! I'll be right there." He hung up and headed for the front stairwell, then turned around and said to Anna, "You coming? Bring your camera." He continued out the door and onto the sidewalk, Anna right behind him. She was beginning to wish she had left the heels at home and worn more sensible shoes.

PACKART'S ORCHARD 197

CHAPTER 23

MIKE SAT ACROSS FROM ANNA AT THE café, sipping the best cup of coffee he'd ever tasted. He hadn't been over to Windsmill in years, but he thought he might have to come up there more often, if for no other reason than to get another cup of this coffee.

Anna was scrolling through her phone when it rang, and she answered it. "Sure, I can come get you, but I'm in Windsmill. You may not be able to get back into your apartment at the moment, though." There was a pause, then she said, "Because number one, I have your keys; number two, there is a policeman at both entrances; and number three, because according to Martha, you haven't been discharged yet and that's why your mother isn't coming to get you either."

She smiled over at Mike as David protested on the other end of the call. "Yes, I'm fully aware that they can't keep you there against your will, but you might want to stay to make sure there aren't any side affects to your poisoning before you leave. Besides, maybe you can play the sympathy card and have them let you in to talk to Albert?" She nodded again and then smiled. "Yeah, you do that." She hung up and looked up at Mike, who had a wide grin on his face.

"You really know how to handle him, don't you?" He chuckled as he looked around the café. Not many people in here this time of day, except a couple of cops at the back table. Mike would prefer to have his back up against a wall too, but Anna had gotten there first. "What is his problem, anyway?"

"He wants to get out so that we can put together a plan of attack and see if we can put an end to all this craziness once and for all. It's been way too long that these deaths have been hanging over the heads of Windsmill's best people." Anna took a deep breath and a good sip of her coffee. "Have you got anything for me regarding yesterday's little game of cat and mouse?" she asked, changing the subject.

"Not much. I'm assuming that was your briefcase that was nailed to the brick wall and your resume that the 'friendly' sign was scribbled on. Impressive, by the way," Mike added with a wink.

"Thanks, and yes. The resume had been in the briefcase along with the laptop and a notepad. Did either of them show up?"

"Nothing yet. They're still canvassing the area to see if anyone might have a camera and might have seen anything. Not a lot of security in that area, unfortunately, and whoever is doing this seems to know the area and where all the CCTV cameras are located. Some of them were jammed pretty good too, so they obviously have some sophisticated tech with them." Mike looked over at the cinnamon bun Anna was eating. "Those any good?" he asked as he pointed to it.

"Good is an understatement!" Anna smiled up at Mike again. "Hey Max, can you bring my friend a cinnamon bun, please?"

The pretty blonde waitress sauntered over to their table a few minutes later, a plate with a cinnamon bun in one hand and the coffee pot in the other. "Here you go," Max said as she smiled at Mike. "Would you like more coffee to go with that?"

"Yes, please!" Mike swallowed what was left in his cup and eagerly handed Max his empty cup.

Anna waved her away as she was going to pour more for her as well. "I've already had three this morning. I won't sleep until next week if I keep this up." She laughed. "Oh by the way, this is Mike; Mike, Max." She pointed to the waitress. "She owns this place," she added absently.

"Impressive. Love the coffee!' Mike said as he bit into a mouthful of cinnamon deliciousness. "My god, that's the best cinnamon roll I've ever tasted," Mike gasped.

"Glad you like it Mike." She turned her attention to Anna. "You keep bringing in these handsome gentlemen and I'll have to start making more pastries." She laughed. "Speaking of which, where's that brother of yours these days? Haven't seen him for awhile,"

"He's in hospital. He'll be out in a day or two," Anna said without thinking.

"Hospital? Is everything okay?" Max gasped at her friend. "Why didn't you tell me?"

PACKART'S ORCHARD   199

The police officer sitting at the back table turned around, then stood up and walked over to their table. "Did I just hear you say David is in hospital?" Charlie asked authoritatively. "That could be why he's not answering his office phone or his cell."

"Why are you looking to talk to him?" Anna questioned suspiciously.

"I have some information for him regarding Marty Faulkon. The sheriff asked me to share and be nice." Charlie air quoted the last part of her statement.

"That would be a change," Anna muttered. "Perhaps I could give it to him."

"Sheriff said to give it to Mr. Allen only."

"Then perhaps you could share it with the Bellcom City Police Department, which is currently investigating an attempted murder that may be relevant to both our cases," Mike said, interrupting the spitting match between the two women.

"Attempted murder?" Charlie asked. "Of who, and why would it be relevant to anything here?"

"Because the victim is one Mr. David Allen, and I believe it is directly related to his investigation into the goings on in Windsmill, Officer Carter." Mike drew out her name.

"Do we know each other?" Charlie scowled at Mike.

"Since we were in the academy together, I'd say we know of each other," Mike responded. "Totally irrelevant to the current situation, however." He took on the 'police stance' and stared stone-faced at the deputy-sheriff. "Or do I have to go over your head to get the information in question?"

"No, of course not." Charlie looked over at Anna again. "I'm sorry to hear about your brother. Is he going to be okay?" she asked with real concern in her voice.

"Thanks to Anna's quick thinking and actions, he will make a full recovery. Now, this information you have on the death of Mr. Faulkon?" Mike looked down at Charlie and raised an eyebrow.

"May I sit down with you for a minute?" She pointed at the empty chair on the other side of the table; she would be facing the door at least. "I'd rather have this conversation in private, but if you insist on having it here, at least we can sit so we aren't as conspicuous."

"How about we move to your table in the back then?" Mike asked. He picked up his coffee and plate and looked pointedly at Anna, who did the same.

200   WENDY SCOTT-ETTINGER

Charlie nodded slightly and proceeded to walk back to her table ahead of Mike and Anna. She leaned down and said something quietly to her partner Marc, who got up and left the table. "Talk to you later, then," Marc said. He paid Maxine for his coffee and lunch, then left.

"That wasn't necessary, I'm sure," Mike said as he sat down where Marc had been a minute ago.

"We're keeping this under wraps for the time being," Charlie said as she sat back down in front of her lunch. "So, tell me, what makes you think that David's situation was intentional and an act to commit murder?" she asked Mike, as if Anna wasn't there.

"You first," Anna spoke up. "What information do you have about Marty's death that the sheriff thought was important to Allen and Associates?"

Charlie raised her eyebrows at Anna's tone but didn't say anything. "The toxicology finally came back from City Labs a couple of days ago. Marty was killed with a lethal dose of ..."

"PCP and cyanide," Anna finished for her.

"How could you already know that?" Charlie asked suspiciously. "Who have you been talking to?"

"Calm down, Deputy," Mike said as he put his hand on Charlie's shoulder and pushed her back down into her chair. "The milk David ingested was spiked with the same mixture. The doctor at Bellcom General phoned it in to us as soon as they were informed of the contents, and they were able to save David's life as a result of that information."

"Milk? What milk?" Charlie asked, still suspicious of what Anna and Mike were saying. So, Anna filled her in on the entire day she had had the day before: about David's condition when she had showed up at the office for work, the milk and the symptoms David was presenting with, giving the milk carton to the nurse who had it analyzed, and how it saved her brother's life. She said that had they been able to determine the cause of death of the people twenty-two years ago, maybe they could have saved her husband's life and Marty's. Maybe if the police hadn't been so quick to judge, they would have requested tox screens on Red and known this information in the spring before anyone else had to die.

Mike put his hand gently on Anna's shoulder and she stopped talking.

"Sorry," she said to both officers. "This whole situation just makes me so angry!"

"Okay," Charlie said seriously. "So, we now know what's been killing people. What we don't know is how, at least not with everyone other than David. We also have no clue as to who or why!"

DAVID HOBBLED HIS WAY OVER TO THE elevator and pushed the UP button. His family was right about him needing to take it easy for a few days and not rush his exit from the hospital. He still felt like hell, but he wasn't going to admit that to any other them, least of all Anna. David smirked as he thought of his sister. The elevator doors opened, and he pushed the top floor button. The doors closed, but the elevator didn't move. A voice came over the speaker system saying, "Are you aware of the floor you have chosen?" The therapist he'd talked to earlier had warned him about this part of his journey.

"Yes, I have been cleared to visit a patient," David answered quickly.

"And who gave you that permission?"

David gave the disembodied voice the therapist's name.

"And who are you trying to visit and for what purpose?" the voice asked.

"I'm here to talk to Albert Packart about some issues at and around his orchard," David responded.

The elevator started to move. It did not stop at any of the other floors. When it dinged and the doors opened, David was greeted by a stern looking orderly in an all-white outfit. "Mr. Allen, I assume." The orderly almost smiled. "Please follow me. I understand you have requested a private area to meet with Mr. Packart." He began to walk toward the locked doors at the end of a short hallway. "Please, this way sir." David followed him reluctantly. *Maybe this wasn't such a good idea after all*, he thought as he looked at the large, jail-like double doors. It appeared as if they had double-paned, bullet-proof glass in them and there was metal mesh between the panes. This wasn't just a psychiatric watch area; this was high security.

"Mr. Allen." A nurse behind the glass startled David out of his thoughts. "If you could just sign in, Barry here will take you to a small office down the hall. I'll bring Mr. Packart down to meet with you shortly." She looked up at David and smiled. "Don't worry, we won't forget you're back there." She chuckled as she pushed a button to open the heavy doors. The lock on the door clunked and Barry pushed them open.

"After you, sir." Barry held the door opened for David. "Once we get into the office, I'll go over a few safety features we have in there, and an intercom that will allow you to inform the front desk when you're ready to exit.

They entered a brightly lit office with a desk and two chairs at the far wall. A pitcher of water had been placed in the centre of the desk with two plastic cups. There was nothing else in the room. No plants, no stationary, no pens or pencils, nothing. The walls were a pale-yellow colour, and there was no natural light in the room at all. Hopefully the whole place didn't look this clinical, David thought as he was asked to sit on the other side of the desk with his back to the wall.

Barry showed him where the intercom button was (under the desktop on the right-hand side), and told him that if he needed anything else, he was to push the button and ask. Barry went through several scenarios with David that made it sound like he was meeting a violent offender. He hadn't thought Albert was dangerous, just delusional, and he said as much to Barry. Barry raised his eyebrows but didn't respond. "I'll be right outside the door; if you need immediate assistance, please just holler."

The door opened a few seconds later and in came an old man of about seventy or more. He looked confused and tired. He looked at David and started to back out of the room again. "What is this? Who are you? Who sent you?" Albert asked, frightened.

"Mr. Packart." David stood from his chair. "My name is David Allen, sir. I'm Jenny and AJ Allen's son."

Slight recognition sparked in Albert's eyes. "Mary's people," Albert said absently.

"Yes, sir. Aunt Mary is actually my biological mother."

"What? You're that David?" Albert rushed into the room and tried to reach over to hug David, but Barry stopped him. Albert pushed away from Barry and sat in the chair that had been designated for him. He sighed heavily.

"Thank you, Barry," David said to the orderly. "We'll be fine here, so some privacy would be appreciated." Barry left the room, closing the door behind him. David heard the lock whir as the door was secured.

"What can I do for you?" Albert looked at David with an inquisitive stare. "Why have you come to visit me and why all the secrecy?"

"Have we met before, Mr. Packart? You look very familiar, but I can't place where we might have seen each other."

"Don't think so," Albert responded. "As least not since you were a little gaffer. Don't imagine you remember much from back then, though."

"No, unfortunately not," David answered. He couldn't shake the feeling that he'd seen him somewhere in the past couple of weeks, but he just shook

PACKART'S ORCHARD 203

his head to remove the idea. "I'd like to talk to you about the orchard and about the deaths that have happened in and around them. It may help me to figure out who was responsible back then and to solve some current issues that have happened to me and to Anna recently." Albert raised his eyebrows in an interested yet non-committal way but didn't respond to David.

"I have a number of questions for you, but first let me tell you what's been happening over the last few weeks." David pushed his telephone to the centre of the desk, close enough for the microphone to pick up both their voices, but not so close that Albert could grab it. "I'd like to record our conversation, if that's okay with you." David looked over at Albert to make sure he understood what was going on.

"Yes, that's fine," Albert responded. "What have you got to tell me that I might be interested in?"

He told Albert about how Anna had come to his office hoping to hire him to investigate Jack's death. He told him about their conversation with Amelia and how they had been the ones to find Marty Faulkon's body at the rest area. He told him about the Windsmill police, and when he did, Albert smiled and raised his hand. "You spoke to Harpy, did you?" Albert asked.

"Yes, he and Deputy Sheriff Carter, as well as a Dr. Redding, the day after we found Marty."

"Poor Becky and Marvin. I'm sure they must be beside themselves." Albert hung his head and shook it. "That should not have happened to them again."

David waited to see if Albert would say anything else, but he remained silent. "Well, go on, finish your telling then," Albert finally said when David remained quiet as well.

"Yes, sir." David continued. He told Albert about talking to Mary about Paul's death and what they'd found when they got back to David's office the next day. He told Albert about his long conversation with Marvin just a few days after Marty's funeral, and how he'd told David about Manny and Malcolm's deaths and the issues at Carson Police Department. He told him how Mary, Marvin and his own dad, AJ, told him he needed to talk to Albert about what happened to Darren and ask if he had any insight into who the investigator was and what had happened to him as well. He told Albert about how he'd ended up in emergency a couple of days earlier, having been poisoned in his own apartment. David looked over at Albert to see if he was getting any reaction, but there was none that he could see.

"So, you see, sir," David said, bringing Albert back to the current conversation, "I could really use your assistance with getting this sorted out."

"Yes, I suppose you could." Albert smiled at him for the first time. "It sounds like you've gotten further in just a few short weeks than any of the police from here to Kendall have been able to accomplish in twenty years." He stood up and shook David's hand. "I'll be out of here tomorrow, maybe the next day if the paperwork doesn't get signed today," Albert said to the camera in the corner. "I'll meet you at your office and I'll answer all the questions I can about that time. But not in here." He glanced up to the cameras again. "Prying eyes and ears and all that," he said to David with a conspiratorial look in his eyes.

"That would be fine." David reached over and turned off the recording on his cell phone. "I didn't realize they were releasing you."

"Oh, they haven't been keeping me in here," Albert answered "I have. After Jack died, I just couldn't face going back to the orchard or to Amelia and her total denial that anything was wrong or that who was doing these horrible things was really who I'd said it was. She is trying to convince Harpy and the Bellcom Police Department that it was me who was doing these horrible things. Now that others have died, and all the things that have happened to you and your property, there's no way that it could have been me." Albert's smile got bigger. "This place will provide me with proof, with a big bow on top!" He was practically dancing. "Now, if you'd push your little button, we can both start getting some answers, and I can get my freedom back!"

David pushed the button, and Barry quickly opened the door. "I assume you'll be wanting to talk to Dr. Baden about your paperwork, Albert?"

"Yes, please. I can wait here if he's in the building." Albert smiled at Barry. "I told you I'd be getting out of here soon."

Barry turned to David. "I know you didn't get all your questions answered, sir, but I think you've made an old man very happy." He smiled. "Please follow me, I'll get you out of here."

David got off the elevator and walked back down to his ward. He let the nurses know he was back. They asked that he wait in his room, as the doctor was looking for him a few minutes earlier. He sat down in the chair beside the window in his room and stared out into the sunshine. How he would hate to have to stay upstairs for long. No natural light and no way to get out for fresh air. What a horrible way to live. He thought about what Albert had said and whether he could have done that to himself if he was in his shoes.

PACKART'S ORCHARD   205

Why was everyone so quick to not believe Albert when he went to them with his story? How could his own wife be so cruel?

As David was pondering everything he had just learned, his phone rang. Without looking at it, he answered, "Hello."

"You've just signed his death warrant," a voice said.

David looked down at his phone to see if there was a name or number on it, but it only said "unknown number." "Who is this?"

"The Grim Reaper." The voice chuckled menacingly. "I'll come for you again too, and next time I won't miss." The line went dead.

"David, I see you're back with us earlier than I expected." The doctor's voice startled David and he jumped.

"Dr. Handling!"

"David, are you okay? You look like you've seen a ghost."

"Yes, I'm fine, but I really need to make a few phone calls urgently." David wiped his face with his hand. "I just got a threatening phone call, and I need to let the police know about it right away." He turned his back on the doctor and hit Mike's number. When Mike answered, David told him about the call he'd just received. He asked if the Bellcom police could provide protection to Mr. Packart when and if he was able to get out of the hospital, and if they could step up security at his office.

He then dialed Anna's number, and she answered saying, "I'm on it. You just look after yourself. Are you being discharged today? I can come get you right away. I don't think you should be staying in Bellcom City right now."

"How did you know?" David asked puzzled.

"Mike and I are just going over everything at your office, so he told me what you said. Like I said, I can come get you whenever you're ready." They hung up.

"Doctor Handling, I'm sorry I didn't realize you were still here." David turned to look at the doctor who had been looking after him the last couple of days.

"That's quite the story you just told your friend," Dr. Handling said. "I was going to release you this afternoon, but perhaps we should keep you here."

"No, no, I need to get out of here. The sooner I can figure out who is causing all this havoc the better off everyone will be. Please, I'll be fine," David pleaded.

"Okay." The doctor looked at David worriedly. "I have no medical reason to keep you here. But you need to try to take it easy for a few more days. The drugs in your system will take a few days to completely clear. You need to drink plenty of liquids, preferably water, and eat a little healthier than you're used to doing. I know, I know," he added when David groaned, "but you really must be careful right now. I don't want to see you back here in worse shape than you were two days ago."

"I get it," David said and agreed to come into the doctor's office for a full check the following week. "Thank you."

He hurriedly gathered up all his belongs and phoned Anna back to have her or Mike come get him. He then called his mom to let her know that he had been discharged and that Anna was coming for him. He told her everything was fine and not to worry about him. "Yes, I'll be careful. Love you, Mom." He said goodbye to all the nursing staff and headed back to the elevators. He needed to get out of there!

PACKART'S ORCHARD   207

CHAPTER 24

DAVID SAT IN HIS OFFICE WITH ANNA and Mike. He and Mike had spent the night in his apartment after a long argument with Mike and Anna about him staying there by himself. He wasn't going to be run out of his building by a cowardly killer, no matter what anyone said. But he wasn't sure how much longer the Bellcom PD would keep his doors manned, especially when there was so much talk about them losing funding. David shook his head and stared at his phone. "What's the Packarts' phone number?" he asked, then looked up to see if Anna was looking it up. She rattled off the numbers and David entered them into his contacts. "I think I should call and see if Albert made it home okay. Do you think the sheriff's department in Windsmill will provide him with protection?"

"David, Albert isn't in Windsmill," Anna said. "At least, not that Amelia knows about."

David looked up from his phone again. "How do you know that?"

"I ran into Amelia at the grocery store yesterday after I left here. I picked up some stuff for you, by the way." Anna smiled at her brother. "You're welcome." She grinned when David didn't say anything. "Anyway, I asked her how she was holding up and how Albert was doing. She was gruff and scowled at me and said 'how do you think he's doing? Have you ever seen those places?' I told her I hadn't, but if they were that bad why didn't she just let him come home, and she said he needed more help than she could give him." Anna sighed. "I really feel so bad for both of them."

"Okay, I'll call Karen." He scrolled through his phone to find her number, then added, "She's the therapist who gave me permission to see Albert" when two sets of eyes looked at him questioningly. When he hung up, he shook his head.

"What's up?" Mike asked.

"Karen says Albert was released yesterday afternoon about the same time I was. She doesn't have a phone number or address on file other than the one for Windsmill. Where could he go? Does he have friends or family in the area?" He looked at Anna for answers.

"Not that I'm aware of. His parents are long gone, before I was born, I think. He had a brother someone mentioned but I think he died in one of the wars we've had over the last fifty years. Vietnam, maybe?" she questioned herself. "Darren was their only child, and you know what happened to him."

"Okay, friends maybe then. I'll call Dad and see if he might know. I'm worried about him. What if whoever phoned me got to him before he could get home?"

"The chief went over to the hospital and talked to Albert and his doctor after I called in your phone threat. He tried to get Albert to stay a couple more days, but he refused," Mike explained. "He said that the killer wouldn't hurt him and that the police should look after you," Mike pointed to David, "but wouldn't tell the chief who he was talking about."

"Okay, so now what do we do? We really need to find him and get him to talk before someone else gets hurt." David looked from Mike to Anna and back again, hoping one of them had an idea.

"Well, the first thing we need to do is find someplace for you to stay while we sort this all out." Anna looked pointedly at her brother. "You can't stay here! It's not safe."

"I'm not leaving!" David stood up abruptly and pushed his chair back with his legs. "This is the best place to be if he's going to come after me. I'm not running from him, Anna, I won't!"

Anna looked over at Mike for support but got none. "Are you going to be with him twenty-four-seven?" she asked Mike. "Whoever is doing this seems to be able to slip in and out of here without anyone ever noticing. We were in the office when he went out the back door and we didn't even know he was here!"

"I will be here until I have to be somewhere else," Mike informed her. "I'll sleep in the spare room, and we can bunk together like we did in college." He smiled at David.

"Okay, but you might have to sleep on the couch in here." David nodded to the old couch up against the freshly painted wall. "If I find Albert, I'm going to try to talk him into staying here until this is over once and for all."

"Well, okay then." Anna looked from one man to the other. "So, I've called a security company to come and install cameras and motion sensors on the outside of the building. I mentioned the parking area, but they asked about ownership and permits to secure a public space. I wasn't sure what to tell them. Maybe you can explain to them exactly what you wanted when they get here." She glanced at her phone for the time and then added, "in about half an hour."

"You called a security company? Who did you call?" David asked, then looked at Mike again. "Did you know she was doing this?"

"Yes, I gave her Kevin's number and told her to talk to him directly." Mike rolled his eyes. "You know, she's good at this stuff, and you could start trusting that she knows what she's doing."

"Really?" David raised his eyebrows at Mike and grinned.

"Yes, really," Mike answered. "Now back to finding Albert."

As they sat waiting for inspiration, the phone rang. David glanced at the call display, but it just said "unknown name or number." He glanced at Mike, who walked into the apartment area and nodded to David. David held up his hand, counting silently to three, and they both lifted the land line receivers at the same time. "Good morning, Allen and Associates Investigations. David Allen speaking."

"Hello, David, it's Albert. Is your phone secured? I can hear someone breathing like they're listening in."

Mike held the phone out away from his face. "It's a friend on the extension in my apartment. The line is secured," David answered. "Where are you? Are you in a secure area?"

"I'm staying with a friend, and he's making sure no one knows I'm here. Listen, I don't want to be on the phone long in case it's been compromised. Can I meet you someplace in the next day or two?"

"How about you come here today? I have people at both entrances as well as one in the building. We should be safe here."

"Okay, I guess that would be alright, but not today. I'll call you back when I'm sure it's safe. They'll be watching. Are there cameras anywhere near your building?" Albert was sounding a little paranoid, and David was worried that he'd just asked a killer or his accomplice into his building.

"No, not yet, why?" David responded.

"Because he's very savvy technically and will be able to watch from any security system around. If not, then he'll be there physically, but you won't be able to see him." Albert sighed. "Which door do you and your friends come in and out of most of the time?"

"The front door. That's the business door, so it has the most traffic."

"Then I'll come to your back door when I do come to see you. Is there a problem with me getting past your police presence?"

"We'll meet you at the back. How long before you can get here? We'd really like to get this done and over with once and for all."

"I'll call when I'm ready. Not today." Albert hung up.

"That was a little strange," David said as he hung up the phone.

Mike walked back into the office a few minutes later. "I've informed the guy at the back to be on the lookout. Told him we were expecting someone to come up to the apartment through the back in the next day or two. Also told him to be extra vigilant and to report any movement back there. I'll let the guy out front know the same thing."

"Can't you just use your radio?" Anna asked.

"Not right now. Especially after what Albert just said." Mike headed for the front door and jogged down the stairs. When he returned, he started looking out all the windows. Then he turned to David again. "Have you looked upstairs at all since all of this started?"

"No, never thought of it. The attic is just storage, there's really nothing up there of interest."

"But it's big enough for someone to stay in comfortably," Mike said as he headed for the attic entrance. "Is it locked?"

"Usually," David said, "but with the way things have been going around here the last few weeks, who knows?" He shrugged.

Mike reached out and pulled on the door, but it didn't budge. David handed him a key from his key chain and Mike turned the lock easily. He opened the door slowly to make sure that it hadn't been booby-trapped and nothing was going to blow up or jump out at him. When nothing happened, he headed up the stairs slowly and as quietly as he could. David and Anna watched from for the bottom of the stairs. "All clear," he hollered as he rounded the upstairs landing and looked around. It really was full of junk, he thought as he shook his head. "What is all this stuff?" he asked when David appeared behind him.

"Oh, you know, this and that." David smiled impishly.

"Is that a kid's baseball glove over there?" Mike pointed. "And aww, you kept your participation trophies." He started to laugh.

PACKART'S ORCHARD   211

"Funny, very funny." David scowled at him. "Since there's nothing of interest up here, can we leave my trip down memory lane for some other time?" He turned toward the door to get his friend and sister to leave the attic when something caught his eye. "What the…?" he said as he walked slowly toward the object he had spotted. He turned his head and made the "shhh" motion with his hand then turned back. He unburied something from the junk that had been piled around it and looked for wires or a power source. Mike came over quietly to help him, and Anna stood watching over their shoulders. When David finally found a power cord plugged into the wall, he pulled it out and looked for any other equipment that might be in there. He looked up into the rafters and spotted a camera. He waved at it as he pulled it out of the ceiling, expecting to get wiring, but there wasn't anything obvious that led back to the recording and listening devices he'd just unplugged.

He whispered to Mike, "How many more downstairs?" and Mike shrugged. He made a sign to David to indicate they'd look around when they got down there. David leaned into his sister and whispered, "You stay up here for the time being and see if you can find anything else. So far, we have three cameras and a recording/listening device and what looks like a makeshift power source of some sort. Mike will look around in the office while I search the apartment." He and Mike headed for the stairwell and down into the apartment.

Anna knew that David had asked her to stay up there for her own safety, but she was going to do a thorough job of looking for any more technical devices, even if her brother didn't think she was capable. She started at the recording and listening device David had originally spotted and followed all the wiring to make sure it didn't lead anywhere else. The cameras appeared to be wireless, so they must have been connected to the Wi-Fi router somehow. She looked in and around all the boxes and finally found an extender plugged into a wall socket behind an old filing cabinet.

Because of the location, she didn't think it was something David had installed, at least not up here, so she unplugged it and wrapped it up in an old blanket with the rest of the equipment they'd found. She picked it all up and headed for the stairs, then decided to look around in the stairwell to make sure there wasn't anything there. Sure enough, in the far corner, looking down at the apartment door, was another small camera. She reached up on her tiptoes and pulled on it. It came crashing down on top of her. "Son of a b— … gun," she said and looked at the device that now lay at the bottom of the stairs in pieces.

"Well, no one's using that one again any time soon." She chuckled as David and Mike whipped open the door and stared up at her. She pointed to their feet and when they looked down, they realized what they'd heard.

"Where was this one?" David asked as he began to pick up the pieces.

"Up there." Anna pointed to the top of the stairwell opening. "It slipped out of my grasp when it released from its position. I wouldn't bother picking those up. I'll sweep when I get down there." She turned around and picked up the blanket with the other devices from the floor where she'd placed it.

"What you got there?" Mike asked as he took the blanket from Anna.

"The device and cameras we already found before you came downstairs, and an extender behind an old cabinet. I assume you didn't put it there?" she asked David.

"What's an extender, and where did you find it?"

"Never mind. Anyway, I did a thorough sweep of the attic. I assume you did the same in the office, Mike?" He nodded at her. "So, what did you find in here?" she asked her brother.

"Not much. A small device in the back behind that door over there, and a camera beside the back door."

"There'll be more than what we've found," Anna said matter-of-factly. "Mike, can you call Kevin and let him know we'll need a full bug sweep before his guys install anything? We'll also need a bug blocker installed on any equipment that they do put in the building. Whoever this guy is, he's smart and he knows his stuff, so we'll need to be one step ahead of him."

"If you think there's still stuff we haven't found, should we be standing around talking about it?" David said indignantly.

"If he still has eyes and ears on us, he already knows we're on to him," Anna replied. "He would have watched as we all walked around and looked for his devices. He's likely sitting somewhere right now laughing at us. Hopefully finding the extender upstairs will have weakened his signal, but if you didn't find one down here yet, he's likely still got some left to play with."

"How do you know so much about this stuff?" David asked curiously.

"Because this is what my degree was in."

"If what you say is true, he may be moving around outside the building trying to regain connection," Mike said as he looked around the apartment again, trying to locate any other equipment they may have missed.

David looked out the back windows and down the alley. "Now we need to meet our visitor somewhere beside here. We don't have any way of contacting

PACKART'S ORCHARD   213

him and we don't even know when he might show up." He was exasperated at the situation.

"You go out the front, turn toward the parking lot, and then around to the alley to the right. I'll go out this way and turn right around the building and back to the front door. I'll alert our guys of what we've found and tell them if anyone comes near or around the building, to wave them off and notify me ASAP," Mike said as he headed down the stairs to the alley below.

David and Anna headed down the front stairwell as Mike had suggested. David mentioned to the police officer that they may be expecting someone, but that they could no longer meet him here so to stop him and tell him to wait by David's car. David then headed over to the parking lot to make sure that Albert hadn't parked there already, even though he'd said he wouldn't be there today. He went to say something to Anna, but she was gone.

"Damn it, Anna!" he called out but got no response. He looked around and spotted her heading the other way around the building. "Fine!" he mumbled as he crossed the street again. He was about to turn right at the corner when he ran into someone coming the other way.

"So sorry," the man said as he hurried by staring at his telephone. "I'm so late and wasn't paying any attention."

"No problem," David said as he waved the man away and continued around to the alley. He started walking down the alley when it dawned on him why Albert had looked so familiar to him. He headed back toward where the man had gone and looked around, but he was gone. He watched as an old, rusted-out red truck pulled out of the parking lot and headed east. "Damn it!" David exclaimed as he watched him leave.

David called his mother to let her know what was going on, then let the restaurant owners both know that he had a security firm coming in to sweep for any viruses or bugs in the building's Wi-Fi and internet services, so they'd need access to their shops early tomorrow.

Anna told them they would be installing security systems, including cameras inside and out. "They may need access to your shops for a bit, but I've asked them not to disturb your businesses any more than is absolutely necessary," she advised them. After answering a few questions about the new system, Anna and David said their goodbyes and made sure his master keys still worked on the door. He'd told Kevin to meet them around 8:00 a.m. the next day to get the keys and to have as much of the system installation in the restaurants done before the 11:00 a.m. rush as possible.

The next day, David and Anna were waiting for Kevin and his crew and then he'd let Mike know they were ready to head out in Mike's private vehicle. Kevin pulled up in front of the building and David handed Kevin the master keys, explained what they had found in the second and third floors of the building, and said he could be reached at his mother's home number for a few days. As he was finishing up with the security team, David's phone rang.

"Hello, Allen and Associates Investigations," David answered absently.

"It's Albert. I'm in the parking lot of your building. Is it safe to come up?" Albert said quickly. David told him to come over to the sandwich shop on the main floor of his office building and wait with him and Anna. Mike pulled his vehicle up to the front door of David's building and honked the horn. David escorted Anna and Albert out to the back seat of the car. David then climbed into the front of his friend's car and they headed west.

"So, what's going on at your building now and where are we going?" Albert asked. He looked tired and defeated.

"Not sure, some place we can talk without being interrupted and without worrying about spyglasses," Mike said, winking at David. He turned toward Bellcom City Centre and then took the Allensville exit. Albert and Anna watched intently.

"We all turned off our phones, right?" Anna said as she checked hers again.

"Yes, I did," came a chorus from all three men.

"Good. Hopefully he won't be able to track us then," Anna confirmed.

They drove to Allensville and pulled up the long drive to AJ and Jenny's house. Jenny was standing on the porch waiting for them. David had phoned her from the sandwich shop in his building and asked her if it was okay if they came there to use his dad's home office for awhile. He'd told her he wasn't using his cell phone for the time being in case they were being followed or someone was listening in, so she wouldn't be able to get hold of any of them until they arrived.

"Hi Mom." David reached over and kissed her on her forehead. "You remember Mike?" he asked as Mike walked up the steps behind him. "And of course, Anna." He smiled. "And this is Mr. Packart. I don't know if you would remember him from Windsmill."

"Of course, I do." Jenny smiled at Albert. "How have you been feeling, Albert? I hear you've been in hospital for a spell?"

"I'm fine, Jenny, thanks for asking. It's good to see you again." Albert hugged her gently. "I really appreciate you allowing us to come out here and

PACKART'S ORCHARD   215

use your home for some nasty business." He frowned. "I'm sure we'll try our best to stay out of your way."

"Oh, no problem at all. It's nice to see everyone occasionally." She escorted them into the house, showing them where the home office they'd be using was, as well as where the washroom was. She pointed down the hall, in the direction of the kitchen, in case they needed anything that wasn't already in the office kitchenette, or if they needed to find her. She then left them to their discussions.

"I'm just going to call Mom and let her know where I am and that I'll likely not be home again tonight." Anna reached for the landline sitting on the large oak desk. She unscrewed the receiver and made sure there was nothing in it that looked out of place, then put the phone back together and dialed her mother's place.

Mary answered on the first ring. "Hi, AJ, what's up?"

"Hi Mom, it's Anna. I just called to let you know that there's been more issues in Bellcom and so I'm out here. I likely won't be home again tonight, if that's okay with you?"

"Of course. Is everything okay?"

"It's fine, just a little delay is all. Give Johnny a hug for me and tell him I told him to be good for you and that I love him."

"He's always good for me, sweetie. Talk to you soon."

Anna turned back to the office area and found the three men sitting comfortably at a round table with four chairs. Each had a coffee in their hands, and they were chatting informally.

"Coffee is behind you, and then come join us." David smiled at her.

She poured a coffee then brought the pot with her and set it on the table. "In case anyone wants more," she said as she sat down.

"Thank you for not telling Mary I was with you," Albert said to her and patted her hand.

"No problem. The fewer people that know what we're up to out here, the better for now."

"Okay, so let's get started," David said as he opened the recording app on his phone. "Where would you like to start, Albert?"

"Can we turn that off for a bit while we discuss the best approach to all of this? I understand that you're anxious to get all the details, but I have a few questions of my own first."

"Sure." David reached over and turned off his phone again. "Better not leave that on too long right now anyway." He looked at Mike and then Anna for confirmation.

"I think we should just forgo the cell phone usage for now." Mike pulled out an old-fashioned tape-recording device and set it on the table. "This will likely do the trick when we're ready, although you'll have to watch the tape doesn't run out." He chuckled.

"Okay, so what questions do you have for us?" David directed at Albert.

"First of all, the old red pick-up truck you watched leaving your parking area yesterday. How many times have you seen it before?"

"I don't know. I remember it from the first time we had issues with Anna's car. I was really tired but wanted to talk to the two restaurant owners in my building. I didn't want to disturb their lunch rush, so I was sitting in my car waiting and I must have fallen asleep. This older man knocked on my window on his way by me and asked if I was okay. I watched him climb into that same truck." David stopped but didn't look at anyone at the table. "The next time I spotted that truck was just before someone called me and asked if I liked the mess. I'd looked out the front window to see if Mike was still there so he could come up and help me with the mess in my office, and I saw that same truck in the parking lot again. I didn't think too much of it since the last time I'd seen him, he had a sandwich bag in his hand. I figured he was likely just a regular customer." David scrubbed his face with his hand. "I don't think I saw it again until today."

"If you did, you likely wouldn't have paid any attention to it. Like you said, you thought he was a regular at Joe's place, so it wouldn't have registered as something out of place," Mike confirmed for him.

"Yeah, likely." David nodded. "He looks very much like you, though, so that's why you looked so familiar to me at the hospital," he directed to Albert.

"Yeah, I figured you'd probably seen Austin around. When you asked me if we'd met before I knew he'd likely been stalking you."

"Stalking me?" David looked startled. "You mean he's been following me around?"

"Oh, for sure. Likely since whenever he got back into the area." Albert looked over at Anna. "I'm sure he's been following you around since then too. Since before …" Albert hesitated.

"You mean since before Jack died!" Anna said pointedly. "Did you know he was back in town then?"

PACKART'S ORCHARD   217

"No, not really," Albert said. "Jack had come to me and asked if there was someone living in the old homestead again. He said he'd seen lights on in it the night before and wanted to know if I wanted him to investigate." Albert shook his head. "After Darren was killed, I wanted Austin gone! I went to talk to him, but he just laughed at me. Told me he didn't have anything to do with all the damn deaths around the orchard. So I went to the sheriff's office but both the sheriff and Harpy – he was a sergeant back then – they thought I'd lost my mind. Everyone in town thought that Austin was dead; missing in action in Vietnam was what the official letter had said. An official government vehicle had come to the door to hand-deliver it and to provide us with their sincere condolences. They said they'd let us know if he was ever found dead or alive, but they never came back," Albert scoffed.

"That's when you came into Bellcom City and talked to a police officer there?" Mike asked.

"Yes, I talked to a Sergeant McCall, I think his name was." Albert looked up at Mike. "You look a lot like him, but obviously this was twenty-two years ago, so it couldn't have been you."

"No, it was my father, sir," Mike said to him. "He never let go of that case; it was his one that got away."

"Well, you should call him and see if he'd like to join in on the capture," Albert said with a smile. "Poetic justice, that would be."

"Anyway, I called in an environmental inspector from the EPS, hoping that he could find some evidence of chemicals or something that would get the police to pay attention. I know they had some evidence at the Carson morgue, but they weren't saying much. I know Malcolm was trying to help them out after his brother died. There was an arson fire up there between the Faulkon boys' deaths. They'd gone to the Kendall Regional Police for assistance, since their chief and the sheriff in Windsmill, Sheriff Dobson, what an ass!" Albert shook his head in memory of the old sheriff. "They weren't getting along at all at the time. Not that anyone really got along with Dobson. So anyway, that left us kind of hanging with no real answers. Lots of speculation, though." Albert shook his head again as he recalled the nineties situation. He still couldn't believe there were five deaths with no real police involvement in any of them.

"This EPS investigator, was he the fifth one that died back then?" David asked curiously.

"Yes, unfortunately, Austin got to him before he could get a report out to anyone. He'd made a few calls back to his office the day he'd come out to inspect the orchards and all the outbuildings. Something had caught his attention, but he didn't tell me what it was. I went into town to talk to him and the clerk at the hotel told me he had gone over to Don's Place for a couple of beer and some supper. She told me that he didn't look very well when he left. I headed over there to talk to him and make sure he was okay, but I could tell I was too late. I tried calling the doctor's office, but no one was answering. Don himself called the police once Jim passed out. It was too late to save him, and I never found out what he'd found or what might have killed him."

"Was an autopsy done in Windsmill before his body was sent to his next of kin?" David asked.

"Yeah, I think so. Again, the Windsmill Sheriff's Department was being tight-lipped about the whole thing. I assume they would have released that information to the Lister family, though." Albert looked over at Anna expectantly, but she had a blank look on her face.

"Why would they give Jack and I that information?" Anna asked, confused.

"Oh no, not you and Jack, but Jack's mother or perhaps his grandparents?" Albert asked. Anna just shook her head. She had no idea what Albert was talking about.

"The EPS inspector that came out here was Jim Lister. He told me all about his little boy and how he was so proud of him. Jim's face would light right up when he talked about his family." Albert smiled at the memory. "I thought you and Jack knew that."

"The fifth death back in the nineties was Jack's father?" Anna asked, in total shock. "Jack never said anything to me about that. I'm not sure he even knew."

"I'm sorry." Albert patted the back of Anna's hand. "I just assumed you and he knew. I thought that's likely what brought Jack out this way in the first place. Trying to find out what really happened to his father. He never said anything to me about it, I just assumed ..." Albert trailed off.

Anna stared at Albert in disbelief. This thing, this person, took her father away from her and David and now she finds out that he took Jack's father too? And then, so many years later, to start up again with killing Jack? "I don't understand. Why would a man kill all of these people? Why us and the Listers and the Faulkons and no one else? What is he getting out of all of

PACKART'S ORCHARD   219

this?" Anna asked the group. They shook their heads as if the same questions were swirling in their heads too.

"Let's take a break and try to regroup. I'll go see if Mom has anything we can steal from the kitchen for lunch and then maybe we can start back with Darren's death and any other details you have about Jim Lister." David looked at the group to see if everyone agreed. No one said anything. They just nodded in agreement.

"Okay, so let's get back together in, say, ten to fifteen minutes?" he asked.

"Sure, that would be fine," Albert finally said. "I'd like to use the washroom if I could?"

They dispersed for a few minutes, and David and Jenny came back with plates of sandwiches, pastries, and a variety of drinks. "Hopefully this will satisfy everyone until suppertime." David smiled as the others gathered around the table. They ate and drank and chatted about what was happening in everyone's lives and what they wanted to do with their summers. Anything but death and bugs and orchards.

"I'd like to take a walk around the grounds, if that would be okay," Albert said before David could ask any more questions. "I promise to come back shortly. I just need a bit of fresh air."

They all decided that fresh air and exercise would do them good, so they headed outside. It was a beautiful spring day in the valley, with not a cloud in the sky!

Albert came back from his walk feeling less like talking over past events then he did before they broke for lunch. He felt they were wasting time talking about what happened in the past when they should be looking for Austin and making sure no one else died at his hands. He felt they were hiding out away from everything in Windsmill when they should get a lynch mob together and storm the damned orchards!

Oh well, he thought as he took a deep breath. *The kids don't know what happened all those years ago, at least not all of it.* Mary and Marvin had told David about some of it and that was good, but Albert knew there were holes in their knowledge. He'd take the time to tell them about Darren and Jim and Austin. They needed to know what they were up against.

When he walked back into the office area, he almost ran right into AJ. "Oh, I'm sorry," Albert said as he backed away. "I didn't realize you were here."

"My fault," AJ said with a smile. "Jenny neglected to tell me my home office had been overrun with David's business." He chuckled. "It's nice to see you again, Albert. How are you feeling these days?" he asked sympathetically.

"Amazingly relaxed, actually." Albert smiled at him. "Thank you for letting us use your space."

"Not a problem. David and Mike were just telling me what's been going on in Bellcom City. I'll leave you all to the telling and the planning. Hopefully all of this will be over soon, and we can get back to living life the way it was meant to be." AJ turned to walk out of the office, then turned back and asked David, "You have the keys to the back cabinets?"

David nodded knowingly at his father. "Yes, Mom gave me the whole set. Hopefully we won't deplete too many of your resources."

AJ chuckled at him as he left the room. He held the door as Anna came rushing in from her jog and she stopped to place a loving peck on his cheek before she continued into the office to join her colleagues.

"Aw, there you are. I was about to send out a search party." David smiled at her. "You look like you've had a good run."

"I did. Helps clear the mind a bit. Are we ready to get back at it?"

"I suppose so." Albert sat heavily into his chair. He looked around the office and then got back up and walked over to a wall full of pictures. There, in the middle of the wall, was a picture of AJ, Marvin, Paul, and Darren. Albert reached up and touched the picture, then pulled it off the wall and sat back down at the table. "I hadn't noticed this before," he said, staring at the 8 x 10 photo in his hands. "This must have been taken during one of the few trips Darren made home when he was in university." Albert set the picture down on the table in front of him. "These boys were thick as thieves and about as much trouble back then too." He smiled down at the young faces staring up at him. A tear slipped down his face as he remembered an unspoken memory. He shook it off.

"Darren was heartbroken when Paul died. He was moody to the point of being dangerous at times. He'd go from being quiet and moody, not wanting to talk to anyone or even be in the same room as other people, including his own wife, to wild and ready to do anything that anyone suggested. He'd play his music so loud he'd wake up the babies and do the most dangerous things, like life just didn't mean anything anymore. I felt sorry for Amy. A strange place with no real friends or family close by to talk to. Two tiny babies to look after, a demanding mother-in-law that was just trying in her own way to help, and a father-in-law that was beside himself trying to figure out what was going on.

"When Manny and Malcolm both died, Darren was so angry I thought he was going to single-handedly tear down every outbuilding and orchard tree from Carson to the northwest end of the valley. He and Amy would take trips up and down the valley every weekend. They'd stay in hotels and B&Bs off the highway. Must have cost a fortune." Albert looked up from the picture and saw three intense faces watching him. He reached over and turned on the tape recorder that Mike had set down earlier. "I assume that Mary and Marvin told you what happened to Paul, Manny, and Malcolm. They likely knew more about those deaths than I did, anyway," Albert said, looking directly at David.

"Yes," David responded, his pen in hand and a notebook in front of him. "I'll let you listen to the recordings if you'd like when we're done."

"I'd like that," Albert said. He sighed heavily. "I don't know that I'll be able to handle this in one sitting, but I'll try. Let's see, where to start?" He pushed the picture away from him and looked up over David's head, like he was searching for the memories in his head. "The night Malcolm died is likely a good place to begin, I suppose.

"Darren had spent the night in the treehouse. He started doing that a lot after Paul died. Said he couldn't sleep and would keep everyone else awake too if he stayed in the house. I think it was more because he and Amy were having difficulties, and being in the mansion was hard on them both..."

DARREN'S STORY — 1990:

"Let's just move back to Kendall and forget all this craziness." Amy paced the floor, a baby on her shoulder. She was trying to get a burp before she laid him back down. "You know this isn't working for either of us. I don't know how much more of this I can take!" Tears started to slip down her face.

"I can't just up and leave in the middle of all of this." Darren raised his voice. "You must know that this craziness is not easy for my father to handle. If we'd come back here earlier, before you were pregnant, it would have been an easier transition, but NO, you didn't want to. You thought your feelings and your family were more important than mine. And I was so lovesick I let you get away with it!"

Darren started to walk out the door, then turned back to her. "If you want to leave, go!" He slammed the door to their room and headed down the hallway. His mother met him at the top of the staircase.

"Everything alright?" Amelia raised her eyebrows at her son.

"No! And it's none of your business!" Darren tried to push past his mother.

Amelia put her hand on the top railing so he couldn't pass without pushing her away, and she knew he wouldn't do that. "It is my business, when I can hear you two screaming at each other from the other side of the mansion," she said crossly. "You have a family in there that you need to look after. You haven't been there for her since she came back from Kendall after the boys were born."

"I just lost my best friend!" He matched his mother's anger. "She has been nothing but difficult through this whole move. Before she ever got down here, she decided she wasn't going to like it or the people here. I can't make her like it here. I can't make her accept you and Dad and this place." He stared at her, expecting her to argue with him. It startled him when his mother didn't say anything. He saw her fighting to stop the tears that were trying to pour from her eyes. He'd never seen his mother cry before.

"I'm sorry, Mom." Darren put his arm around his mother's shoulders and hugged her gently. "I didn't mean to make you cry." Amelia returned his hug, then patted him on his back and headed back into her own room. She closed the door gently without looking back at him.

Darren watched as she left him at the top of the stairs. He'd stocked the mini fridge in the treehouse office with beer and junk food. He might even have some leftover sandwiches from earlier that he'd put in there. Too bad the place didn't have a TV. He could use a distraction from his own thoughts right now. He'd have to look into putting one up there if he and Amy stayed here much longer.

He pulled a golf cart out of the shed without turning on any of the lights. It was already dark, so he was hoping to find signs of whatever was killing people out there. He knew everyone kept saying that Paul died of a heart attack, but Darren knew that wasn't true. Now that Manny was gone too, the police would have to take it more seriously, right? He hoped so, although he didn't have much faith in the bumbling idiots in Windsmill.

He drove slowly down the path, weaving in and out around the trees, trying to spot anything. He saw a car pull up to the cabins as he passed behind them. "Good. Malcolm got back okay," he said out loud as he saw the

PACKART'S ORCHARD   223

boy get out of his car. Darren thought he'd stop by and say hi but changed his mind at the last minute. He wasn't in the mood to have friendly chats with anyone. He pulled quietly away from the cabins and headed over to the treehouse. He wasn't going to see anything out here tonight anyway.

After his third, or was it fourth, beer, Darren was feeling no pain. He was feeling tired, though, so he started to strip off his clothes to lay down. He'd pulled an old cot out of one of the cabins and dragged it up the stairs into the office on one of his many late-night adventures through the orchard. He'd even found some old blankets and a quilt that his mother had made when he was just a boy. It was comfortable enough for his needs. He was almost asleep when he heard someone yelling out back toward the old homestead. He pulled himself up off the cot, slid open the back window, and looked around.

There, on the roadway walking toward the old house, was Malcolm. He looked and sounded like he'd had one too many too. Darren chuckled as he watched. He walked down the staircase and toward the river, where he could see Malcolm better. "What are you doing out there, Malcolm?" he hollered at the boy.

Malcolm turned quickly and looked in the direction of the voice. "Darren, is that you?"

"Sure is." Darren smirked. "What are you doing out here so late at night?"

"I was just taking a late-night walk. It's been a crazy day," Malcolm responded. "How about you?"

"Oh, just trying to get some quiet time," Darren responded. "You should really try to stay close to the cabins this time of night. Dad says there's coyotes out this way." Darren snorted at the thought. He knew damn well there wasn't any coyotes out this way, ever, but that was his dad's standard line when the crew asked why Albert was so adamant about not being out in the orchards at night.

"Sounds like a plan," Malcolm said as he turned back toward the cabins. "I should probably try to get some sleep, anyway."

"Good night, then," Darren said as he waved at Malcolm and watched him walk back down the dirt road toward the cabins. Darren looked the other way. What the hell was that out in the field? It almost looked like an animal, but it was walking hunched over, like a person trying to stay low. He squinted his eyes, trying to see in the dark. Nothing moved. It was like whatever, or whoever, it was knew he had spotted them.

Darren stood still for a long time staring out into the darkness, until he realized he was standing in the middle of the orchard in bare feet, with no shirt or jacket on. He shivered and walked back up the stairs again. He grabbed his shirt off the office chair and slipped it back on. "Well, I'm wide awake again," he said to himself as he looked out the window he'd opened earlier. No sign of Malcolm or anything else out there. He pulled the window closed and locked it, then went back and locked the office door before opening the fridge and grabbing another beer. *What the hell*, he thought as he sat on the side of the cot and stared out into the fields behind the outbuildings. He turned the radio on full blast to try to drown out all his thoughts of what might be out there. Good thing he was on the other side of the orchard, or he'd have the whole mansion swearing at him, he thought as he smiled into his beer.

CHAPTER 25

DARREN WOKE UP WITH A START AS someone pounded on the office door. He could hear old Red hollering for some help. "What time is it?" Darren rolled over and looked at the clock on the office desk. "Damn, its only six-thirty in the damn morning." He looked down at himself to make sure he had something on, then walked over to the door and pulled it open. "Red, what the hell's wrong? You look like you've seen a ghost!

"The boy," Red huffed out. "Call the cops, call a doctor. Someone needs to help him!" he said as tears started rolling down his face. He swiped at them and stared at Darren.

"Red, whoa! What are you talking about?" Darren didn't know what was going on, but he knew something was wrong. He'd never seen Red this upset before – ever.

Red went back out to the golf cart and headed toward the mansion. Darren watched him drive like a madman down the pathway. He pulled his boots and shirt on and headed over to the cabins to see what Red was talking about. When he saw Malcolm's body lying in the grass by his cabin, Darren felt sick. Maybe he should have called Malcolm into the treehouse the night before. Maybe there had been something out in the field that did this. He ran back to the office as fast as his hungover body would go and called 9-1-1. The operator told him that Albert had already called it in, so Darren hung up and phoned Carson PD to let them know what was going on.

He then made the hardest call he'd ever made in his life, to his friend Marvin. He walked back over to the cabins to wait for the shitshow. Albert, Red, and Marvin made it there about the same time and they all stood in silence waiting for the emergency vehicles to show up.

By the time all was said and done, Malcolm's body was taken to the coroner's office in Windsmill because the Carson building was still under investigation due to a suspicious fire that had happened the night before. The two police stations decided that cooperating with each other would be a better approach than fighting each other over who was responsible for dealing with the Faulkon brothers' case.

Darren watched in the background as Marvin talked to the Carson PD about letting his uncle know what was happening, then asked the Windsmill Sheriff's Department about when he could clear out their personal affects from the cabin. The police informed everyone that they'd be doing a thorough investigation and would keep everyone informed as they finished looking around. As the police started to disperse, Marvin stood staring out into the field to the east of the cabins. Darren came over and put his arm around Marvin as best he could to give the big man a hug. "I saw him last night," Darren said as he too stared out into the field. "He was out walking the gravel road at about ten-thirty. I heard him hollering out into the field, like Paul did, remember?" he asked Marvin.

"Yeah, I remember," Marvin said quietly. "There's something out there Darren. Even if we can't see it, there's something there. I've seen it on the cameras where Manny died."

"Yeah," Darren agreed. "There's definitely something out there. I think I saw something last night, but I didn't pay any attention. I'm so sorry. Maybe if I'd told Malcolm to come up and talk about what was going on ... he seemed so angry last night."

"Yeah, I know the feeling. I dismissed him from my place last night too. It was late and we haven't been sleeping since Marty came home. I should have taken the time to talk to Malcolm last night too." Marvin shook his head and stepped back from Darren. "What the hell is going on, Darren? What's killing everyone out here?" Marvin scrubbed his face with his hands.

"I think I know who it is, but I can't quite figure out how. Or why," Darren said almost to himself. "But I'm damn well going to find out whether Dad likes it or not!" Darren turned away from the quiet group of people watching the police scurrying around and headed back toward the treehouse. He'd better get his act together and go let the women know what's happening out here. Then he was going to have a long talk with his dad about all this crap. "He knows something," Darren said out loud, as he hopped onto his golf cart, "and I'm damn well going to find out what it is!" He sped out onto the pathway and headed to the house.

He got to the mansion, pulled his cart up to the front steps, and jumped off. He was more determined than ever to get to the bottom of all of this. He'd better talk to Amy first, though, and put a plan together about what her next steps were going to be. It wasn't safe for her and the boys to be here. As much as he hated to do it, he needed to send her back to Kendall and away from all this death.

Darren pulled the big door open and walked with purpose into the kitchen, where he could hear the women chatting. His wife and his mother were sitting at the kitchen table, each with a baby over her shoulder, patting their backs and rocking back and forth like all women seemed to do when they held a baby. *What a happy sight*, he thought as he walked into the kitchen and up to the table. *This is the way it should be all the time.* Him and his dad working together in the orchard; Amy and Mom in the kitchen with the babies, chatting about whatever they were talking about. He smiled and leaned down to kiss his wife.

Amy looked up and frowned at him. "What's going on out there?" she asked. "Red came flying into the office with Albert and then left again without a word. We heard sirens. Is everything okay?" Amy and Amelia looked at him with worried eyes.

"No, everything is not okay," Darren said despondently. "Red found Malcolm dead beside his cabin this morning about six-thirty. The coroner's office has taken him away and the police are out searching the orchard and surrounding area for clues." Darren sat down at the table between the two women and placed a kiss on the tops of each baby's head.

Amy gasped and put her free hand over her mouth. Tears formed in her eyes and she squeezed the baby tighter to her chest. "Oh, not Malcolm too," she said softly. "Not another one."

Amelia just stared out the window into the morning shadows in the backyard. "What's going on here?" she said to no one in particular.

"I don't know but I'm going to find out!" Darren stood up again and grabbed a cup of coffee from the coffee station. "As soon as Dad gets back to the house, he and I are going to talk about what's going on. He knows more than he's letting on, and I want to know what he's hiding!" Darren spun around and looked pointedly at his mother. "You know too, don't you?" he accused.

228   WENDY SCOTT-ETTINGER

"Me?" Amelia was startled by her son's sudden change in attitude. "I don't know anything about any of this!" she responded indignantly. "Why would you say such a thing?"

Darren started to walk out of the kitchen, then turned back and said to Amy, "You and I need to talk about your next steps and whether you and the boys should stay here any longer. When you have a minute," Darren raised his eyebrows at her to indicate that now would be the preferred timeframe. He then headed out of the kitchen and up the back staircase to his suite of rooms upstairs. He'd wait for her to bring the boys up and then they'd make a plan.

Albert walked into the kitchen to grab a coffee and see if there was anything to eat. He knew Amelia hated to have off-schedule meals prepared but these were unusual circumstances and hopefully she'd be able to pull something together for him and Darren before they got to work. He looked around, wondering what had happened to Darren. He hadn't been in the treehouse when Albert stopped to see if he was okay, so he assumed he'd be in the mansion somewhere. A golf cart had been left at the front door, so he figured Darren had to be around.

He spotted Amelia sitting at the kitchen table, teacup in her hands, staring out at the garden that Red and Malcolm had just finished planting yesterday. He noticed the tear tracks on her cheeks as he got closer, so he picked up the Kleenex box that sat on a shelf behind the nook and set it in front of her. "I take it Darren told you?" he asked quietly.

Amelia nodded as she reached for the Kleenex and wiped at her face. "I must look a mess," she said absently.

"You're beautiful, as always." Albert leaned down and kissed the cheek she just wiped dry.

"Darren wants to talk to you as soon as possible. I think he and Amy are going to leave and go back to Kendall." Amelia sighed deeply. She looked up at Albert, expecting him to have all the answers. He had always had the answers she needed when she was feeling lost.

Albert sat down heavily beside her. "I don't know why this is happening, Millie." He called her by the pet name Austin and Albert had called her when they were younger. He whispered to her, "I think I might know who, but the how and why are still a mystery."

"Darren accused me of hiding something from him that would help solve all of this, but I don't know what he's talking about."

PACKART'S ORCHARD   229

Albert hung his head and didn't respond for a long pause. "I know you're going to think I'm crazy, Millie, but I really think that this has something to do with Austin. I just don't know what or how."

"Austin!" Amelia stared in disbelief at her husband. "Austin died years ago, Albert! You can't possibly think he's come back from the dead to randomly kill these people!" She pushed herself away from the table and picked up all the cups. "I suppose you're wanting something to eat now?" she asked as she went over to the fridge and pulled the doors open. "I can make eggs and toast but it's too late for bacon or sausages. It'll be lunchtime soon and the crew will want something cold, I suppose."

"Amelia," Albert interrupted her. "I think Red has gone into town to get something from the café. I don't know where Darren and his family are, but there isn't any other crew out here now."

Amelia whirled around and stared at him. She opened her mouth to say something, but nothing came out. She closed the refrigerator door again and slammed the egg carton on the counter, breaking most of the eggs. She then burst into tears and ran out of the kitchen.

When Darren entered the kitchen for the second time that morning, he found his father standing at the stove trying to cook scrambled eggs. He reached over and pulled the toast out of the toaster and started to butter it for his dad. "Where's Mom?" he asked conversationally.

"Upstairs, I assume," Albert answered.

"Why are you making so many scrambled eggs?"

"Because she broke most of them before she went upstairs."

"Okay?" Darren looked confused. "Why did she do that?"

Albert whirled around to stare at his son. "Because everything is falling apart, and I don't have any answers to help her put it back together again. And your attitude lately has not been helping!" Albert pointed the egg-flipper at Darren, then turned back to the frying pan. He looked down and realized the eggs were now more than brown, moving toward black. Albert picked up the frying pan and threw it into the trash can beside the counter. "Damn it!" he said as he walked away from his son. "I'm not hungry anyway!"

Darren watched as his father headed toward the house office. He'd let him cool down a bit and then he'd go in and talk to him. He and Amy had talked, and they collectively decided that they'd stay until Darren and the police had resolved whatever was going on here. Then they'd go back to Kendall and let Albert continue to do whatever he needed or wanted to do with the orchard.

Darren's heart wasn't in the orchard business; never had been if he was being honest with himself. He'd need to have that conversation with his dad too, but maybe not today.

He walked over to the coffee station and realized there wasn't any left in the pot. He pulled out a filter and fresh coffee grounds from the cupboard and busied himself making another pot of coffee. He figured it was at least a two-pot-of-coffee kind of day. As he finished pouring water into the machine and turned it on, he heard someone behind him.

"You sure you know how to do that?" his mother asked quietly.

"I'm sure," Darren responded without looking behind him. He waited for the first few drops to start coming out of the machine, then turned around to see his mother standing by the counter looking at the mess in the trash.

"Did you do this?"

"No, Dad was trying to make scrambled eggs when I came down. It didn't go well."

"I see," Amelia said with a quick smirk. "This toast looks about as appetizing as the eggs." She picked it up and tossed it on top of the frying pan in the trash. She looked up at Darren and some of the sadness left her eyes. Then she started to giggle.

"Do you want me to wash that pan?" Darren asked as he pointed into the top of the trashcan. He smiled at his mother.

"Leave it." Amelia began to laugh harder. "I've wanted new pots and pans for the kitchen anyway. It will give me an excuse to go shopping." Tears of laughter started down her face. She held onto the counter. "Oh my sides," she said as she bent over.

"Mom, are you okay?" Darren was trying to hold back his own laughter and look concerned.

They laughed together until their cheeks and sides hurt. They giggled like school children at everything and at nothing. They finally sat down at the nook table and stared out at the garden. And the giggling stopped. It felt good to just sit and be silly with his mother, Darren thought as he looked at her sitting quietly and looking out at nothing. She looked so tired and old now, he thought.

"I'm sorry, Mom," he whispered. "I'm sorry for everything."

Amelia stood up and hugged her son. "It's going to get better, Darren. I promise."

He patted her hands, then stood and moved toward the coffee station. "Would you like some?" he asked as he poured himself a cup.

"No but take some into your father. I know he'll need some by now." Amelia walked over to the counter and began to tidy everything back up. "I assume you'll be wanting to talk to him about what he thinks is going on around here."

"Yeah, I really want to put a plan together. I really don't trust that the police will do much about all this. There's three dead people in our orchard and they still don't seem to take it seriously. Someone needs to." Darren shrugged and apologized to his mother for the second time. She waved him away and he took two cups of hot coffee toward his father's office.

Darren rapped lightly on the bottom of the door with his foot. When Albert didn't answer, he kicked it a little harder. Albert pulled the door open and glared at his son. "Why are you kicking the door? It's not locked!" Darren didn't answer. He held out the coffee cup in both hands as if that would give Albert a hint as to why he'd used his feet to knock. Albert took one of the cups and turned back into the office without a word. This was going to be a fun conversation, Darren thought as he pushed the door closed again with his elbow and moved to sit at the other side of his father's desk.

Albert sat staring at the computer screen. He hated these machines. It was so much faster and easier when he just held pieces of paper and read them that way. When you got to the bottom of page one, you turned it over and continued to read. The stuff on the computer screen was hard to read, and you couldn't just make corrections on it with your pen like you used to be able to do. "Damn it!" Albert swore at the screen. "Why can't I just get a paper copy of this shit instead of having to read it on here!"

Darren reached over and pushed the on button on the printer beside the computer. He then reached over his father's hands and pushed Ctrl P and the printer came to life. It printed the document Albert had opened, which ended up being about five pages, and then turned itself off again.

"Thank you." Albert reached over and picked up the pages. "I need to hire more crew if we're going to make sure the orchard runs smoothly this year." He busied himself with the papers in his hands.

"Dad," Darren said firmly. "Can that not wait until Malcolm's body is at least cold, before you start replacing him?"

Albert looked up, startled. "You may not have noticed, but I have a business to run here," he responded indignantly and returned to his reading.

"You aren't even really reading that, are you?" Darren stood up and placed his coffee cup firmly on the desk so that it clunked beside Albert's cup. "I'm going to go look through the field on the other side of the trunk road. Then I'm going to go see who's been living in the old homestead. Lights are on every night in the top floor windows. Someone is there, and I'm going to find out who. If you don't want to talk to me about it, then fine, I'll figure it out myself." Darren swung around and walked toward the door. "I'll be taking the golf cart with me, if that's okay with you, Mr. Packart." Darren drawled out his father's last name sarcastically.

"What do you mean, someone's living in the homestead? There's no one out there." Albert rounded the desk and grabbed his son's arm and spun him around. "There's no one in the old homestead buildings. No one!" he said adamantly.

"Dad, I've been sleeping in the treehouse almost every night since Paul died. There are lights coming from the upstairs windows in the old house. There's also someone wandering around out in the fields at night. You and I both know it. I've also seen that red pickup truck that picked up the barrels that Marvin's crew found and Paul questioned you about. Whoever it is drives out late after the crew stops working for the day and heads north toward Carson. They sometimes don't come back until early in the morning or even a few days later. Then the lights go back on out there. Who is it, Dad?!"

You won't believe me if I tell you." Albert hung his head and turned back toward his desk. "I told your mother this morning and she thinks I've lost what little sense I ever had."

"Who, Dad?" Darren demanded.

"Austin." Albert looked up at his son defiantly. "It's Austin that's been living out there. He's the one that put the barrels in the watermill. He's the one that wrote all over them and the plans Paul had in his office. He's the one that's been walking out at night. But I won't believe he's killing people. I can't believe he'd do that!" Albert shook his head as if to get the thoughts out of his head. He looked up at Darren, who hadn't said a word.

Darren just stared at his father. He didn't know what to say about all of this. Austin had been declared "missing in action" before Darren was born. He'd never known much about him, except that he had been dad's twin brother. His parents never talked about him. He knew that his grandfather had left the homestead buildings to Austin in his will, and the business of running the orchard was left to Albert. Albert had built the mansion after he'd

PACKART'S ORCHARD   233

married Amelia and his grandmother had lived with them in the mansion wing that Darren and Amy were now living in. He figured Albert didn't want to have the old homestead house taken down because it really belonged to Austin, and Albert always held out hope that his brother would come home to claim it. But it had been almost thirty years now and he'd never shown up. At least, not that Darren knew of.

"If Austin is back, why hasn't he come up to the mansion and had a meal with us? Introduced himself to those of us who never knew him? Why is he being so sneaky? Why did you give those barrels back to him and what was in them? Where are they now?" Darren looked pointedly at his father. "If it is Austin that has done all these things, why haven't you told anyone before now? Why haven't you told the police?"

Albert didn't answer Darren. He just looked down at the floor, thinking about all the questions Darren had just asked. "I don't know!" he finally said. "He's different than he used to be. He won't talk about where he's been or how long he's been back in the country. He won't tell me anything about the last thirty or more years. He was only eighteen when he enlisted and left for boot camp. He seemed to love being in the armed forces. Then, just before he got shipped over to 'Nam, he became really quiet. He used to write letters every week and tell Pops all about everything that was happening. Then one of his last letters before he left the country said something about him being transferred to security or something. The letters stopped coming after that. A few years later Pops got the letter from the armed forces saying that he was missing and presumed dead. That's what killed Pops. He just stopped living after we got that letter. But I never believed it. I could feel it in my bones that Austin was still out there."

Darren sat back down in the chair in front of his dad's desk. He couldn't believe what he was hearing, but his dad was so sure. *Now what?* he thought as he stared into space. How could he go barging out to the homestead and ask the uncle he never knew why he was killing people? Why he'd killed Darren's best friend?

DARREN SAT ON THE EDGE OF THE bed beside his wife and watched the babies sleep in their bassinets. They were getting so big already. With everything that had been happening this spring, Darren felt like he had missed watching his boys grow. He hadn't felt like cuddling them or helping Amy with looking after them. He'd been so self-absorbed.

"I'm sorry, Amy," he said as he kissed her cheeks. "I know all this craziness is hard on you and Mom. I'm going to try to be here more and not sleep out in the treehouse all the time."

"Not to worry, Darren. I know Paul was more like a brother to you than a friend. It's been hard on everyone. And now with the Faulkon boys gone, it just makes it harder. What did your father say again?" Amy looked into Darren's face. She couldn't believe what he'd told her about what Albert said.

"Dad seems to think that his dead brother Austin is back from the armed forces and living in the old homestead. There's no electricity or running water out there anymore, so I can't imagine anyone wanting to live out there. The place is falling apart." Darren was rambling and he knew it. He stopped talking.

"So, your dad thinks Austin is responsible for these deaths? I thought Paul died of heart failure or something. Isn't that what the doctors told us?"

Amy was worried about her husband. He hadn't been himself since they'd come to Windsmill, and she wasn't liking what she was seeing. Maybe Darren was right. Maybe they should have come down here before the wedding and stayed for awhile. Maybe she would have seen this side of him before they had gotten married and definitely before they had the twins. She shook her head to get rid of that train of thought. Life didn't work like that. You can't go back and change what's already done.

"Paul died in the same way as Manny and Malcolm. Mysteriously in the orchard. They didn't do any investigation with Paul's death, even after those barrels were found and the crazy notes were written all over his office. Paul kept talking about bugs big as his head, but the doctors just said he was delirious." Darren stood up and walked over to the bedroom window. It was mid-afternoon and no one was doing anything in the gardens or in the orchards today. He wondered where Red had disappeared to, then he remembered Dad told him Red had gone into town. Wouldn't likely see him for a few days now. He paced back toward the back wall and then to the window again. He felt like a caged animal.

He grabbed his keys off the bedside table. "Let's get out of here. Let's go down the valley and stay by the lake for a few days. We can pack up what we need for the twins and just go." He looked hopefully over at his wife.

"No, Darren. This is not the time to be walking away. Your dad needs you now more than ever. I think your mom knows more than she's letting on too. I think we need to stay here for awhile longer."

PACKART'S ORCHARD   235

Darren looked at Amy in disbelief. She was the one that was always wanting to get away from here and his parents. Now she wanted to stick around. It didn't make any sense.

"Come on, Amy. You never wanted to be here in the first place. You were right, we should never have come down here. I'm sure if I called them, Kendall Environmental Investigations would take me back in a heartbeat. Maybe not in the same position, but they'd find something."

"Darren, please. Let's just stick it out here until things settle down again. Then you can have a serious discussion with your dad about you not wanting to be here, and we'll go where you can find work from there. Now is not the time to be doing that. It would kill your parents if we left now."

Darren paced the floor again. He couldn't believe his ears, but he knew in his heart that Amy was right. Them leaving right now was not going to end well. "I'm going to go down to the office and make some calls. I think I can find some information out about Austin from the armed forces offices on the coast. They should have the final records for his service and whether he ever came back to Canada or not. That should settle that argument. Then I'm going to call up to Carson and find out what ever happened to those barrels that dad supposedly had shipped up there. There must be some record for them somewhere." Darren gathered up his jacket and slipped his work boots on. "You going to be okay here by yourself for a little while?" he asked his wife.

"I'll make do." Amy smiled at him. "You go look into all this craziness and come up with some answers. The sooner you do that, the sooner we can get on with our lives." She leaned into his chest and gave her husband a hug. He kissed her like they used to before they came here.

"We'll figure all this out. I promise." Darren left the bedroom feeling more like himself than he had in months. *I'm not going to sit around and mope about this any longer*, he thought as he took the stairs down to the main office two at a time. *This is going to end now!*

A SHORT WHILE LATER, DARREN CAME BACK into the mansion foyer shaking his head and feeling more confused than ever. He'd made a number of calls to the armed forces offices in the province but ended up getting passed from one area office to the next and then finally all the way up to national headquarters, and no one had any records of an Austin Packart ever being in the services. They finally passed him onto someone in the Security Services

Agency, but they weren't any help either. In fact, they left Darren with more questions than he'd had before he'd made any of the calls.

After deciding to let that sit for awhile, he called around Carson and all the way up to Kendall trying to find a chemical disposal place that had taken six barrels from the orchards in March. There was no registered chemical disposal place within a fifty-mile radius of Carson, and none of the registered places in Kendall or Allensville had ever heard of such a disposal request. He was going to talk to his dad again about what actually happened to the barrels and who picked them up. He was not going to let him sluff off his questions again.

Darren swung the office door open and burst into his father's office, right into the middle of a heated argument between his parents. His father was red-faced as he tried to calmly explain to his wife why he truly believed that he'd seen and talked to Austin at the homestead, and why he was now going to phone the EPS and have an investigator come in to look for and dispose of the barrels properly.

"Whatever's in those barrels, Millie, is likely responsible for killing Paul and the others. Do you want more people to die before we do something about this?" Albert yelled at Amelia.

"You are crazy, Al. Those barrels went to Carson and got disposed of properly. I have the receipt right here!" She waved a piece of paper at her husband.

"I'll take that, thank you." Darren reached over his mother's shoulder and grabbed the piece of paper before she even realized he was there.

"Darren!" Amelia held her hand to her chest. "How long have you been standing there?"

"Long enough to hear that dad is finally going to do the right thing and have a certified inspector come in to investigate the strange barrels and their whereabouts." Darren glanced down at the receipt. "Who is Carson Jackson Disposal Services?" he asked, reading off the receipt in his hand.

"They're a good company." Amelia tried to take the receipt back from her son, but he anticipated her move and stuffed it into his jeans pocket quickly.

"I've been phoning up and down the valley from Kendall all the way to Allensville and beyond trying to find any registered disposal company that took those barrels. No one has ever heard of a disposal company in or around Carson. Nor have they ever heard of themselves or anyone else taking those barrels off orchard property." Darren looked from his father to his mother and back again. "What's really going on here?" he asked quietly.

PACKART'S ORCHARD   237

When neither of them answered, Darren turned around and walked out of the office. "I'm going to go find out who is living in the old homestead, and then I'm going to call the police and have whoever it is physically removed from our property."

Darren almost made it to the front door when his mother caught up to him. She grabbed hold of the back of his jacket. "Darren, please don't go out there."

"Why not, Mom?" he asked pointedly as he ripped his jacket from her grasp.

"It's not safe," she responded unemotionally.

"What's not safe, Mom? Or should I say WHO'S not safe?"

"Darren, please just leave it alone. Please."

Darren walked out of the mansion and down the steps. He didn't know who he was going to find out there but damn it, he was going to find out right now. He jumped onto the nearest golf cart and headed toward the other side of the orchard. It was starting to get dark, but he could still see enough through the trees that he didn't bother to turn on the headlights. No use in warning whoever it was out there that he was coming.

He rounded the cabins and hit the gravel road a little too quickly. The golf cart slid sideways, and Darren figured for sure he was going to flip it. He pulled off the throttle and came to a stop just as the cart was about to tip. He stuck out his foot and twisted around to stop the momentum. He twisted his ankle in the process, but the cart hit back onto four wheels and came to a stop.

He needed to stop and take stock of his emotions before he confronted whoever was in the homestead. He looked down the road but didn't see the usual light in the upstairs window. He looked back at the cabins, but they were all dark too. Strange that not even the streetlights were on at the highway entrance. Darren couldn't remember the last time they were all off at the same time. He rubbed his ankle and wondered if he should just go back, pack up his family, and leave all the craziness behind. But he knew he couldn't do that. He needed to find out what was happening out here and why Paul had been killed.

Darren pulled himself back into the driver's seat of the cart and flipped on the headlights. He jumped with a start when he saw two people standing about half a mile down the road from him. They turned and looked his way, like they hadn't realized he was there. He squinted his eyes, as if that would make them see more clearly in the dark. He needed to find out who was out there and what they were doing on Packart property. He started the cart and slowly drove up the gravel road. But as he got closer, he realized that the people were no longer on the road. "Where did they go?" Darren asked. He stopped driving and got out off the cart.

"Hello! Is there anyone out here?" Darren looked around but he couldn't see anything – shadows and strange movements but nothing distinguishable. "Hello! Who's there?" Nothing. Just as he was getting back into the cart to go back to the homestead, he heard what sounded like a laugh or maybe a cough. He turned his head in the direction of the noise but saw nothing. "Damn it, who's out here?" he hollered. No response. He continued down the road and came to a stop in front of a worn-out wooden door. It was likely very distinguished in its day, but now it just looked sad. Darren walked up to it and tried to open the door, but it didn't budge. He pushed on it again, but still nothing.

"That door hasn't opened in probably thirty years," a voice said from behind him.

Darren swung around and found himself staring into his father's face. But not his father. Someone that looked just like him. "Austin?" he whispered.

"That's right. I'm Austin Packart. Who are you and why are you trying to get into my house?"

"Your house? This property belongs to my father," Darren said indignantly.

"Darren? Is that you?" Austin came a few steps closer.

"Stay back!" Darren had his back up against the homestead door. He didn't trust this man and didn't want him to get too close. "Why are you killing people?"

"I'm not. I haven't killed anyone since 'Nam. I told Albert that when he came out to talk." Austin air-quoted that last word and chuckled. "Albert was always a little emotional," he finished.

"What are you doing out here? Why haven't you come to the mansion to help Mom and Dad in this crazy time? Why are you hiding out in a rundown old building with no heat, electricity, water?"

"I've got enough light to read by, and enough blankets to keep from freezing. Water's plentiful in the creek, and the irrigation system is easy to tap into."

"That doesn't explain why you're out here. Why no one knows who you are or that you ever existed."

"You've been making some phone calls, I take it." Austin stepped back off the homestead porch and leaned up against a tree. "You'll not get any information from the forces about me or any of my company. As far as they're concerned, we never existed. They'll keep it that way no matter what."

"Were you in the forces? Did you serve our country in the Vietnam War, or were you one of those rogue mercenaries we read about?"

Austin lit a cigarette and let out a hardy laugh. He took a big drag from his cigarette and blew circles of smoke in the air above his head. "No, I was in the forces. But they're not going to have a record of me or any of my missions. We weren't officially in the war, you know. We weren't ever there as far as the world is concerned, and they'll keep it that way. When we went missing, they didn't look for us. They couldn't."

"So how are you here then? How did you get back?" Darren was more curious than afraid now. He wanted to know about this man standing in front of him. He looked like his father, but he was more slender, in better shape. Not that dad was in bad shape, just maybe better fed, Darren thought. This version in front of him had a weathered face like dad's but in a different way, and his hair was almost entirely white, like he was older than his years.

"Let's just say I came with the deal." Austin drew on his cigarette again and stared out into space. "I don't think they figured me and the guys were still alive and surely not as healthy as we were. The Cons kept us just barely fed, but we were still alive. This place," Austin nodded at the old building in front of him, "this is a palace compared to where I've been the last twenty years." Austin threw his cigarette butt in front of him and ground it into the gravel with the toe of his boot. "Now, if you'll excuse me, I'd like to have my own quiet time." He started to walk toward the field, away from the front door.

"Wait, where are you going? You haven't answered my questions. Why have you been killing the people around the orchard?"

"I told you I never killed no one." Austin said and then just disappeared.

Darren looked around, bewildered. *Where the hell did he go? You can't just disappear like that in an open field!* But he was gone. Austin just disappeared in front of Darren's eyes.

Darren climbed back into the golf cart and turned on the headlights. They illuminated the porch and front door, but nothing else. Darren decided he'd come back in the daylight and see if he could find out where Austin had disappeared to. As he backed the golf cart away from the house to get a better place to turn around, the upstairs windows lit up. Austin appeared in the window and waved at Darren, then closed the curtains again.

Darren turned the golf cart around and headed back down the road toward the cabins. As he was about to turn into the orchard and find a pathway back to the mansion, a light went on in the end cabin. Red must have come home tonight after all, Darren thought as he turned slowly, this time, into the orchard grove behind the row of cabins. *That means work will get done tomorrow by someone.* Darren smiled at himself. As he was turning to go into the treehouse office, he changed his mind. He'd promised Amy he'd stop spending his nights out here, so he swerved back onto the pathway toward the main house.

It was the same pathway where they'd found Paul a few months ago. *The one the big black bugs were on*, Darren thought as he started to investigate the trees and drive the cart just a little faster. By the time he made it to the cart shed to put his golf cart in its place, his imagination was running wild. He quickly locked up the shed and turned toward the parking lot. A few more steps and he'd be home free, but then something caught his eye. And what was that sound? Birds? No! Bugs! Darren turned to run but something hit him in the head. Then another in the back of his neck. *What the hell was that?* he thought as he began to sway. *Why do I suddenly feel like I've been out on an all-night drunk?* he wondered as his knees hit the gravel parking lot. Then everything went black.

PACKART'S ORCHARD 241

CHAPTER 26

ALBERT BLINKED AND SWIPED AT THE TEARS that had started to pour down his cheeks. He looked around the table and saw that the eyes of everyone in the office were the same. "I'm sorry. I'm going to need some fresh air for a bit," he said quietly as he stood up from his chair. "It's been a very long time since I've had to tell anyone about my boy. About Darren's death. Red found him the next morning lying face down in the gravel. His face and neck were swollen up like he'd had an allergic reaction to something. I knew right away. I knew he'd gotten my boy too." Albert wiped at his face again and walked out of the room.

David turned off the recorder, stretched his back, and looked at his colleagues. "What do you think?" he asked no one specifically.

"Interesting," Mike said as he stood up too.

Anna reached over and picked up the picture Albert had taken down off the wall. She walked over and put the picture back in its place. "Does what he said even make sense? How does he know that Darren talked to Austin before he died? And if Austin is the killer, why go up into the homestead and then somehow get these killer bugs to the mansion miles away to kill him in front of his parents' house?" She looked at David, then Mike and back to David, but neither of them responded. "We need to ask more questions," she said as she walked toward the outside patio. "Where did he go, anyway?" Both men shrugged and followed Anna outside into the fresh air. They looked around but didn't see Albert anywhere.

"He can't have gone too far," David said as he turned back into the house. "Maybe he headed to the washroom, or into the kitchen or something."

"I'll check the bathrooms; you head to the kitchen. Anna, can you check outside again and make sure he isn't out there?" Mike directed as he headed down the hallway toward the first washroom.

David looked at Anna, shrugged, and headed toward the kitchen. "I'll see if mom or dad saw him anywhere," he said as he left the office area.

Anna turned back toward the patio door and walked out into the sunshine. "Now, where have you gotten to, Albert?" she said as she turned onto the pathway she'd been running on earlier.

Jenny had prepared a big deli buffet-style meal and called everyone in to have a bite to eat and recharge themselves. They'd all been out walking and driving the acreage, and the roads around it for hours, with no sign of Albert anywhere. Jenny was worried about all of them. This whole situation was getting out of hand.

As they straggled into the kitchen, they filled their plates and sat down at the kitchen table. None of them said a word.

"I'll drive around Allensville after we eat," declared David as he grabbed a cold beer out of his parents' fridge before sitting with the rest of them.

"I'll go with you," Mike said as he took the beer from David's hand and downed it. David grabbed a couple more out of the fridge and asked if anyone else wanted something to drink before he sat back down.

Jenny pulled a bottle of wine out of the same fridge and poured two glasses, handing one to Anna as she sat at the table.

"Do you really think he's walked into town and is just sitting around waiting to be found?" Jenny asked.

"I don't know, but he has to be somewhere, and unless his friend from Bellcom City drove out and picked him up ..." David stopped. "Maybe that's exactly what happened!" he declared to the table.

"I've thought of that myself," Mike said, "but I don't know who his friend is, or anything about them. Hard to follow up on that line when we literally don't have any information."

"This whole situation doesn't make any sense," Anna finally said as she pushed herself away from the meal and started to clean up.

"I agree," David said as he started to help his sister. "Maybe we should call the police stations in and around the area and see if anyone has spotted him, or any strange vehicles, in the area?" He looked over at his friend for confirmation, but Mike just shook his head.

PACKART'S ORCHARD   243

"We can't put out an all-points bulletin on a man that hasn't done anything other than leave a discussion about something that happened twenty years ago," Mike said. "We can't even put out a missing persons bulletin, because he's only been gone for a few hours."

"So do you think us driving around Allensville will even do anything other than make us feel better?" Anna asked as she cleared more plates from the table.

"No, not really," Mike sighed. "I just don't know how he got out of here so quickly, without any of us seeing which direction he left in." He looked around the room for any inspiration from any of them, but none was forthcoming.

"Maybe he went into the bathroom down the hall and called his friend. If they had a rendezvous place sorted out, he just headed out that way." Jenny looked around at the people staring at her. "Well, it's as plausible as anything else I've heard." She shrugged.

"Actually, that makes a lot of sense." Mike pulled up a map of the area on his phone. "Bellcom City limits is only about twenty minutes from the outskirts of Allensville and then another ten to fifteen minutes out this way on the highway. If Albert snuck passed everyone as we were stretching our legs in the office, he could have walked out to the main road and headed toward Allensville without us noticing."

"By the time we noticed him missing, he could have walked a fair distance. Albert is used to walking the orchards all the time," Anna continued. "He could move pretty fast when he wanted to."

"Yes, but even so," David joined it, "he'd have to stay out of sight, wouldn't he? We started looking for him and calling out to him within a few minutes of him leaving."

"Did we?" Mike raised his eyebrows. "We spent a lot of time looking around the house and the yard before we figured out he had left the acreage. He could have been anywhere by the time we started calling out to him in earnest."

"Actually ..." AJ spoke up for the first time since they'd all sat down. He drank what was left of his beer and looked around the table. "If I was Albert, I would head out around the back and head toward Bellcom from there. The back road is gravel, but it's a lot faster than going through Allensville."

"Yeah, you're right! How did I forget about the back road? We used to use it all the time when I was in college. There's no traffic back there either, so no one would see him walking and think it was strange." David grabbed the keys to his dad's car and headed for the back door out to the yard.

"Where are you heading?" Mike asked as he followed him out.

"To the back road. See if we can see anyone or anything out of place. If Albert's friend is familiar with the place, it would be pretty easy to meet up with him. But if he isn't, it could take awhile to find the right turn-off. Most of the roads out here aren't marked anymore."

AJ headed out the door with the men, leaving Anna and Jenny in the kitchen.

"Well, I guess we're on clean-up duty." Jenny laughed as she looked around. "Or maybe you were and most of it's done already."

"I think better when I'm busy. There's just a few things left to put away. I wasn't sure where to put them," Anna said as she pointed toward the counter where she'd placed the offending items on. "I was hoping David would get around to putting them away."

"That boy likely didn't even notice them there." Jenny chuckled as she tidied up the counter and poured more wine into each of their glasses. "So why do you suppose Albert took off like that, anyway?" she asked as she handed the wine glass to Anna and sat back down.

"Good question." Anna sat with her chair twisted so she could see out the back window. Not that there was anything to look at, but she needed to continue scanning the yard.

"Was something said or implied that would scare him off? Did anyone say anything to him?" Jenny asked as she stared out the window with Anna.

"No, he was telling us about the meeting Darren had with Austin, and then how he died before he made it back to the mansion. I'm not sure how Albert knew about the discussion Darren and Austin had, and we didn't have a chance to ask any questions or make any comments at all."

"I don't remember much about that whole situation." Jenny sighed into her wine glass. "It was such a horrible time, and that's about the time that David came to live here. Everything was all upside down and backwards back then. Poor Amy was beside herself, and Amelia was acting really weird." Jenny looked over at Anna. "At least, weirder than normal, anyway." She smiled.

"Amelia always seemed so standoffish, like she was better than everyone else." Anna drank some wine, then set the glass on the table. "I can't imagine having to live with her like Amy did. And poor Albert seems so dead set against going back to his own family home right now. He says Amelia tried to have him arrested after Red died." Anna didn't look over at Jenny, but she could feel the tension increase.

"Amelia accused Albert of Red's death?" Jenny said indignantly. "Albert is one of the most gentle, caring people you'd ever want to meet. After David came out here to live, Albert would call and make sure everything was alright. He'd ask us what we needed, or just send little care packages for David. I know he did the same thing for Mary, with having to raise you by herself and look after everything."

"Really?" Anna was shocked at what she'd just heard. "Mom never mentioned any of that to me."

"No, I don't imagine she mentioned it to anyone," Jenny said matter-of-factly. "We talked about it some and decided we needed to put our foot down and stop him. People were going to start to get suspicious with all the money and new toys for the kids. We sat down and talked to him about it one day when he was out doing some business with the cannery. I remember he looked so dejected but said he understood." Jenny finished off her glass of wine and stood up. "He did, however, set up a nice college fund for all the kids. You, David, Amy's boys, even for Marty and Michael." Jenny walked over and put a new pot of coffee on. "I think the boys are home again."

Anna stood up and looked out the window. It was starting to get dark, so there wouldn't be any use looking for Albert now until morning. "Maybe they found him," she said as she walked over to the back door and pulled it open.

"Anything?" she asked as they walked back into the kitchen.

"We drove all the way down the back road to the Bellcom turnoff," AJ said.

"Someone nailed a big business envelope to a signpost just before the turn-off." Mike shook his head.

"It was a note from Albert," David said. "Took me awhile to convince these two to stop and investigate." He pointed at his companions.

"So, what did it say?" Anna asked curiously.

David handed her the envelope. "Read it for yourself." He walked to the fridge and opened it, staring into it like he used to when he was a teenager.

"*I'm so sorry. I will call you later. I needed to get away to re-think all that has happened. After retelling Darren's death, I realized it didn't make any sense. Austin couldn't have killed him; he wouldn't have killed his own son.*" Anna looked up from the note. "His own son?" She looked around the room. "What does that even mean?"

There were shrugs from everyone in the room, but no words, as they sat at the kitchen table staring at Anna.

"Wonderful, more questions with no answers." She sat down and joined them. "Now what?"

CHAPTER 27

DAVID SAT IN AN EXTREMELY UNCOMFORTABLE CHAIR, waiting for the sheriff to show up. They'd made a tentative appointment to talk to Sheriff Harper for 9:00 a.m., but David was told that he would be a few minutes late. Something about a phone call. Anyway, if he didn't show soon, he'd head up to Carson to talk to whoever up there might remember what happened twenty years ago.

David rubbed his face. Although a lot of what Albert had told them last night made some sense, there were too many holes, and David didn't like holes. He glanced over at his sister, who had insisted on coming with him. She sat quietly, flipping through a magazine that must have been as old as this case was. David chuckled at the thought.

"What are you laughing at now?" Anna put the magazine back on the table and looked at her brother.

"Just wondered if there was anything in there about the Windsmill deaths in 1990. That magazine looks about old enough." David chuckled again at his own joke.

"Not quite, but pretty close, I'd say," Harpy's voice chimed in behind them, making them both jump. "Sorry, didn't mean to startle you." Harpy pointed down the hallway. "Sorry to make you wait so long, I was on an urgent call. Please come on in."

They stood up, gathered their belongings, and followed Harpy down to his office. "Nothing too serious, I hope," Anna commented.

"Maybe, maybe not." Harpy shrugged as he walked into his office and pointed to the couch on the far wall. "Make yourself comfortable. Can I get you anything?

"No. we're good for now, thanks" David answered for both of them.

247

"So, what can I do for you two this morning? I hear you've been having more trouble at your office, David?"

"Yes, we have, but that's not what we're here for now. We're still digging into the old cases to see if we can piece together what happened back in 1990 with what's going on here now. I really think whoever is harassing Anna and I, and ransacking my office, is trying to stop us from investigating what happened back then." David searched the sheriff's face for any signs of, well, anything, but didn't see any emotion in his eyes. He took a deep breath and continued. "We spoke at length to Albert yesterday afternoon, and I have a few questions about what happened back then that I'm hoping you can fill in."

Harpy raised his hand in a stop motion before David could continue. "You've spoken to Albert? At the hospital?" Harpy raised his eyebrows in disbelief.

"No. I did speak to Albert at the hospital a few days ago when I was being kept for observation after my poisoning. It was a rather short conversation at that time. He seemed concerned that he was being watched and his conversations were being listened to. He was released from the hospital a couple of days after that."

"Oh, really? I haven't seen him in town, and when I ran into Amelia yesterday at the general store, she didn't say anything about him being back."

Anna stepped in as David was about to continue. "Albert didn't come home after he was released, and he doesn't want Amelia or anyone else to know that he's out. Once we continue our questioning, it will be clear why he isn't anxious to come back to Windsmill."

Harpy raised his eyebrows again but didn't say anything more. He motioned for David to continue.

"Albert is convinced that Austin was the one that killed all of the people back in 1990 and that he has somehow come back to Windsmill to continue whatever he thinks his mission is. Albert tried talking to Amelia about it, but she became quite hysterical and figured Albert had lost his mind. She insists that Austin died in Vietnam back in the seventies and that Albert must be the one killing all these people. Albert indicated that after a particularly bad verbal fight with Amelia she threatened to come to you and give you evidence that it is Albert who is guilty."

"And you want to know if she did come to me, is that it?" Harpy asked.

"I was hoping you might have some information on what actually happened to Austin, and yes, did Amelia come in to talk to you after Albert was admitted to hospital?" David raised his eyebrows like the sheriff had earlier.

Harpy looked down at his desk and stared at a piece of paper he'd obviously been scribbling on during his telephone conversation. He looked back up at David and Anna and sighed. He said quietly, "You two aren't going to stop until you find out what's going on or you end up dead, are you?"

"No, sir, I won't," David said quickly. "Whoever is doing these things has made it very personal for me and my family, Sheriff. I don't plan on stopping until I know who and why, nor do I plan on ending up dead."

"Okay, I get it." Harpy stood up and passed between his desk and the couch where David and Anna were sitting. They could tell he was agitated about something and debating telling them anything. He sat heavily in his office chair and stared at them. "Okay, fine. I'll tell you what I know. I will also tell you that Austin Packart is definitely not responsible for young Marty's death, or for your attempted murder or the vandalism of your property or Anna's car."

"Okay, so what can you tell us about Austin Packart?" David asked sternly.

"I'll need to start with what happened back in 1990. I think you know most of what happened to Paul, the Faulkon twins, and Darren. Did Albert tell you about the investigator, Jim Lister?"

"Yes, he filled us in on who he was and how he died," Anna said sadly. "Jack never mentioned his father. I wasn't aware that he'd died in the same manner as my own father; in the same way my ... Jack, how Jack died."

"I actually didn't make the connection myself until I was going back through all the files from back then. It dawned on me that Jim and Jack were most likely related." Harpy stared at Anna with sadness in his eyes. "I'm sorry, Anna. None of this can be easy on you."

"I need to find out who killed all these hard-working men and why!" Anna screamed as she stood up.

David reached over and touched her arm. "It's okay, sis. We'll get to the bottom of all this," he said quietly. "Please, continue, Sheriff." Anna glared at the sheriff before calming herself down and sitting back beside her brother.

"Anyway," Harpy continued, "Austin was declared missing in action, along with a lot of other men and women who had been sent overseas during that time. Canada wasn't officially in the Vietnam War, but we did have some participation in partnership with the US. Anyway, Austin had been in some top-secret area of the armed forces and was sent over to gather specific intelligence that was supposed to help end the war. Of course, I have no idea what that was or why he specifically was sent over. The armed forces and CSIS are very tight-lipped about those sorts of things. Anyway ..." Harpy sighed and looked out his office window.

AUSTIN'S STORY – 1990:

"What do you mean they won't talk to you!" Sheriff Dobson scowled at Sergeant Harper. "Who do they think they are? We have two dead boys in our jurisdiction that they took out from under our noses because the grieving father won't believe our tox screens and now they're shutting up!" Dobson paced the floor of his office. "What the hell are they hiding?"

"I don't think they're hiding anything," Harpy said to his boss. "I think they're in the middle of their own shit show."

"What the hell does that mean?!" Dobson got up into Harpy's face.

"They had a fire at the precinct the night Malcolm Faulkon died. The place is in bad shape. All the coroner's files were used as accelerant to start the blaze, and the coroner himself was killed and stuffed into one of the coolers with the other Faulkon kid." Harpy walked away from the sheriff and then turned back again. "Tony's over there now trying to determine cause of death."

"Our coroner is up there helping them, and that screwball of a sheriff won't even talk to us?!" Dobson started to pace again. "Did that idiot Redford at least keep copies of the reports he gave them last week in all that ruckus?"

"I don't know." Harpy stared at his boots. Not having answers when the sheriff was in this mood was not a good idea, but Harpy really didn't know what Tony had kept in his office.

"Well, go down there and find out. That secretary he hired must have some idea of where the files are kept!" Dobson watched as Harpy left his office and headed for the back stairs. The sheriff really didn't think that there was anything to find, but he needed Harper out of his office. He hollered out his office door, "Janet, where's my coffee! And bring me Chief Baxter's private number, I'm going to get answers if I have to get him out of bed!"

"Hey, Harper." Dobson was accustomed to hollering at anyone that walked past his office. Unfortunately, Harpy needed to go back downstairs

250   WENDY SCOTT-ETTINGER

today to see if Tony had returned to the office. He'd snuck past yesterday after getting nowhere with the secretary, but no such luck today.

"Yes sir," Harper said as he stood in the office doorway.

"What did you get from Redford and his secretary yesterday?"

"Nothing, sir. The file that he had with the Faulkons' name on it was empty, sir." Harper looked down at his boots, expecting a reaming out like the sheriff always meted out, but it didn't come.

"So why were you down there again today? You sweet on the girl?" The sheriff coughed to cover the chuckle that tried to escape his throat.

"No, sir," Harper said with a blush. "I was hoping that Tony, er, Dr. Redford would be in the office this morning so I could ask him directly, but he's not expected back from Carson until tomorrow."

"Thank you, Harper," Dobson said in a dismissive tone. "Let me know if you catch up to him."

"Yes, sir." Harper exited the hallway quickly so Dobson couldn't change his mind and ream him out anyway. Damn Tony for not keeping proper control over case evidence. If they did ever catch whoever was doing this shit, they'd lose it in court with this incompetence. Harper shook his head as he walked right into a solid frame of a man. "Ooof. I'm so sorry," Harper exclaimed as he backed up a step. "Did I hurt you, sir?" he asked as he looked into Mr. Packart's face.

"Not at all," Albert said as he put his hands on Harpy's shoulders. "Are you all right, Harpy? You look a little upset."

"I'm fine, sir. What can I do for you today?"

"I just came in to let your office know that I've called in the EPS to investigate those barrels and to determine if their contents had anything to do with Paul, Manny, and Malcolm's deaths."

"Why would you do that now, Mr. Packart? I thought you had those barrels disposed of. Didn't you give us a copy of a receipt from some disposal company in Carson for those things before Paul even died?"

"Yeah, I did. Amelia gave me the receipt and I originally accepted it as fact. But now I'm not convinced." Albert hesitated. "Anyway," he stumbled on his words. "Yeah, the guy from the Environmental Protection Services will be here in the next couple of days. I just thought you should know." Albert turned to leave and then changed his mind. He turned back to the sergeant. "I think Austin is back in town. I think he's living in the old homestead building."

"Austin? Your brother Austin that died in Vietnam?" Harpy couldn't believe what he was hearing. "Are you saying your dead brother is back in town and killing random people in your orchard?"

"Austin didn't die in 'Nam. He was declared missing in action, but he was found and released a few years ago in some deal that the States made with North Vietnam. He's been back in Canada for a few years now." The look on Albert's face told a long story. He turned back to the front door. "Never mind. I'll find out myself what's going on at my property. Maybe the Carson police will have better luck." Albert left before Harpy could ask him more questions.

Harper walked over to the door and watched the man he'd known all his life walk slowly down the steps toward the hotel. He walked much slower than Harpy had ever seen him walk before. He looked almost defeated. Hopefully he and Darren could get things back on track and they could all put this behind them. Harper turned back toward his boss's office. Should he tell him about this new information, or just wait and see if anything came of it before he mentioned it? Either way, Dobson was going to be pissed. *Might just as well get it over with*, Harpy thought as he headed back down the hall toward Dobson's office.

"Now what?" Dobson hollered as Harper approached. "Don't you have anything productive to do?"

"Yes, sir. I just thought you'd like to know about the conversation I just had with Mr. Packart. It was a little strange."

"Strange? How?"

Harper told Dobson about Albert calling the EPS about the barrels, even though they'd been disposed of earlier. He also told Dobson what Albert had said about Austin being alive, and Albert's belief that Austin was the one responsible for what was going on out there.

"Austin's dead. What the hell are you on about, Harper!" Dobson yelled at Harpy and looked at him as if he was the crazy one.

"Apparently Austin wasn't dead, just missing. Anyway, apparently Austin is alive and brought back to Canada."

"Whatever." The sheriff waved him off. "Go find something to do that doesn't involve crazy-assed stories of dead-not-dead brothers that are murderers. Jesus Christ, Harper, get a grip!"

Harpy hurried down the hallway, anxious to get out before Dobson wanted something else from him. These cases were getting more convoluted

252 WENDY SCOTT-ETTINGER

with every turn, and Harper was worried he was somehow going to get caught in the web that was being spun.

ALBERT WALKED OVER TO THE HOTEL AND talked to the day clerk about getting a reservation for an EPS Investigator from the coast. "I think he'll be coming into Windsmill in the morning," Albert informed her. "I don't know if he'll need to stay longer than the one night, but can we reserve a room for two nights and then if he doesn't need the second, we'll just cancel."

"Actually, Mr. Packart, Mr. Lister from the Environmental Protection Agency has already booked a two-night stay with us. I assume that's the investigator you were expecting?" Janelle looked at him expectantly.

"I suppose so," Albert said, a little dejected. "When is he expected to arrive?"

"Sometime tomorrow, sir." Janelle looked at her registry for confirmation. "He indicated he'd be looking around the Packart Orchard and meeting with you, then sending a preliminary report to his office and talking to anyone else that he'd deemed necessary, so he asked for the second night – just in case." She smiled at Mr. Packart, realizing that he'd asked for a second night for the same reason.

"Good," Albert said under his breath. "Hopefully he'll have some answers for me tomorrow as well." Albert headed back out onto the street. He really didn't feel like going back to the mansion just yet, but there wasn't anywhere else he needed to go. He glanced over at Don's Place but shook his head. That would likely cause more friction between him and Amelia than there already was, and he just couldn't handle that right now either. He started walking toward the city park; maybe he'd just walk around the park for a while and clear his head.

"Albert? Is that you?" a voice sounded from behind him as he turned a corner around a small grove of trees. He startled and looked around but couldn't see anyone.

"Hello?" he said tentatively.

"Sorry." Mary came through the gate from her back yard and joined Albert. "I didn't mean to startle you. What are you doing in the park at this time of day? Are you alone?" Mary looked around to see if she could spot Amelia but didn't see anyone.

"Yes, alone," Albert said quietly. "I had some things to take care of in town, and it's such a nice day I thought I'd take a stroll before heading back

PACKART'S ORCHARD   253

into the orchards. They really look after this park, don't they?" He smiled at Mary. It had only been a few months since Paul's passing, and he really didn't know what to say to her. He hadn't seen her since the funeral, and that wasn't very neighbourly of him. He continued to walk back toward town square.

"Mind if I join you in your walk for a bit? I'm headed over to the grocery store to pick up some supplies before Anna and David get home from kindergarten." Mary walked quickly to catch up to him. "I really miss seeing you and Amelia. I heard about the Faulkon twins, and I'm really sorry it happened. It must be very difficult at the moment."

"It is," Albert said quietly. "Especially when neither the Windsmill sheriff's office or the Carson Police Station have any answers for me or the Faulkon family. No one seems to know or care about what happened." Albert looked over at Mary. "Or the Jackson family either." He paused and looked directly into Mary's eyes. "I'm so sorry for what happened to Paul. I really liked the boy. He was more like a son to me than …" He drifted off.

"Thank you, Albert." Mary patted him on his arm. "I know you and Paul were close. Darren was his best friend pretty much all their lives. I'm sure you saw more of him than his parents did." Mary smiled at the thought. She remembered her mother-in-law saying just that before they moved into the valley.

"Yes, I suppose I did." Albert smiled at the memories. "Well, I best be heading back home." He frowned down at his boots. "I'm sure there's something that needs to be done, and until I can get more crew out there It's just me, Darren and Red." He waved at Mary and headed back toward the sheriff's office parking lot where he'd left his truck.

Mary waved back at him. "That was a strange interaction," she thought as she turned down the path toward the general store.

HARPY WAS AWAKENED BY HIS WORK PHONE ringing. He'd gotten to bed late after tracking down Tony in Carson and getting the low-down at what was going on up there. He'd gone back into the office to get some paperwork done, hoping that Dobson would have left for the day, but no such luck. He decided that everything that had happened up in Carson and at Packart's Orchard was somehow Harpy's doing, and he listened to the lecture for what seemed like all night. He'd finally got his reports written up and sent to Dobson's secretary at close to midnight. Now the phone! "Hello, Sergeant Harper speaking," Harpy said groggily.

"Harper, get your ass out to the Packart's place right now!" Dobson yelled into the phone. "We've got another body and we sure as hell are not going to lose this one to those Carson idiots!" He hung up before Harpy could say anything or ask any questions.

By the time Harpy made it to Packart's mansion, there was already a full contingent of police, medical professionals, and the coroner's van in the yard. Harper parked at the far end and walked over to what appeared to be the lead on the scene, but the officer was busy shouting orders.

"Sergeant Harper, what are you doing here?" Dr. Redford wandered over and stood beside him.

"Dobson called me a few minutes ago. Was worried you'd be giving this one away to Carson too." Harpy winked at Tony. "So what have we got so early in the morning?"

"Unfortunately, we've got Darren Packart. Red found him this morning on his way to check on the garden over there." Tony pointed to the large garden area to the west of the house.

"It's what," Harpy glanced at his watch, "Three forty-five in the damned morning. What's Red doing wandering around the orchard at that time of night?"

"Good question." Tony shrugged. "He's in pretty bad shape, both physically and mentally right now." He pointed in the direction of the mansion steps. "I think he's been drinking pretty heavily since the Faulkon boys died. Now this is going to send him right over the edge." Tony walked away, toward the crowd of officials between the cart shed and the house.

Harpy walked over and sat beside Red. He'd known the man all of his own life and would put Red at about fifty-five or sixty; the same age as Albert and Amelia. "You okay, Red?" he asked softly.

Red lifted his head from his hands and stared at Harpy, taking a few seconds to recognize the policeman. "Yeah, sure, just another dead body in the orchard. No one seems to care that they're dropping like flies around here," Red slurred at him. "Can I go now?"

"Just a few more minutes, Red." Harpy patted him on his shoulder. "Can I get you a cup of coffee or something?"

Red shook his head and didn't say anything else, so Harpy looked around to see if the Packarts were out in the yard or if he'd have to bother them in their home. As if on queue, Amelia came out onto the porch. Her face was tear-streaked and her hair was in curlers. She looked like she had hurriedly

PACKART'S ORCHARD 255

thrown on some day clothes, but they looked mismatched and wrinkled, like she'd pulled them out of the laundry. She looked more angry than emotionally upset, but everyone dealt with these types of situations differently, Harpy thought.

He stood up. "Mrs. Packart," he started as he took a couple of steps up toward her.

"What are you doing here? You no-brained incompetent idiots should have solved all this before my Darren died!" She scowled at him and pushed him backward, almost toppling him over.

"I'm sorry for your loss, ma'am," Harpy said sadly. "I really liked Darren."

"And that helps me how?" she screamed at him. "Get these idiots off my property, right now! Where are they taking my boy?" she asked as she watched the coroner's crew load the body into the van.

"To the morgue, ma'am," Harpy said, as he walked away from her. He spotted Red walking up the steps to hug Mrs. Packart. They spoke quietly to each other, then Red headed back down the steps and out into the orchard. Harper let him go. There was no use trying to talk to him tonight anyway.

"Has Albert been out here at all?" Harpy asked a passing officer.

"Yes, Mr. Packart was the one that phoned it in," the rookie said as he continued passed Harpy. "Don't know where he is now though."

Harpy looked around. He could bet his next paycheque that Albert was over at the old homestead, but would he really go over there with this many police on the premises? Harpy decided he'd drive over as close to the old house as he could get, rather than take a chance of getting lost in the orchard. He hopped back into his cruiser and headed down the highway, turning onto the access road in front of the cabins. He spotted lights on in the first cabin and assumed Red had made it home alright. He drove as carefully as possible to the end of the road and parked the cruiser by the foot bridge that crossed the river in front of the old building. There he saw two men standing on the front porch having a rather loud and angry conversation.

Harpy walked quietly toward the two men, hoping to hear what they were saying without them knowing he was there. The minute his foot hit the bridge, the first of the two men stopped and looked right at him.

"What the hell do you want?" he asked angerly.

"Who is it?" Albert asked as he turned around to look toward Harpy. "Is that you, Harpy? What are you doing out here?"

256   WENDY SCOTT-ETTINGER

"I was looking for you, Albert," Harpy said cautiously. "Who's that with you?" He nodded toward Austin.

"My brother," Albert snarled at the other man. "I was letting him know I was onto him."

"And I was telling him I had nothing to do with this or any of the deaths in the orchard," Austin responded.

"Okay, so why are you two yelling at each other, and why are you way out here? Shouldn't you be at the house trying to figure out what's been happening?" Harpy questioned them.

The two men looked from Harpy to each other and back again, then burst out laughing like he'd just told the funniest joke.

"Come on in," Austin said as he opened the front door. "Watch your step, though, this floor is pretty much rotted through." He took a large step over a smaller hole in the floor as he said this.

Albert took the same large step and then quickly headed for the back parlour. Harpy took a leap over the hole and almost missed but kept his balance on his toes. "That's not exactly a safe entry," Harpy suggested as he followed the two men into the back kitchen area.

"Better than any security system." Austin laughed as he took an old coffee pot off a big pot-bellied wood stove and poured himself a cup.

"So, let me get this straight," Harpy started. "You've been living out in this rotten old building for how long now?"

"I've been out here off and on for a couple of years. I've been back this time a few months now," Austin replied, "but before you start accusing me of anything, you need to know that I wasn't back here yet when Paul died." He looked over at Albert for confirmation but didn't get any. "I came to town just as Albert's crew was finishing up the irrigation system upgrades. I ran into a couple of the crew by accident one day, and they just assumed I was Albert. They asked me how Paul was doing and if he'd be back to work anytime soon. I told them that I hoped so, and just kept walking toward the cabins. They seemed to accept that and didn't ask any more questions.

"Look, I know the timing of me being here is not good. If I was you, I'd be checking me out very carefully too. But I can honestly say I didn't know Paul, I didn't hurt those two boys that were staying in the cabin beside Red's, and I sure as hell didn't kill Darren. I'd never hurt my own boy! Especially since I just got to meet him yesterday!" Austin turned away from his company and stared out the window. He seemed to attract a shitshow no matter where he went, he thought as he looked into the field toward another access road behind the homestead.

"Wait, what do you mean 'your boy'?" Harpy questioned.

"It's a long story, Harpy. I'll tell you about it sometime."

"Look, you want to look around the place, go ahead. Just be careful where you're stepping. Most of the floorboards and stairs in the place aren't much better than the front entrance." Austin headed out the back door and disappeared.

Harpy looked at Albert. "So you believe his story?"

"Austin is a lot of things. Some of them I don't really understand. But one thing I'm sure of he's not a killer. He may have done his share during his time in 'Nam, but that's not what I'm talking about." Albert walked toward the back door himself. "Like he said, look around, but be careful. If your cruiser is still sitting here after breakfast, I'll assume you fell in somewhere." Albert disappeared out the back the same way his brother did.

If I hadn't seen them together, I wouldn't have believed there was two of them, Harpy thought as he looked around the kitchen. It was warm in here because of the pot-belly stove, but it looked dilapidated. He spotted a door at the far end of the room and walked over, being careful to test each board before putting his full weight on it. He swung the door opened and was met with a staircase going down toward the basement. *Or maybe just a cellar*, Harpy thought as he looked around for a light source but didn't find one. No way he was going down there without some light, and he'd left his flashlight in the car. He closed the door.

Harpy turned toward what looked like a sitting room and saw stairs going up. He figured they had to be safe enough, because he'd been told several times that lights were seen in the upstairs windows. He gingerly climbed the stairs, being careful not to put his full weight on each stair until he was sure it would hold him. There were three rooms up here. Each looked like a bedroom, with a small water closet to one side and a porcelain pitcher and basin beside it. No running water that Harpy could see. *Austin must be bringing it in from the river*, he thought.

A bedroll lay in the corner of the room that looked out onto the fields in front of the house. A lantern sat on a stack of books beside the bedroll. A duffle bag sat at the end of the sleep area and a few shirts hung from a rafter board close to the basin. *Small, but comfortable*, Harpy thought as he walked down the hallway to the next room. It had a similar layout to the previous room, but this one didn't look like it had been touched in many years. Spiderwebs and cobwebs hung from the ceiling. Window had more dust than glass left, and the basin was chipped, and the pitcher was missing. Harpy looked into the next room and it was much the same. This one had an old-fashioned baby's crib at the far end of the room.

Harpy noticed an identical crib on the other side of the room. This must have been where Albert and Austin slept, Harpy thought, then shook his head. That didn't make sense. Albert and Amelia stayed here with Albert's parents until old Mr. Packart had died. Albert built the mansion and moved his wife and mother into it shortly after that. Maybe this was where Darren slept as a baby, but why two cribs? Harpy closed the door.

There really wasn't anything in the house that looked out of place. Unless there was something strange in the basement, it didn't look like Austin was up to no good.

Harpy headed back down the stairs and turned toward the front door, then changed his mind. Both Austin and Albert had used the back door to exit, so that's the way Harpy was going to go. As he made his way around to the front of the house and started walking toward the bridge to get back to his cruiser, he noticed someone walking down the access road. Harpy couldn't make out who it was from this distance, but it didn't look like Albert or Austin. As he stood beside his car watching the figure walk, the person turned into the orchard behind the cabins and disappeared. "Maybe Red?" Harpy speculated out loud as he got into his cruiser and maneuvered his car around so it was pointing toward the highway. As he passed the last cabin, he noticed Red sitting on his steps. Harpy stopped and rolled down his window.

"How are you feeling, Red?" he asked softly.

Red looked up, startled. "I'm doing okay," he said despondently. "Hey, Harpy. You find anything over in the old house?"

"Nothing too exciting," Harpy answered. "Hey, listen. Did you see someone walking down this way a few minutes ago?"

"Nah, didn't see nothing. Wasn't really looking, though. Why?"

"Just thought I'd seen someone walk in behind the cabins here when I came out of the old homestead. Was just wondering who it might have been."

"No one's left in the orchard sep me and the Packarts. Don't suppose it was any of them. I'll keep an eye out," Red responded as he stood up and turned to go into his cabin. He looked over his shoulder with a worried look. "Hey, Harpy," he asked, "you think I'm safe out here?"

PACKART'S ORCHARD   259

"I think you're as safe as you've ever been, Red. But I can come look in on you occasionally if you'd like me to."

"That would be nice," he said as he walked into his cabin and closed the door.

Harpy rolled up his window and headed forward. As he stopped at the end of the access road before entering the highway, he thought he spotted someone walking along the treeline. He squinted to try to see better, but there wasn't anything there. *My imagination, I guess,* he thought as he pulled onto the highway toward Windsmill. "Stranger things are coming, I think," he said out loud as he drove into town.

THE NEXT DAY, ALBERT CAME INTO THE precinct looking to talk to Harpy. Harpy came around the corner just as the desk officer was telling him Harpy hadn't come in yet.

"Good morning, Mr. Packart," Harpy said from behind him. "What can I do for you today?"

"Can we go someplace private to talk?" Albert asked.

"Yes, of course, follow me." Harpy escorted him into a large boardroom. "This should give us some privacy."

"Thank you." Albert looked around. "This is secure?" he asked.

"Yes, I'm sure it is. We use it for general meetings with witnesses and that sort of thing."

"Okay." Albert looked around again.

"Just to be sure …" Harpy hesitated. "Am I talking to Albert or Austin?" he asked quietly.

Albert laughed out loud. "Albert." He smiled at Harpy. "I think Austin's hair is a lot whiter than mine, and his face shows a lot of hard living from his years in a prisoner-of-war camp. At least, I hope I don't look that old and haggard." He laughed again.

"Sorry," Harpy said as he pointed to a chair and then sat down across from him. "What can I do for you today?"

"Just wanted to let you know that the EPS guy is in town. He'll be wandering around the grounds today and possibly tomorrow, depending on what he finds." Albert sat. "I also thought you'd like to know that Austin is getting on a plane out of Bellcom City this afternoon. He asked me to give you his flight information and a copy of his itinerary." Albert handed Harpy a small envelope.

260   WENDY SCOTT-ETTINGER

"Thank you." Harpy took the envelope and put it into his uniform pocket. "Why is he leaving?"

"Too much crazy and suspicion. Besides, he really came back for Amelia and Darren. Now that Darren is gone and Amelia refuses to believe he's back and not dead, there's really nothing here for him." Albert rubbed his face as if to try to push the emotions away.

"What are you talking about?" Harpy asked in disbelief. "Why would Austin come for Amelia and Darren?"

"Austin and Amelia met in basic training in the armed forces back in the early sixties. They fell in love and were as inseparable as possible at that time. She was in electronics and robotics and some other stuff I don't understand, and Austin was pretty good at all that stuff too. They hit it off and were going to get married.

"Just before Austin was shipped overseas, Amelia found out she was pregnant. They quietly tied the knot at the base chaplain's office, who filled out all the paperwork for them, and the next week Austin was gone. Before he left, he phoned me and asked if I would look after Amelia for him." Albert sighed heavily. He'd never told anyone about this before and it felt good to let it all out.

"I flew east to meet with them just before Austin left the country. Austin gave me the paperwork that the chaplain had given them and showed me that it just had 'A. Packart' on it. He said that Amelia could be my wife and when the baby was born, we were to list the father the same way. Once he was finished in Vietnam he'd come back and collect them, and they'd be together again. Until then, I was to make sure she was happy and healthy.

"I brought her back to Windsmill with me about a month or so after I'd gone east. Everyone thought it was a love at first sight kind of a situation. The only ones that knew the truth were us and my parents. Darren didn't even know." Albert hung his head. It's broken Austin's heart that Amelia didn't recognize him. She kept calling him by my name and telling me to stop all the craziness about Austin. She accused us of doing it to hurt her.

"Anyway, I need to get back to the orchard. There's no one else now, and Amelia is beside herself. Hopefully the ESP guy will find some answers for us." Albert stood up and went to leave, then turned back to where Harpy was sitting. "Please, don't breathe a word of what I just told you to anyone. No one, you understand?"

Harpy stood and shook Albert's hand. "Not a word, Albert, I promise," Harpy said as he followed him back out into the hallway and out to the main entrance. "Let me know what, if anything, the ESP investigator says, and if he gives you a report, I'm sure the sheriff would like to have it for our records too."

"Will do. And Sergeant," Albert looked sincerely into Harpy's face, "Thank you for everything."

THE SHERIFF SHOOK HIS HEAD AS IF to bring himself back into the present. He looked up and saw David and Anna staring at him in disbelief.

"Albert drove Austin into Bellcom City the previous day, and Austin stayed at the airport hotel. His flight left that day early in the afternoon. There's no way he could have been responsible for Jim Lister's death." Harpy stood up and pushed the intercom on his desk. When Sarah responded, Harpy asked for the special carafe and three glasses. Sarah came into the office with a small bottle of gold liquid and three small drinking glasses and set them on the table in front of David and Anna. "Will there be anything else?" she asked. Harpy shook his head and thanked her as she left the room.

He poured a small amount of the liquid into each glass and handed the twins each a glass. "Here's to family secrets that now only we and the Packarts are privy to," he said, then downed his scotch in one gulp. He sat, and watched as they drank. "You can't tell anyone about what I just told you," he warned them. "I made a promise twenty-two years ago, and I've kept it until now. You must promise me you'll never breathe a word of it to anyone."

"So, you're saying that Austin was actually living in the old homestead during that summer?" David questioned. "Why wasn't there more of an investigation into that part of the property?"

"There was no cause. Remember, Paul's death was declared a stress-related heart attack. The Carson PD may have done a more thorough look around than I did back when the Faulkon boys died, but if they did, I never heard about it. I know Albert went to Bellcom City Police after Darren died, insisting that they investigate Austin and what was really killing all these men, but I'm pretty sure Sergeant McCall didn't get very far with that request. Dobson was kicking up a big fuss about everyone butting into Windsmill's jurisdiction. He didn't want to do anything more than was absolutely necessary, but he didn't want anyone else to either." Harpy shook his head as he thought about his old boss. He learned a lot from him, but most of it was what not to

262   WENDY SCOTT-ETTINGER

do. Harpy took another swig of the scotch and offered Anna and David more as well, but both declined.

"So, if Austin was cleared, why does Albert continue to accuse him of all these deaths? None of this makes any sense at all," Anna said in frustration. She just couldn't fathom blaming her own brother for such atrocities after talking to him and helping him leave town.

"I'd say that Albert is grasping at straws. It's possible that he's doing it himself, and in a psychotic state doesn't remember after the fact. Or it could be someone else completely away from the orchard. Someone with a vendetta against the Packarts, or that is looking to run them off their land so they can buy it up." Harpy looked thoughtful, then shook his head again. "I can't image Albert killing any of these people. He loved your father like his own son, and he doted on Darren. It just doesn't fit. And I don't know of anyone that would wait around twenty-two years to get hold of a dilapidated old orchard."

Just as David was about to say something the phone rang again. Harpy glanced at it, then said, "I need to take this, if you'll excuse me for a few minutes." He answered the call as David and Anna stood up to leave.

"Sheriff Harley Harper, Windsmill Sheriff's Department. What can I do for you?" he said as he watched the twins depart. "Yes, can you hold for a minute, please, I have company in my office." He held the phone to his chest and then hollered out at David and Anna. "Dr. Redford will be around in a few minutes if you'd like to wait. Otherwise, you can leave and come back later." He went back to his call.

CHAPTER 28

DAVID SAT AT HIS USUAL TABLE AT Maxine's, drinking another cup of coffee and hoping his sister and best friend got back soon. He loved sitting in Max's place, but he'd read through all the autopsy reports and medical records that Dr. Redford had given him. He was able to get his hands on his father's medical files after Mary signed a release for Dr. Redding to get the records from Bellcom City Hospital and then give a copy to David. He was also going to be able to get hold of Jim Lister's information once Anna got back to town to sign the release papers for them. Apparently, she was the only living relative at this point since Jack was an only child, and his mother was out of country and unreachable.

Anna had already given David a copy of Jack's reports that David had read before but was now reading again in the same context as the rest. Dr. Redding was also trying to track down any relatives for Red. He didn't seem to have any family in the area, and there wasn't any at the funeral that Dr. Redding could remember seeing. But he needed to confirm that before he was able to release the toxicology and autopsy reports to David. Dr. Redding was hopeful that he could get that one to him in the next few days. David had asked him if he could give him any verbal indication of what may have killed Red, but all he would say was, "It fits with the others, with slight variations," whatever that might mean, David thought as he waved at Max for another refill.

Dr. Redding had been able to find Malcolm's reports in his records, and since Marvin had signed all the release papers for all three Faulkon boys' deaths, he gave a copy of Malcolm's reports, along with Marty's, to David. Manny's reports had been lost in the Carson fire, but Marvin was going to call his Aunt Agnes and ask if she had been able to find the copies the police had given to Uncle Mo. David assumed that Manny's would be similar, if not the same as Malcolm's, but it would be nice to have the original take on that death as well. He'd also asked Marvin if he had a copy of the security tape that he had pulled from his security system the night Manny had died. Depending on the medium, David might not be able to view it anymore, but he may be able to get his friend Kevin to look at it and see what he could do with it. Marvin said he'd look around and see if he could find the copy he'd made for himself. David was hoping to hear back from him soon too.

Anna had gone up to Carson to see if there was anyone at the police station there that might be able to provide any information on the Faulkon brothers investigation or the fire that had occurred back then. Maybe she would bring back some good information from that end.

Mike had driven back into Bellcom City to talk to his dad and see if he would give them his investigation files on the Packart deaths. That might fill in some of the questions about Darren and Austin that Albert may have forgotten to tell them now.

Max walked up with a fresh pot of coffee and a new pastry she was trying to sell in addition to the cinnamon buns. "You look like you could use a little sugar in your life." She winked at David. "Maybe you'll try this for me and let me know if they're any good." She set the plate down in front of him and filled his coffee cup. "Can I get you anything else at the moment?"

"No, I'm good, thanks." David smiled at her then took a big bite out of the pastry. "My god, that's good!" he exclaimed. "It's melt-in-your-mouth delicious." He finished it off in a single bite and handed her the plate back. "Can I have some more please, sir," he said with a grin in his best Cockney accent.

"Yes, you can. As long as you never use that accent again." Max laughed at him as she headed back to the kitchen area.

As if they'd planned and rehearsed it, Anna and Mike pulled up in front of Maxine's Café at the same time. They parked on opposite sides of the street and waved at each other as they exited their vehicles. Mike reached into the back seat and retrieved two big boxes.

"You need some help with those?" Anna yelled across the street when she saw him turn around with his arms full.

"Sure, can you grab the manilla folder in the back seat for me? It seems to have escaped the boxes somehow." He smiled at her inquisitive look.

"Okay." She looked both ways then ran across the road. She retrieved the folder and then locked the doors of his car. "You got your keys?" she asked, and when he nodded, she closed the door.

PACKART'S ORCHARD   265

They both paused to let a light-blue pick-up pass in front of them, then crossed the road again and entered the café. "Wonder where Marvin is off to?" Anna commented as they sat down at David's table.

"Hopefully he's coming to bring me Manny's reports, and the security tape from the night he died," David said, answering his sister's question as he carefully gathered up all the reports he'd strewn all over the table.

"Coffee for my friends here, please, Max, and maybe a plate of those delicious pastries for them to try as well," David called over to her.

"I saw they were coming," she said as she entered the dining room with a full coffee pot, sugar, and cream for Mike, and a plate of pastries.

After a short reprieve from their investigation, David looked up and said, "So what have you two found out for me?"

"Dad said 'fill your boots, but there's not much there.'" Mike pointed at the boxes he'd set behind David's chair up by the wall. "I haven't looked in them yet, but we can do that in your office tonight."

"Oh, and this was with those." Anna handed the folder to Mike, who passed it over to David. David looked down at it and saw his name written on it.

"What's this?" David asked Mike as he turned the folder over a few times in his hands. His friend shrugged at him and grabbed another pastry. David pulled the folder open.

He began to read it to himself when Anna nudged him with her elbow. "Well?" she asked, "what's in it?"

"A note from Mr. McCall and a number of handwritten notes pulled out of a wire-spined notebook," he answered absently as he continued to read the top note. He looked up at the table and summarized, "It says these are his own notes and thoughts on what was going on in the spring and summer of 1990. He said he had no proof of any of this, but that he figured maybe it was time someone looked into it properly."

"Into what?" both Anna and Mike said together.

"I haven't had a chance to read it yet," David said in frustration. "Give me a minute."

"Does this have anything to do with all the mining and water culvert tunnels in and around the hills and valleys between Windsmill and Carson?" Mike asked as he tried to look at the file in David's hand.

"I have not read it yet," David annunciated every word slowly. He then closed the file and said, "We'll look at it in detail tonight."

266   WENDY SCOTT-ETTINGER

"That's an interesting detail to look in to for sure," Anna said, eating another pastry. "It could explain how whoever is doing these things can move from place to place so quickly without anyone seeing them."

"True," David said thoughtfully. "Maybe you have something there. So," he looked at his sister. "What, if anything, have you found out from the Carson PD?"

Anna dug around in her purse and pulled out an envelope and her notepad. "First of all," she handed the envelope to her brother, "Marvin called me as I was getting out of the police station and asked if I could stop by his aunt's house and pick this up. He said you were asking for it," she added as David smiled at her.

"This should be Manny's autopsy reports," David said as he ripped open the envelope. As he did, a floppy disc came out with the report. "Okay!" David exclaimed. "This will be the security tape from Manny's death." He turned the disc over a few times in his hands. "Does anyone have anything that will open this?" he asked.

"Maybe Uncle AJ would have something?" Anna suggested. "I don't think those three-and-a-half-inch discs have been used in years."

David and Mike shrugged. "I'll call Dad later too. If he doesn't have anything, maybe Kevin knows how to retrieve the information from it." Mike said as David put the report and disc with the other files he'd piled up beside him.

"Anything else?" he asked her.

"Well, the chief in charge is one Sarge Chernoff." Anna smiled. "He was the police officer that Malcolm had talked to and gave the tape to back when Manny first died. He's also the cop that Malcolm had helped with the fire and the strange cleaner the evening before Malcolm died." Anna paused for effect.

"And?" David asked impatiently. "Was he able to give you anything?"

"He said he was glad that someone was finally trying to pull it all together. He confirmed that the coroner had died that night and his body had been stuffed into the cooler with Manny. He confirmed that the fire at the entrance had been started using the autopsy files and investigation reports they had initiated on Manny. He also told me something interesting." Anna paused and took a sip of her coffee. Before either of the men could say anything, she continued. "Apparently, the police officers in the building at the time, I think there were four of them," she confirmed as she looked at her note, "yes, four. Anyway, they had been drugged with PCP. When I asked Sarge if

PACKART'S ORCHARD   267

there was anything else detected, he shook his head. He said they'd dusted the ventilation system for trace evidence and found a large deposit in the vents in the lunchroom. Whoever did that must have known that, at shift-change, the policemen gathered in that room to discuss the daily calls."

She looked over at Mike for confirmation. He nodded, then added, "That's a common area for them to do the changeovers and discuss the evening ahead. Usually over a cup of coffee and whatever's been left for snacks by the day shift."

"Okay," Anna continued. "Anyway, I guess one of the officers was in pretty bad shape and almost died from the experience. Not only the PCP interacting with some medication he'd been taking, but I guess he was also asthmatic, and the smoke hit him bad. He apparently quit the force and moved to the coast where his family was. The rest were back to work and trying to figure out what happened to Malcolm by the following week."

"Did they find anything of interest?" David asked.

"Not that Sarge could, or would, say to me, at least. He did say that he'd been talking to the Windsmill Sheriff's Office off and on all day, and that he had texted the e-files to the sheriff as we were speaking."

"That must have been who Harpy was talking to before and maybe as we were leaving," David commented, mostly to himself.

The bell over the café door interrupted their discussion and as they looked toward the door, in walked Marvin. He smiled over at them, then approached their table. "Is this a private party or can anyone join in on the fun?"

David pulled the files off the table and placed them on the boxes Mike had set on the floor. "Of course you can join us," he said as he moved a chair back so Marvin could sit down.

"Just coffee, Marvin, or would you like something else?" Max asked as she set a cup of coffee and a few packets of sugar down in front of him.

"Thanks, Max." Marvin opened the sugar and dumped it into the cup. "Those pastries look good." He pointed at the now-depleted plate in the middle of the table. "You got any more of them?"

"I will bring out another assortment as long as you promise to be honest with me about which ones you might be willing to purchase some day." She handed the lonely pastry left on the plate to Marvin, then walked back into the kitchen with the empty plate.

"I assume," Marvin began as he finished swallowing his pastry, "that you were able to get the information you needed from Aunt Agnes?" He directed this at Anna.

268   WENDY SCOTT-ETTINGER

"Yes, I did." Anna smiled. "You really need to visit her more often, though. I think she's lonely."

"Yes, I'm sure she is." Marvin took a sip of his coffee. "Becky has been trying to convince her to sell the place in Carson and move down here with us. I don't think she will do that as long as this case is still hanging in the air."

"I think you're right," Anna said sympathetically. "She said she wanted us to get to the bottom of what happened to her boys and wished us luck."

"Sounds like Agnes," Marvin confirmed. "My dad lives up there too and he says the same thing. I think the two of them visit back and forth quite a lot, so they aren't completely alone up there."

"I think he was the one that was at Agnes's when I got up there. He was the one that gave me the tape and said it might be of some use to us."

"Oh good." Marvin sighed in relief. "I've been looking for that thing since we talked earlier." He pointed at David. "I couldn't for the life of me figure out what I did with it. I must have given it to Mo for his records."

"I'm glad it was found," David said. "Now all we have to do is find someone that has equipment that old and can get a copy off the disc."

They talked conversationally for awhile while they tried another plate of freshly bakes pastries, then Marvin stood up and stretched his back as he seemed to always do. "Well, I best pay for my coffee and pastries and get back to the house. I'm sure Becky will be happy to hear that the disc has been found."

"Your coffee and pastries are on our business tab, Marvin, don't worry about that. And thank you again for the paperwork and the disc," David said.

He thanked David for everything they were doing and went to leave, when Anna said, "Oh, by the way, I like that new baby-blue truck you're driving around in."

"Not so new, actually." Marvin smiled at her. "It belonged to a friend of mine. I'm just having it cleaned up and a new decal made for the door." He waved at them and exited before anyone could ask any more questions about the truck.

Marvin held the door open and spoke to someone on the sidewalk before letting the door go, and Deputy Sheriff Charlene Carter entered the dining room. She looked over at the three sitting at what used to be her favourite table and walked over to them as quickly as she could.

"Good afternoon." She nodded as she approached. "Sheriff Harper has some urgent information he would like to share with you that he says may assist in your investigation." She looked at each of them as if waiting for a response. When none was forthcoming, she continued, "So if you could just follow me, we can go back to the conference room and he can share his findings."

"Oh, you mean right now?" David faked a look of shock.

"Yes, Mr. Allen, now," Charlie snarled at him.

"Are we under arrest, or being officially summoned to report?" Mike responded in a more professional voice.

"Of course not!" Charlie said in frustration. "The sheriff is quite adamant that you come as quickly as possible. However, if you aren't willing to cooperate with the sheriff's department, we will proceed with the information we have without your assistance." She turned on her heels and headed for the door.

"Tell Harpy we'll be there in five minutes. It will take that long for us to wrap up here and pack everything in our vehicles." Anna stood up and started to gather some of the loose papers.

"Yes, and Charlie," David called after her. "You might want to try a little honey rather than vinegar if you really are interested in cooperation."

Charlie left in a huff. "Five minutes," she confirmed as the door swung closed.

CHAPTER 29

THEY WERE ESCORTED IMMEDIATELY TO THE CONFERENCE room across from the sheriff's office, and when they entered, they were greeted by Harpy, Sarge and Charlie.

"Please come in." Harpy motioned for them to enter the room and have a seat. "Thank you for coming over so quickly," he continued. "I understand from Charlie that you had quite a bit of paperwork to move into your vehicles." Harpy winked at them as he said the last part.

"Yes, we've been pouring over all the information that we've just recently been provided," David smiled then looked over at Sarge. He extended his hand and said, "I don't think we've met. I'm David Allen."

"Yes, you look very much like your sister." Sarge smiled over at Anna. "I'm Chief Sergei Chernoff from the Carson PD. Most people call me Sarge, though."

"Nice to meet you, Sarge." David looked over at his friend. "This is Sergeant Mike McCall from the Bellcom City Police. He's been investigating some of the strange goings-on at my office in Bellcom, as well as assisting in our investigation here."

"Yes, the sheriff has been filling me in on some of those goings-on. Hopefully after today we'll be closer to closing a lot of investigation files." He reached over and shook Mike's hand.

"So, what have you got that's so promising?" Anna asked as she sat down across the table from Charlie.

"Well, it may be nothing but," he began, "I'm really hoping that this information will be helpful in at least providing a way that the person we're looking for can move so quickly from one place to another, without being

271

spotted." Sarge opened a surveyor's map on the overhead computer, and it lit up the screen on the far end of the room.

"I received a request from a surveying company to do some ground-penetrating radar in and around the Carson area. Harpy here received a similar request from the same company. They were looking for old mining tunnels from the late 1800s and early 1900s that might lead them to gold and copper in the area." Sarge looked over at Harpy.

"Yes, they called a few months ago and I asked a few questions about this equipment and how invasive it would be to the people in the area. They assured me that no one would notice them and that there would be no harm done to the ground, the environment, or the people," Harpy explained. "I'd kind of forgot about even giving them the go-ahead until they phoned a few days ago to ask if the sheriff's department would like a copy of what they found."

"They called me about the same time," Sarge confirmed.

"Anyway, the two of us received the same email with this file attachment. My equipment wouldn't open it up, so I asked Sarge if he was having the same issues. Apparently, they'd sent an encrypted file without letting us know what the passwords were. Once we got that sorted out," Harpy pointed at the screen, "this is what we have."

"Doesn't look like much at this detail level," Sarge continued, "but if you zoom in to the Packarts' Orchard and the Faulkon farmhouse ..." Sarge pushed a few buttons on the keyboard, and the picture zoomed in so you could see an aerial view of the two homes that they were talking about. "It's a bit complicated to explain in one sitting, but as you can see," he pointed out the old homestead on the far side of the river, "there's a number of small, decommissioned mining shafts around this house that extend all the way under the highway and up the hill behind this rest area."

"Is that where we found Marty?" Anna asked quickly.

"Yes, that's the same rest area," Charlie responded. "That's also where Red Lightfeather's body was found."

"If you look up the hill where the Faulkon driveway ascends from the highway," Sarge used his pointer again to indicate the area where Manny's body had been found, "there's an access from that tunnel just down the hill from where we found Manny Faulkon."

"Okay, so what exactly does all of this mean?" David asked as he squinted at the screen to try to figure out the punchline to this meeting.

272   WENDY SCOTT-ETTINGER

"Well, that's just the beginning." Sarge zoomed in again, this time right about where the golf cart shed was built. Behind the shed there were several small squiggly lines, but they didn't look like the mine shaft lines from the other two locations. "These," Sarge started, "are old irrigation lines that run from the field in front of the cabins to the current residence."

"Irrigation lines?" Mike asked skeptically. "Those usually aren't very deep and are not bigger than a two-to- three-inch pipe."

"If these were new systems, I'd agree with you." Sarge nodded. "I was thinking the same thing, but after doing a little digging around, I found some information on the original irrigation systems that were used in the early thirties and forties. That would have been about the time that Mr. and Mrs. Packart senior started the orchard. The parents before them were gold miners and prospectors, so the irrigation wouldn't have been put in until Albert's parents decided to change direction in the family business."

"Okay, so what did you find?" David was becoming impatient. He would have preferred to have this information on his own computer so he could look at it himself.

"These lines here represent culvert style metal pipes. They'd have been about three to four feet high and would have run from the river into the Orchard. When they were decommissioned and a more modern system was put in place in the sixties and seventies, the water would have been blocked from entering the piping and the watermill would have been used as a central pumping system for both water and electricity." Sarge looked over at Harpy, who nodded for him to continue.

"This," Sarge pointed at the pathway between the shed and the mansion, "is where Paul's body was found. And this over here," he pointed to the parking lot of the mansion, "is where Darren's body was located."

"Okay, so I'm assuming you'll show us another underground access in the field across from the cabin." Anna looked closely at the map. "At the top of the screen there, right?"

Sarge smiled at her. "Yes, that's right." He moved the view of the screen, so the area Anna had pointed to was now in the middle of the screen. "This is cabin two." Sarge pointed to the cabin that the Faulkon twins had been staying in. "This here," he moved the pointer again, "is another mining access tunnel. We aren't sure if this one is connected to the others that we already pointed out. That's were our next steps come in." He set the pointer down beside the keyboard but left the screen up.

"So, what exactly do you have in mind?" David was curious again. "Some kind of raid?"

"Not exactly." Harpy smiled and got up from his chair. "We have a couple of other guests with us today that will be helping us find out what exactly is going on out there."

"And who has been doing all this killing," Sarge added.

Harpy walked out into the hallway and opened his office door. He talked to someone in the office, then turned back toward the conference room. "For those of you who may not know who these two men are," Harpy began as two identical figures entered the conference room, "may I introduce you to Albert ..." he pointed to the man standing on the left. He was hanging his head and looked very nervous. "And Austin Packart." He pointed to the man standing on the right. Austin stood with a slight smile on his face, as if the shock on everyone's faces amused him. He was slighter than Albert and dressed in an armed forces green shirt and pants, whereas Albert was in his usual overalls and plaid. Otherwise, you would have a hard time telling them apart.

"Thank you for joining us, gentlemen." Harpy pointed to a few empty chairs and said, "Sit where you're most comfortable."

"Before I sit down," Albert looked up for the first time, "I owe these three young people a major apology." He nodded at Anna, David, and Mike. "I left you hanging a couple of days ago by running out in the middle of our conversation about my," he glanced over at his brother who'd already sat down, "or should I say *our* son's death. As I was telling you about what had happened, I remembered my conversation with Harpy here many years ago. I remember helping Austin to leave the area and believing him then when he said he didn't do it." Albert glanced over at his brother again, tears glistening in his eyes. "I knew as I finished up the telling, that I had been so focussed on all the wrongs that Austin did to me that I had blinders on to anything else. I had to get away and think it through."

He glanced over at the three young people again. "Will you ever forgive me?"

Anna rose from her stair and hugged Albert tightly. That seemed to end that line of discussion, and everyone sat back down.

"So." Harpy looked around. "What's our plan for dealing with these tunnels and trying to figure out who has been using them for the last twenty-two years?"

"Albert and I have been talking a lot over the last few months," Austin said. "I knew he still believed that I was the one doing all the killings, and that I'd somehow snuck back into town and was living in the old homestead again. I wasn't, and it took me until just recently to convince him of that."

"Yes, the old fool that I was, wasn't seeing things for what they really were. But now I think we've figured it out and we'll need your help to get the proof." Albert smiled for the first time. "It will be good to have this over with once and for all."

CHAPTER 30

AMELIA SAT STARING OUT THE UPSTAIRS WINDOW like she had for many years. Now that Albert had been taken care of, she only had to wait a short while for the paperwork from the hospital to come through so she could legally take over the orchard as Albert's conservator. This would give her the power and the money needed to sell the place that has been her prison for so many years. *Finally*, she thought as she turned away from the window. If only Austin hadn't felt he needed to tie her to his family when he left. If only he had come back and not died overseas. Her life would have been so much different, and she wouldn't find herself so alone in this god-forsaken place.

It was a beautiful sunny day in this part of the world today. Amelia had put on her jeans, a lightweight pullover sweater, and her old pair of army boots. She decided she could now walk through the orchard and into the old homestead the way it always should have been. Now that there wasn't anyone around these parts to see her, she could wear what she liked, not those horrible house dresses that others considered proper ladies' attire back in the day that became Amelia's signature dress code. She hated those dresses. She could walk through the orchard and go wherever she wanted instead of always having to walk the perimeter behind those cedar trees. She'd had Albert plant them for her when he built the mansion. He hated the look of those trees; he was always complaining about how they blocked the views and gave the orchard trees too much shade, but he'd planted them anyway. He'd never asked why she wanted them, and she never said.

Amelia walked out to the parking lot and looked around. She always found this part of the orchard so sad. It reminded her too much of Darren and what could have been … no, should have been. He was the heir apparent for this orchard and all the land around it. He was the one that should be standing here right now admiring his land and all the money in the mines below it. *But that stupid woman he brought home with him didn't want anything to do with us or the inheritance Darren should have had.* She'd heard them talking the day before he died about how they would stay only until they settled the deaths and then go back to Kendall where she'd come from. That would have broken Albert's heart if Darren had left this all behind. Hers too, as a matter of fact. She had needed him to take over the business so she and Albert could leave town and get on with their lives. Their dreams may be different in that regard, but they could part without their secrets getting out to all these nosy residents in this stupid town.

She continued toward the back of the orchard on the pathway beside the cart shed. No one had used any of the carts since Red died that spring. *Stupid drunk that he was*, she thought as she continued up the path. He should have kept his nose out of her business, but no! He stopped her on the other side of the highway and started asking too many questions about how she got there and what she was doing. She only kept him around this long because he was Austin's friend. She should have disposed of him long before now.

She paused when she reached the spot where Paul had been found. He was another one that should have minded his own business. Should have remembered his place as an employee of the Packarts and not a family member, as he tried so hard to convince Albert he was. She shook her head in disgust. Only one son in this family, she told herself as she continued toward the treehouse. Paul's treehouse. She sneered at the strange-looking structure. "What is a grown man doing building an office in a tree, anyway? Up there drawing all his plans of what HE wanted to do with this land – almost had Albert convinced too," she said out loud to herself. "Stupid men. Both of them!"

Jack was the same, stupid boy. He wanted to resurrect all of Paul's plans and then some of his own. Said the orchard trees were no longer viable or some crap. *Who cared about the damned trees anyway*, she thought. He probably knew what his father had found out too!

She rounded the short corner to the watermill and pulled open the door. No need having everything out here locked up anymore, she thought as she flipped the light on and walked to the back of the millhouse. She'd made sure that no one could see the door back here when she'd installed it so many years ago. It was her way of hiding in plain sight, as she needed to in those days. She pulled open the wooden door with a piece of rope hanging from the rafters. It had been so easy to come and go without anyone knowing any better. It was

PACKART'S ORCHARD   277

her way of getting over to the old homestead without anyone seeing her. Until that stupid Marvin had come to fix the irrigation systems and decided that the electrical and plumbing in here needed to be worked on too.

She shook her head in disgust again then smiled at herself as she remembered the barrels and the fun she'd had bringing them in here from the homestead basement. No one could figure out how they'd just appeared and who would have put them there. Not even those bumbling police officers from town. Then she put her best "Austin" face on and came and got them back from Albert. "That was so much fun!" she laughed out loud. "He didn't even blink when I walked up and asked him what he wanted done with them."

It was fun messing with Paul's desk and his drawing too. She'd originally thought she would just poison his food or coffee or something but decided better of that approach. Someone was bound to want to check that out if he just keeled over at his desk with a sandwich in his hand. No, she thought, her way was much better. She'd found those old barrels of industrial-strength cyanide in one of the mine shafts and had moved them up closer to the homestead. She knew they'd come in handy some day.

She walked through the opening and let the door slide back down into place. She would walk through the tunnels into the basement this way one last time, she thought. For old time's sake. She laughed out loud. No one could hear or see her down here, so she could say and do anything she felt like. She reached up and unhooked the lantern from the wall and lit it.

Then that inspector showed up snooping around, she remembered as she headed down the tunnel. *He made the mistake of asking me about the decommissioned irrigation canals under the orchard.* She shook her head at his audacity. *Wanted to know if anyone had cleaned them out or had them checked for contamination recently. Couldn't have him asking Albert about that now, could she?* They'd find her little hiding places for sure. No, her way was much better.

It was time to finish what she started, she thought as she pushed the door to her basement lab opened and set the lantern on her workbench. Time she got out of this god-forsaken hell hole Albert loved so much.

She looked around her workbench and shelving. It was all gone! Gone!

She screamed and fell to her knees.

ALBERT WALKED BACK OVER TO WHERE THE others had gathered. They'd made the second cabin their headquarters and had put up drawings of the area on the walls and pulled the kitchen table to the centre of the room with all the computer and telecommunications equipment on it. It looked like something out of the movies, Albert thought as he looked around. But he didn't have time for that right now.

"Amelia isn't in the house anywhere and her car is still in the parking lot. I noticed the old red truck behind the homestead, so she could already be in there, but no way of telling. I took a cart and brought that over here so if she is around, she wouldn't think much of me being out in the orchard, although she still thinks I'm in hospital, so it might be a bit of a shock." Albert chuckled to himself as he thought of what her face would look like when she saw them all in her old house. She was the one that didn't want him to tear it down. Now they knew why.

"That's a strange-looking mask you have there, Anna." Albert walked over to it.

"David and Mike found these in the basement of the old homestead earlier this morning. There were a few more there too, but they only brought these ones out for now. This one looks like you and Austin." She lifted it up to show him. "And this one Sarge thinks is the old man in the Carson PD that killed the coroner and started the fire. There's also a small device on the table by that other stuff" Anna pointed over to the coffee table. "It goes in your mouth and will change your voice to higher or lower, so when she talked to people when she was wearing the masks, you wouldn't recognize her. Those were also down there."

Albert walked over to where Austin and Harpy were talking about the strange-looking little machines.

"She always was very handy with making whatever surveillance or combat contraptions we ever needed," Austin was saying. "That's how we met, trying to get something that wouldn't be conspicuous in the bushes if the enemy spotted them. She had come up with something similar to this back then."

"Pretty sophisticated equipment for the early sixties, wasn't it?" Harpy asked as he looked at the bugs on the table.

"If you weren't in the spy business, it sure was." Austin laughed. "This is only a small sampling of what the government was playing with back in the day."

"Where's David and Mike?" Albert looked at the stuff strewn on the table with worried eyes. He'd never forgive himself if something happened to those boys too.

"One's in the homestead kitchen and the other is on the front porch," Sarge called from the kitchen area. "We have eyes and ears on them in case something goes sideways," he said, trying to reassure Albert and Anna.

PACKART'S ORCHARD   279

"What's the plan then, just sit around and wait for her to show up? What if she comes in a different way and surprises them?" Anna sounded as worried as Albert had.

"We have a heartbeat in the culvert between the treehouse and homestead," said Charlie. "Ready for action," she said into one of the mics on the table.

"Roger that, we're ready," Mike's voice said over the communication system.

"How did she get into that culvert?" Harpy looked at the drawing on the wall and back at Sarge. "There doesn't seem to be any way into it from the orchard side of that particular tunnel."

"Obviously an entrance that no one has seen before." Sarge shrugged. "What's going on, Charlie? You still have a position on her?"

"Lost it for a bit, but it's back on. Seems we can't hear when they're under the river." Charlie watched the screen in front of her. "She's in the building," she said to the room, then pushed the mic button, and said "the mouse has landed, the mouse has landed. Appears underground."

Everything went silent. They could hear breathing over the comm-system, but nothing else.

They all stood still, not wanting to make any noise. They held their breath and only sucked in air a small amount at a time.

"She's going to know," Austin whispered. "She's going to know that her inventory has been tampered with." Just as he finished his sentence, a very loud and angry scream broke the silence from the comm-system.

"Who in the hell has been in my lab?" Amelia yelled as she stormed up the basement stairs and swung open the door. "Whoever you are, you'll be sorry when I get my hands on you!" she continued as she looked around the room.

David came into the back kitchen door, looking like he was worried about something. "Oh, Mrs. Packart, are you alright?" he asked innocently. "I heard someone screaming and thought maybe they'd fallen through these rotten boards." He pushed his toes gingerly on the kitchen floor. "Are you okay, ma'am?"

"You!" Amelia screamed at him as she started toward David. "You! I should have killed you when I had the chance!" She reached over to grab him, but something stopped her. She was suddenly being held up off the ground by someone behind her.

"Put me down!" She flailed around, kicking and swinging her arms franticly. "Put me down right this minute!"

Mike chuckled as he held her steady. "I don't think so, ma'am. You're a lot stronger than you look."

She continued to flail and swing around until David couldn't take it anymore. "Why'd you do it, Mrs. P? Why'd you kill all of those men?"

She stopped flailing and stared at him, blinking rapidly. "They needed to go. They were in the way. I needed out," she stammered.

"How were they in the way? Of what?" David asked her intrigued.

"Your father was a meddling fool, always trying to have Albert change this or that. Always with the big plans and the bigger drawings. He was going to find them you know. It was just a matter of time. He was going to find the tunnels." She stopped talking and started flailing again, but Mike held steady.

"And the Faulkon boys, what about them?" David said angrily. "Why did they have to die?"

"That first one, what was his name again?" She looked over at David for an answer.

"Manny?"

"Yeah, that one," Amelia continued. "He was a mistake. He shouldn't have been where he was. It was the other one, his brother. He was the nosy one. Always looking around and asking too many questions. He was a good worker, though," she said as she thought back to the days when Malcolm and Red worked the garden and helped with building the fruit and vegetable stand for her. They worked good together. She began to kick again, and this time landed a good one, but Mike still held on.

"Okay." David looked at her with sad eyes. "And what about Darren, your own son. Did he have to die too?"

"He was going to leave us!" she screamed at David. "Him and that too-good-for-us wife of his!" Tears began to pour down her cheeks. "He was my ticket out of this god-forsaken place, and he was going to leave me here to die!"

Mike carried her out the back door and around the corner to the front porch. There in front of them stood Albert and Austin. Amelia looked up and shook her head violently. "What kind of trickery is this? Who's wearing one of my prosthetic masks?" she yelled. "Take it off. Take it off right now!"

"No one, Millie." Austin started to walk toward her. "It's me, Austin," he said as he reached for her.

PACKART'S ORCHARD   281

"No! Don't touch me! You're dead, you can't be here!"

"No, Millie, I'm not dead." Austin rubbed her hand as he spoke to her. "I was missing in action, but they brought me home back in 1989. I was here back then, living in the old house."

"No no no no no no no, you aren't him!" she cried. "Albert, please stop this. Stop torturing me this way," she sobbed.

Albert walked over and stood beside his brother. He took Amelia out of Mike's arms and set her down on the old porch. Albert and Austin sat down beside her, one on each side.

"I'm sorry I didn't try harder to convince you when I was here twenty years ago," Austin said as he held her hand. "The thought of being back with you and my son was the only thing that kept me alive in that hell hole the Congs were keeping me in."

"Amelia, I'm sorry I kept you here in Windsmill all those years. If you'd only talked to me about leaving, we could have come to some agreement. Even if Darren wasn't staying, that didn't mean we couldn't go away." Albert held her other hand and rubbed it softly.

Amelia didn't look up at either of the men sitting next to her. She went limp and continued to sob softly. "I just want to be on my own. I just want to get back to being myself again." When she felt both men loosen their holds on her she suddenly jerked away from them and sprinted forward. Mike and David ran after her. They grabbed her as she ran, knocking them all to the ground before she could make it to the bridge.

"Good act, though, Amelia," Harpy said as he pulled his cuffs off his belt. "You always were a good actress." He cuffed her hands around her back and lifted her back up to her feet. "You may have had the hearts of these two gentlemen, but you had the scorn of the townspeople," he continued as he walked her over to a waiting cruiser. "You always acted like you were better than everyone else. Like they were all your servants and were expendable if they got in your way." He pushed her head down and sat her in the back. "That's why you thought you could just kill them all at will, isn't it, Amelia?"

She glared at him with contempt in her eyes. "They were expendable. All of them!" She sneered at him. "And those two so-called 'gentlemen'," she nodded toward Albert and Austin, "destroyed my life!"

Harpy closed the cruiser door. He'd heard enough for the time being. "That's a wrap, ladies and gentlemen," he said into his lapel mic. "Good job, everyone!"

THE NEXT DAY THEY WERE ALL BACK over at the homestead clearing out evidence from the basement. David and Anna followed the basement tunnel under the river back toward the orchard. When they reached the end, it looked like there was no way out, but there had to be. Anna felt around and spotted a rope hanging above her. She pulled on it and a door slid open. "Slick," she said as she held the rope and moved carefully through the opening. David slipped in behind her. She let the rope go slowly and the door slid back down and clicked closed. Anna stared at the wall that she and her brother had just walked through. "Where are we?" she asked.

David held the flashlight up over his head and shone it around the large room. "I'm not sure," he said as he looked around. "Looks like some sort of equipment or utilities room."

"There's a door over there on the opposite side of the room." Anna pointed as she made her way over to it. "Hopefully its not locked," she said as she turned the handle. The door swung opened easily, and the room filled immediately with sunshine. Anna covered her eyes and walked out on a grassy area and looked up. "It's Dad's treehouse!" she said as she stared up at the house in the tree around the corner. "I haven't been out here since -- since Jack..."

David walked out of the watermill and looked around. "This must be the watermill house where Marvin and his crew found the barrels." He looked up toward the treehouse Anna was staring at. "Cool house!" he said as he stood beside his sister.

"What are you two doing over there?" Mike hollered at them from the access road to the homestead. "How did you get there?"

"We came through the tunnel from the basement to see where it came out," David hollered back. "Turns out it comes out in the watermill building." They walked toward the access road and watched as the police carried out boxes and boxes of evidence. Austin and Albert were also watching. They stood in front of the cabins with another man.

"Hey, David, Anna, come over and join us." Austin waved at them. "We have cold beers." He laughed as he held up his can.

Anna started walking over, but David stopped as Mike hollered at him again. "Hey David, guess what we found?" he said as he lifted a box up over the car hood.

"What've you got?" David asked as he walked over to the other side of the car.

PACKART'S ORCHARD   283

"You know those files from your other clients that you couldn't find after the break-in?" Mike asked with a smirk. "Well, we just found them. Along with tape recordings and video feeds all over the computer down there. They show Amelia coming into the back door and up the attic steps. Then a bunch of stuff with you talking to various people, including Anna and me. Also, a bunch of old files that you'd closed already, and a copy of the recording you took of Mary telling Paul's story."

"Shit." David shook his head. "She was thorough, I'll give her that!"

"Yes," Mike agreed, "but that thoroughness is going to get her locked up for a long time. She even had video surveillance from each of the deaths. They figure it must have been hooked up to the electronic bugs she used to kill them."

"How'd that all work anyway?" David asked. He'd seen the bugs on the coffee table but hadn't had a chance to ask any questions before he and Mike were sent to the homestead.

"They had a blow hole in the front of them that released a powdered PCP into the victims faces. They figure that made the victims dizzy and hallucinate. There's also a pressure injection on the back end of the bug, like an epi-pen. She had one loaded with enough cyanide to kill a bull! She controlled them from a remote control that also allowed her to see from the bug's perspective. She would release the PCP into the victim's faces and then swing the backend around and run it into them. That's why Paul had a large, bite-like welt on his neck. Jack's was on his forehead, and apparently after re-reviewing the coroner's reports, Harpy said each of them had similar marks on them. They were dismissed at the time as bug bites, likely from insects in the area."

"Why did she have one all loaded up like that?" David wondered out loud. "Had she picked her next victim already?"

"They were speculating about that while they packed everything up in there. They figure it was likely either you, Anna, or maybe Albert. We don't figure she would have killed Anna, though. She didn't see any of the women as threats to her, just nuisances."

"Man, she sure had it all figured out, didn't she?" David commented, then turned around to walk over to the cabins. "She'll be gone for a very long time."

THE END

Printed in the USA
CPSIA information can be obtained
at www.ICGtesting.com
LVHW041259070624
782576LV00007B/634